D0732237

THE
SINGLETON
TARGET: CUBA

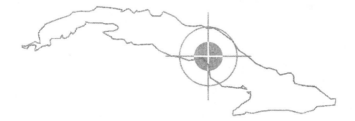

THE
SINGLETON
TARGET: CUBA

BY

ROBIN MOORE

AND

MAJOR GENERAL (RET.)
JEFF LAMBERT

Affiliated Writers of America / Wichita, Kansas
Imprint of Alexander & Fraser, Inc.

ISBN: 1-879915-19-7

Library of Congress Control Number: 2004115899

Published by Affiliated Writers of America
An Imprint of Alexander & Fraser, Inc.
507 Barlow
Wichita, Kansas 67207
316-706-7875

Manufactured in the United States of America

To the fallen Special Forces and CIA operators who have made the ultimate sacrifice for the nation.

ACKNOWLEDGMENTS

First, Robin wants to thank his good and long-time friend and Green Beret Officer, Major General (Ret.) Geoffrey "Jeff" Lambert, whose initial concept of this novel has finally led to the completion of this book. The General's wife, Bonnie, was also a great help in making it possible for Jeff to put in the time needed.

Also, Robin would like to thank Chris Thompson who once again stood by and provided great help in editing and conceptualizing this not-so-fictional story.

Naturally, when the manuscript was ready to go to the publisher (that only happened at the end of September, 2004), we wanted to get the book out quickly. Robin called his long-time publishing friend, Jay Fraser, and within a few days he had taken over the entire project promising to get it onto the bookshelves by Christmas, 2004—a difficult deadline. He did a terrific job on the final edit.

Of course, always in the background and sometimes foreground, Helen Edelston, who has been unbelievable help in all of Robin's writings recently, especially this one, which was completed and put to bed so quickly.

A great friend of Robin's, Marie Reed, who has read many of his books and who has always given good advice, has been a great help in the final days of getting this book into publication.

We thank Jerry and Nancy Jaax, and the National Agricultural Biosecurity Center, for their great work and for their expert assistance regarding agro-terror in this book.

A special thanks to Linda Robinson, author of *Masters of Chaos*, and Doug Stanton, author of *In Harm's Way*, for encouraging Jeff Lambert to put pen to paper.

And to Robert D. Kaplan, Thomas Friedman and others who appreciate the nuances of combating terrorism.

GLOSSARY

AC-130 – A propeller driven, four engine gunship dating to the Vietnam era. Famous for its precision weapons that fire from the side of the aircraft: 105mm and 40mm. Nickname: Spectre

Air America – The Central Intelligence Agency's secret civilian airline in Laos during the Vietnam conflict

AK-47 – World's most popular automatic rifle. 7.62. Soviet design

AQ – Al-Qaeda. Also term used for individual terrorists

Barrio - Neighborhood

BG – Brigadier General (one-star General)

Blood Diamonds – African Diamonds traded illegitimately, frequently obtained by violent actions

Bohio – Grass roofed shelter, usually without walls

Bona Fides – Means of verbal identification without stating the actual purpose of the conversation

Bursting radius – The casualty producing radius of an explosive round

BW – Biological Warfare

Café con leche – Coffee with milk

Campesino – Field hand

Cerveza - Beer

CIA – Central Intelligence Agency

Cuba Libre – A rum and coke, entitled "Free Cuba"

Cuchillo - knife

C2 – Command and Control

C-17 – The U.S. Air Force's premier strategic reach aircraft. The "Globemaster" can lift 170,000 pounds of equipment

DEA – Drug Enforcement Agency

DGI – General Intelligence Directorate (Cuba)

DIA – Defense Intelligence Agency

DOD – Department of Defense

DOJ – Department of Justice

Dress Greens – Slang for the Army's Dress Uniform

EEP – emergency extraction point

El Lider – The Leader, term of respect

ELN – National Liberation Army. A small leftist rebel movement in
    Colombia allied with the FARC

FARC – Revolutionary Armed Forces of Colombia.
    Communist/narco- trafficking rebels

FBI – Federal Bureau of Investigation

Field Strip – From WWII. Filterless cigarettes were torn
    apart, tobacco dispersed, and the remaining white paper
    balled up and placed in a pocket to preclude the enemy
    from finding evidence and being able to derive the number
    of soldiers at a given location

Finding – A Presidential document containing an authoritative
    conclusion or decision

Flash – The unit insignia on the front of a U.S. military beret

FMLN – Communist guerrillas in El Salvador. The Farabundo Marti
    National Liberation Front

Glock – A popular brand of semi auto handguns, particularly the
Model 17 9mm pistol

GPS – Ground Positioning System

Guayabera – A fancy dress shirt worn instead of a coat and tie in the
    tropics

GWOT – Global War on Terrorism

HAMAS – Terrorist organization created in 1987. Popular for
    charitable activities for the poor, particularly among Palestinians

HUMINT – Human Intelligence

INMARSAT – Common slang for satellite communications system
    that provides voice, data, and fax transmissions from anywhere
    in the world. Derived from International Maritime Satellite
    Organization

IR - Infrared

IV – Intravenous fluids introduced through a suspended bag, tube
     and catheter needle

JSOTF – Joint Special Operations Task Force

J2 – Intelligence Office of a Joint Headquarters

KGB – All-powerful intelligence service of the U.S.S.R

KSK – The Kommandos Spezialkrafte, the German Special Forces

KV – Kevlar, material for bulletproof vests, helmets, other uses

Latina – Latin American woman

La Patria – The Fatherland

La Policia – The Police

LBJ – Load Bearing Junk, slang for Load Bearing Equipment (LBE);
     also a term from Vietnam for Long Binh Jail or President
     Lyndon Baines Johnson

LTG – Lieutenant General (three stars)

MACV-SOG – Military Assistance Command, Vietnam – Special
     Operations Group

Manos sucios – dirty hands

MC-130 – Propeller-driven, four-engine C-130 aircraft. Highly
     modified "penetrator" designed to fly behind enemy lines
     Also known as the Combat Talon.

MEDEVAC – Medical Evacuation (usually used for air evacuation)

Merengue – Fast tempo dance originating in the Dominican
     Republic

MH-53 – The U.S. Air Force's most powerful helicopter. Capable of
     long-range penetration of sophisticated enemy defenses in all
     weather conditions.

MID – Cuba's Ministry of the Interior Directorate

Mi Vida – Term of endearment. Literally, "My Life." Equivalent
     in English is "Honey"

MX – Small portable radio with a stubby antenna and limited range.
     Sometimes called a "brick"

MI-6 – The United Kingdom's Secret Intelligence Service

M-4 – Modified/shorter version of the M16 rifle. Used initially by
     Special Operations troops, then accepted by light infantry

M-79 – Vietnam-era, breach-loaded single shot 40mm grenade
     launcher

NATO – North Atlantic Treaty Organization

NCO – Non-Commissioned Officer. Refers to soldiers, sailors, airmen or marines in the grades generally referred to as sergeants or mid-level leaders; the "backbone" of the armed services

NCAA – National Collegiate Athletic Association

NRO – National Reconnaissance Office

NSA – National Security Agency

O Club – Officer's Club

Okie – Slang for a person from Oklahoma

OPSEC – Operational Security

OSS – Office of Strategic Services. The U.S. Army organization in WWII disbanded after the war and later resurrected as the CIA.

OU – University of Oklahoma

PLF – Parachute Landing Fall. A technique to roll after impact with the ground, lessening the chance of injury while landing

POTUS – President Of The United States.

RUF – Revolutionary United Front

Salsa – sensuous Latin music, dominated by horn-based ensembles

SAS – Special Air Service; the United Kingdom's Special Forces

Sendero Luminoso – A communist guerrilla movement in Peru. In English, the Shining Path

SNAFU – Military slang for Situation Normal, All F— Up

SOCEUR – Special Operations Command Europe

SOUTHCOM – Southern Command

STABO – Straps, frequently sewn into other gear that allow soldiers to quickly attach themselves to winches or ropes from helicopters for quick extraction from the ground

STOL – Short Take Off and Landing. Descriptive name for special light aircraft with the capability to land in small, unimproved locations

UBL – Usama (Osama) Bin Laden; special ops abbreviation for the terrorist leader

UK – United Kingdom

UNITA – National Union for the Total Independence of Angola

USAF – United States Air Force

USSPACECOM – United States Space Command

VR – Virtual reality

WILCO – Will Comply

WMD – Weapons of Mass Destruction
WME – Weapons of Mass Effect
WWII – World War Two
Zero/zero – Virtually impossible conditions for landing an aircraft:
    no ceiling and no visibility.

CHAPTER ONE

Panama City, Panama

As usual, during the rainy season in Panama, the tropical deluge let up around four in the afternoon.

A stooped, old man of Cuban descent shuffled out of a small Chinese restaurant in a poor *barrio*, and onto the beaten path overlooking the tourist attractions of "Old Panama," now far removed in time and place from the ancient colonial city that had once served as the crossroads for the New World.

A medium-sized *mola* he had purchased from a *Cuna* Indian street vendor reposed in his backpack. A white dove in flight—a signal of freedom and hope—was sewn above a green and blue globe on the colorful *mola* cloth wrapped around a cheap, wooden frame that enclosed two powerful documents. The old man smiled as he thought back a few hours to his bargaining for the colorful *mola* cloth.

He had long since fled Fidel's cruel regime and had lived in Panama for many years. The last instructions he had received from the few surviving anti-Castro activists in Havana were to get the two documents that had been handed to him into the hands of the British government, and this became his single, most-important mission.

Stepping out onto the bustling street, the old man walked towards the main thoroughfare and then boarded a bus, heading downtown.

He loved the *"chiva chivas."* Many of the Panamanians did not know why the buses were called "rams," but many years ago one of the bus company owners had been fond of the ornaments put on Dodge cars and had mounted the most ostentatious versions on every bus. This bus was no exception and was also covered with art varying in theme from the crucifixion of Jesus to Elvis's career and flashing lights. The bus was enveloped in boisterous salsa music and the noisy, animated chatter of the crowded passengers.

In his sunglasses and scruffy beard the old man's true identity was well hidden. In the past he had been one of Fidel Castro's best human intelligence operators, a leftover from the heady days of 1958, but he was now on the run from the communist revolutionary.

His most difficult task had been making absolutely certain that he would be able to make sterile contact with British Intelligence in Panama, whose Embassy was close to the bus stop at which he alighted. The arrangement had been made through British Intelligence in Honduras.

As he lifted and adjusted his tattered baseball cap, he could see his much-younger counterpart, Enrique, across the street. Enrique recognized the old man's signal—the pre-rehearsed adjusting of the baseball cap. He reached into his pocket and gripped his pistol—firmly picking up his pace—scanning 360 degrees and looking for signs of imminent danger. With typical Latin nonchalance, he swaggered across the street and joined the crowd—just a few paces in front of the old man.

No longer looking at the old man, Enrique resembled the other residents of the *barrio*. His hair, jewelry, swagger, and even his fingernails were designed to blend. To the locals he was invisible. Panama was Enrique's turf. No one worked it better. His family had fled Cuba when he was just a young child and now, like many Cubans in exile, he was actively working against Fidel.

Soon after the old man stepped off the bus close to the British Embassy and almost immediately after signaling Enrique he spotted two young Latinos in *guayabaras* and business slacks walking in his direction. One had a pistol already pulled. Because of the growing crowd of women and children getting ready to mount the next *chiva chiva*, the Latinos who had been closing in on the old man stopped dead in their tracks. Suddenly, they turned in unison and put two rounds into Enrique—both professional head and chest shots.

The old man knew he had been made.

The two Latinos were Castro's Cubans. As they turned to approach him, the crowds scrambled clear of the street. The *viejo*, now nearly eighty-five years old, would use denial and his cover story as a last-ditch defense. He could no longer out run or out fight younger men, he would have to talk his way out.

Suddenly, and silently, the chests of both his pursuers exploded and they fell to the ground at the *viejo's* feet. A frail but curiously tall old woman with graying hair and wearing a native shawl hanging down almost to her feet hobbled past him saying in Spanish, "I think this means you may go to the British Embassy without fear."

She then quickly disappeared down an alley, where she concealed her gun. She dropped the shawl to the ground and took off her wig revealing a cascade of golden, blonde hair.

The old man, heartbroken over the sudden death of Enrique, approached the British Embassy where two waiting embassy staff eagerly met him and removed the rucksack from his back.

As the old man left the Embassy's front gate, he brushed by a stunning young blonde, briskly entering the grounds.

The old man's task was over. He had delivered the *mola*-covered evidence over to the Brits—documents that so many Cubans against Castro had worked and given their lives to get out of Cuba and into the hands of British Intelligence. It was safely on its way.

CHAPTER TWO

Washington DC—In the Oval Office
11 May 04

An officer wearing the dress uniform of the British Navy walked into the Oval Office carrying a package wrapped in heavy paper. "British intelligence, MI6, sir. Directly from Prime Minister Blair."

"Yes, I've been expecting it," President Bush replied.

The British officer continued, "I have been instructed to remain until you have opened this," and handed the package into the President's outstretched hands.

The President nodded. "Yes, I did promise Tony I would do that. He attached the greatest importance to this item."

He opened the packet and found the colorful *mola* which the Cubans had wrapped around the reports. He rummaged through the pages and soon called in Condaleeza Rice, his pretty, young National Security Advisor. He had already called an 8:00 a.m. meeting with his top three cabinet officers in anticipation of the arrival of the original documents smuggled out of Cuba.

Rice came in and greeted the British officer by his first name. She noted that the President himself had opened the package. "I'll be in touch with you later today, Ian," She said and took him out a back entrance as the President glanced through the pages the British officer had delivered.

Secretary of Defense Donald Rumsfeld, CIA Director George Tenet, and Secretary of State Colin Powell sat outside the White House Oval Office in the waiting room. Traditionally, it was presided over by the President's private secretary. She had not yet arrived for work.

The atmosphere was cordial, but worrisome, since the agenda was unknown to them. Bush was about to brief Rumsfeld, Tenet and Powell. Usually it was the other way around.

Condoleeza opened the door slowly and gestured for the three to come in. The atmosphere became tense as President Bush opened the proceedings. "We've just had a rough three days in Iraq. After the media released the Abu Ghraib prison photos indicating harsh treatment by Americans against Iraqi prisoners, it was bad enough. Now a terrorist named Zarqawi has beheaded an American civilian in Baghdad, claiming retaliation for the Abu Ghraib prison incidents."

Tenet spoke up. "We're trying to get confirmation on Zarqawi's participation as we speak, Mr. President."

Bush paused, and nodded to Tenet. "I know you people have been working day and night for months, and I can never relay how much I appreciate your personal sacrifice. But now, there is even more I have to add to your agendas."

For a moment, Bush's stern face turned into a sympathetic smile; Rumsfeld was about to leave on a spur-of-the-moment trip to Baghdad in the face of all the torture recriminations, and Secretary Powell's journey to speak at an Arab leaders' conference was also slated for this week. Both were to make these appearances for damage control over the Abu Ghraib prison incidents. The fallout from this fiasco had literally swamped the administration. Iraqi citizens were coming out of the woodwork, claiming to the eager press that they had been victims of mistreatment at Abu Ghraib, even though some of the Iraqis who were hamming it up for the cameras hadn't even been prisoners there. The entire incident was becoming another totally unexpected nightmare.

Bush's smile narrowed, and was replaced with a look of concentration. "As if we didn't have enough on our plates already, Prime Minister Blair has just sent me something quite shocking. It began with some documents smuggled out of Cuba and delivered to British Intelligence in Panama. The Prime Minister assured me that the British have worked very hard to verify the information. In addition, they are sending over one of their top intelligence agents to be imbedded with us on this project."

The President continued. "Castro has developed a biological weapons program which is progressing at an alarming rate. We must take immediate and positive action and either derail or destroy his program. The U.S. is obviously the target, and I totally believe the case laid out for us."

He raised the thick manila diplomatic envelope and held it in his hand. "The British Embassy has the best intelligence set up in Cuba of any Western power. Tony Blair told me personally and confidentially that Fidel is building a capability that is truly a strategic threat to the United States. Making matters worse, President Chavez of Venezuela is also involved in the project."

The President then laid the thick manila packet in the hands of George Tenet. "Here's the intelligence. I promised the British PM total security on these reports—which are accompanied by more than fifty CDs of additional data. If the Cubans see any of this, it will destroy British intelligence operations in Cuba for many years to come."

The CIA chief accepted the package. "How do we sign or account for it, Mr. President?"

"We don't. This didn't go through proper intelligence channels, and you must realize what a political hole Blair could find himself in by going into another conflict with us right now. The British will help us, and already have, but there can be absolutely no leaks on this project."

The President added, "In addition, Fidel has stirred up the old communist FMLN in El Salvador and the Sandinistas in Nicaragua. The supposedly democratic parties are sending covert representatives to Venezuela to plot their resurgence, and to try to overthrow the elected governments in the region. From what I've gleaned from this packet, intel indicates they secretly gather on the island of Margarita, off the coast of Caracas. So now, Cuba must be added to our heavy work load as a very high priority for national defense."

Bush paused and took a deep breath. He then spoke slowly and with conviction. "Since September 11, 2001, the progress at breaking our nation's archaic, stove-piped operational channels has been less than optimal. The congressional investigation of the intelligence available to us before September 11 has not been kind. Even though we are sharing information better than ever in our nation's history, the State, Defense, Homeland Defense Department, the CIA, and, of course"—the president's voice lowered a register—"the FBI, have continued to move forward separately—not as a cohesive team."

He paused again. "Therefore, I am choosing the lead federal agency for the Cuban matter right now."

He allowed a moment for this last to sink in, and then Bush fixed his gaze on Director Tenet. "George, you take the lead in development of intelligence and field operations. When it's time to go operational, I want Secretary Rumsfeld to provide the very best support available. The same goes with the other government agencies."

Rumsfeld interjected: "This is relatively simple. We could put two Tomahawks on any laboratories or facilities and back it up with some smart bombs—ground penetrating—so that we obliterate any above- or below-ground structures."

There was a brief pause in the room and then Tenet said, "Mr. President, I appreciate Don's proposed solution. The Department of Defense relies heavily on kinetic missions. But I recommend a more sophisticated approach. The kinetic solution will not eliminate the scientific knowledge, the infrastructure, other hidden or additional facilities, or Castro's will to continue the program and rebuild. It's a temporary solution which will not guarantee the long-term safety of the United States. The only way to address the long-term strategic issue is to convince Fidel that it is not in his interest to continue."

The President thought for a few moments and then said, "Thank you, George, and Don. After our experience in Iraq, I don't think the kinetic approach is the answer. An air strike on Cuba would carry some very heavy political consequences, and unknown second- and third-order effects that would ripple throughout Latin America. This could also seriously affect our plans for the upcoming election. I think the real center of gravity in this issue is Castro's *motivation*. We must destroy his motivation to continue this program, and the best capability we have would be your people, George. You, therefore, are going to be the lead federal agency on this project."

He looked from one person to the next and then continued. "I need a collective analysis of the road ahead—*a hybrid*—if you will—

of determined action—with all agencies working together. Our purpose is the elimination of Cuba's biological WMD capability and Castro's will to continue it."

Again the President paused, the characteristic half-smile coming to his face. "Let me tell you what *a hybrid* means to me," Bush said. "According to the dictionary, it's *a blend of several unlike sources, combined to utilize the best qualities of each.* In Texas, we cross horses and donkeys to make mules—which don't act like jackasses"—he paused and grinned—"to do the heavy hauling."

A slight chuckle echoed around the room and cut the tense mood for a moment.

"Remember, I want this done in the shadows. No fingerprints. I want nothing attributable to the United States. That is why the CIA has the lead. I'm not sure that any other agency can still keep a secret." The President smiled one of those Bush grimaces that didn't exactly exude good cheer.

"Prime Minister Blair cannot afford any risk on another operation with us after the public outcry from his people about the war in Iraq. Despite his problems with the split in the British Labor Party, Blair has agreed to help us. But the hybrid must be completely clandestine. No leaks. British Intelligence will be working closely with us and it is probable that there will be at least one of their Intelligence officers seconded to us. The history and details necessary to start planning the mission are in this packet."

President Bush stood up and turned to Rumsfeld: "We'll continue our discussion on the prison mess while you're airborne on Air Force Two to Iraq."

As they stood up to leave, President Bush overheard Tenet say to Rumsfeld, "We may need the best singleton we can find for this mission, Donald."

Asking his national security advisor to stay behind for a moment, the President and Rice said goodbye to Tenet, Rumsfeld, and Powell as they exited the Oval Office.

"What is a Singleton?" Bush asked her.

"I don't know but I'll find out."

* * * * *

After their meeting with Bush, the State Department, Agency, Defense Department heads, and all other associated staffers rapidly "passed the word" about the presidential comment over their lack of teamwork on past operations. Whatever loyalties each of the agencies had for their own, it was time to come together or be replaced. That much was clear.

Digging into the British intelligence, Tenet rang Secretary Rumsfeld just before he left for Baghdad. "I have a tentative collaborative structure in mind to accomplish the mission. We will need to work together closely. My team will brief you when you get back from Baghdad. I would like to illustrate our cooperation by using the President's exact words—the mission will be executed by an interagency team called *The Hybrid*."

CHAPTER THREE

Afghanistan
05 Nov 2002

On an isolated, sandy road outside the Bamiyan region of Afghanistan, Captain Mike Trantor—a dirty, bearded U.S. Army Green Beret—suffered from labored breathing. He had struggled all night on foot to reach a point where he could mark a landing zone for an Agency STOL (short take off and landing), five-seater, light aircraft. He pulled several small infrared strobe lights from his rucksack and paused to check his global positioning system one more time to gain exact coordinates for the pilot's makeshift landing zone.

He was on a *singleton,* or solo mission. He was honored to wear the legendary ruby Special Forces ring that had been passed from soldier to soldier over the last thirty years—the first into combat, or those chosen to perform the most secret and dangerous of missions.

Somewhere, deep in the annals of Fort Bragg, North Carolina, his name would be added to the list following Master Sergeant John Bolduc, the first Green Beret to have gone behind the lines in Afghanistan the year before.

Captain Mike Trantor had successfully completed his mission. Mike had managed to link up with a group of indigenous Hazara rebels that held a fierce hatred for the Taliban. They had promised to join the Northern Alliance if Special Forces advisors, equipment and funding could be provided to them.

The war in Afghanistan had been over, as far as the media was concerned, for more than six months. But after Operation Anaconda and the end of the "official" war in the spring of 2002, U.S. Special

Forces had remained and continued to support the indigenous people. In fact, Afghanistan had grown more dangerous in the past several months, and the Taliban and Al-Qaeda continued to re-spawn and regroup.

Mike and his four short, dark-skinned Hazara bodyguards had been ambushed as they moved on horseback to his extraction point. His night vision goggles had helped him spot the enemy and survive, but sadly, his Hazara companions did not. Mike couldn't warn them quickly enough. The Taliban fighters faded back into the darkness after Mike killed two of them with headshots from his M4 assault weapon.

Abandoning his horse, he continued on foot, alone, and crept stealthily and cautiously away from the ambush site to find a suitable location for his extraction. He relayed the Taliban situation and reassured the pilots that the road was a safe distance from the enemy patrol. He switched on the strobe lights and put a pressure bandage on the bleeding near his ribcage. Mike had been hit by a Taliban AK-47 round, nothing critical.

Mike was extracted by an MH-47 helicopter and taken to the Special Forces camp called K2 in Uzbekistan. Then he was evacuated to the military hospital in Landstuhl, Germany, and finally flown to Walter Reed Army Hospital in Washington, D.C. Mike Trantor was different from the other Special Forces men who had been wounded. He asked the Army doctors that his wife not be notified of his wounds—a rare occurrence. He would wait to tell Kirsten himself.

Following his release from Walter Reed, Mike visited his assignment manager in the Pentagon. There, he received some great news for both himself and Kirsten. After being briefed by his Special Forces personnel officer, he learned that the Army was going to send him to college in Oklahoma, fully funded.

As Mike was about to leave, the Special Forces branch secretary opened her desk drawer and handed him a folder. "Here you go, sir. I almost forgot," the cute, young secretary said.

Mike opened up the folder and his jaw dropped. He was staring down at promotion orders—Major! Mike had been so busy fighting the war that he didn't realize that his promotion board had met. Mike had never cared much about promotions, but being a Major would mean more pay, more responsibility, and possibly a Special Forces company command.

Mike was absolutely ecstatic. His new post at the college in Norman, Oklahoma, would be only a few hours away from his family home. He hadn't spent much time with his mother and old dad for many years. Kirsten would be pleased to learn that she could continue her college education, full time, and he would get his M.A. as he had always hoped.

The nation's capital city always enthralled Mike. Despite it being a dreary morning with the impending threat of thundershowers, he went for a final walk on The Mall before he was to be driven to Reagan International Airport for his flight home. He finally felt a deep satisfaction at the way his military career had turned out after all. He had told Kirsten so many times that this would happen as a reward for his singleton activities.

As Mike strolled towards the Vietnam Memorial, he pulled his collar up as he felt the first few raindrops. A few moments later he stopped. He found himself staring—not at the wall, but at the bronze statue of the Vietnam veterans. The soldiers were slick with rain, and the drops ran down the bronze figures. Mike saw what looked like perspiration streaming down their faces and felt their fatigue and fear.

He shook his head. The sculptures had been real for a nanosecond. Maybe it was a flashback. Maybe he was heading for the Technicolor nightmares Vietnam vets frequently mentioned. Perhaps he had been in too many fights in dark and lonely places.

As he turned to leave, a tall man with graying, dark hair and wearing a black trench coat walked up to Mike. The Green Beret on his head dripped with water, and a single star stood out on the center of the flash.

"I was just thinking about you, Joe."

"Welcome home, Mike. A little bird told me you had a close call," the aging general said, giving him a hug and a pat on the back.

Mike grabbed his side where the general had inadvertently squeezed his wound from Afghanistan and gasped slightly.

"Sorry, Mike. I forgot for a moment," the general apologized.

"Just a flesh wound," he said in his phoniest British accent. Monty Python had played the part of the wounded Brit in *The Search for the Holy Grail* and it was one of their favorite movies. And it wasn't the first time Mike had made that joke with the general following his return from the wars with honorable battle scars. The Purple Heart with two oak-leaf clusters on his chest reflected that.

After a few more words, standing in the light rain, they shook hands. Mike looked into the general's green eyes. After their shake, the gold and ruby Special Forces ring glinted in the general's open palm. Joe Cordell looked down at the ring with a nod, and closed his fist around it for a moment before slipping it into his breast pocket. Mike was standing down from combat. It was time to pass the sacred SF ring back to its steward.

The tall, dark-haired general simply said, "Bless you, Mike," and briskly walked off into the distance. He would pass the sacred ring to the first man into the next SF conflict. Mike shook his head—as tall as General Joe Cordell was, he had the smallest pair of feet you could imagine.

Now he needed to get home, heal, spend time with Kirsten, and prepare to work hard in graduate school. There was one sticky issue. Mike couldn't hide his wounds from Kirsten, so he had to steel himself for a verbal ass-whipping. Prior to going to Afghanistan, he had told Kirsten that he was going out on a lengthy training exercise. She would know he had lied. Mike Trantor was a singleton, and covertly operating by himself complicated life at home.

CHAPTER FOUR

The Pentagon
June 04

A long, black sedan pulled up before the Pentagon's west entrance. A diminutive man in a dark, pinstripe suit carrying an attaché case stepped out onto the marble steps. He shook hands with a Defense Department civilian awaiting him. They moved quickly inside, out of the hot sun and into the foyer to exchange pleasantries.

Once settled into an intimate, private room arranged by the intelligence arm of the Pentagon, the CIA analyst in the dark suit unlocked his case. He was carrying research developed during his rapid ferreting through MI6's case against Castro. After the uproar following the Bush Administration's comments regarding Iraqi weapons of mass destruction, the Agency was walking on eggshells and triple-checking everything.

Eric Beckham had been one of the Agency's top Cuban analysts for forty-one years. A mid-level civilian, he was greatly respected in interagency intelligence circles.

After half an hour, allocated for Eric to set up his brief, six men and two women were ushered into the dark, mahogany-paneled room. Their collective wisdom spanned the entire intelligence and counter-intelligence spectrum, from space-based electronic spying to running agents.

The invited were subject-matter experts from the National Security Agency, the Defense Intelligence Agency, the CIA, the Counter-Terror Joint Fusion Center, the Joint Chiefs of Staff's operations center, the FBI, and the newly formed National Agricultural Biosecurity Center in Kansas.

Eric wasn't nervous regarding the veracity of his information and sources; he was just worried that he wouldn't be able to sell his conclusions to the people in attendance. The ultimate purpose of this gathering of "the best and the brightest" was either to agree with his analysis or to reject it. The highest levels of government and the military establishment would immediately know the results of the briefing as soon as the decision was made. Eric was literally breathless—this was his chance to make a difference.

The task at hand was a serious matter. Few in America would believe that the fading and increasingly fanatical leader of a third-rate communist republic like Cuba, with virtually no external assistance, could possess the capability to wreak strategic havoc within America.

The intelligence review team had been long accustomed to dealing with classic abductions and hostage scenarios along with nuclear, biological, and chemical (NBC) terrorism, but this situation presented a new challenge altogether.

Eric began unhurriedly, quoting President Clinton's Secretary of Defense, Bill Cohen, in his report to Congress in 1998, "The Cuban Threat to U.S. National Security." The Defense Intelligence Agency (DIA) had summarized by saying, "Cuba's current scientific facilities and expertise could support an offensive biological weapons program at least in the research and development stage. Cuba's biotech industry is one of the most advanced in emerging countries and would be capable of producing biological warfare agents."

The most damning quotation Eric presented was that of high-ranking Soviet defector Ken Alibek, the Soviet Union's former Deputy Director of Research and Production of biological weapons. Wary that much of the false or misleading testimony regarding Saddam Hussein's weapons of mass destruction had come from defectors, Eric tried to articulate Alibek's record of integrity, stating many instances where his statements had been exactly correct when verified by the CIA and other intelligence sources. Alibek was on record as stating that his superiors were convinced that Cuba had an active biological weapons program in existence in 1990. He also traced other suspicions to 1997, which became an irrefutable biological weapons program by 2000.

Also, as far back as 1988, personnel involved in South Africa's ostensibly abandoned weapons of mass destruction program publicly offered that Cuba had used chemical warfare on South African troops in Angola. Military, CIA, and even Congressional investigations concluded by late 2001 that Cuba had an active WMD program, Eric explained.

Next, Eric quoted Dr. Maida Donate-Armada, who had once reported that Cuba's biotechnology center was under the strictest military control despite apparent civilian authority and participation in leadership. The suspected bioweapons facility itself was in the form of an animal feed plant, yet one needed the highest security clearance to gain entrance. Centrifuges and other BW manufacturing and processing equipment had been bought from a company with close ties to an Italian arms fabricator in Milan, and shipped to the animal feed plant by way of a Panamanian-registered ship with Cuban crew, via Venezuela.

In 1992, Carlos Wotzkow was forced to leave Cuba because of his condemnation of Cuba's ecological policies. He related how, as far back as 1981, Castro created a bogus institution to serve as a front for biological research.

Carlos had also made another allegation: the spread of the biological warfare agents to the United States was to be by the most unsuspected carriers—birds. Birds!

This possibility was given further credibility when Dr. Luis Roberto Hernandez defected from Cuba in 1995. According to Eric, when Hernandez had safely arrived in exile, he stated the following:

"We had a front organization for a biological warfare program. I cannot be sure, but we were troubled by the knowledge that at the same time, the organization had Cuban agents working with birds on farms in Puerto Rico, concentrating on species that migrate deep into the United States."

Funding was traced as well. In the last decade and a half, Cuba had spent the equivalent of over a billion U.S. dollars on biotech industries, yet the reported earnings had never covered the sustained investment. In addition, Eric had laid out the virtually unimpeachable proof that Cuba, through Angola, had been using profits from the illicit diamond trade in Sierra Leone to provide additional hidden financing for the program.

Next, Eric moved on to describe potential bio-weapons facilities. He started out this portion of the briefing by laying satellite photography of six reported BW sites in Cuba on the table in front of his audience. Eric explained in detail the construction of each potential site, and how intelligence sources had selected them as probable locations. He briefed no data that had not been verified by at least two sources, recalling Secretary of State Colin Powell's now embarrassing briefing about Iraq to the United Nations with similar photos. However, he noted, one facility in particular would be most interesting to them.

Unbeknownst to the Cubans, British Intelligence (MI6) had found that the facility was in the hands of a Mr. Matos, Fidel Castro's best counter-intelligence officer. According to MI6, Fidel trusted Matos as much as any other man alive, and to find him in charge of a potential BW location was extremely enticing.

Worse yet, NSA had found indicators that Cuban agents had exchanged information with a famous Russian scientist by the name of Viktor Latshev. Doctor Latshev had been in charge of the research program that would guarantee a famine in the United States after the advent of World War III.

The Soviet layers of strategic attack were: first, nuclear attack; second, massive bio attacks of smallpox and other diseases on a nation virtually without medical resources left after nuclear conflagration; third, Latshev's agro-terror plan was to be unleashed to starve the survivors of the first two attacks to death.

Dr. Latshev was the Soviet Union's most brilliant designer in its secret arsenal of agro-terror weapons, weapons keyed on the destruction of U.S. agricultural crops. Latshev had succeeded in developing a terrifying strategic capability for his masters, by working with an unlimited budget and the best minds available in the Soviet biological research inventory. Mutant strains of every imaginable pestilence were brewed, cooked, grown, defeated, and then made more resilient. Genetic engineering opportunities multiplied. Wheat and grain crops would be attacked first, fruits were attacked next, and then wild grasses that protected major American riverbanks from erosion.

Eric then asked the scientist from the National Agricultural Biosecurity Center (NABC) at Kansas State University to speak, and she addressed the others in the room. "It is important to understand the *magnitude* of the threat. It is believed that the Former Soviet Union (FSU) could have had as many as fifty to sixty thousand scientists and technicians working in offensive biological weapons (BW) programs. Sixty thousand people—working in dozens of secret sites scattered in isolation across the Soviet Union. And thousands of the workers were involved in programs developing agricultural bioweapons. Let me give you an example.

"Foot and mouth disease (FMD) is caused by a highly contagious virus that occurs in much of the rest of the world. There hasn't been a case of FMD in the U.S. for over seventy years. Even though it does not affect people, it is one of the diseases that is especially dangerous from an agricultural perspective, since it would have a devastating effect on the U.S. economy if it were to reoccur here. Even a *limited* outbreak would certainly cost billions of dollars to our economy.

"Additionally, foot and mouth disease could be introduced without a sophisticated delivery system. Infected food, smuggled in by migrant workers, could be the source—with millions of cattle concentrated in the nation's heartland as the target.

"A Soviet agricultural facility in Pokrov was ostensibly used to produce foot and mouth disease (FMD) vaccine. This facility had the capability of producing FMD virus on a massive scale, up to twenty-four tons of virus per production run. Curiously, this agricultural research and development (R&D) complex included five nuclear-hardened bunkers for its products. Interestingly, with little retrofitting, this facility would also be capable of producing dozens of tons of smallpox virus. Logic would certainly question whether this massive production and security capability was not obscene over-kill for a facility producing an agricultural vaccine, no pun intended."

Several in the room smiled briefly, and the scientist continued.

"Of course, the really critical question for us here is, *where are all of those scientists now?* Obviously, the vast majority of them would not be a danger to us or anyone else. But many could be, because of their unique technical expertise. Perhaps worse, they could possess or have access to biological agents that have been modified or enhanced as weapons during the old offensive BW programs. It is well known that the 'brain drain' of scientists out of Russia has reached crisis proportions.

"Unbelievably, the average research scientist in the FSU is being paid an average salary of $1644 a year. It doesn't take a rocket scientist, or even a molecular biologist for that matter, to see that this has created a huge potential for the proliferation, or escape of dangerous expertise, technology, or even biological agents out of the old FSU offensive programs. Some of these scientists could certainly be susceptible to recruitment by rogue countries or even terrorist groups. Aside from the obvious financial incentives, it is not hard to suppose that some veterans of cold war bioweapons programs might be sympathetic to those ideologically opposed to the interests of the U.S."

"I get it, Doctor. What about the birds and wheat?"

"First, the birds. There are numerous species of migratory birds that traverse the Caribbean and the U.S. That part's easy. For example, hummingbirds migrate from here to South America.

"It would be theoretically possible to use birds to deliver an engineered mold or other pathogen which would attack wheat or grain crops. After being fed contaminated food, the agent could be delivered through natural foraging and waste elimination. This would certainly not be the most efficient method, but it is indeed feasible. A novel, or unknown pathogen might well escape initial detection here, thus allowing a widespread disease outbreak to occur.

"The agent could also be optimized to have a more dramatic or pathogenic effect on the crops, increasing the ultimate damage to our economy. The fact is that intensive use of a relative few, highly productive varieties of crops has greatly increased our production capabilities. But, since we have selected for less biodiversity, this practice has increased our vulnerability to an engineered disease that would efficiently attack a specific variety.

"If a country like Cuba gets a top Russian scientist with the right expertise, it is possible we could be hit with unique plant pathogens which would be undetectable and untraceable. There is a crop corridor in the United States where we grow nearly all our wheat, from Dallas, Texas, north to North Dakota and the Canadian border. They could conceivably take it all out. And it wouldn't stop at the border, either. Canadian crops would probably be affected as well.

"The real trick would be to modify the agent to have these unique characteristics and then be able to transport it, or deliver it in some 'natural' way—such as in birds. This would certainly provide Castro and the Cubans with what in the arms control business is called *plausible deniability*. That is, without indisputable proof that they, or someone else for that matter had purposefully introduced the disease, it would be arguable that it was a natural exposure. The Cubans could simply say it was a natural disaster. It would be very hard to prove otherwise."

"Could we prove it?" Eric asked.

She paused and shook her head. "Probably not, unless we had irrefutable intelligence, a unique genetic fingerprint, a defector, or some other smoking gun to ID the Cubans.

"One other example, and then I'm done. Speaking of birds— again!" she said with an emphasis that elicited a nervous ripple of laughter, "When the first cluster of human cases of West Nile Fever occurred in New York, it was obviously looked at very closely by the public health community.

"A bank of known antigens for commonly occurring viral encephalitis diseases was used to make a diagnosis. Based on the results, the cases were diagnosed as St Louis Encephalitis (SLE). SLE is a serious disease that is endemic, or naturally occurring in this country, but was not a particularly alarming diagnosis. Those were the diagnostic reagents commonly available, and SLE just happens to be in the same viral family as West Nile Virus.

"Luckily, there was an astute veterinary pathologist at the Bronx Zoo, who noticed that not only were crows dying all over the city, but so were other species of birds at the zoo that she knew were not susceptible to lethal infections of St. Louis Encephalitis virus.

"Fortunately, she made the connection between the human and bird disease outbreak quickly, performed diagnostics on several of the dead birds in the zoo population, and suspected the correct etiologic, or causative agent. She contacted military veterinary pathologists at the U.S. Army Medical Research Institute of Infectious Diseases (USAMRIID) who confirmed the diagnosis and quickly identified the exact species of WNV.

"Of course, now, West Nile is endemic in the U.S., and has rapidly spread from New York to California, and everywhere in-between through a bird-mosquito cycle. The West Nile emergence was a classic case of diagnostic tunnel vision. No one expected to see West Nile, and predictably, no one saw it. That initial tunnel vision was costly in public health terms, but it points out how novel or unexpected diseases can easily be missed or misdiagnosed.

"Incidentally, it has been reported that the Cubans were at one time working with West Nile virus. Would it be paranoia to suspect that West Nile came from Cuba? Perhaps, but we can't really say for sure where it came from. But let's just for argument's sake say it did come from Cuba. There it is—*plausible deniability*—virtually impossible to prove one way or the other. This is one of the perverse beauties of using biology as a weapon."

The room was very quiet. Eric said, "Thank you Doctor. You've been most enlightening. The Cubans may be further along than we thought.

"Simply stated, Fidel wants the capability to create economic chaos in America. I firmly believe that Cuba is on the brink of developing agro-terror weapons that could do so. In addition, fear of spreading contagion would cause the world to literally quarantine the United States, damaging our entire economy beyond belief. Our exports would be cut off and our food supply radically reduced."

Eric then quoted Undersecretary of State John Bolton, from a speech in May of 2002. According to Eric, Bolton had stated that Cuba was, at that time, developing "...a limited offensive biological warfare..." program.

"The ramifications are horrendous. The costs and chaos would rend the nation's fabric. Democracy would be challenged and an attack could force our society to fight just to survive," Eric said emphatically.

Eric's faith in his analysis seemed quite justifiable. The strategic potential of the previously unknown Cuban threat made even the most skeptical of those in the room rethink their position, and a consensus was rapidly achieved. All those in attendance would leave with the entire British package, and all that Eric had developed. Their orders were to, in turn, either verify or refute the evidence that had been presented to them by Eric. Their charter was clear: no more "Iraqs." Intelligence had to be unimpeachably sound. In ten days, the CIA would brief the collective findings to the President.

Time was of the essence as the assembled officers left the briefing room. With each passing day, Fidel Castro vacillated more and more. He was harassing and imprisoning increasing numbers of Cuban citizens that peacefully opposed his regime. He was squandering the goodwill he had built by carefully stroking both the Third World and the Hollywood elite. Seventy-seven years old, Castro was desperate; the realization was beginning to take hold that his communist regime would barely outlast him. Fidel's days were numbered, and he knew it. To some, it seemed he wanted to go out with a bang.

01 Jun 2004

Rumsfeld's secure, red phone began to ring. It was George Tenet. The Director of the NSA and Colin Powell were already on the phone when Rumsfeld picked up the receiver, on conference call. Their subject: *agro-terrorism* and the collective assessment of the threat to go to the President.

After several minutes of hushed discussion, Mr. Tenet said, "Our men and women on the executive committee have done a great job thus far putting the intelligence picture together, and I fully agree with the vetting of the threat. I'll take the lead to schedule a brief to the National Security Council and President Bush."

The next day, June 2nd, Tenet, Rumsfeld, and Powell were again in the White House. The President was in a good mood, and receptive to their briefing, presented with some alterations from his original ten days earlier. Condoleeza Rice walked into the Oval Office at the last minute.

Upon completion, the President asked one question: "When will the threat be operational and capable of being employed against the United States?"

"Our estimate is between six to nine months from today," Tenet said. Rumsfeld nodded his agreement.

"Fine, I want you to put an intelligence full-court press on obtaining details articulating threat development," The President explained. "OPSEC (operational security) is of the highest importance. I want no leaks. Lock this one down."

Bush continued, speaking candidly:

"Tragic as the last three years have been, this threat makes Al-Qaeda's best effort look like a gas station holdup. Think what it would do to our international trade deficit if we lost our wheat crop—*just our wheat crop*! The stock market would crash and consumer confidence would go to zero. It would be an economic disaster.

"The great engine of our prosperity in this country is our ability to produce safe, plentiful, inexpensive food. And we must protect that. We have a desperate, geriatric, Cuban idiot building a capability that could destroy it, and spread, and take down Canada and the entire hemisphere. We're going to stop him from doing that. Now I truly believe the 1960s reports that he asked the Soviets to nuke the United States even if Cuba was destroyed in retaliation. His hate for us is unfathomable.

"Six to nine months is not a lot of time for us to react. UK resources can be used as well, but I don't want to let Prime Minister Blair get within the political bursting radius. We've damaged him enough already.

"Remember: everyone must support the CIA with the very best they have in terms of resources and personnel. Colin, I want you to guarantee that our plans include appropriate strategic informational contingencies. We don't need to have President Chavez in Venezuela, the FARC and ELN rebels in Colombia, or the Shining Path in Peru exploding over U.S. intervention in the region. Brief me regularly on the progress." The President smiled confidingly. "This is a 'no-fail' operation. Thanks."

Tenet returned to his office and ordered his lawyers to draw up an interagency memorandum of understanding to put the CIA, with him at the helm, in charge of intelligence collaboration and operations for the Cuban issue at hand.

Near the end of the day, Tenet called for his deputy and right-hand "number two" man, Lieutenant General (LTG) Paul Hanscom.

LTG Hanscom sighed. Murphy's Law dictated that every crisis in Washington would hit at the end of the day. He walked into Mr. Tenet's office and came back out an hour later with a legal pad full of notes. Director Tenet had selected him to run a project against Castro, which would take him completely away from all other duties until it was complete.

Paul Hanscom returned to his office, noting that his secretary had already set a steaming hot cup of black coffee on his large conference table. Paul ripped off all the pages of notes, and, after writing "*TOP SECRET WORKING PAPERS*" on the top of each sheet, he sat down to reread his notes and to think, creatively doodling as he went along.

His first note was "OPSEC." His second was "Clandestine/no links to the U.S." His third was "Effects-based planning." The fourth: "Use old-timers and multiple cut-outs." The fifth: "Use, but protect UK interests and the Prime Minister." This last will be very delicate, he thought, since Castro will never deal with the United States. We must paint the UK as responsible for all actions in Cuba, and then bring both of them to the table together at the end of the operation— while not letting the world believe that the UK is involved at all.

He continued to make notes as he read and re-read his instructions, adding comments to his list from the specified and implied tasks in the mission, as he perceived it, prior to detailed intelligence briefings.

After several cups of coffee, he had distilled the mission down to three possible courses of action, but final shaping would be determined by the intelligence available. At least he would have some comments that would drive intelligence requirements and collection, starting bright and early the next morning.

Paul was mentally formulating a tentative force list: men, women, and equipment that might be required to support each of his broad concepts. Before long, Paul's thoughts drifted to his wife, Dana, waiting for him at home. For almost forty years she had stood by his side. A selfless partner and wonderful mother to their sons, she was one of the most admired women in the military establishment. She cared about every soldier, and everyone she contacted realized it.

The General knew she would support yet another late night. As always, he would call and explain that work necessitated another evening apart, adding as always, how much he loved her. He reached for his black, unsecure phone and pushed the speed-dial button to his quarters.

Immediately thereafter, he called his aide in to arrange for two more calls.

*   *   *   *   *

The next day, June 3rd, General Hanscom arranged for a meeting over lunch with Mr. Tenet. He also invited the Chief of the NSA, a State Department representative, a Department of Defense intelligence officer, and a State Department advisor who had been hand picked by Secretary Powell. Condoleeza Rice sent a National Security Council representative as well.

LTG Hanscom began. "Gentlemen, Director Tenet gave me the responsibility to move on the Cuban problem. Unfortunately, as you may have heard, Mr. Tenet officially resigned as Director today, June 3rd, 2004. He will hold his post until the 11th of August, and he has put me in charge of this operation until its completion. Deputy McLaughlin will be temporarily taking the reins from Mr. Tenet. He has been instructed that nothing regarding The Hybrid will change, in any respect, due to postings of new or interim Directors or Deputies.

"With that much to ease your minds, I will need a hundred and ten percent in the intelligence arena if we are to meet the President's instructions to brief him on our progress in at the most two weeks, or thirteen days the way we're moving." Hanscom paused for a moment to let the words sink in before continuing:

"I will build invisible planning and command and control cells on a distributive basis that will find ways to destroy the Cuban capability by truly integrating the various agencies into a joint operation. I envision a plan that uses all sorts of devious means and tricks to coerce Cuba into compliance with our wishes. I see electronic warfare and informational tools in the lead, complemented by 'military muscle' when required. I want absolute secrecy. I need your personal pledge to work as a team, or it's a 'no go.'"

LTG Hanscom, speaking slowly, noted the heads nodding around the room. "I will sign whatever directives and authorities are required. I, and my organization, will take full responsibility for this project's outcomes. I want your complete and loyal support and you have my pledge that if we fail the nation I will ensure that all of your equities are protected, including an offer of my resignation, if need be."

The room was silent. Mr. Tenet had fully empowered LTG Hanscom: an incredible testament to trust, faith, and confidence in a subordinate. No comment from his luncheon companions was forthcoming: everyone had the message. Further discussion on the subject of both Tenet's resignation and The Hybrid lasted another ten minutes. They reached a positive consensus—to break down the remaining Cold War interagency walls and stovepipes that had impeded effective cooperation in the past—The Hybrid would be known among them as Tenet's legacy, and Hanscom held the swagger stick now.

The attendees, now newly bonded associates, discussed how to communicate while ensuring that their respective staffs thought everything was business as usual, with interagency feuds flying. For now, they agreed to deal only by red phone, leaving no paper trails at all. Only the principle bosses would know what was going on. Having them come from different sources and different projects would hopefully mask all intelligence requests.

Finally, Hanscom concluded his talk. "We are going where others have never been. Our hybrid organization will apply all the means of national power in coordinated fashion. My goal is to destroy the Cuban *agro-terror* initiative, possibly without firing a single bullet."

He paused a moment, inspired that the normally taciturn bureaucrats were excited about working together. "The team we are going to put together may be a template for the future."

* * * * *

After the others had gone, Paul Hanscom spoke privately to Tenet in his office.

"I am going to build independent cells for this operation. For now, I will construct one for Angola, Cuba, Germany, Mexico, and Venezuela. I may need more. No more than a few individuals will ever know how it all ties together. The independent parts will be disassembled when their functions are over. I intend to accomplish the mission without risk to President Bush or Prime Minister Blair. The cells will also be front organizations, thus making any attempt to piece this effort together virtually impossible for an outsider. In fact, with your permission, I am not going to brief anyone in the administration on the mechanics. Most will know almost nothing beyond the fact that we need intelligence support."

He turned to Mr. Tenet. "From the CIA, I want John Jones, your best planner. I will select Mr. Ellis, a retired Army infantryman, to be the cutout for the efforts of us in this room. Ellis will be the sole conduit from operational personnel to us. I will also pull in tough, old, General Joe Cordell to work with John. I promise there will be no leaks.

"I'm worried about the ramifications of this threat for Homeland Security. Secretary Ridge ought to be given planning time to research how to help the American people just in case Castro somehow succeeds in developing this capability. I'm not sure about OPSEC, or timing. I will leave that to you and the senior leaders of the nation, while I focus strictly on threat elimination."

Tenet agreed, and LTG Hanscom warmly shook his hand.

* * * * *

Ellis was already waiting outside when LTG Hanscom returned to his office. Once inside, the men embraced and swapped old war stories to catch up. After over fifteen minutes of discussion, Hanscom broke the ice:

"This is an opportunity to work together to conduct sophisticated operations to take apart a Cuban threat. Delicate, synchronized, interagency, clandestine, covert and carefully coordinated actions are part of the fabric we will weave. We'll build an invisible organization that has no permanent headquarters; an organization that "morphs" for each mission; an organization that continually changes its size, location and functions. One that is effects-based.

"I'm going to trust you to get the right people, operators, commo men, and staff. Find them. I'll write the checks," Hanscom explained.

"The division of labor will be this: I want Brigadier General Joe Cordell to lead the execution of the Cuba mission when it 'goes hot'—I'll get him energized, along with John Jones; you should use Jones to plan and direct singleton employment.

"You are the sole portal to senior leaders of this administration. I want you to find quality operators that will succeed in other countries that need our attention. All operators in other countries must deal through cutouts and be totally independent. Since the most dangerous and complex part is Cuba, I want you and John to communicate several times daily; we can't afford any risks in that department."

Ellis was thinking to himself, mentally scrolling through hundreds of personal sources. "I know exactly where to find the right kind of people for such an organization—seasoned operatives from the CIA and the U.S. Army Special Forces."

CHAPTER FIVE

10 Aug 2003

Mike and Kirsten pulled into Norman, Oklahoma, after spending two weeks with Mike's family in the western part of the state. Mike was being put into the Army's school account for eighteen months of graduate study at the University of Oklahoma, as promised. He would graduate just prior to the Christmas break in December of 2004.

Mike was already accepted for admission; the Army had worked his application for him, using his academic records and Graduate Record Exam score on file at the Army's personnel center in Alexandria, Virginia. His major was to be Latin American Studies. Perhaps he would be going to 7th Special Forces Group as a commander; maybe they were short on experience in South America. They had something in mind for Mike, and it had something to do with Latin America. Of that much he was sure.

Mike was authorized to move his wife and all of his possessions as part of a permanent change of station. He had two weeks to report to his administrative command in Indiana, letting them know that the family had made it, his address, phone number, and other particulars, and that he had completed enrollment. Officers in the educational account were supported in all administrative matters from the small holding unit. His tuition and books were fully funded.

The first week in Oklahoma was a time of settling in. Mike had found a reasonable home and had signed a year-and-a-half lease. Mike's wife, Kirsten, a saucy redhead from Virginia, had only one semester of college, so she also enrolled. She wanted to teach English, having a passion for picaresque novels.

Their home took shape. Kirsten bustled about hanging drapes, thoroughly enjoying making a home for her husband, who, for the first time in their marriage, was going to be at home.

"Oh, Mike, this is really great. I can't believe you come home every night—that I cook for a husband that is actually home. And I wake up with you beside me in the morning. It is wonderful."

Kirsten was a reasonably contented wife. But being an army wife, she still had that nagging worry—that apprehension—always wondering—not if, but when—orders would arrive to deprive her of her husband. She knew it was the one thing that spoiled their happiness together. Her insecurity would flair up from time to time, leading to huge, destructive rows.

But she was so grateful to have time with Mike. He had been repeatedly deployed, and his cumulative time away from home equated to seven years of their eight-year marriage. She wanted to get to know him better. A whirlwind courtship had preceded their wedding. Shortly thereafter, it became apparent that the main thing they did together was pack and unpack Mike's bags. Frequent and wonderful but too-short vacations had been their only quality time, available only because Mike had to expend accumulated Army leave.

All in all, Kirsten remained supportive of his secretive disappearances, but her tolerance was wearing thin. She had expected more from their relationship.

Kirsten was not from a military family but she sincerely tried to understand Mike and his motivation. She embraced the fact that Mike loved her, loved his men, and loved the mission. Asking him to choose priorities among the three would be futile.

One thing Mike wouldn't discuss was his wounds. Once, he had told her he was going away to a six-week survival course, and he came back with a bandage taped just below the knee on his left calf. A small-caliber round had gone through, hitting only soft tissue, nothing vital. Mike had nothing to say except that it was a training accident. Kirsten didn't believe him. Now he had come home from Afghanistan, again wounded—once again after deploying without telling her he was going into danger. She was not pleased.

But for now, life seemed great.

* * * * *

Football fever was sweeping the campus like a Great-Plains tornado, and Mike found himself caught up in the middle of it. Coach Stoops had roared into Norman five years before and was already hinting at yet another NCAA National Football Championship.

Oklahoma's football team meant more to the average citizen of the state than would be understood by college fans elsewhere. The disaster of the dust bowl had forced millions of "Okies" to leave to survive. Steinbeck's depiction of the pain and suffering in *The Grapes of Wrath* clearly showed that something had to be done to change the image of the state and the Okies from semi-literate, starving refugees to one of winners.

The oil industry supplied the solution; members of the Touchdown Club supplied the money. Oklahoma literally bought the nation's best athletes for winning teams from the late 1940s until the late 1950s—outbidding other coaches—until the National Collegiate Athletic Association grew punitive teeth. The longest winning streak, lasting forty-seven games, still stands as the national record. Pride in the state and OU football swelled accordingly, intertwining the fortunes of the football team with the state's appreciation of well-being.

George Cross, the president of the university, when speaking to the Senate of the Great State of Oklahoma in 1952, asked for a significant budget increase. When questioned as to his purpose, he replied, "I would like to build a university the football team can be proud of."

Mike and Kirsten quickly found out that the University of Oklahoma, in the intervening fifty years, actually had become an institution of quality, largely due to the efforts of a dynamic president, Dr. David L. Boren. The average SAT scores, endowed faculty positions, number of Rhodes scholars, and improved research facilities were impressive. Both Kirsten and Mike found that they needed to "hit the library hard" to stay afloat.

On Thursday nights, many of the grad students would gather at O'Connell's pub, a block away from the football stadium, to drink beer and analyze the next weekend's opposition. Mike couldn't help but take a second look at many of the busty Soonerettes that hung out in the pub, and being in their presence made him feel years younger. But he didn't do more than look, because Mike knew whom he truly loved. He had always stayed faithful to Kirsten.

CHAPTER SIX

05 Jun 2004

The President slowly signed the document and handed it to his chief of staff in front of the assembled few that knew about the Cuban project.

The paper was a "Presidential Finding" that authorized the CIA, with other governmental agency support as well as collaboration with British Intelligence, to conduct clandestine and covert operations to destroy WMD programs in Cuba. Worldwide supportive actions were authorized in pursuit of the destruction of Fidel's growing capability, to include preemptive action.

Following the President's briefing, the same team had gone to Vice President Dick Cheney, as ordered by President Bush, in order to gather his impressions. The VP agreed that the threat was credible and that action must begin as soon as possible.

No operational details were explained or offered. George Tenet planned on returning when his courses of action gelled for a verbal-only presentation regarding execution of the plan on the ground.

Riding in his car on the road beside the Potomac River, Tenet keyed his secure telephone. "Paul," he said, "You have the green light."

President Bush looked out of his window down on the rose garden. He was thinking of the horrible weapons the Cold War had spawned—worried that there was no longer any safe haven for the citizens of his beloved country. He prayed for a better future.

06 Jun 2004

On a Sunday afternoon near the end of the spring semester of 2004, Mike Trantor ambled happily across the campus. He had just checked the results posted for his last exam and was quite pleased. His grades were solid, and his thesis was coming along. Summer school was coming up, and then after the fall semester he would graduate with his M.A.

Kirsten was well aware of the war in Afghanistan and Iraq. She worried constantly that Mike would be called away to combat. Things between them had been really good lately. Her worries were justified.

Mike had to get across town for a post-wedding party one of his retired reconnaissance buddies was hosting. Kirsten was busy studying and had given Mike a "kitchen pass" to have a few cold ones on his own.

Splat! The wedding cake hit the ceiling fan. Icing-laced trajectories followed on the ceiling, walls and floors. The new husband and wife rocked to and fro, dirty dancing. Mike eased out of the room. In a modest home, Rocky, a retired Command Sergeant Major from the 75th Ranger Regiment, was hosting a wedding for his son's best friend and his bride from Midwest City, Oklahoma. His son had followed his father into the Regiment and had brought ten of his best teammates back for the festivities.

Rocky and Mike Trantor had been friends in one of the Ranger battalions. Both had made the cut. Rocky had stayed a pure Ranger, while Mike had later diversified by moving on to become a well-known and highly respected Special Forces officer. Rocky was pleased that Mike, somewhat a celebrity, could and would attend the wedding. After all, there would be a keg of Coors: a guaranteed Mike-magnet.

Mike always appreciated it when sergeants thought enough of him to invite him to their parties and functions. He was the son of poor, Oklahoma dirt farmers, and still believed that men who worked with their hands, with *manos sucios*, were more honorable than most.

Mike also believed his word was more valuable than his life. He had helped himself to a cold beer from the Coors keg and went out on the back porch for a smoke. He lit up a cigarette and took a long drag. Through the smoke, he saw a shape in the shadows approaching the screened-in porch from the road beyond where a 4x4 truck was parked. In the dark he saw a tall man with a distinctive crew cut. A second or two later he "made" the individual. The dead giveaway was abnormally small feet. It was Brigadier General Joe Cordell. Shit. Something was up. Mike smiled, and stepped off the porch, remembering the old days during Phase One of the SF Qualification Course with his legendary buddy . . . back then, Colonel Cordell was the meanest son of a bitch on the planet, and ran the Q-course like a concentration camp.

Many regarded General Joe as the best tactician in Special Forces. Some even said that Joe Cordell was the "second-coming" of Bull Simons, the legendary colonel who had also led the Son Tay raid into North Vietnam in an attempt to rescue American POWs held just outside of Hanoi. Mike stepped out into the dark and saluted, even though both men were in blue jeans. General Joe returned the salute. This was undoubtedly business, and Mike was curious.

General Joe's haircut hadn't changed since the 1960s; he was a strict disciplinarian. Like Patton, he was death on anyone violating Army or unit standards. Mike was unprepared for what followed. Joe started his conversation slowly.

"Mike, I want you to stop cutting your hair. I want you to grow a beard and a mustache. That is all you need to know. When you get orders eventually, execute them. Regardless of their wording, we will be working the same project. Be patient with this one."

The old warrior continued, "I am putting you in a pipeline. What happens in that pipeline is still to be exactly determined. Obey your instructions; we are going to need you." Joe paused and stared deeply into Mike's eyes. "Are you willing to sign on for another singleton?"

The long definition of a singleton was a Special Forces soldier who would perform the key or critical portion of a mission alone. Detailed preparation was the norm, and typically, unlimited resources would be available. Preferably these missions would fall to a soldier who was unmarried. Too many couples had been shattered, either by the strain of total lack of communication during an extensive mission—or worse, by the never to be explained circumstances of the volunteer's death.

Nothing was more painful to Special Forces commanders than having to notify a young wife that her husband had perished; and in the war against terrorism, many commanders were, sadly, well versed in the practice. Old-timers remembered that in 1965, the 101st Airborne Division used to ensure that the infantry platoons had evenly distributed percentages of married men. That way, when a platoon was wiped out, the number of widows would be minimized.

Mike replied, "Sir, I'll do anything you ask. You know me; I'm best on my own. I'll take any singleton you offer, in the blind. But, before I get pumped up, I just want to make sure it is for real. We've both lived through too many phony alerts and warning orders."

Joe quietly chuckled and put his hand on Mike's shoulder. "I guarantee this is the real thing, *potentially*. I have contacted you because you *are* the best on your own. Not only are you an ornery rascal, you have incredible instincts and an uncanny ability to survive. Most of all, I want you because you are all heart. The only problem is you aren't single, and I hate to repeatedly put you at risk. As you know you can't tell Kirsten anything about this."

Joe started to slowly walk away, and then turned back to Mike.

"It's no secret that you have some issues with Kirsten at home. I initially considered not choosing you, because you need time for 'marriage maintenance' and are a bit long in the tooth for this business. However"—he paused, smiling—"it's your reputation. You always deliver, and even better, you always come home."

Mike answered quickly, "Kirsten will be okay. Even though there's a difference in our ages, she is mature when it comes to handling my time away from home. She understands what I do for a living. Besides, we've had a good nine months together, a whole school year. The pay increase to Major didn't hurt things on the home front, either." Mike's voice raised a decibel. "She knows, in Special Forces context, what the War on Terror means."

Joe nodded. "Okay. But after you finish this one, you will come back and…" Joe gave Mike a significant stare for a moment.

"You are going to have to accept change, and the fact that you are getting older. Soon it will be your turn to train and launch a new generation of singletons. Okay?"

"Got it, sir," Mike replied. "I'll put everything I have in this last one." His eyes followed General Joe who abruptly turned and was out of sight in a few seconds. Mike was surprised that Joe knew about the sandpaper between him and Kirsten. Their time in Norman together had been good, but not great. Kirsten complained constantly about how much she dreaded returning to Army routine.

Nonetheless, Mike was supercharged. He walked back into the house and refilled his beer, grabbing an empty glass so he could have one for each hand. Wondering if anyone could feel his joy and corresponding increase in his heart rate, he went outside, sat under a tree, and chain-smoked more Marlboros. He was ready for whatever was coming.

General Joe was right. His life would soon permanently change. For now, though, Mike was savoring the moment. He would simply wait and discreetly pick up his physical training load while preparing for summer school.

As the party wound down, Rocky joined Mike under the tree asking if anything was the matter. Mike said, "Not a single thing." They spoke late into the evening, as only special operations men can do, of old firefights, friends, and sacrifice. During lulls in the conversation, Mike thought of General Joe. The veteran infantryman and Special Forces officer was his cherished mentor. Eccentric and brilliant, Joe was a clandestine poet, dreamer, and friend. For Joe, Mike would do anything.

11 Jun 2004

In O'Connell's Pub on the evening of June 11, while playing a game of shuffleboard, Mike bumped into a short African-American male wearing a baseball cap and wrap-around sunglasses.

In a hushed voice, the man asked, "Could you please step outside and have a word with me?"

Mike hesitated. It was getting dark. There were still a few hippie screwball panhandlers left around campus, throwbacks to the 1960s and 70s. He responded, "Why should I?"

The young kid leaned toward his ear and whispered, "I want to talk about the camouflage contest at Ranger School."

Mike paused, and then let out a laugh, remembering how he won by having the men in his squad camouflage their buttocks. He grabbed his beer to take it outside.

Outside the pub, the young Afro-American quietly spoke, "Your instructions will arrive in blank, white, sealed envelopes in a student mailbox in Cross Towers. The box is number 303. Here are two keys. The box is not in your name. In two days start checking the box daily, Monday through Friday."

He continued, "Never conduct business from any phone other than the one in your house. Do not use phone booths or your cellular except to call home. Your home phone has been tailored for your protection; look at it as your umbilical cord. Take this small envelope. In it is a credit card; the pin number is taped on the back. Memorize it. Sign receipts with your real name. The credit card is for any expenses you incur on official business."

He concluded, "Don't watch me leave. Go inside and enjoy your beer. I asked you for a few bucks out here for gas. You told me no." The black kid walked around the corner and disappeared.

Mike smiled. He was going into the pipeline. Someone was going to check him out to see if he had the right stuff for whatever program was operational. He was ready, and would follow instructions to the letter, and then make the best judgment calls if he had to break them. Someone would be monitoring.

14 Jun 2004

Mike walked across the southern part of the campus, the same as any other day, casually swinging by Cross Towers. It was tempting to try to determine who could be watching the drop, if anyone, but Mike knew better than to act suspiciously. When he opened the mailbox, there was a plain white envelope, as promised. He took it and placed it in his backpack (still a rucksack in his military lingo). On a break, he opened the envelope and read the contents:

    You have several weeks to polish your
    Spanish. Learn to operate in social

environments that will convince observers that you are a frequent and confident traveler in South America. There are excellent tutors in the university area. Select one from the yellow pages, and get to work.

Mike smoked a cigarette under the trees that lined the University Mall. He took the note, lit it with a match—no small feat in the summer winds, and let it burn away in his fingers.

He went home. Kirsten was working out in the gym again, so Mike took advantage of her absence to begin his search for a tutor. Opening the yellow pages, he found a promising ad. He dialed.

The technician shouted across the small room, "This is a hit from Norman, Oklahoma. He's calling OU Language Tutoring. Take it, Lisa!" The call was automatically routed to Lisa's desk. She picked up the phone.

"OU Language Tutoring. How may I help you?"

"Well, I need to brush up on my Spanish. How quickly can something be arranged?"

"We can get you started right away."

In a few minutes, she had coordinated a tutoring program to be conducted in one of the graduate study rooms in the new library annex. She outlined the hours for study, and agreed to supply appropriate textbooks. She then spoke Spanish with Mike for about five minutes to explore his capabilities. An agreement was reached to begin lessons in three days, in the OU library. A credit card was okay for payment.

Lisa looked out of her window, at the Washington Monument in the distance, as she closed the deal. Mike knew his phone was probably bugged, but he didn't have an inkling that Lisa was in Arlington, Virginia. There were two other girls and a young man in the same room. They complemented Lisa on her sale. If she had failed, they were the back-ups in place for his next and any subsequent calls in search of a tutor. They went back to their other tasks—ready for the many roles they would play that day.

The technician pushed a preset button on his phone, stating, "Launch Marcella. Details to follow by secure e-mail in two minutes. Thanks."

*   *   *   *   *

Mike, of course, didn't tell Kirsten about the tutor. It would not only be an operational risk, she would be absolutely furious that the Army's promise of an eighteen-month sojourn from duty was being broken. Besides, if he didn't make the cut for the mission, Kirsten would have been concerned over nothing.

Since Mike had already set a pattern of spending much of his time in the evenings in the library anyway, the effort to upgrade his Spanish wouldn't cost him any additional time away from Kirsten. He would go about business as usual as summer school started. If Kirsten stumbled onto the lessons, he would say he needed them to help in conducting original research from Spanish documents.

17 Jun 2004

Mike looked down at his watch. He was reading in the OU library's Great Room. He had five minutes to hit the latrine and walk to the linkup with his newly acquired tutor. He was tired, and not looking forward to the first session. After the latrine, he ambled down the hallway to the designated room. He walked in and sat down. Another student, a girl, was in the room, reading. She was attractive, reminding him of Jennifer Lopez, the movie star. He asked her if she had permission to be in the small study, since he had it reserved. She replied, "*No hay problema. Hola, Mike,* let's begin. *Me llamo Marcella.*"

One hour later Mike was exhausted. She had wrung him out. Her technique was role-playing. He had rented a hotel room, by phone and in person, at least ten times. He had coordinated for laundry pickup, practiced how to tip, he had complained about the service, had asked for his bags to be delivered, and had been attuned to be arrogant to the staff, and therefore be more respected and, correspondingly receive better service.

At the end of the session, she said, "I want you to have all this dialogue memorized before your next class."

His next class was only forty-eight hours away. Marcella was a pro, and a tough taskmistress.

He left with a small book for the next lesson, in which he was to go to a bank and open accounts for savings and checking.

Marcella drove back to her hotel room. She lay on the bed relaxing after a shower. She picked up her cell phone, dialing the secure code. It rang. She said, "He will be competent enough in six weeks to accomplish what you described, though I would have liked to be given more details to be absolutely sure. I guarantee he will study." She smiled, and turned on the TV.

* * * * *

As summer school kicked in, Mike found that Spanish had significantly increased his academic workload. It was becoming more and more difficult to do course work and upgrade his Spanish at the same time, particularly with increasingly difficult scenarios Marcella was making him memorize before each session.

However, no matter how frustrated he was with the increasing load, seeing her made him happy. He felt like a schoolboy with a crush on his teacher. This time, however, he was the older one in the relationship.

After six weeks, Marcella surprised him by saying, "Come to the next session wearing a suit and tie and meet me in front of the library."

Twice, Mike had left the house for an evening class in a suit, to honor a guest lecturer at OU. Kirsten, now almost as busy as he was with course work, wouldn't notice.

At the designated time, Mike arrived at the library and stood outside. Marcella was not to be seen, so he lit a Marlboro to kill time. She hated his *cigarillos,* so he never asked for a smoke break during lessons.

He stared as a black Mercedes with tinted windows pulled up. The passenger's window came down and inside, Marcella was dressed to the hilt. Mike was speechless. She winked and said the Spanish equivalent of, "Are you going my way?" Mike couldn't believe the plunging neckline of her evening dress. He averted his eyes and quickly pulled the door open and swung into the passenger's seat, worrying that Kirsten might see them.

Marcella sped up the interstate to Oklahoma City, all business. She described the meal they would have, how he would treat her, what she expected of him, and that the cost of the trip would be in his first bill from the course.

She pulled up two blocks short of a five-star Latino restaurant.

"OK, Mike," she said as she handed him the keys to the car. "Change places with me. You're in charge now and I'm just your girlfriend for the evening. We'll speak only in Spanish. Not a word of English, please."

Mike handled the evening in impeccable style. He obtained a good table, and ordering well off the menu. He needed her help a bit in finding a good Chilean wine, but overall he was earning a passable grade, he was sure. Ending with an after-dinner drink, she instructed, "Ask me to dance." Mike stammered. Marcella laughed with glee, grabbing his hand and elegantly heading for the dance floor.

In Spanish, she said, "Hold me like this." Then, she reviewed the *merengue* and showed him how to modify some of his steps to varying Latin rhythms.

They were having a blast, even though Mike occasionally had two left feet, and was unable to keep up with Marcella's quick pace on the dance floor. After approximately forty-five minutes, she said, "Now if you dance with a *Latina* she will know that you've been in Latin America before."

When they were about to leave, Marcella said, "Mike, please stay for this song. It's one of my favorites." She put her head on his shoulder, and for one dance only, held him very close.

As soon as they entered the car, she began a severe critique from behind the wheel that lasted all the way back to campus. She scrutinized every single action he had taken, and he realized that she was a serious professional, mature well beyond her apparent years. Mike sensed how silly his crush on her truly was, especially when she handed him his homework for the next week.

After she dropped him off, Mike waved goodbye. Dying for a smoke all night, he lit a Marlboro and slowly walked home, laughing heartily at himself. He felt like a fool for thinking his obviously professional instructress shared his juvenile romantic notions.

Arriving at home a little after midnight, it would appear he had stayed in the library until it closed. Kirsten was asleep on the couch, a book lying on the floor beside her. Mike went upstairs and showered. Scared that perfume might be on his clothes, he put them in a bag that he could sneak out of the house in the morning and drop at the laundry.

He gently kissed Kirsten awake and took her hand. "Come on sweetheart. It's time for bed." He was feeling somewhat ashamed of himself and as he crawled into bed, taking Kirsten into his arms, he harbored inexplicable feelings of guilt.

CHAPTER SEVEN

02 Aug 2004

The President was livid. The U.S. Telestar-12 communications satellite orbiting 22,000 miles above the Atlantic Ocean was under attack.

The Telestar-12 is used to relay Voice of America broadcasts around the world, to include nations that desired to limit the information their citizens could access. North Korea, Cuba, Iran, the People's Republic of China, and others were among those that were offered a window to the world.

Jamming attacks emanating from Cuba began on June 6, 2003, the day that Voice of America began transmitting Farsi language programming to Iran. Since the repressive theocracy in Iran lacks the wherewithal to jam satellites in the western hemisphere, Cuba stepped in with its sophisticated electronic warfare capability.

In fact, Fidel's arsenal includes an electronic espionage base located at Bejucal, a town near Havana. With Russian installed equipment, Cuba can wage denial of service attacks for computers and telecommunications systems, and can listen in to non-secure telephonic communication anywhere in the continental United States.

The President put the packet down on his desk. "I agree. This is another indicator that Fidel's judgment is slipping. His human rights assaults, and now an open and flagrant challenge to us clearly indicate that we have to take action to preclude having strategic agro-terror weapons at his disposal. In layman's terms, Castro may be 'losing it.'"

*   *   *   *   *

After a short pause to rearrange the chairs in front of the President's desk, LTG Hanscom was prepared to begin his brief. Only he, new interim Agency Director John McLaughlin, and Secretary Rumsfeld were in the room with President Bush. The room had been swept for bugs a last time one hour before the briefing.

The audience was limited and OPSEC was being stressed because Paul Hanscom wanted the President to hear, to a degree, the operational details of the Hybrid's plan to scuttle Castro's agro-terror program.

After forty minutes and several questions from President Bush, General Hanscom summarized the briefing:

"Sir, we will present the Cubans with multiple simultaneous dilemmas, none of which they can successfully solve without a massive amount of resources, which we know they simply don't have. Their agro-terror program will collapse from a global assault of a 'thousand cuts,' and the U.S. will not be identified as the agent of the collapse."

LTG Hanscom continued: "If our plan fails, and the agro-terror capability continues to be developed, we will defer to the Department of Defense as the lead and join ranks to support a kinetic plan with the main effort being conventional forces."

Secretary Rumsfeld interjected, "Today, we have a small cell initiating planning to use our military power to remove the threat, if required. They are working in CIA headquarters and he controls all the information. There will be no compromise of information that could endanger the CIA's extremely detailed plan."

The President quietly added, "Make sure, once again, that this doesn't leak and endanger our clandestine operators. Also, it is worth the risk to try the clandestine option first. I want the kinetic option developed, but only in concept. Rummy, you and the Agency come brief me on it when it is outlined."

He paused, "I approve the plan for execution. I'll sign the execution order today. A courier will deliver the single copy. Thanks for your hard work. I'm available, twenty-four hours a day, if there is anything you need."

"One other thing, please, before you leave. General Hanscom, early in the briefing you used a term that is new to me. What is the exact definition of a singleton?" the President asked. Condoleeza had already provided her definition—but the President wanted to be sure.

"A singleton is a special operator who is deployed on missions best accomplished by a lone man or woman," Hanscom explained.

"Those chosen for duty must meet the training, physical and psychological profiles engendered by the task at hand. We invest heavily to ensure that singletons are optimally prepared. They fully know the risks involved in their assigned missions."

03 Aug 2004

After the night out on the town, it had taken Marcella several hours to write her final report on Mike. She had reread the personal assessment on her secure computer numerous times before sending it to D.C. for the psychiatrists for study. Her boss had demanded blind, absolute candor. For some reason Mike was an extremely important subject.

Marcella's report concluded: "I have exactly delineated my assessment of the subject's ability to operate in Spanish and in a Latin American culture. I have also answered the detailed questions posed by the psychiatrists.

There is an additional comment. This man is truly in love with his wife. He had many opportunities to make advances and he never tried. He may be a man with unimpeachable character and morals. We do not need to worry about women agents penetrating his cover or interfering with any operation.

"Mike is charismatic and unassuming. He appears to not have an egotistical bone in his body. Best descriptions: principled, focused, even-keeled, multi-talented and patriotic."

* * * * *

Two weeks earlier, while smoking a Marlboro by the University Mall, Mike opened what was to be his second-to-last envelope.

The instructions were clear: He was going "hot."

Prepare to leave during the next two weeks. Your wife can stay and continue school. Inform

her that you may be gone up to nine months and
that you will be unable to contact her during
that time period. See your professors;
withdraw from the courses for the fall
semester. The intent is to return you to
school to eventually re-initiate study. Travel
light: you will be receiving a clothing
allowance. You will not be able to return home
after departure. Bring your civilian and
official passport and your shot records. No
other military gear of any type will be
carried. Continue growing a beard. Your ticket
will be in the mailbox prior to your
departure.

Mike's Special Forces pulse was pounding. At the same time, he
hated to leave Kirsten—even though the past school year in Norman
had been busy, and he had appreciated being at home every night.

He walked to the florist, just off campus. He purchased a dozen
roses in a vase, and centered them on the dining table, so that Kirsten
would see them as soon as she came home from class. It was going to
be a difficult evening. Mike was sure this one would really hurt.

He went home after his last lecture and found Kirsten with tears
in her eyes. She had seen the flowers; the card he had left was open
on the table. Mike immediately tried to tell her how much he loved
her.

Kirsten was upset and on the offensive. "Mike, what is it this
time? Just once I would like flowers that aren't a precursor to bad
news! I want it up front. You know I read you like a book. Our time
in school together was to be our reward for all of your hard work and
our sacrifice. What's going on?"

It took Mike thirty minutes to calm her down. "I'll be leaving in
two weeks," he said. "We have one more weekend together, and I
thought we'd go to Colorado and spend it there. Would you like
that?"

"That sounds nice. But we hardly spend any time together. We
need more time together. I want a promise from you, Mike. Promise

me that this is the last mission—that after this, we'll be able to settle down and have a proper marriage. Maybe start a family?"

"That sounds good to me, and yes, I'll do everything I can to be with you. I'll come back and work on my degree, spoil you rotten, and even help you finish school."

He assured her that he would complete his degree eventually, and they'd have more time then. He also assured her that she would be able to continue school.

Kirsten begrudgingly accepted the news and the weekend in the mountains. And the fact that she would continue her education, possibly for more than the eighteen months, helped a bit. But she did not relish doing any of it on her own.

Mike slowly arranged things for departure. He turned finances over to Kirsten since he would live on his credit card or travel advances. Anything else could be traced to Major Mike Trantor.

The trip to the Rockies was medicinal. It helped soothe the wound of Mike's departure. After a wonderful afternoon riding up to Pike's Peak on the railroad, they had a bottle of wine at a small café and then returned to their hotel.

They kissed and Kirsten said, "It tickles! I think I like your beard. It's become quite soft—and could become nicer than your sandpaper growth when you want to be passionate in the mornings. Mmmm. . . . Oh, Mike!"

She was very happy for several moments, but then she started thinking about him leaving again. Although she was less than happy about being abandoned soon, she was still, but barely, willing to accept it. She was still feeling insecure and needed continuous reassurance: "It is the last time, isn't it, Mike? Promise me that this is really the last time."

"Kirsten, you have my word. I will do everything I can to spend time with you."

*   *   *   *   *

When they got back to Oklahoma, Mike made preparations to leave. Mike's professors all understood that the Army could recall students, and there were no difficulties in gaining their support. Marcella helped wind things up by bringing him a bill for the entire Spanish course, including their night on the town. She copied his credit card number, and said he would see the charges on his billing statement. He spent most of his free time during his last two weeks studying Spanish with all the concentration he could muster, preparing for each remaining session with Marcella.

Mike met Kirsten every day for lunch at the Crossroads or in the student union. She liked the deli, and her schedule meant that a lunch break everyday at 11:30 was a perfect time to meet. Kirsten seemed to be accepting the inevitable, and her English courses continued to inspire her. Mike finally felt that she was going to be fine.

Two days before his departure, Mike picked up his ticket making his final visit to the post office box. Miami International was his first destination. There were no other instructions. Later, he had his last class with Marcella.

At the end of the hour, they said goodbye to each other, told a few jokes about his more horrendous errors in Spanish during the crash course, hugged warmly, and went their respective ways. Mike was thinking how little Marcella knew of his life, and how she would never suspect that he was going to disappear. Marcella was wondering if Mike had ever realized she wasn't from Norman, Oklahoma.

*   *   *   *   *

The final night with Kristin was awful. Although their weekend in the mountains had brought them closer together, and she had been warm and loving that morning, that night the tension in the house was incredible. He was totally nonplussed about her sudden change of attitude. Nothing Mike could say or do was right.

"Kirsten, please don't be this way," he pleaded. "It's our last night together before I leave."

"You want me to pretend to be happy? Well, I'm not. I'm not happy that my husband is going away. Again!"

"We've already been through this."

"Yes we have. Way too many times."

"I know you don't like it. Please, let's just have a lovely evening together."

"Lovely? Where's the love going to be for the next nine months? Out of our nine years of marriage we've had twenty-one months together. You call that *lovely*?"

There was no warmth or affection from Kirsten the entire night. When they went to bed she rolled over and turned her back to him. It was like they slept totally alone.

The next morning, Kirsten said she didn't want to miss class to see him off, so he called a taxi to take him to the airport. It was better for operational security anyway, he rationalized, since Kirsten wouldn't see the flight destination, even though she could call and find out if she really wanted to track him.

At the door, as Mike was leaving, Kirsten quickly gave him a kiss and then stepped back.

"Take care of yourself, Mike."

"I will, sweetheart. And I love you. Always remember that," he said, fighting the hollowness of the moment.

Instead of saying, *I love you too*, she said nothing and slowly closed the door.

When Mike got to the airport, he wanted to call her but had no idea what he could say. Besides, he was forbidden to call anyway now that he had started the journey. He was hurting, and he knew he just had to take the pain. Feeling like his guts had been kicked out, he decided to displace the emotions by throwing himself into the mission.

After Mike left the house, Kirsten had gone to the couch where she lay, thinking about him and the military, and love. It seemed that all he really cared about was the Army, and didn't understand the meaning of the word *love*. Nonetheless, she regretted not saying, *I love you too*, as he stood at the door, and now she wished he would call from the airport so she could say it.

As Mike's plane took off, Kirsten sipped coffee in the Crossroads. She was depressed, and in a black mood. In the library the day before, she had searched for Mike, so they could spend their last afternoon together reading in his beloved Great Room. Afterwards, Kirsten had planned to walk home and surprise Mike with a bottle of wine, his favorite desert, and more. Looking for Mike, she had peered into one of the graduate study rooms. A strikingly beautiful *latina* and Mike were hugging and laughing.

She thought about entering the room and confronting the situation, but decided against it. She kept her faith that it was innocent, that it was somehow related to his military assignment, and decided to wait and see if he told her about it later. But the jealousy lingered, and grew, and she blew off the idea of the wine and dessert. When he didn't mention the encounter with the other woman, she became angry and even more jealous.

She now realized as she thought about it that she had been horrid to Mike. The last night had been a bitch. And she regretted it, but it was too late. He was gone. And that depressed her even more. The bitter pill was when he didn't even call her from the airport.

Kirsten had been hit on frequently since walking on campus, but had remained true blue. Mike's damned career, coupled with his personal treachery, Kirsten realized, was making her dangerously angry and bitter. She turned her thoughts to a tremendously attractive young man, also an English major, who had befriended her.

CHAPTER EIGHT

Mike, at the same time, landed in Miami. Kirsten's mood bothered him to no end, yet it was time to be on his toes. He had to get the hollow feeling out of his stomach and out of his thoughts, so he focused on the mission.

After landing, he stopped at the nearest airport bar. He sat down with an empty stool on each side of him. Being static would help his contact spot him.

It was odd having no established *bona fides* or link-up plan. He also wondered why General Joe used an old fashioned dead drop instead of speaking over a secure cell phone or hitting him on the Internet. He sipped Crown Royal on the rocks and struggled to control his thoughts, which continuously drifted back to Kirsten. Sooner or later everything would become clear, he decided.

A younger man, about thirty, in a business suit, light blue shirt, and carrying a computer case and a hanging bag, sat down next to him. Soon they were discussing college football and then the young fellow leaned toward him and quietly asked, "You look like an old airborne soldier, did you ever do parachute landing falls off a roof?"

Mike smiled. He was glad to get started. *Bona fides* were never given in code; it should always be part of a normal conversation. Such a comment could be overheard by anyone, yet it would be meaningless unless one were in the system. He chuckled and nodded. General Joe was using personal knowledge of Mike's past to link up.

He remembered the PLFs—parachute landing falls—and a party at night when they had practiced jumping off the roof.

Then the stranger next to him asked Mike if he was staying at the Miami Marriott; Mike played along, saying that he was. The stranger responded, "Great, would you like to share a taxi?" Mike agreed.

At the hotel, where Mike found his reservation, the two checked in together. While waiting for a taxi the stranger said, "My name is Gary. We are old friends working together on a job." This was enough information to allow them to enter the hotel together, check in, exchange room numbers, and plan to meet for dinner.

Mike had been slipped a new credit card with a different last name; he would destroy his old one as soon as possible. He was glad to retain "Mike" so the change would be easy, and it would serve him well if any old friends inadvertently bumped into him. Though Mike wasn't registered in his real name, had a false address, and there was no reference to the Army, there wasn't any cover at all. He carried his own passport and driver's license. The only thing accomplished was to place a thin veil between himself and the University of Oklahoma.

He went to the gym and hit the Nautilus machines for about an hour, showered, and dressed for dinner. He was ready for the evening, except that he couldn't seem to shake the burning desire to call Kirsten.

He then met Gary in the pub, and they spoke about current events and sports until after dinner. Gary seemed to be a great fellow, and they were hitting it off nicely.

In a corner of the hotel pub, Gary began to discuss business. He said he was a "professional contract trainer." His charter was to train selected personnel on equipment techniques and procedures to help them succeed in urban environments, particularly overseas. He explained that he had ordered two rental cars to be delivered the next day: a Mustang convertible and an old Toyota. The workday would start at 8:00 a.m.

The next morning, Gary and Mike took off in the Mustang and drove for hours as Gary quizzed him. Subjects included how to tail someone in a car, how to spot a tail, how to shake someone, what to do if stopped by armed gunmen, how to hop curbs, and how to do 180-degree "J-turns" without stopping.

Gary's questioning technique was first-class. He never leaned towards a correct answer. When the verbal examination was over, Gary concluded that Mike was well trained.

Gary drove all day. He wanted Mike just to observe. It took Mike a little while to pick up the fact that they were being tailed, giving Gary reason for a critique. The rest of the day consisted of breaking tails and tailing other vehicles. Mike estimated the supporting cast to be up to ten personnel and four vehicles. Gary clearly was a pro and had a great program of instruction.

That night, Gary told Mike to meet him at the Toyota. They drove for about an hour to a deserted racetrack. Gary gave Mike the wheel, and really put him through the paces. After an hour and a half, Mike had been refreshed on just about everything one could do with a civilian car except roll it.

Gary was pleased. "Well done, Mike. We'll meet at ten for breakfast. Remember, don't use the phone."

"OK. See you in the morning. But just one thing. Is there a secure phone anywhere that I can use. I really need to call my wife."

"Sorry, Mike. No outside contact."

Mike still couldn't shake the bad feeling he had about Kirsten.

*   *   *   *   *

Gary had given Mike permission to leave the hotel, mentioning that he was free to venture out for short periods of time to stretch his legs and avoid cabin fever. So he did.

The next morning, Mike took his suit and a shirt to a laundry that was a few blocks from the Marriott. Mike had spotted the Cuban laundry the day before and wanted to try his Spanish. He chatted with the lady at the desk and eventually was introduced to the extended family working in the back. The mom-and-pop laundry appeared to be doing well, even though the family could speak virtually no English. Mike was proud when he didn't miss a word or an innuendo.

At 10:00 a.m., as planned, he met Gary for a late breakfast. During the meal Gary asked Mike if he had spotted the tail on him en route to or while he was coming back from the Cuban laundry. Mike said he hadn't noticed a thing because he wasn't looking. Gary then told him the next two days of training would be on human tails, not vehicular ones.

For the following thirty-six hours, Mike tailed and then was tailed. He practiced every technique he knew to slip away from observation, or to retain observation on a target. The effort was terminated with videos and full critiques in Gary's motel room. The only security measures they took were to speak quietly.

Mike was given another break for the following day. He asked if he was covered to drive one of the rentals and Gary said fine. Mike took the sporty red Mustang, lowered the top, and drove all over the city. The "combat zone," which tourists were warned against entering, was traced in yellow on his city map. The car rental companies made sure their customers knew the boundaries. Mike noticed guards with automatic rifles outside of a McDonald's. Something new every day, he acknowledged, wondering what had happened to America.

As he drove the red Mustang, he spotted a vehicular tail and quickly gave them the slip. His training was serving him well.

Then he discovered what looked like a nice Irish pub on Red River Road. It turned out to be a family place that seemed very friendly. The clientele was from the neighborhood. The black and tans tasted great. Mike chuckled to himself, easily spotting his tail in the restaurant. Everyone else in the place had one or two children.

He left the restaurant and drove around restlessly, heading toward the beach. When he got there, he pulled his car into a slot facing a strip of lonely beach, got out of the car, and gazed up at the moon. He lit a cigarette and smoked it, thinking of Kirsten. When he finished the cigarette, he tore the remains open, sprinkling the bits of tobacco and ash on the ground. Then he dropped the twisted paper ball into a pocket for later disposal and turned back to the car.

Suddenly, a car roared up behind the Mustang and screeched to a halt, blocking any attempt to back up. Three young black men were in the vehicle. Mike was about two steps from the driver's side door of his convertible. The keys were in his pocket. One young man fixed a pistol on Mike and told him to raise his hands and step away from his car. The other opened the Mustang's driver side door and stepped forward, leaning over to check if the keys were in the ignition. He also had a pistol in his hand, a Glock 9mm.

The scar-faced youth with the pistol pointed at Mike was agitated. Mike immediately assessed him as being on drugs and severely unstable. The driver was quiet, under control, and appeared unarmed. The man looking for the keys was excited but seemed rational.

The most dangerous and unstable one would have to go down first. Mike made a side step forward, kicked the gun out of his hand, and struck him with a paralyzing blow to the throat. As smooth as a karate sequence, where a drill is finished with a board break, Mike threw his entire body weight against the Mustang door, crushing the legs of the man who was looking for the keys. In shock, he was an easy target. Mike broke the young black thug's wrist while taking away his pistol. He turned and immediately shot out two tires on the criminals' vehicle, then zeroed his weapon between the eyes of the driver. The young man slowly raised empty hands—eyes locked on a large Glock that Mike had snatched from the second assailant. Suddenly police sirens screamed in the night, coming fast a few blocks away. They must have been nearby and heard the shots, Mike thought as he reacted to the sound and quickly re-assessed the situation.

Mike instantly shouted at the driver, "Back your car out and block the road or you're toast. Now!" The driver immediately slammed the vehicle into reverse cut the wheel hard and blocked the road. Shielded momentarily from police pursuit, Mike yanked the twitching body out of the Mustang, started the car, stomped it in reverse and then threw it into first gear.

The tires squealed, jackrabbiting the convertible forward. Simultaneously, he screamed at the driver, "Run, you dumb son-of-a-bitch, get away while you can!" The driver took off running like a scalded cat, disappearing in the night.

Mike slowed down as he broke contact with the scene. The Mustang's left door was sprung, but after repeated slamming, it finally latched.

Mike cursed himself, his mind racing. Driving a criminal magnet like the Mustang in unknown sectors of Miami had been extremely foolish. He probably was at the edge of the combat zone.

Mike mulled over the incident as he drove to the hotel. He thought of his shallow cover, the false name on his credit card, and the rental car in Gary's name. Even worse, his fingerprints were all over everything. He visualized himself in court testifying. He had blown it. His training to make instantaneous life and death decisions, in this instance, had let him down. Mike could have chosen to just give up the car, except that the fellow with the pistol was a flake and a wild card.

Balancing Mike's concern was the fact that in the past his instinctive reflexes had always proven to be correct. Finally he envisioned himself lying in the street, next to the Mustang, bleeding to death—and felt better about his reactions.

He pulled up to the Marriott and headed straight for Gary's hangout, the swimming pool bar under the grass-roofed *bohio*. Mike thought Gary might be sweet on the big-breasted girl in the bikini that served the drinks. He told Gary the story, relating that he might have severely hurt the first criminal with the blow to the throat. He explained that he had ordered the escape of the one that had the most time to study him and could make the best identification. The full beard, to which he was unaccustomed, would certainly be a point of recognition. The bottom line was that the car was hot and needed to be washed off the books immediately. He had parked it in the darkest corner of the parking lot so it wouldn't stand out.

Overall, Mike was afraid he would be pulled from his assignment. What he hated the most in the world was even the slightest hint of failure. Gary calmly took the news and the keys. He told Mike not to worry, to pick up his clothes from the laundry in the morning, and be prepared to check out.

Gary took a sip of his drink before he continued.

"Mike, we saw you field strip a Marlboro when you were standing in front of the Mustang, just before the three hoods hit you. Never do it again. It marks you as an American military man. Hereafter, concentrate on twenty-four hour a day situational awareness: 360 degrees. I'll see you off in the lobby at 0700."

Impressed, Mike turned away, thinking about the field strip. The practice was part of "litter discipline" in the woods to keep the enemy from easily tracking an opponent. Mike's dad, an Army veteran from the Korean Conflict, had taught him how to do it.

10 Aug 2004

At 0700, Gary handed Mike a ticket to Atlanta along with a Florida driver's license in a name that matched the ticket. He took Mike's credit card and gave him five hundred dollars.

"After you land in Atlanta, go to any lounge you like in Annex E, the international wing. You'll be met. You stunk it up a bit here, but there is no residual odor. We'll stay on course. Stick with it. So long."

After picking up his laundry, having breakfast, and checking out, Mike went to Miami International, a bit depressed about the beach incident. But he was comforted by still being in the program: down but not out. At least they were still investing in him.

10 Aug 2004

Meanwhile, a special group of former intelligence and special operators convened a meeting. They were an ad hoc organization indirectly created by Mr. Ellis to evaluate the teams being put together to deploy around the globe to attack the Cuban threat. They were Mr. Ellis' sounding board.

As the first order of business, the group had given its blessing to SOCEUR's (Special Operations Command-Europe) plan to destroy the diamond mine in Sierra Leone, an action to take place a few days hence. The special operators at SOCEUR knew nothing else other than their mission to destroy the mine and that they had been ordered to make it appear that the United Kingdom had executed the raid. Mr. Ellis had made sure that the instructions for the raid had emanated from the Chairman of the Joint Chiefs of Staff. It was a Department of Defense operation, with no apparent linkage to The Hybrid.

A Mr. Peters, the eldest member, nearly seventy-years old, was clearly in charge. Some referred to the group as "the graybeards," old timers blessed with the wisdom that comes from years of being professional clandestine operators.

There wasn't another man or woman in the group of six that was less than fifty years of age. They were all dressed conservatively in expensive business wear. The bare mahogany table in the meeting room was perfectly shined and spotless. No one was taking notes; none had writing or recording instruments before them; none had coffee.

It was clear that they only exchanged information verbally. An interagency working group, they met only on call, and at times remained dormant. Their charter was to ensure that candidates for employment as singletons or in small groups had the requisite skills to accomplish assigned missions. Employment was the word always used, in the weapons sense, as in "employ nuclear weapons." They evaluated human weapon systems, and Mike was one of them.

The briefer finished his update on Mike with a video of his actions against the unfortunate bandits in Florida. He took the hard drive out of his computer that he had used for the presentation and laid it on the table, exiting smartly.

The elderly man opened. "Comments on what we have seen so far?"

The youngest gentleman said, "I'm impressed with Mike's ability to follow orders. He has not contacted his wife, even though he could use a letter to a surrogate such as his brother. He also has never used a telephone without being instructed to do so.

"I am confident that he will stay on course, even when his instructions make no apparent sense, as may happen with the abstract scenario we have been given for his employment. My overall impression thus far is that Mike has the right stuff."

Ms. Winthrop, a crusty middle-aged CIA veteran, peered over her glasses, canvassing the others with a stern look. "I am not convinced that he will make appropriate calls under stress, as we witnessed in the Miami scene.

"He reminds me of the MACVSOG veterans that became policemen on the West Coast during and after Vietnam. These veterans had tremendous problems evaluating when not to shoot. Their responses had been refined to tripwire tolerance, and what they saw they hit. It seemed that the synapses between seeing a threat and killing it were overly streamlined.

"The Seattle SWAT team, as I recall, generally wouldn't hire veterans until at least two years after their MACV-SOG or Special Forces tour. Do any of you have similar concerns?"

She paused, staring questioningly at the others, one by one. "I'm simply not sure if he won't fail to wait a precious fraction of a second at some crucial juncture and thus compromise or terminate the mission."

A distinguished looking gentleman across the table countered with: "The same observation, in my opinion, can be used to illustrate that he has incredible survivability, which is absolutely necessary for success as a singleton."

Silence followed, then the senior member concluded: "If none of you has anything else to say, let me comment on another subject, operational security, or OPSEC. One group handled the Oklahoma move and preparation without a hitch. Another worked the Miami portion.

"None of the operatives know what the others have done, and none will care. Overall, the effort is on track, and Mike Trantor is disappearing, as planned. I have no security concerns."

He continued. "We will continue to convene periodically when those in charge of this operation want advice or assessment."

Peters, a former Army military intelligence general, watched the others leave the room. He personally went over, picked up the hard drive, and took it into a back room where he put it into a compactor so powerful that the disc was reduced to a flat plate. He was thinking to himself how good their OPSEC really was. For now, only he knew the graybeard's point of contact was a Mr. Ellis—no first name.

Later in the day, Ellis called Lieutenant General Hanscom at the CIA. Via secure phone, he gave him his updates on SOCEUR's upcoming mission in Africa and Mike's preparation.

10 Aug 2004

Mike had a sour taste in his mouth after his performance in Miami. He was sipping a diet Coke. The fellow next to him had been sipping a beer. He nonchalantly looked over and asked, "Haven't I seen you here before?"

"I doubt it," Mike replied.

"I recall you used to pass through here a lot. I seem to picture you in a Hawaiian shirt and sandals," the stranger replied.

Mike looked closely at the stranger and replied, "You have a good memory," recalling an impromptu brief he once gave to a four-star General while dressed in a Hawaiian shirt and sandals.

The stranger smiled. "Mike, I'm Ray. I'm your escort. Are you ready to get moving?" Mike nodded. Ray picked up the tab and asked Mike if he needed help with his luggage.

Their first stop after getting out of the airport was a photo shop where they ordered a dozen passport shots of the bearded Mike and waited to get the copies. Paying cash, they moved down the road. Ray pulled over at a gas station two miles later and handed Mike a small canister of shaving cream and a razor. He told Mike to step into the rest room and shave. "But keep the moustache," he suggested.

It was obvious they were going to backdate any phony passports they created for him. His less than attractive beard would help "age" the photos, indicating that enough time had passed from issuance to the present. Visas would be another matter.

Mike gladly scratched away the itchy beard. *Sans* beard, Mike had less chance of being linked to the Mustang and Miami. He kept the moustache, since virtually all Latinos his age had them and it might ease crossing a cultural barrier somewhere down the unknown road ahead.

They pulled up to a run-of-the-mill Holiday Inn. Mike was given a room key. Ray came into his room and said to Mike, "Hand over anything you might have that links you with Mike Trantor."

Mike had virtually nothing. He handed over his driver's license and the fake Florida one he had used to board in Miami. Mike realized that he was being distanced from himself; he was being "washed." Mike Trantor had ceased to exist in Miami. He couldn't be traced any further.

Ray took the licenses and said, "Stay in your room, Mike, until I return."

There were some soft drinks and sandwiches on the nightstand. Mike turned the TV on to *Telemundo*, figuring that he might as well start immersing himself in Spanish.

He hadn't expected to stay in the room all night long. He did push-ups and sit-ups for exercise. He watched TV. He was dying for something to read, but orders were orders. He saved one of the sandwiches for breakfast just in case.

In the morning, he shaved, showered, and dressed. He made coffee from the motel machine, ate his last sandwich and watched CNN. Finally, around ten in the morning, there was a knock on the door.

It was Ray. He moved over to the small desk, sat down and was all business. Mike wondered if Ray wasn't off his time schedule. He quickly went through Mike's new documents and paraphernalia: British passport, international driver's license, rental agreement for his car, extended for thirty days to include all insurance, and a small notebook with his "family" addresses in England and their phone numbers.

It was all there, his full cover, including a copy of *Country Life*—a rather upscale English magazine—and a two-day old copy of *The London Times*. The shaving kit was English through and through. Pens, pencils, and notepads were European. His credit card was from Barclaycard. A nice, soft, leather briefcase was provided to enclose it all.

Ray finished, handing him a new leather wallet—the "Made in Bradford" clearly visible—amply supplied with British pounds and U.S. dollars, and said, "This is as far as I take you. Your first name is still retained as Michael. The black Neon sedan outside is yours. I was told to give you this envelope, then leave. Just walk out of the hotel when you are done." Ray left.

Ray was done, handing Mike over. Mike read his instructions:
Drive to a warehouse one block to the north of the northernmost corner of the coffee stain on the enclosed map of Atlanta. The warehouse is split into sections for small businesses. It is the pale yellow building. Walk into Southern Design, Inc. The secretary is waiting for you. Destroy this note.

Starting the car, Mike was practicing his British accent. He had served for three years as an exchange officer with the SAS, the UK equivalent of Special Forces. He had noticed that the goods just received from Ray placed his residence near Hereford, his old SAS stomping grounds. His knowledge of the area would help sustain his cover, at least for a little while, if he was under stress.

An hour later, Mike found Southern Design, Inc., obviously a small, struggling, start-up company. He was sure he hadn't been tailed.

He walked in and the secretary welcomed him. She was middle aged, frumpy and maybe fifty pounds overweight. She was clearly recruited not to attract attention, a decision based on simple traffic management. It was clear that employees of the other businesses in the warehouse complex wouldn't be stopping by to hit on her.

Looks were deceiving. In a few short minutes, the secretary proved to be witty, charming, and kind. She put Mike at ease, and without further preamble said, "Go down the hall, past the two bathrooms, and you will see a red button on the wall. Push it and you will be allowed entry into the back office."

Mike stopped on the way and used the nondescript bathroom. While washing his hands he tried to see any evidence of bugs or cameras; there were none. He was becoming operational; he was being conditioned, situational awareness, every minute.

He walked down the hall and pushed the red button. He was under observation from a camera, overt. Hanging from the ceiling, it looked him in the face.

A few seconds later he heard a dead-bolt move, and a young man in blue jeans and a sweatshirt met him. The young fellow ushered him into a small room with a full-length mirror and surprised him by expertly taping him head to foot, exactly as a professional tailor would.

Included was a UK scale to measure his feet. Mike recalled that his shoes in Britain were about one size smaller. The young man said his work was completed and ushered Mike to the bolted door. His instructions were to see the secretary.

The secretary said, "You need to find a nice hotel to stay in and then come back here at noon, the day after tomorrow. Pay for the hotel in cash and check out before you come back here."

Just before he got to the door, she added, "Don't bother to do laundry." Mike shrugged and left.

That evening he watched *Telemundo*. As he fell asleep, he wondered where General Joe was in the organizational diagram. He felt like one of the three blind men that touched an elephant; one the tail, one a tusk, one a leg.

12 Aug 2004
Mike killed the time on his day off reading the Spanish newspapers from Miami available in the hotel. *Telemundo* and two sessions for exercise—one in the weight room and one in the pool—helped fill the day. Mike hated days with lots of down time; his thoughts inevitably turned to Kirsten. He had a bad feeling about her and wished he could call.

The next morning, he checked out and drove back to the warehouse. The secretary was pleasant as ever. She asked him to bring his luggage into the building and to carry it back to the door by the red button.

Mike did, and the tailor from the day before was back. A rack of brand new suits, slacks and jackets hung in the room—all sporting Saville Row, Dax, Burberry, and other well-known British labels. On the floor were several pairs of Clarks shoes and a large pile of socks.

"I hope our offering here will please you," the young man began. "In addition to what you see, the cabinet in the corner contains British underwear, shirts of several styles, ties—a bit wider in Britain than in the U.S. right now—and other items you might need.

"It's time for you to change clothes and pack your new wardrobe. We will destroy your current clothes; please place them in the plastic bags provided. I hope the new luggage is satisfactory. The only exception to turning over your possessions is your running shoes. We know how much exercise means to you, and your brand is available worldwide, so feel free to keep them.

"I will step out for a short time to allow you to disrobe and dress. As you pack, please think about anything else you might need."

Undressing quickly, Mike found the clothes to be to his liking. He put on a two-button gray pinstriped suit and selected a light blue shirt with a conservative tie.

He was impressed, particularly with the tan raincoat. If he were in a quality clothing store, he would have picked exactly the same items. The young man, oddly still in what looked like the same jeans from two days ago, really knew his business.

Rapping lightly on the door, he walked in without waiting for a reply, asking if there was anything Mike needed. When Mike said that everything was perfect, the Brit beamed, proud of his work. "Then you'd better be off," he said with his slight Yorkshire burr.

Mike stopped at the secretary's desk where she handed him an envelope and said, "Good luck on your travels."

He put his new bags in the car. The letter informed him that the dental appointment he had requested was at 4:00 p.m. across town in a medical complex. It was signed by a dentist and was absolutely clean.

Mike grabbed a healthy lunch, thinking that he might be out of commission for a while after what might turn out to be a significant dental treatment.

He found the medical center with little difficulty. Walking in, he presented his letter, and the receptionist was pleasant. She then surprised Mike a bit, asking, "How will you be paying, sir?"

Mike, with no apparent sign that he was ruffled, replied in his best British accent, "Would cash be acceptable?"

"That will be excellent, sir," she replied. Mike realized that, unlike the secretary in the warehouse, this lady wasn't read on to anything.

After fifteen minutes in the waiting room, Mike was called. He had filled out the preliminary worksheet that asked if he was allergic to Novocain and such. The dentist, a seemingly nice fellow named Bill, said, "When we are done discussing elementary preliminaries on your sheet, depart and return at 5:30. I normally close at 4:30, so my receptionist and assistants will be cleared out when you re-enter. I'll be waiting. Just knock on the door."

At 4:25 Bill walked him out and thanked him for coming by. It was neatly done for all to see. Promptly at 5:30, Mike knocked. The door opened and Bill was standing with another dentist. Mike's assumption was quickly corrected when Bill introduced his partner as a doctor, a specialist in plastic surgery and implants. As they discussed the plan, Mike had a flashback, remembering a rugby game he'd played in Hereford, England against a team from Vancouver,

Canada. In the game he'd hit head-on into a 240-pound running back, splitting his forehead open to the skull and breaking off his two front teeth, which were now capped.

Bill started speaking, bringing Mike back to the present moment. "I am going to change your panoramic dental record. Since all your other teeth are perfect, this should be easy. I'm going to pull off your crowns, drill out the fillings you have, and replace them. Anyone that could have acquired your dental x-rays will not be able to identify you. I will make sure by comparing your new x-rays with the old ones when we finish."

Mike replied, "What you mean is that if my body is held by the enemy it will be more difficult to link my corpse to the United States."

Bill replied, "You are correct, but we are more concerned about helping you if you are captured. Your covers must be protected. Also, my friend here needs to brief you on your surgical procedure tonight."

The briefing was short. "Right after your dental appointment, I will use a local anesthesia to prepare an area behind your ear. I am going to insert a tracking device that we can activate from space behind your right ear. We will use it only in emergencies."

Mike asked, "Why?"

The reply was, "Battery life is less than six days, and we will use this as a last resort if we lose you."

Mike nodded that he understood, telling them to get on with it.

The dentist and the doctor were finished with Mike before midnight. They provided mild pain medicine, and briefed him fully on what he could or could not do. He was to take it easy for a day, and was given the address for another hotel. He was told to pay cash, and check for delivery of an envelope during the evening. Bill also gave him a phone number to call if there were any medical complications. Mike said he felt pretty good, and that he wasn't woozy. Bill told him to hold off on hot drinks until the afternoon of the following day. The doctor provided an extra bandage and coached him on how to wash the small incision behind his ear. The stitches would be absorbed over time. There was no need to return for follow-up unless an infection occurred.

Mike was dead tired. He drove to the designated hotel, got a room, hung out the "Do Not Disturb" sign, and went to bed.

13 Aug 2004

Mike Trantor woke up around noon feeling rested, even though his teeth bothered him. He went into the bathroom and looked at the reflection of his new dental work. Using his shaving mirror he was able to study the incision behind his ear. Miniaturization in military technology was becoming quite impressive. The bulge under his skin was barely noticeable. He had refrained from asking the obvious question. *Why would my handlers bother to disguise my natural teeth from any existing record, military or otherwise, and then implant technology that could identify me as a foreign agent?* He was sure an x-ray would find the tag in his head. Even though the tag would be sterile and therefore untraceable, Mike would be in a world of hurt.

Delivered that night were Mike's instructions to return, not later than 8:00 a.m., to the same warehouse that had provided his new wardrobe.

Mike walked into the warehouse the next morning at 7:55 a.m. The secretary was pleasant and offered him a cup of coffee. Mike declined because of his dental work and strolled down the hall to the controlled doorway. He hit the red button and entered. The interior of the warehouse had been completely transformed. The walls were covered with satellite photography; workspaces, secured phones, computers, faxes and copiers abounded.

Most interesting were the simulation machines. Mike recognized one of them immediately—the suspended parachute—where a soldier could be placed in a harness about two feet off the ground. He would then put on the virtual reality headset and literally "see" his drop zone in enemy territory.

The computer would be set for the speed and altitude of the plane making the drop. The soldier would rehearse different winds, memorizing the shape of the drop zone and locations of obstacles such as trees, power lines, rivers, and buildings. For high-risk jumps, the computer could plug in enemy positions or (for agents) link-up parties on or near the drop zone.

Most valuable was that the parachute had its actual toggle lines. The parachute would do whatever the soldier commanded. He received immediate input, good or bad, successful landing or crashing into a house, for instance.

Another innovation caught Mike's eye. It was a large flat-screen computer hanging on a wall. Through manipulation of satellite photos an almost three-dimensional product appeared. From several feet away, one could see what his target looked like at whatever altitude chosen. This device was extremely valuable for pilots flying in unfamiliar urban settings.

There were four men in the room and one woman. The oldest man approached. He and the rest were wearing the clothes of mid-level managers in Atlanta. Shaking Mike's hand firmly, he introduced himself as John. LTG Hanscom had specifically requested John Jones. He was from the CIA and was grown in a different garden from Mike, yet they converged in their innate ability to plan and conduct coherent and effective special operations.

John had gone to boarding school at Hoskins and had spent a year studying Russian language and culture in what was then Leningrad. He returned to the United States, went to Yale, and was then recruited into the Central Intelligence Agency.

John had made his bones by studying patterns of travel by various surrogate *HAMAS* organizations. His conclusions led to detailed analysis of clandestine attempts to radicalize the Muslim government in Bosnia. He had gone beyond normal compartmentalized analysis. He had developed a complete campaign to negate the effort, using economic incentives, psychological pressure, military threat, espionage, bribery and blackmail.

His superiors were impressed. Not only had John's analysis of the threat been brilliant, but his plan to neutralize the threat was first-class, innovative, and relatively low-risk. The plan, virtually unchanged, was endorsed by the Departments of State, Justice, and Defense. The President himself had written a congratulatory note to John when the project succeeded.

John opened by telling Mike that his staff in Atlanta was charged with ensuring optimal preparation for the mission. He followed by introducing the team. Two of the men were technical intelligence experts. One of them said that he could tap into any classified system in the Department of Defense, CIA, NSA, NRO, Department of Justice or any other governmental data bank to obtain intelligence packages that might help Mike plan details of his mission.

The second, after being introduced, explained that he could go worldwide to obtain open-source information. A master surfer, he could literally reach around the world, into any academic society, anywhere that was wired, to help in preparation. Mike asked who he was when using the open net, and the man gave a straightforward answer; he was an employee in a haberdashery in Pool, England.

The third man was a Department of Justice (DOJ) lawyer, assigned full time to Mike's preparation. The inclusion of a DOJ lawyer meant that the team could move quickly because they would have continuous legal oversight. The lawyer would make sure that American citizens' privacy was protected and that no statutes were violated by the team's activities. By daily keeping the effort legally squeaky-clean, thousands of hours of bureaucratic questioning and hand-wringing would be avoided later in Washington.

Mike liked the structure. The spooks were wired worldwide for classified and open source, so they could reach anywhere into the collaborative intelligence net to dig for his or other emergent requirements. The lawyer was a critical additional key to gaining permission to execute if a rapid launch were required.

John introduced the woman last, as Angela. She was an obviously fit, approximately thirty-year old English girl with blue eyes and blond hair. She said she was his personal trainer in mission preparation: physical fitness, English idiom, and fluency in Spanish. They would meet every morning and at times, in the evening. They would start work by focusing on sprints. Mike wondered how far and under what conditions he would have to run.

Angela spoke to him in Spanish. He was amazed at her fluency—her accent was almost the same as Marcella's. Then she switched to an upper-class English accent and explained that her father had been a diplomat in Latin America for many years. He looked at her closely, thinking that there was a lot to this woman. She was stunningly beautiful, and Mike assumed an overly businesslike demeanor to compensate.

Suddenly, the entire crew, including the lawyer, switched to British accents. Mike followed suit. After a short discussion of the necessity for Mike to be able to operate as a Spanish speaking Brit, Mike said, "Right," which caused chuckles in the small gathering. "Right," in Britain, means, *I've got the message, I'm tired of talking about this subject, and I'm ready to move on.*

Someone had assembled and funded an impressive organization. Mike sincerely acknowledged the effort by saying, "I am truly pleased to meet all of you and I am glad to be part of the team. Let's get to work."

John agreed. "Right. It's time for your mission brief."

Finally, thought Mike, as he looked at his watch. Noticing the date, he winced. Kirsten's birthday was coming in two days. He couldn't even call.

CHAPTER NINE

13 Aug 2004

It was Friday the 13th on an aircraft carrier in the Atlantic Ocean off the West African coast. Preparations were underway for a nighttime landing and almost immediate re-launch. The aircraft were helicopters from SOCEUR's 352nd Special Operations Group in Mildenhall, England.

The helicopters had been flown for eighteen hours, refueled along the way by special airborne penetrator tankers. The soldiers on board for the mission were Green Berets from the 10th Special Forces Group stationed in Bad Tolz, Germany. The men were lying on mats trying to get as much sleep as possible while aboard the aircraft.

Fresh, fully rested flight crews were brought in from SOCEUR two days earlier to take over the aircraft. The pilots had more hours flying at night than whole squadrons of Navy helicopter pilots. The special operations aircraft were capable of seeing at night and were authorized to land in "zero/zero" visibility—i.e. flying through solid clouds and landing in dense fog.

Their radar systems were more advanced than any others in the world. In addition, their computers automatically downloaded and updated intelligence available by NRO (National Reconnaissance Office) satellite imagery and processed it to tell the pilots what the enemy threat was in real time, without middlemen to process or classify it. The immediate raw data increased platform survivability over a hundred-fold.

The pilots had spent the whole day "flying" their missions for the last time with virtual reality headsets plugged into their lightweight computers. The secure computers reached all the way back to the USAF Special Operations Lab at Eglin Air Force Base, near Tampa, Florida. Tonight, with their night vision goggles (NVGs) on, the pilots would be seeing the same terrain they had "flown" in virtual training for weeks on end.

Their flight plan would take the Special Forces operators deep into the jungles of Sierra Leone: a hot, humid tropical nation, roughly the size of South Carolina. Situated between Guinea to the north and Liberia to the south, along the Atlantic coast, its wealth is mostly mineral: titanium, gold, iron ore and diamonds make up the bulk of the banana republic's Gross Domestic Product. Sierra Leone's population of over five million lived mostly on meager subsistence farming, however, and had an average lifespan of scarcely forty-two years.

The enemy forces were one of the few remaining armed remnants of the nearly defunct Revolutionary United Front, or RUF, known worldwide for cutting hands, arms, and feet off opponents and innocents, from children to old women. The remnants of the RUF, badly damaged by the British Army and the Sierra Leone peacekeeping forces, only held onto a few key remote locations. Their stock in trade was diamonds. Diamonds for the highest bidder; diamonds for Al-Qaeda and other terrorist groups; diamonds paid for by the blood of many; hence the name "blood diamonds."

The SOCEUR mission: destroy the RUF's main source of blood diamonds. Years earlier, Liberian President Charles Taylor and the RUF had an agreement—together, they would use diamonds and diamond income to buy weapons and terrorize numerous West African states for their own ends.

Now, with Charles Taylor gone, the diamonds funded activities even more sinister; the CIA along with many others had determined that the precious jewels funded terrorism operations in Latin America. Many of the current inhabitants of the prison camp at Guantanamo Bay in Cuba were discovered to have diamonds from Sierra Leone when they underwent the final deep search.

The terror was directed against the United States of America. Now it was up to the special operators to take them out.

*   *   *   *   *

The Special Forces engineers readied their demolitions—shaped charges that would wreak havoc and collapse the walls of the diamond mines by changing their inherent geology. The SF demolitions experts had gone to civilian sources for advice after obtaining guidance from the Army's engineering and explosive ordnance disposal (EOD) experts at Fort Leonardwood, Missouri. Others prepared standard demolitions for ancillary tasks, cutting charges, and preparing fuses.

The mission commander, from SOCEUR, had wisely sent the demolitions on two aircraft, and fuses on another two. One reason for this precaution was to prevent an accidental explosion. Another reason was to guarantee that if an aircraft had to "ditch" in the sea due to a malfunction, the mission-essential equipment would still make it to the aircraft carrier. In addition to the demolitions, the capabilities and equipment of the special operators had all been balanced and the principals cross-loaded, so that even in the event that any one chopper had to ditch the mission would remain successful.

The men put on their camouflage, test-fired their weapons off the side of the ship, and checked their communications gear and other technical equipment. They "chalk-talked" their actions one last time, put on black, "Mitch" helmets, checked their bone mikes and back-up radios sewn into their vests, did a final check on their NVGs, and gave a thumbs-up.

*   *   *   *   *

Meanwhile, deep in the jungles of Sierra Leone in the Kono diamond mine district, a retired U.S. Army colonel named Bert McNab was "closing shop" for the day. Graying, tan, and blue-eyed, Bert played by 1960s rules he had learned in Vietnam as a MACVSOG operations officer in the Phoenix assassination program.

He still loved agrarian societies, threatening environments, ad hoc organizations, camps constructed in strange and terrifying places, arming and training tribesmen and surrogate forces, foreign languages, foreign women, rum, and guns—not necessarily in that order. When the Vietnam War ended, and the Army modernized and changed, Bert simply chose not to do so.

Years after the war, while still on active duty, Bert ran out of luck and finally was forced to resign from the Army. One of Bert's subordinates reported him for landing a helicopter at night, using only night vision goggles. Bert's superiors were furious since Bert *wasn't a pilot*. While old Special Forces friends stood behind him, other officers had ostracized Bert on the way out. He didn't help matters by immediately seeking employment with Arena Linea, a shady mercenary group subordinate to the Strategic Effects conglomerate in Britain.

Bert had trained his mine security force well. His immediate subordinates were South African, including infantrymen, communicators and medics. Defenses were correctly emplaced; guarding all routes of access to the mine complex that any foe might choose to take. Defensive positions—manned bunkers with overhead cover—were arrayed in depth, with an inner perimeter surrounded by concertina and razor wire.

Every night as the sun went down, Bert walked the perimeter to ensure that all roads and trails, both in and out, were closed and secure. In addition, he checked each manned position to ensure his native African soldiers were alert, properly armed, aware of their duties, and witting of all actions to take if attacked.

Bert normally scheduled his tour to last two hours, affording ample time to talk with the men individually. He always took along an interpreter in case his two African languages failed. One was *Temne*, spoken along Sierra Leone's northern border, exactly where his mine was located. There were many dialects in this area, and they varied from tribe to tribe. The "night shift" knew Colonel Bert McNab would come back sometime between 11:00 p.m. (2300 hrs) and 4:00 a.m. (0400 hrs) to check again. Any man found asleep in his fighting position, drunk or not, was fined a month's wages.

Bert was proud of his security force and confident they could handle any threat in the region. Bert's men respected him; he was tough but fair, and he kept his word. He enjoyed the walks each night, feeling as if he were twenty-one years old and back in

Vietnam. He hoped it would never end, though he knew he was rapidly aging and slowing down. His tough body was still tanned and sinewy, but at night his joints ached with the beginnings of arthritis.

One big change in his life was Amy, a Wisconsin girl twenty-five years younger than him. Bert had fallen for the young Air Force veteran when he first met her in Washington, D.C. Amy was on the Montgomery GI Bill at George Mason Law School, but dropped out in her second year to follow Bert to Africa.

The security force occupied tiny plywood hooches with corrugated iron roofs, but Bert and Amy had managed to acquire a small air conditioner for their hooch, which they fitted into a hole cut in the wall. Amy's prized "cheese-head" hat hung from a nail on one wall. The tribesmen couldn't comprehend why she wore it to their plywood team house, or "club" on the weekends, where she drank too many beers and spoke incessantly about a place called Green Bay. Life was large for Amy and Bert.

*   *   *   *   *

Out on the aircraft carrier, SOCEUR's force loaded onto the birds for take off. Two aircraft would set down. Two would remain in the air as fire support, with back up roles as search and rescue on the way to the target, or as emergency extraction from the mine during the action. Each helicopter had door gunners with mini-guns and a .50 caliber machine-gunner in the tail. As they lifted off, they dropped to only thirty feet above the sea. The Special Forces troopers were comforted when all machine-guns and mini-guns worked, as proven by the test-fired tracers skipping across the Atlantic all around them.

When the first bird went "feet dry" (crossing from over sea to over land), it was totally dark. The pilots and gunners had so much gear on they looked like robots. No skin showed through the adornments of special helmets, suits, gloves, night vision devices, and communication links. In addition, not only did each man have on Kevlar (KV) body armor, the floor of each helicopter was covered with a bulletproof KV blanket.

The aircraft hit the timelines right on the money. They were turning at a key river bend to head on their final leg into the target.

The mission commander put himself on the ground, but kept the air mission commander flying. The air mission commander was his "2IC," or Second in Command. If things went sour on the ground, he would be fresh and unengaged, ready to take charge.

The two aircraft set down out of nowhere into the middle of the diamond mine complex. Bert had not prepared for a sophisticated assault, one that would land *inside* his defenses. The birds were to sit still, placing them in severe jeopardy for the five minutes of allotted ground time. Five minutes that, to the operators, would seem like hours.

Defensive teams spread out to protect the aircraft, moving to predetermined guard positions to ensure no one could approach unopposed. Total surprise was achieved.

The Special Forces shooters dismounted quickly and moved past the defense teams. Silenced M4 carbines quickly dropped two armed guards on roving patrol duty. The Special Forces engineers quietly disposed of two more stationary guards just outside the main tunnel into the mine.

Two SF soldiers posted themselves at each side of the entrance. The demo team cautiously began to move deep into the mine. As they moved, confidence grew. The human intelligence (HUMINT) boys had done their job. The mineshafts matched the reports and their rehearsals and no other enemy was found inside them. They went about their main business, finding exactly the right locations to set their charges. The other Special Forces troopers fanned out to their targets. Their orders were to kill anyone who tried to interfere with the explosives being placed in the mines. They were additionally tasked to destroy several key items of engineering heavy equipment, the fuel dump, and the camp's communications center.

Things were going well, and all demolitions were in place in less than four minutes. Meanwhile, a South African radio operator in the communications shed had to be eliminated to allow plastic explosive to be emplaced on a critically important satellite relay.

On the other side of the camp, Bert and his men were enjoying their evening meal, cold beer, and loud music in the "club." Many were dancing with camp followers, girls from Liberia that had come to the mine to illicitly earn a living.

Amy was sitting on a stool at the bar, and Bert had just joined her. He was dirty from the day's work, and his khaki shirt was wet with sweat from the perimeter walk.

The club had some overhead vents and mosquito netting covering large openings to allow the breeze to pass through. The music was growing too loud for Bert, another sign of aging, he thought, as he stood with a rum and coke in his left hand and his arm gently on Amy's shoulder. Then the stereo went quiet while the bartender changed a CD on the portable player that sat underneath the bar.

Suddenly, Bert heard the helicopters over the noise of the camp generators. The choppers were starting to rev their engines preparatory to pulling the teams out.

The Special Forces soldiers were collapsing back to their aircraft a bit late, five minutes and thirty seconds after they had landed. Simultaneously, the two airborne craft rolled in, prepared to chew up anyone interfering with their mates' departure.

Bert knew immediately that a helicopter at night meant a major operation was underway. He automatically assumed it was British SAS. They had done excellent work in Sierra Leone previously.

"Oh, shit!" Bert grabbed his M4, hanging by its sling on a nail by the door of the bar, and fired a burst through the roof to get everyone's attention. He shouted one word: "Helicopters!"

Bert had meticulously rehearsed his men on alert procedure, but, sadly for his employers, Sunday night was when his Arena Linea mercenary force was at it weakest, with the CD blasting music into the darkness accompanied by rampant consumption of beer and rum. Clumsily, Bert's men grabbed their weapons and scrambled out of the bar to designated fighting positions, while the women lay down flat in the club awaiting orders. The selection of a Sunday night was made on SOCEUR intelligence that each weekend security was less than optimal.

Medics scrambled to man the aide station, electrically illuminated, fully sandbagged, and containing supplies and a few beds. As selected guards tumbled inside the protected Command bunker, the two helicopters were fully torqued, waiting for the last SF soldier to retreat past the defense teams.

Bert ignored his duty station, the sandbagged command bunker. As he ran straight towards the aircraft, he couldn't believe what he was hearing. The distinctive deep-throated whine as the engines revved up was characteristic of the MH-53, which meant a U.S. operation!

As Bert closed in on the helicopters, he rounded a building and suddenly froze. In the dark, he saw a camouflaged soldier not more than twenty meters ahead of him.

He could distinctly see two MH-53's behind the defender. Suddenly he was aware of a laser red dot dead centered on his chest. Bert dropped his M4, raising his hands up in the air, wide apart. Quickly he backed away, expecting at any moment to be torn to pieces by automatic fire.

Ducking around the corner of a building, Bert exhaled deeply and peeked back warily. The choppers were lifting off. He could barely make out the 53's pulling out in the moonlight. As he moved forward to retrieve his M4, one of his perimeter positions opened up on the aircraft. Rounds went through the thin skin of the bottom of one bird, causing the SF soldiers to bounce in the air as the KV blanket rippled from catching the bullets. The pilot immediately reported that his ship was hit.

Rounds from the mini-guns of the aircraft watching over their brothers ripped into the guards and their defensive position. Bodies, sandbags, and timbers flew into the air. The rain of tracers from the mini-gun looked like fire hurtling from the night sky, terrorizing the camp. Not another guard position fired after the display.

As soon as the two choppers with the ground troops aboard cleared the edge of the camp, the chief Green Beret engineer looked down and squeezed his remote-firing device. All of the charges, except the special munitions deep in the mine, blew at once.

The communications center, the heavy engineering equipment, and the fuel dump blew up simultaneously. The helicopters hovered about a kilometer away, and then paused in offset orbit to observe one more blast of their handiwork from a safe distance.

The camp was in chaos, with a background of flames from the fuel dump. Then it got worse. The main charges, with the greatest blast potency, set deep in the mine, exploded. The demolitions had been on a timer, along with a back-up timer and a duplicate firing system.

The floor of the camp rolled. The men who had just regained their feet from dodging the helicopter fire were toppled to the heaving ground, as if a magnitude-eight Richter scale earthquake was trembling beneath them. With their long-range optics, the SOCEUR team was making videotapes to assist in damage assessment. Satellites had also been cued to watch the whole operation, but clouds had been considered a threat to adequate coverage.

Bert ran back to the club and saw that Amy was unhurt. She was doing a great job calming the women. She gave him a thumbs-up and he simply returned the gesture as he ran to the command bunker to get reports and assess damage.

In a relatively short period of time, the pilots went feet wet. Landing on the aircraft carrier, a replacement special operations crew took each bird over. Without cutting the engines, every bit of extra operations equipment, and all the extra pilots and crews were loaded. The plan was for the formation of helicopters to leave the aircraft carrier in darkness, link up with their special operations tankers, "get a drink" of fuel, and head to an airfield in the Canary Islands.

Via secure radio, the mission commander gave a verbal report to the SOCEUR commander back in Germany. His orders were to be well away from the aircraft carrier before sunrise to avoid satellite coverage. Special Operations maintenance technicians on the ship inspected the hurt bird and gave thumbs up.

Finally, all four aircraft, even the one that had been struck by small arms fire several times, were ordered to fly off the ship. The lead pilot had faith and confidence in the recommendation of the enlisted maintenance crews. They had never failed him in twenty years of flying.

The SOCEUR mission commander then loaded all but minimal personnel and all equipment on the three aircraft that had not been hit. He had the crew in the damaged bird lay out their safety rafts for ready access. The other helicopters checked and rechecked their winches in case someone ended up in the drink. After making sure that valuable incriminating equipment was accounted for and not left accidentally at the mine, the force took off. The wounded bird would lead and the others would follow.

The dead-tired mission commander, assault force, air crews and pilots were preparing to fall asleep on the floors, stacked like logs amid weapons, communication gear, rucksacks, chow, and water containers.

*   *   *   *   *

Bert spent the night laying out the dead, caring for the injured, seeing that weapons and equipment were accounted for, positions were manned, and communications reestablished. Amy had seen to it that Bert was uninterrupted for an hour of solid rest. At sunrise, he went outside to survey the damage in daylight. Bert had two of his South Africans follow him so he could relay orders and set the priorities of repair work.

During the night, when submitting his reports, Bert had purposely not mentioned that the operation was probably U.S.-sponsored. He stated effects, number of helicopters, and supplied generally accurate descriptions; he simply left out that he knew the exact type of aircraft and probably the nation responsible. Although an expatriate, Bert was still a *patriot,* and didn't want to blow the cover on a U.S. operation.

On their walk, Bert and his South Africans had found some detonation cord and a fuse lighter, hidden in an olive green pack that was stuffed into the brush along the side of the trail. The branches of an overhanging tree were snapped downward—the pack was purposely placed there for later discovery. The detonation cord and fuse were both standard UK issue.

Bert also found a cigarette planted in the brush—Dunhill, his favorite brand from England. It was crumpled, but hadn't been lit. He muttered out loud so the South Africans would hear: "Damn Brits!" He reached for his portable satellite phone and reported his additional findings to Strategic Effects' Arena Linea point of contact in London.

Bert thought to himself that after he had cleaned up the mess, he would move on. He didn't want to be at odds with the United States during their Global War on Terrorism. President Bush's administration had taken Uncle Sam's gloves off and they were going for the jugular. Besides, after the raid, Bert was positive that the U.S. had someone inside his defense force on the payroll. The raiders' actions indicated that they had close to perfect intelligence. It was time to try Asia again, maybe the Golden Triangle. He would have to talk to Amy.

*   *   *   *   *

The NSA intercept network was at highest alert during and after the Sierra Leone raid. It was no surprise but rather a confirmation of British intelligence when Arena Linea, from London, passed the news and damage assessment on to valued clients. Instead of Liberia, Nigeria, or other West-African States locked in the Sierra Leone and Liberian peacekeeping efforts, the news of the destruction of the diamond mine was flashed to a bank in Angola, one with ties to Fidel Castro for over two decades. For years the bank had paid the Cuban Army for its services against the UNITA rebels of Joseph Savimbi, paying the Cuban treasury in U.S. dollars or gold bullion.

The second recipient of the news of the mine's destruction was in the western hemisphere, a small office in a sunny tourist resort on the island of Margarita, forty kilometers off the coast of Venezuela. The connection surprised the NSA operations officer.

Even more of an eye opener, there was a new info addressee; the source to which the intelligence just gathered would be forwarded. He shrugged and sent the report, acknowledging to himself that there were some things that, with all of his clearances, he was not to know. The addressee was someone new, someone relatively unimportant, since it was only an info addressee. Something called *The Hybrid*.

15 Aug 2004
The President hung up the secure phone. Secretary Rumsfeld had just informed him of the success of the raid into Sierra Leone to eliminate Fidel's principle source of funding for his biological and agro-terror program. Nothing was in the newspapers. Remembering that Fidel's birthday was the very day of the raid, Bush smiled and said, "Happy birthday, Fidel!"

16 Aug 2004

Kirsten was in the weight room pumping iron. The night before, nude, she had critiqued herself in a full-length mirror. She was quite pleased, having lost thirteen pounds since arriving in Norman. In school she was doing well, too. Her addiction to English literature grew stronger everyday. She was fulfilled and doing what she loved.

She was in her niche, happy. Except Mike was gone, and she couldn't shake the memory of the woman she had seen with Mike their last night in the OU library. Her anger burned daily, needing an explanation to quench the flames.

Even on her birthday, Kirsten knew Mike could neither call nor send a present. "When Special Forces boys go operational, they simply forget loved ones," she muttered to herself between sets on the incline board. Deep inside, Kirsten knew better, but bitterness with the lifestyle was gnawing at her. She remembered her joy on hearing of Mike's graduate school assignment. Now, instead of seven out of nine years apart, it could be almost eight out of ten.

Ted, a muscle-bound pretty boy, also an English major and one of Kirsten's classmates, broke the funk. He had welcomed her invitation to start working out together. Ted was spotting. "Ready for your last set?"

Kirsten nodded. As she completed her last repetition, Ted commented, "You have dropped a few pounds on your lift. Are you injured?" Unexpectedly, she blurted out that it was her birthday and that she was simply depressed, knowing that she would spend it alone.

Ted did his best to comfort her throughout the rest of the workout, wishing her the absolute best for the day. As they finished lifting and headed for the showers, Ted wished her a happy birthday, squeezed her hand, and said everything would be all right. Ted's kind gesture helped. As Kirsten showered, she felt better.

That night, around 8:00 p.m., there was a knock on her door. Frumpy, Kirsten was wearing old blue jeans and a beloved XXL Oklahoma Sooners sweatshirt. She had been curled up for the evening, reading. It was one of the students from her favorite English course. He asked her to please step outside. Her patio furniture had been moved on the front driveway. A cake was lit. A large cardboard sign said, simply, "Happy Birthday, Kirsten!"

The crowd consisted of two boys and two girls from her class, and Ted, who walked around the corner with a bottle of wine and plastic glasses. As her young classmates broke into song, Kirsten self-consciously reached for her hair; it was a mess.

She recovered, eyes misted over, yet laughing simultaneously at how horrible she must look. The cake, plastic forks, paper plates, cheap wine, and plastic glasses were equal to the finest china and fare in New York's Metropolitan Club. She felt better than she had in weeks.

The surprise party lasted less than twenty minutes; the students had to go on their way. It took moments to throw the residue into a garbage bag and return her lawn furniture to the back yard. Ted walked her to the front door, garbage bag in one hand. Kirsten reached up and kissed him on the cheek, simply saying, "Thank you so much."

Ted replied, "See you tomorrow." He walked away without looking back.

Kirsten closed the door. Ted, the body builder, more than pretty, had heart. She turned and shook her head. She was smiling inwardly, embarrassed at what she was thinking.

17 Aug 2004

Mike received his mission brief. Location: Havana, Cuba.

His task seemed simple enough. Grab a briefcase and deliver it to designated U.S. control. The devil was in the details. The briefcase would be carried from a fully secured facility to a waiting car with at least two armed security guards and a driver. In addition, the area where the car would be situated was observable from at least two guard towers.

The man who would be carrying the briefcase was a diminutive scientist. The briefcase was always chained to his wrist. He had become a target because he "patterned" himself—leaving the walled compound at the same moment on the same day of the week. Mike guessed he was a quad-A personality, addicted to fixed structure, routine, and absolute adherence to time schedules.

To Mike's advantage, the compound was in a crowded *barrio* in Havana, which would help his approach. The top-secret biological warfare research facility was well disguised. It looked like a medium security prison, which indeed was its cover.

Surrounded by dense *barrios* meant that any gringo military action against the facility would probably cause civilian casualties, which added to the laboratory's protection. The deception/cover was excellent. The local population was convinced the facility was one of Castro's many prisons.

Mike was told that it had taken intense intelligence scrutiny to identify the bio facility and discover its true purpose. Although he was only told that a substance highly detrimental to U.S. interest was being developed in the former Cuban jail, Mike's target was perfectly clear. The briefcase, if captured, would provide information instrumental in determining the nature of the threat material.

For the first week of training, as Angela commented, they would work only the target. Photos or reports on the site, pictures of the scientist, a model of the scientist with exact height and weight, and a three-dimensional model or mockup of the "prison" were available.

Numerous briefcases of exact size and estimated weight were available for inspection and practice. Unlimited numbers of cuffs were available to include several models, allowing Mike to examine and determine how best to defeat them.

Mike could request any intelligence product or training aid. John's team would do its absolute best to satisfy the requirement. Mike greatly appreciated the team's dedication to ensuring his success. Although there were no scheduled weekends off, Angela and John would listen to Mike as they set the pace. The only rule was to start the daily work schedule at 8:00 a.m. so the others in the warehouse complex would think the front company was operating a normal business.

Mike, in particular, liked the rehearsal area they had built for him, especially the virtual reality kits. He could walk the streets of Havana and through the alleys of the *barrio* and see the prison walls, literally "casing the joint" in his virtual world. He practiced day after day, then returning to the intelligence experts to get increasingly more data fused into the virtual reality (VR) system. Each day the realism improved.

He refined walking times to the point that he knew within five seconds how long it would take to reach his final hide sight before the sprint. The best spot was behind a refuse container, in an alley oblique to where the security vehicle was to park. The distance of the sprint was to be twenty-two meters.

Getting away was another matter, but that would follow full development of actions on the objective.

In addition, Angela was using the evenings to pump him full of information about Havana. She was a world-class regional expert. She was "Cubanizing" his Spanish, and that left him constantly amazed that the language was not her mother tongue. She was also imbuing him with the Cuban culture as forty years of Communism had changed the way people act in public. Mike realized that her efforts could be incredibly valuable, particularly if the plan broke down necessitating evasion on his own.

Mike had never confirmed the Cold War legend about the Taiwanese spy, who after years of training, finally deployed to the mainland. The spy, supposedly, was doing great until he was in a restaurant and ordered a second bowl of soup. In the sixties a second helping of anything was forbidden in starving China. The entire restaurant turned and looked at the offender, and he was caught running out.

One Saturday morning, Angela called. "Meet me at the park a few miles from your hotel—we're going for a jog so bring your running gear."

When Mike showed up, the small park was empty. Seconds later, Angela showed up. She was a stretching enthusiast, and Mike hated it. She was also a tough trainer and refused to listen to his complaints. Angela repeated over and over that she was not going to be responsible for Mike's failure due to a blown hamstring.

As the days went by, Mike began to silently wonder if he knew anything close to the truth about the actual purpose or scope of the mission. As both an experienced handler/trainer and singleton, the extensive investment in preparation and assignment of some of the best talent he had ever seen for a simple bag snatch didn't add up.

The need to employ someone with his particular Green Beret experience and acumen to simply "nick," the word Angela used for an act of petty theft, a bag off some elderly scientist was significant overkill.

He grimaced as Angela led him in a twenty-minute stretching drill. Next she jogged about a mile with him, following with some sprints. Then, she opened the trunk she had brought with her and took out a surprise. She put a set of heavy sunglasses on Mike's head, leading him out into an open field. She worked a small control box and Mike could "see" his start point in Havana. Angela then put a Velcro strap around his biceps, wrists, and ankles. Each strap had small sensors imbedded in them.

She then restarted the computer, telling Mike to run and get the briefcase. It was truly surreal. Unlike the virtual reality walks in the warehouse, this equipment allowed Mike to have full peripheral vision and to run full speed. Mike could see a car pull up, the gate open, and the small man walking out with the case. Mike bolted. He stumbled and almost fell.

Angela closed up to him; she put her hand on his shoulder and helped steady him. "Go slowly," she cautioned and then added, "We have only a short time to work on this. I want you to know it by heart when you face the real thing—we just can't take any chances. We'll only have one bite of the cherry."

Mike thought of his high school football coach, repeating Vince Lombardi over and over again, "Practice doesn't make perfect. Perfect practice makes perfect."

They stayed in the deserted park for almost an hour, until he could sprint at full speed and have faith in what he was seeing. The lab had loaded the car pulling in at fifty different attitudes, with the driver and two guards placed in different positions. The man with the briefcase was more limited in his actions because he had to come though the gate. One interesting rendition was when he stooped over to tie his shoes just before Mike took off at full speed.

Angela was worrying about shoes. She would turn all the intelligence tomorrow to finding out what shoes the populace wore in the barrio around the prison. She was going to have a pair of Mike's favorite running shoes modified accordingly. She needed to have his pants, T-shirt, hat, and backpack all custom tailored for *barrio* acceptance, utility, and speed.

She found herself liking this brave, trusting man. He was all business, yet he had a great sense of humor. Mike was making a final run, and she "tripped" the VR computer, causing him to loose his equilibrium. He fell. She ran to him, laughing. "Great workout. If you'll stretch and cool down for about fifteen minutes, I'll pay for a Starbucks coffee across the street." Mike agreed, glad that the workout was over.

In Starbucks they spoke of current events, sports, and politics. She asked if he liked *salsa*. Mike sighed, saying he was only an average dancer, adding that Latin music made him feel things he shouldn't. Angela disagreed. She said, "*Salsa* makes you uninhibited, it is therapeutic, it relieves all stress."

As he sat talking to Angela, Mike was enjoying himself, until he thought of Kirsten. Suddenly, he terminated the conversation, but in a pleasant way, telling Angela he had to run some errands.

Angela released him for the day. He thanked her for the workout and drove away, troubled. He found himself wanting to know more about her.

CHAPTER TEN

16 Aug 2004

The Angolan banker was in a rage. He had just fired his head accountant, and his vice-presidents were lined up in front of his desk. He threatened them, literally, with execution. None had an answer. All records of the largest secret diamond account had disappeared. Computer files and all electronic records seemed to have instantaneously evaporated. Millions of dollars were missing, as if the money had never existed.

Notifying the point of contact in Cuba was not going to be pleasant. He pulled out his cell phone, placing a card in it from his safe. It was a secure card, one that would scramble the entire conversation.

"*Señor* Matos, *por favor*?" he asked.

Señor Matos answered quickly. The banker gave a crisp report, and was told to calm down and not panic. He then received his instructions: "I will send my best composite team over immediately. Whatever you do, do not touch your computers for any reason. You may contaminate valuable data. A *Señor* Piñon will be in the lead."

Señor Matos looked out his window over a steamy Havana street. It had just rained, and his twenty-year-old air conditioner, a luxury in Cuba, was barely making a difference. There was sweat on his brow. He carefully opened a hidden panel in the woodwork of the old building. It was a small safe, unknown to other workers in the office. He applied the combination and pulled out a file labeled *Mundo Nuevo*, or New World.

Matos wrote out a report by hand, afraid to use electrons to record the phone call. The file was thick. The report on top was a damage assessment of the raid on the diamond mine in Sierra Leone and the impacts of funding for *Mundo Nuevo*. The assessment was now outdated, for if the report from Angola held, *Mundo Nuevo* was penniless.

His project's funding, carefully designed through old Angolan communist Cuban allies from their years in Africa fighting UNITA, was most assuredly under attack. That *Mundo Nuevo* had somehow leaked was a distinct possibility. The project was Fidel's number one TOP SECRET program. Heads would literally roll if the project failed because of incompetence or lack of security within Matos' domain.

After carefully writing down an exact record of the phone conversation, he felt better. He hoped that the attacks were against funding for the remaining thugs in Liberia and the RUF's diamond industry itself in Sierra Leone. Hopefully, there was no linkage to Cuba because of numerous cutouts and firewalls between *Mundo Nuevo* and the Angolan bank. Nonetheless, the computer attack remained a severe and crippling blow.

Although *Mundo Nuevo* might survive as a project, Matos would have to find a totally new means of finance. He thought of the drug cartels, and then shuddered. If Fidel found out, Matos could face a firing squad. Fidel hated drug dealers and drug money.

Matos told his secretary to send in Piñon. Four days later, Matos received a report from Piñon, now in Angola, via a secure phone. He was in the bank.

"*Señor*, there is simply no record of the accounts. I cannot trace the actor that broke into the computer. Worse, the back up records here are useless. To introduce the accounts would make us look like the perpetrators of fraud. In effect, we would look like the criminals." He paused. "However, there is some information available. Many Internet hits occurred against the bank's firewalls for two days before the accounts disappeared. They came from an e-mail address in the United Kingdom. I will bring the information home for more detailed analysis and follow-up."

Piñon concluded, "The accounts have simply disappeared into the ether. I'm sorry I can't give better news."

Matos sagged over his desk. He stopped re-writing his report for a second and replied, "You have done your best as always. See me immediately on your return." He continued to write, preoccupied with *Mundo Nuevo* and his own future.

Matos had thirty-five years of loyal service in Castro's most compartmented intelligence service. He had risen quickly, instrumental in tying all of the party block chiefs into an intelligence pool that made Cuba's population control measures nearly as good as East Germany's. Matos had been ruthless. Torture, imprisonment, and threats of rape or harm to children and innocent relatives were among the tools of his trade. He found out the truth, one way or another. Pursuing spies and disloyal citizens with a vengeance, he had been the key to the complete destruction of the CIA network in Cuba.

Matos was also a master of deception. Some agents that he discovered were simply turned, and on his payroll, and they had been supplying the CIA with bogus information for years.

Fidel himself had handpicked Matos to manage *Mundo Nuevo*. The project was to be his crowning achievement. Matos envisioned his family with him in Fidel's office, receiving a retirement medal and personal thanks for a lifetime of service. He wiped his brow with a handkerchief and looked at the wall. His prize possession was hung on it: a black and white photo of *El Lider*, himself, in fatigues and full beard, hugging Matos.

*   *   *   *   *

General Hanscom was pleased that the first step in shaping the battle space had been successful, and President Bush had passed his sincere thanks regarding the success in Angola. It reinforced the administration's strategy of targeting the financing of organizations that intend to harm the United States. In fact, Treasury General David Aufhauser had recently announced that Al-Qaeda funding had successfully been cut, in less than three years, by almost two-thirds.

21 Aug 2004
During the previous week, Angela had made equipping Mike a priority. She used her British intelligence experience to help him

determine the best clothes for his mission. The result was several sets of hand tailored clothes, rucksacks, bulletproof vests, and several copies of a vest for under loose-fitting shirts that would house his pistol, magazines, and other special equipment. Built into the vest was a STABO harness that would allow him to attach rapidly to extraction cables dropped from a helicopter.

Duplicate sets of all the requisitioned equipment were purchased in case Mike destroyed anything during his extensive full-speed rehearsals. In addition, Mike's kit included several devices brought in by some guest "technicians." Everything was vetted for the Cuban street. Shirt, slacks, rucksack, hat—all of it looked native except under the closest scrutiny.

Early in the week, Angela handed Mike a package from behind her back, wrapped with a colorful bow. "Open it now," she suggested. Mike obliged. His favorite running shoes had been modified on the top and sides to resemble common Havana *barrio* footwear, yet they still retained their fit and flexibility. Mike dropped to the floor and put them on. He jogged in place for a moment, then put one arm around Angela and gave her a hug.

"Fantastic!" he said, "They feel as if they haven't been modified. Thanks." Angela glowed.

Mission-essential equipment included a modified 9mm Berretta with ceramic, hollow point, exploding rounds. Men with bulletproof vests would, at the minimum, be knocked down. Mike would carry only four extra magazines. On the pistol was a laser sight along with a miniaturized high-power laser for cutting off the handcuffs. It added to the weight, so Mike would have to do lots of firing range work in the next few days to get used to the balance and feel. A range had been rented from a local gun club for the purpose. A front organization had said it needed to test some garage industry modifications to some of its pistols. No questions would be asked.

Angela had put Mike through the paces to make sure his new gear was adequate. He fired and fired, and then he ran and ran. Confidence in his gear was high. His faith in the new pistol was improving. Mike was sure that what he saw in the pistol's sights would drop.

It took a while to adjust to the pistol's added weight due to the laser's battery. A flick of the switch would allow Mike to sever the handcuff chain, or the arm of the scientist carrying it. Mike would have to decide on the run. The laser used so much battery power that it was good for only two or three shots, maximum. Only one shot was absolutely guaranteed in the tech specs.

Early in the morning, Mike practiced different runs with the laser, the manikin, and the mock-up of the briefcase. Sometimes the laser would only fire once, sometimes twice. Mike didn't feel too confident about the thing—a pair of bolt-cutters would have done just fine in his book, and they wouldn't run out of juice when it really counted. He planned to buy some for his rucksack.

For communications, Mike was given what appeared to be an everyday international pager. It had embedded security that could be activated with a simple four-digit code. If Mike didn't re-enter the four-digit code every twenty-four hours, the pager's secure function would switch off, and the case officers in the United States would know that the pager had fallen into enemy hands or that Mike was in trouble. The pager was "real time" communication—acceptable to use in any situation except link-up, fire support, or close-in fighting.

Survival had to be a concern, because, as Murphy's Laws of Combat explained, no plan ever stayed the same after the first shot was fired. He was supplied with pressure dressings, bandages, tiny bottles of various drugs and morphine syrettes, and an IV bag and catheter. Everything was labeled and instructions were in Spanish.

Mike added a Leatherman multipurpose tool, fishing line, hooks, a magnifying glass, waterproof matches, and some vials of "bug juice." As tough as Mike was, he had an Achilles heel: he really hated mosquitoes, so he threw in a head net. Also, he added a pair of light cotton gloves, a mini MagLite with extra AA batteries, back-up batteries for his pager and laser cutting tool, and a rubberized night-vision spotting scope.

A critical supplement to his kit was two pairs of prescription glasses, one for sun and one regular, with Cuban government-issued frames. Mike would need them if his time on the ground was extended, or if he had to change his appearance by removing his colored contact lenses. He would also carry a tourist's map of Cuba, available at any corner store in Havana.

Mike added a Taser gun and two tiny canisters of pepper spray for non-lethal defense. Two long sleeve T-shirts and a Cuban-made, light rain jacket rounded out his essential gear. Dried fruit, beef jerky, and iodine water purification pills would keep him self-sufficient for a week or more with no other rations available.

Around his waist, in a tailored fanny pack rode his passport, pounds Sterling, American dollars, Cuban pesos, and other identification. Included was a card with his blood type, just in case he was severely wounded and the enemy chose to help him survive for exploitation.

Weapons and ammunition would be carried in the special flesh-colored, lightweight nylon vest under his baggy T-shirt. The harness, designed especially for Mike, included rolled up straps to convert the harness into a nylon "cage" around him to assist in extraction by helicopter winch.

Angela watched Mike's fluidity and rhythm improve with repetition. She used his own American football analogy when working with him—after the snap, the players don't even feel their pads and equipment. When the whistle blew for Mike's kickoff, she wanted him to be able to concentrate solely on executing his task. As Mike's rehearsals continued, his equipment and his body became one—he was almost ready for the mission.

Towards the end of the week, John called Angela and Mike over to his corner of the warehouse. They had a discussion and agreed that Mike was as prepared for the briefcase snatch as time could allow. It was now time to focus on the three main tasks of the mission. They were simple; get in, do the job, and get out: *infiltration, handing over the briefcase,* and *exfiltration.*

CHAPTER ELEVEN

22 Aug 2004

A portly, graying, sixty-year-old man passed through Athens, Greece. His suit and tie were outdated, and he moved with a slouching shuffle. If anyone could portray an absent-minded professor, it was the Russian. He was Viktor Latshev, brilliant botanist and genetic engineer.

The airport was notorious for weak security and sympathetic support for terrorist groups, as well as deposed Yugoslavian leader Milosevic's cronies from Belgrade. Money talked in regards to the airport security system and the CIA knew it. As Viktor's luggage moved from his Russian plane to the next carrier, a baggage handler with a special ring of keys quickly opened one of the suitcases.

The lining was slit open, and a small package was inserted. Clothes were gently placed as they had been prior to being disturbed, and the luggage was locked once again and sent on its way.

Moments before landing in Mexico City to transfer to a Cuban airline, Viktor was in seventh heaven. For thirty years he had sacrificed the good life to conduct research in a highly classified facility in Chukota, Russia. Fenced into the city of Providence, he had lived in the Arctic Circle, had faced brutal cold and winters ten months in length, and had raised his children away from his beloved home in Saratov, Volga. His suffering was only relieved by periodic holidays at the Black Sea.

He was bitter. After his three decades of sacrifice and absolute loyalty to the Soviet Union and the communist cause, he had been sacked. Even worse, he had lost his wife to cancer the year before, and his children were gone. He was destitute, desperate, and chronically depressed.

Job prospects in Russia offered very low wages for such a top scientist, less than two thousand dollars a year U.S.

Then the Cuban Embassy had contacted him, offering him nearly a hundred times that amount, and finding Viktor quite willing to engage in productive work. He had, via the Internet, engaged *Señor* Matos' cronies, and contributed some startling conceptualizations toward a Cuban biological weapons program. The Cubans were grateful and Viktor began receiving modest emoluments. Self-respect returned. He soon was called to Cuba to be a key contributor to *Mundo Nuevo.* He would be important again; the warm weather and unconstrained scientific research would be therapeutic, healing the wounds of the last decade.

Viktor was an expert in diseases—not curing them, but in creating them. Viktor was way beyond archaic concepts such as Agent Orange defoliant. Release of his products was untraceable. They could be delivered by aerial spray, by hand, by animals and birds, by bombs or missiles. Once present, his diseases would infect, proliferate, and spread geographically, veritably breaching Pandora's original box of pandemics.

Viktor had dreamed for years of the devastating effect of his handiwork on the United States. After infection, and sudden realization that the U.S. could no longer export food, panic would ensue. The world would have to embargo the United States, Mexico, and Canada to prevent spread of the diseases and the specter of worldwide starvation. Viktor visualized an America imploding, abandoned by her allies. As her citizens became more and more desperate, a major breakdown of law and order would follow.

Viktor assumed there would be a temporary respite if the military took over food distribution, but in the long run, chaos would reign. The United States, already Balkanized, might simply fall apart. In the rural areas, survivalists, already fully armed, would fight any urban movement into their smaller towns and villages by the starving masses from the cities.

Viktor was convinced that the U.S. could never stand the stresses of such a challenge. The capitalist citizens were soft and spoiled.

Russia had suffered thirty million dead in the World Wars, and still stood proudly despite her recent difficulties. U.S. democracy, so delicate, so pampered, might just fall apart the way the Soviet Union had done.

But Soviet Prime Minister Gorbachev had pulled the plug on the project shortly before he gave up power. Research was destroyed. Spetznatz units followed his technicians as they made certain all spores and mutations were eliminated.

Finally, Gorbachev himself made a secret trip to inspect the complete destruction of the research labs and associated facilities. Latshev's colleagues, many of whom he had known for years, were dispersed to the four winds. Shortly thereafter, the wall came down and the Soviet Union itself collapsed.

Gorbachev had not destroyed the program out of humanitarian concern. In fact, he had increased the budgetary allowances for WMD each year he was in power. The death knell for Viktor's program was an accidental infection of Russian crops. Even though the infection was eventually contained, the bureaucrats involved had all lied in the cover up. Gorbachev was furious with the scientific community.

When rumors of the incident reached Moscow, an investigation was ordered—to be immediately and ruthlessly conducted. The result was cursory and unsatisfactory. Displeased, Gorbachev commissioned a KGB estimate, separate from the biological warfare scientific community, on the likelihood of the program's threat to the Soviet Union. The KGB's assessment was extremely pessimistic. Eventual contamination of the Soviet Union occurred under most developmental scenarios. In sum, there was simply too great of a threat to allow the program's continuation, despite the protection of conducting research in the Siberian deep freeze.

As a result, Gorbachev, darling of the West, ordered elimination of Viktor's crop destruction program, simultaneously ordering resultant cost savings transferred to more "stable" programs: the development of new strains of small pox, anthrax, and other debilitating diseases.

Now, however, Viktor was celebrating, ordering vodka after vodka from the airline attendants. The KGB may have cleansed the laboratories in Chukota; however, one body of knowledge had not been destroyed—Viktor himself. He wished he would have smuggled out a vial or two, but he had been unable to do so. He was sure that some had, but they were watching him too closely.

A wheat specialist, Viktor knew more about wheat than any scientist in Europe or Asia. Viktor's stock in trade was genetically engineered smut spores, the covered and loose varieties. Infected plants developed wheat kernels with a blackened center; a pocket of black spores. When exposed to the air, thousands would be released to spread the infection. The spores caused the wheat to have a foul, fishy odor and rendered it inedible.

Viktor had dabbled in wheat rust and mosaic disease as well. He had a formidable arsenal in his mental archives. A joke in the Russian lab was that Viktor had built the enemies of wheat into "diseases on steroids," and he was proud of his designer products. He had tested his protégés against many of the wheat strains worldwide, and none had proven resistant.

Now he would continue his work with wheat smut and genetically engineered new pathogens—that it couldn't be detected by tests—create something totally new that would attack the specific hybrids of wheat in the target areas. He would plan exactly how it would spread—from harvesting, in trucks, in graineries, by animals, and on air—and he would enhance its persistence and mask the way the tests are used so that it could not be detected. He was a very patient man and knew that it didn't have to happen with a big bang to get the desired effect.

Viktor's flight closed on Mexico City. How ironic, he mused. Bernhard Warkentin, a German Mennonite immigrant, had taken the wheat strain *Turkey Red* from the Russian Crimea to Halstead, Kansas in 1873, eventually creating the great breadbasket of the free world. Now, a single Russian scientist was bringing, from the same great nation, the capability to destroy it. Fidel Castro would, forty years after losing nuclear weapons during the missile crisis, have his own strategic weapon to terrorize the United States.

Viktor finished his final vodka, landed and entered the airport. He searched happily for directions to *Cubana de Aviación*. His joy was short-lived. A customs agent collected him and escorted him to a private office. His luggage was eventually delivered and a thorough search conducted. Cocaine was discovered in the lining of his suitcase.

Viktor was livid. He had been set up. Worried that the Russian government might have orchestrated the plant, he found his anger taken over by fear, and he quickly became cooperative. But in spite of the Mexican government's tangled web of bureaucracy, and despite the incompetence of its law enforcement units and courts, Viktor was expelled from the country within forty-eight hours. Mexican counter-drug authorities, the DEA, and the CIA had worked well together, resulting in a perfect execution. Viktor was headed back to Moscow, his dreams smashed.

Despite the differences between the countries regarding immigration and the previous year's dust-up about Mexico's lack of support for the invasion of Iraq, *Presidente* Vicente Fox and President Bush could still work well together on issues of mutual strategic interest.

The Russian Embassy was informed of the arrest and subsequent actions, and the Cubans found out about the arrest and deportation via carefully placed news reports in Mexican media. In Havana, next day, Señor Matos was crazed with foreboding. Someone, somewhere, knew about *Mundo Nuevo*. The diamond mines, bank accounts, and now Viktor? The invisible someone was both powerful and professional.

Matos called in his counter-intelligence specialists. A silent inquisition was instituted within his organization. He had to discover the leaks. There would be no mercy for those responsible.

Stuttgart, Germany
23 Aug 2004
The purchase of specially designed stainless steel storage tanks with computer-designed glass linings was imperative for Señor Matos' project. The cadre of scientists he had assembled would be unable to grow their arsenal of spores and agents in quantity without this essential equipment. Three known sources in the world fabricated the tanks. One was in Ohio. Another was in Stuttgart, Germany. The third manufacturer was somewhere in Russia, and was reportedly out

of business. Señor Matos began to contact some old friends who had previously been part of the East German communist intelligence apparatus, and he was able to arrange purchase of five of the tanks with an export license from Greece.

Matos' last report was encouraging: laundered money had moved via electronic banking from Sierra Leone, through Angola, to the Caribbean, on to Italy, and ending in Greece. Product delivery was arranged from Germany to a small Cuban-sponsored front company in Greece, and thence to Havana. Upon final inspection in Greece, if the tanks passed their final rigorous quality-control checks, German technicians would seal each one for shipment. *Señor* Matos was able to breathe a sigh of relief—he had paid for the tanks up-front, prior to the destruction of the diamond mine and the cyber attack on the Angolan bank.

Shortly after midnight, three men clad in German running clothes and shoes slipped over the security fence of the Stuttgart manufacturing company. They carried heavy rucksacks on their backs. The figure in the lead set his pack down for a moment as he picked the tumbler lock on an exterior metal door, while the other two kept a lookout from the shadows.

In an instant, the men were inside a storage facility, where the five tanks sat, awaiting crating for shipment the next day. The tanks were to be moved by large transport to the port in Bremerhaven, then on to Greece. The intruders, U.S. special operators, had restrictive rules of engagement. Use of deadly force was prohibited. In fact, they could be legally charged if they injured some unfortunate German citizens during the mission.

The men in the running suits carried modified M-79 grenade launchers, which they pulled out of their rucksacks. The breeches of the break-open launchers were loaded with 40mm rounds full of non-lethal "sticky foam." If fired, the foam would cover an opponent with a gum-like substance, effectively "gluing" him or her in place for at least an hour, and it could only be completely removed by strong solvents.

One man guarded the recently "picked" door, while the other two climbed on top of each tank in series. There was a sense of déjà vu among the operators; it meant that the rehearsals had been right on the mark.

The tanks were exactly the same as the mock-ups used in training. The seals were first cut off and removed. Next, the men pulled plastic bottles of liquid from their backpacks. They poured a bottle into each tank, closed the tops, and then resealed them with pre-prepared company seals identical to the originals. When they were finished, the tanks appeared undisturbed; there were no signs of tampering.

Their mission complete, the men hopped the fence and moved smartly through the woods into a lush German park about a half mile away from their objective. They quickly pulled off their running suits, revealing a different set of clothes underneath.

The four men were stashing their equipment in the trunk of a BMW when a German policeman stepped out of the woods. He berated the men for being in the park after closure and told them to freeze. The German policeman assumed they were drug dealers. BMW, weapons, changing clothes, it all added up. The policeman was barking at the four operators in German, ordering them to step away from the vehicle.

One of the men stepped sideways and said, *"Englische, bitte."* The policeman paused, and then the foam hit him. As the officer stood helplessly glued to the spot, the men tossed their remaining gear in the trunk, deliberately speaking in English as the officer grunted and struggled helplessly against his chemical bonds.

They sped off into the night, and paused a short distance away to rip off the top license plates, exposing new ones underneath. The BMW headed for the safe house, a place where the men could "stand down" the mission, dispose of equipment, and split up. Two of the intruders would fly back to the United States; the third would remain in Germany.

They were troubled because they had been spotted, but they were not overly worried. They had accomplished their mission; at least the poor German policeman knew they spoke English with British accents, a bonus for the operation's deception to blame the UK. It was unlikely that any link between the tanks and where the men were spotted would occur.

The men wished they could see what was happening inside of the tanks. One of the key ingredients of the "cocktail," as they called the liquid, was an industrial acid that ate through everything except plastic.

*   *   *   *   *

LTG Hanscom called George Tenet at home. Even though he was officially in retirement, that didn't mean he couldn't offer Paul some sound advice.

"The men and their German counterparts have done well. No one was hurt. There should be no indicator that sabotage has taken place, and shipment of the tanks is scheduled for tomorrow. A policeman had to be 'slimed,' but it was far from the site," Hanscom explained.

"I've talked to the head of the Chancellor's Federal Intelligence Service and he agrees that it was a great combined operation. The Germans only know that the tanks were supposed to be used for biological warfare. We did not tell them their ultimate destination. The English speaking report from the policeman should serve us well if the Cuban intelligence network hears of this," the General added.

"Great news and fine work," Tenet boomed. He hung up the phone, musing to himself. It was all coming together. At this rate, the Hybrid could soon go for the jugular. It was nice to leave a legacy, even if only a handful of people knew of its existence.

The Pentagon
24 Aug 2004
Peters, the chief of the vetting committee, was about to meet the day's guest, Ellis. He had just finished setting up the briefing room, deep inside the Pentagon. Entering through the VIP entrance, Ellis was quickly led to the JCS ring corridor. His military escort moved smartly down the wood-paneled halls to the briefing room, where a light lunch was laid out. The men shook hands and sat down.

Peters began. "I trust that the interagency staffs know that for deception purposes, this meeting is to see what we can do to improve our working joint and interagency relationships in the Global War on

Terrorism. Whenever we meet, everyone in Washington wants to know what is going on."

Ellis nodded.

Peters continued, inviting Ellis to eat while he spoke.

"I have been sent here today to provide advice from the gray-beards. The Hybrid has accomplished a great deal. The enemy's finances are disrupted, technical expertise has been limited by the Russian being returned to Russia, and we have sabotaged what was to be the nucleus of the laboratory, the tanks that have just been shipped to Greece. *Mundo Nuevo* is more severely crippled than the Cubans yet know," Peters explained.

"As the gray-beards, we again have consensus: we're nearing the moment when we should administer the *coup de grâce*. Our advice is to now move the effort to direct informational attacks in Cuba to cause the Communists' endemic paranoia to work in our favor, following with direct application of power to the problem. As you all must know, we do not yet have operational details, nor should we unless you decide to provide them. However, in the macro sense, we endorse the course we are on." There was no discussion.

* * * * *

Ellis immediately reported to LTG Hanscom's office. Everything the graybeards had recommended was well-underway. LTG Hanscom began, "We will need the NSA to ensure that our ground attack on the compound is completely tracked. I want our man to be sending strong signals, and the same with his equipment and caches. In addition, our boys downstairs deserve a pat on the back.

"We have found out how to reach out and touch Señor Matos on his computer. Our specialists have, on short order, finished the psychological profile on him and built what messages we can manipulate to ensure that he strongly recommends closure of the program. The wild card is Fidel. We must make sure that he sees no other options available. As one of Fidel's oldest and most trusted advisors, Matos is the lynch pin."

General Hanscom added, "Indeed, we do need Matos' staff to implode from fratricide. To that end, we have succeeded in setting up one of Matos' compatriots as a British agent. The discovery of this false agent will help feed Matos' paranoia, increase his already growing doubts about security and project longevity. This plus some potential direct contacts we are developing may convince him of the futility in continuing the project."

Turning his head to look out of his office window, Hanscom continued: "The NSA has put its best foot forward as well; using satellites and aircraft they have penetrated *Mundo Nuevo* beyond my expectations. I understand they are inside their secure phone system; capturing what Matos is receiving and sending. Right now, he can't make a move without us being ahead of him."

He paused, glancing down at his notes. "On the Hybrid side, as you know, we have selected and are training a lead agent, thanks to Secretary Rumsfeld sending us one of his best. The agent is a free thinker, tough, and a guaranteed survivor. Twice in the past, as a singleton, he has made key strategic contributions, waging small fights with huge strategic impact. In Cuba, we are fully confident that he can punctuate what will be a huge interagency effort."

Ellis then brought up a significant issue. The creation of false British agents meant that it was mandatory that Prime Minister Blair be brought up to speed. A meeting with the President would be required soonest, and prior agreement between all players to include the Secretary of State, Colin Powell, would be a must.

General Hanscom summarized: "It is critically important to have the President's full endorsement of our scheme of maneuver and the role we need for him to play in bringing Prime Minister Blair fully onboard. I'll take the lead preparing the brief."

CHAPTER TWELVE

The practice mission for Mike's infiltration would begin in the Florida Everglades. A spot similar to his designated drop zone in Cuba was marked out for the critical rehearsal.

Mike was breathing from his oxygen bottle, wearing a jumpsuit, special boots to cushion his landing and brace his ankles, gloves to protect his hands from the cold at high altitudes, a safety helmet, and a facemask. His equipment was attached to a small bag, which was strapped below his parachute harness. All of his equipment was European in origin; Angela had ensured that he was completely comfortable with the variances from Special Forces-issued gear. In addition, the pilot, copilot, Mike, and the civilian-registered small plane had no links to the U.S. government. It was the same with the jumpmaster and John, who was "strap-hanging" along as an observer.

The jumpmaster checked his portable instrument panel strapped to the floor near the open door. He leaned out several times trying to orient the lights of a large city below to confirm the plane's vector. He, too, was bundled against the cold, with goggles for eye protection. All of the lights inside of the aircraft were red to save Mike's "visual purple" and allow him to see as well as possible as he fell through the void.

"Two minutes" was indicated by a loud shout from the jumpmaster and the extension of two of his fingers. John caught Mike's eye through his goggles and gave his charge a pat on the back and thumbs up.

"One minute," the jumpmaster shouted, expressing it visibly by a single finger. Pulling himself back inside the open door, he shouted, "Stand by!" Mike took over the door position, standing ready. The jumpmaster got on one knee and stared at his control panel on the floor. He then looked up at Mike and shouted, "Go!" Mike disappeared into the darkness.

A heads-up display in Mike's goggles gave him a directional arrow to follow during his descent as well as a reading in meters to the desired impact point. Laden with the technology he would need for a successful Cuban infiltration, Mike checked his wrist altimeter to judge his exact distance from the ground. Leaving the aircraft at 30,000 feet and opening his chute as soon as he was stable, Mike could literally "fly" tens of miles across the face of the earth. This would allow him to leave the aircraft in an international traffic pattern before making his run into Cuban territory when he executed the actual infiltration.

With a jolt, Mike's canopy ballooned successfully. He looked up to check the chute, making sure it hadn't deployed improperly; a difficult confirmation to make at night, but the bright stars helped. The shape of the parachute was right. Mike jerked the toggle lines to guide the parachute, and assumed control for the long ride down and across country.

During his silent, high-altitude descent through the chill air, Mike wondered why a parachute infiltration was necessary—he was quite sure that he could have entered Cuba with nothing more than an airline ticket and a cover story. Cuba was a popular holiday destination for British tourists. His gear could have been dead-dropped or delivered by a covert Agency plane. His best guess was that the Cuban intelligence system must be so proficient that the U.S. couldn't have absolutely guaranteed successful delivery any other way.

Mike came off his oxygen at eight thousand feet. He was freezing, steering left or right, at times "crabbing" the chute to stay on the virtual track in front of his right eye. At a little over three thousand feet, he knew he was going to be right on the money. The drop zone was a large pasture with a distinctive tree line. Mike quickly determined the corner for his landing, which was previously selected from satellite photography. Turning into the wind on final approach, he stalled the chute, and then flared for his landing by yanking back on both toggles. His landing was nearly perfect. He stumbled on the rough ground and rolled, but was uninjured.

Mike grabbed his chute and his rucksack, slinging it onto his back. He jogged quickly into the nearby wood line, where he crouched perfectly motionless for almost five minutes. He controlled his breathing and listened for any movement in the area; a simulated aggressor-force had been stationed in the area to test his evasion skills. For twenty minutes, Mike ran through his mind all of the tasks he would have to perform on the actual infiltration, including digging a hole with an entrenching tool to bury the parachute, harness, extra rucksack and gear for future recovery.

Mike stripped off the black coveralls he wore over the *barrio* clothes he had been issued—at first glance he looked like a Cuban peasant. He moved out to a narrow asphalt road, and then stepped back into the woods, where he patiently waited, even though his heartbeat was drumming in his ears.

In the distance, he could hear the sound of an engine approaching. Soon, a black Mercedes pulled up into the clearing. Mike stepped out of the brush, scanning back and forth for any signs of danger before he sprinted forward and swung into the passenger seat, gingerly closing the door, trying not to slam it too loud.

Angela was in the driver's seat. She nodded and gave a smile.

"We're Brits on a dirty weekend, Mike. Great jump rehearsal. We'll stop for breakfast in a minute. The recovery crew is digging your equipment up now."

She stomped the accelerator and the black Mercedes sedan tore off, gravel spitting out behind the tires. "For the rest of the day we'll repeat memorization drill—thoroughly going over all the contingencies related to infiltration."

Mike had memorized the list over and over; he knew it by heart. He had memorized in excruciating detail what he would do if he wasn't met; landed on the wrong drop zone; was severely injured, or was spotted and pursued. There were fifteen contingency plans on the infiltration alone, including Mike's private and sealed "go to hell" plan—get to an isolated beach, put out a pre-designated marker, and try to survive until help arrived.

Mike returned to the tasks at hand, and grabbed a plastic box of moistened "baby wipes" to clean his face and hands. He followed by removing his shirt, wiping his upper body the best he could, rubbing on some stick deodorant, and putting on a freshly starched *guayabara* shirt. Pushing the seat back, he removed his pants, and pulled on a pair of respectable trousers, followed by a change of socks and shoes. Combing his hair back, Mike folded the barrio clothes and stuffed them into a small nylon bag he grabbed from behind the back seat. His cover: he was a guest of a friend from the British Embassy. He was there to explore tourism investment opportunities within Cuba.

Using their British accents, Angela and Mike ordered breakfast at a hotel coffee shop. Then Angela asked, "Are you ready for tonight? We need a break from training. Will that be OK with you?"

"It's about time!" Mike replied.

But Mike did have a problem with it. After his actual Cuban infiltration, a Mercedes was going to take him to one of the best hotels in Cuba, where he would relax and stage for his mission. He would ostensibly be staying with his British "girlfriend," a female agent attached to the embassy in Havana. A woman he didn't know. The coming part of the rehearsal, staying in the same hotel room with Angela, while posing as lovers, made him feel a little bit apprehensive.

The reason for his concern was not because he was inexperienced at role-playing; the problem was that Mike had become more than a little fond of her. She was beautiful, fun to be with, and his respect for her had grown—for her dedication to thorough mission preparation and technical and tactical skills.

Mike's thoughts drifted to Kirsten. She might understand the mission, but nonetheless, she would have trouble dealing with this rehearsal. The fact that she would never know didn't help his guilty conscience.

22 Aug 2004

Angela and Mike drove the Mercedes back towards Miami. Mike sent in his initial entry report via secure pager, in mission format. As Angela drove, he practiced changing his clothes once again. The route was planned to take the same length of time as would be required to reach the Cuban hotel on the real mission.

Mike checked them into the Miami hotel where they acted like lovers on holiday—not a difficult task for Mike because he was captivated by her. They spent the afternoon relaxing around the pool, holding hands and whispering endearments to each other. As the sun dropped low in the sky, they went up to their room to shower and change for dinner.

They knew they were practicing in a room that was bugged and/or under observation. Mike said, "Darling, you look stunning—come here—dinner can wait," and held his arms out for her.

"No no no," she said as she walked over to his arms. "I'm starving."

"But honey—"

She kissed him on the lips and he pulled her close, his passion rising. Then she pulled away gently and said, "Let's wait, sweatheart. We have all night."

Angela was a load of fun during dinner, and Mike relaxed, enjoying himself. He ate a Delmonico steak, cooked rare, and was feeling great. The meal was in accordance with what Angela and her nutritionist contacts thought would be best for Mike and his mission. Mike was allowed only one glass of Merlot.

They spoke in Spanish the entire evening, an everyday occurrence in Miami. The only thing he dreaded was the dancing, soon to begin on the top floor of the hotel. There would be no mistaking him as a full gringo once he started.

Eventually they went upstairs to the nightclub. The booming music deafened Mike. He could barely tolerate the noise even though they sat at the table furthest from the band. It was great *salsa*, but the decibels were off the top of the scale. They ordered drinks—Coke for Mike, and another glass of wine for Angela.

She reached for his hand, took it firmly, and led him to the dance floor. Mike tried to display his best Latin rhythm, but he could barely concentrate. Angela was one of the best dancers he had ever held in his arms. Every movement was subdued, yet suggestive and hypnotic.

Returning to their table, Mike got a hold of himself. She was beautiful and magical, yes, but he was married. A slow dance started and Angela reached for his hand. Out on the floor Mike felt her uncovered back, and the touch of her skin invited him closer. He resisted slightly, but Angela held him close and kissed him at the end as actual lovers do. She scolded him laughingly, yet appropriately. "How would two lovers on vacation really be acting? You can do better." Eventually, they agreed to call it a night and go to bed.

In the room Mike worried about bugs and hidden optics, even in training. He showered first, and came out of the bathroom wearing his underwear only. Angela had the TV on and was sipping another glass of wine. She headed for the shower.

Mike got in bed and flicked the channels, finally finding an old war movie he recognized. He had turned off all the lights in the room. Angela came out of the shower, and in the indirect light of the television, Mike could see that she was completely naked. She crawled into bed and snuggled up to him. She kissed him and he kissed her in return. She put her head on his shoulder, and in moments, she was asleep. Mike was relieved. He watched the TV for another twenty minutes, slowly pulled his arm from around her, turned off the TV with the remote and, with difficulty, finally dozed off.

The wake up call came on time, and they ate breakfast and checked out. Mike sent in another coded situation report on his pager, stating that he was leaving the hotel. Once they were moving, with luggage placed in the back seat, Mike practiced changing clothes into his mission set. The mission set, weapons, combat gear, and clothes were kept overnight in a special locked box in the trunk. On the mission vehicle, the box was going to be welded to the floor of the trunk. Cuban agents could search Mike's room, but a search of a car with diplomatic plates from the UK was simply not allowed. If they did pop the trunk, they would face a high-decibel alarm system and a formidable metal box with multiple locks. Angela again timed him. He did well.

At a pre-selected alleyway, she stopped. Mike stepped out. He strolled down to the end of the alley, acting like a rag picker going through the trash. His adrenaline went up. He was ready to make his run. He shopped through the trash for a few minutes before returning to the car. Rehearsal was over.

They flew back to Atlanta. All the way back on the flight, Mike read a novel he had picked up in the Miami airport. He kept thinking about Angela, his mind's eye replaying over and over again how beautiful she was leaving the shower and how gloriously soft she felt lying next to him.

Angela, sitting next to him, was mentally editing her report. One paragraph would include, "Mike will function well under observation. He is an excellent role player who can survive direct optical and audio monitoring. No matter what he encounters, he maintains his poise and reacts in accordance with his cover. I have no concerns remaining on his ability to complete the infiltration phase successfully." Left out of the report would be how Angela wished the stay in Miami could have lasted a week, or even longer, as long as she could have more time with Mike Trantor.

After landing in Atlanta, Mike and Angela drove straight to the warehouse. John met them. He said bluntly, "We still have several weeks, by our best estimate, before we will go hot. Make sure we make best use of our available time." Next, the team of Angela and Mike had to ensure that actions after capture of the briefcase were planned to the *nth* degree.

25 Aug 2004

Mike was pleased and excited to be counting days. He had practiced the virtual parachute infiltration hundreds of times. He'd memorized the shooting range. The infinite number of possibilities for armed guard intervention had become finite. He couldn't think of a scenario he had not live-fired with his weapon. He had done his equipment drills blindfolded; he and his rucksack, weapons, and special vest/STABO were one. He had used his laser to cut the briefcase from a mannequin's wrist hundreds of times. Mike was ready.

The last elements of total preparation, the handover of the suitcase and his pick-up and exfiltration from Cuba were coming together as well.

Prior to exfiltration rehearsal for the day, Mike told John he needed to be excused. Mike was Roman Catholic, but rarely attended

Mass. Although no one could observe it, he prayed several times a day. He found a nearby Catholic Church in the yellow pages, looking to see if priests were available for Confession. Alone, he left the warehouse.

Mike prayed for his family and his beloved, deceased father, mother and brother. He asked God to guide and take care of his Special Forces and Ranger brothers. Years earlier, Mike had found that if he never prayed for himself or for selfish reasons, almost all unspoken prayers would be answered. God truly seemed to reward the selfless and the meek.

The confession booth was open. Entering slowly, Mike got on his knees, crossed himself and speaking clearly to the priest, he said, "Father, I confess all my sins. I have not worked hard enough to get ready for a great challenge ahead. I am afraid of failure, afraid of letting those down that have faith in me."

The priest asked if Mike could tell him more about what was troubling him. Mike said that he couldn't, but added that he found inspiration in the book of Isaiah. He slowly recited from memory, "…and the Lord asked, who will speak for us? Whom shall we send? And I answered, send me."

Sensing that Mike would not open up with more information, the priest simply replied, "Son, though I lack detail on what is facing you, I can guarantee your faith in God will sustain you. Let us pray."

John had stuck a small bug on Mike's jacket. The surprise request to go to Confession worried him. Mike's mental state was all-important. Listening, John and Angela looked each other in the eye. John spoke, "This goes into today's report. Mike is fine."

Mistily, Angela nodded slightly, looked deep into John's eyes, and quietly added, "I feel soiled for listening. Mike would die for us."

She turned away, walking towards her desk. As she sat down, back towards him, John saw her hand reach into a drawer. Angela pulled out a Kleenex.

Mike returned. John slipped away to remove the bug while Angela and Mike began memorization drills for exfiltration.

The plan was virtually complete. Mike was to sprint into an opposing alley with the briefcase. As he left the alley, a Cuban taxi, a pale green 1957 Chevy would be parked, engine running, with a taxi driver leaning up against the right rear fender. The taxi driver would have on a red baseball cap.

Mike was to slow down in the alley, walk calmly up to the taxi driver, place the briefcase on the ground by the driver's leg, and ask directions to *El Prado*, a famous street. The answer was to be crisp and fast. Mike could start walking immediately giving a *muchas gracias* over his shoulder. The briefcase was to stay on the ground. The taxi driver would simply pick it up, go around the car, and drive away.

The handover was to take less than 15 seconds. Mike had to keep moving crisply in case there was any pursuit from the *Mundo Nuevo* compound. Another block covered, turning left into an alley, Mike would run again. At the end of the alley the black Mercedes, with plates, the engine running, would be waiting, a woman driver inside. Mike had practiced slowing down in the alley, then entering the car nonchalantly.

As they drove away, Mike was to dump his mission gear as he changed clothes. A route was selected with turns and other opportunities to discard clothing and equipment. Mike would be taken directly to Havana airport, making an immediate flight out of Cuba. The car supposedly could not be stopped or searched by the Cuban police or military. Nevertheless, it was crucial to get rid of incriminating evidence as soon as possible.

There were many contingencies. First of all, if the 1957 Chevy was missing, Mike was to take the briefcase into the second alley and deposit it in a large dumpster for recovery by other agents. He was instructed to try and accomplish the act without observation and to cover the briefcase with refuse. Recovery personnel were to be in the area at the time of the hit. Mike would have no idea who they were. Mike also knew the recovery personnel could not help him in a fight. Their covers would have been lost forever, probably along with their lives.

Second, if the airport was not open due to military or police activity, such as roadblocks, and thorough searches of foreigners, the British Embassy was to be the contingency location. Passports and documentation of Mike and his driver were backstopped, and the Embassy could serve as a safety valve and safe haven.

Third, Mike had picked two seedy hotels in poor neighborhoods that could serve as locations for the driver and himself to stay overnight in Havana as the situation demanded. From the two locations, he memorized routes to move out of Havana overland to dig up the cached equipment near the original drop zone.

Fourth, if Mike and his partner were forced to leave the city, they would go to pre-designated evacuation sites to be met by an agent from the British Embassy. The Embassy would time the pick-up based on the Havana situation, and Embassy employee freedom of movement.

On link-up Mike and the woman agent accompanying him would be placed in a vehicle's trunk and taken straight to the Embassy. They would be held, hidden incommunicado, until the U.S. and Britain determined it was safe for their removal from Cuba.

A fifth option would be the use of U.S. helicopters to pull them out. Numerous helicopter-landing zones in remote areas had been implanted upon his memory as possible pick up points. Mike would use his pager to identify the one he needed to have "serviced."

If communications were completely lost there was yet a sixth contingency, a backup pager in his cache. In the worst case, he could risk dialing from a Cuban telephone. He had instructions on how to place an international call from Cuba, another memorization drill item on the growing checklist.

If all else failed, Mike would go into unilateral evasion. Mike wrote the evasion plan himself, and left it in a sealed envelope, along with other documents. No one would read it unless everything went to hell. His plan ran through some incredibly nasty terrain, and he hoped his female partner was in good physical condition. Without communication, Mike and his partner would hide during the days. At night they would be ready for pickup, waiting in the treeline to be found. The recovery team would be prepared to operate with weapons on safe, so as not to mistake them for the enemy. Appropriate code words and flashlight signals were developed for close-in recognition.

Every single action, secondary action, alternate action, and contingency action was recorded after memorization. John told Mike he would be his primary case officer. No matter how bad the situation might be, John would be monitoring Mike's progress and know what Mike had planned to do. John was responsible to literally *be* Mike in crisis. If Mike were incommunicado, John's conclusions about Mike's decision-making could mean the difference between life and death.

Angela took Mike out to the park. She placed the virtual reality shades on him. He ran through the alleys and to his pick up car time and time again. The next day, they would go into the city and begin rehearsals on actual urban terrain.

A street pattern exactly like that in Havana had been found in a condemned Housing and Urban Development neighborhood. They had permission from the Mayor to use the area, representing themselves as an Army unit conducting urban training. A film team went along to video Mike's last rehearsals in on-the-spot critiques. Mike ran and ran and ran. On one of the rehearsals, with a scenario requiring Mike to shoot two guards, he made the sprint from the alley to sitting down in the Mercedes in 58 seconds. He was razor-sharp, mission ready.

Later, when they were back at the warehouse, John was tempted to tell Mike the truth about Angela. But, he knew that for her protection during the first few hours in Cuba it was better that Mike not know about her continued role. There was always the grizzly possibility that Mike might be captured on the drop zone and tortured into compromising others. The fact that Angela would be his link-up on the drop zone, his wheelman, would, for now, remain secret. She would drop him off, start his run, and by then he would know it was she sitting in the black Mercedes to pick him up when he came out of that alley.

Angela was a British citizen, and her cover was to be the new assistant to the Vice Consul at the embassy in Havana. She would be traveling on a diplomatic passport. She had made reservations for two, through the embassy, at a carefully selected Cuban resort within twenty miles of the drop zone.

British intelligence and the CIA were working closely together on this assignment and the embassy had been instructed to provide her with a vehicle with diplomatic plates. The secure metal box for mission gear would be welded down in the trunk. Angela would have both keys to the vehicle and the trunk when her flight landed. The vehicle would be sitting in a pre-determined location. Angela's cover was simple. She would be taking a few days accumulated local leave and spending the time with her fiancé at the beach.

Mike was told that the woman picking him up would look like Angela, in height, weight, and overall appearance. Mike worried out loud: "It is unconscionable that I will go into this not having rehearsed with my actual partner!"

John answered, "Normally I would agree, but we have kept you separate just in case you are captured before your linkup at the first site. It is best that you know little in advance. Otherwise, torture could result in the loss of two operators instead of one."

Mike grasped the logic; he would accept the OPSEC price he had to pay. He also pondered why they had spent so much time on cultural training. Whoever it was, the overall operations director of this mission had made him do a lot of skill development, way over normal requirements. And the whole planning and acclimatization timetable was unusually drawn out. Possibly, the organization was just incredibly thorough. A final thought was perhaps, when preparation started, requirements for him had not yet fully jelled, so they just kept preparing while waiting for the go-ahead.

Daydreaming, Mike shook his head. He had imagined a woman that looked like Angela screaming, tears running down her face. She was in a dark basement of one of Fidel's political prisons. Her hand had just been crushed with a hammer. She was blurting out what little information she knew about Mike's mission. Mike paused, praying to himself that his partner would be okay until they could get together in the vicinity of the drop zone.

CHAPTER THIRTEEN

25 Aug 2004

Kirsten sat down for lunch in the Crossroads, the coffee shop in the center of campus. She had just ordered her favorite: a turkey sub and a Diet Coke. Canvassing the room, she finally spotted him.

It was Ted. He had started dropping by for lunch, and now they met almost everyday. Kirsten was ashamed of her affection for the younger student, but she couldn't seem to help herself. He loved literature as much as she did. Their conversations were lively and, for once, weren't about people and things, they were about topics that really mattered: theory, interpretation, and ideas.

Kirsten didn't worry about Ted having a crush on her - she worried about the crush she already had on him. She couldn't wait to see him in the gym, and her pulse raced like a schoolgirl's when he showed up for lunch. She was falling, hard.

Ted ordered his meal, saw her, and came over with his tray. He sat down, and they began to banter about the day's lecture, current events, and student movements on campus. She wished they could stay and talk forever. Just prior to standing up to leave, Ted asked, "Would you like to study together tomorrow? If you would like, we could meet on the second floor of the Student Union at seven."

Kirsten gushed, "Of course, I'll be there," trying to contain her enthusiasm.

Ted replied, "Great, and by the way, I love your new earrings. I'll see you tonight." Kirsten was flattered, and all of a sudden, her face felt hot.

weekend and had three new earrings in one ear. Mike probably wouldn't approve, but *damn it*, she concluded, *Mike has taken off again and I can do whatever I want.* The big age difference between Mike and Kirsten had also created some cracks in the relationship. A differing appreciation of current fads and music was one of them.

That night, Ted and Kirsten met on the second floor of the OU Student Union. A piano was in the corner; and a student was softly playing. The unwritten rule was that no one spoke above a whisper. Ted and Kirsten found their way to a huge leather couch with two stuffed footstools. They kicked off their shoes, pulled out their notes, and began studying.

Close to midnight, Ted woke Kirsten up. She was cuddled on his shoulder. "Time to go, he said." Kirsten was embarrassed. She had run out of gas an hour ago. She hoped she hadn't snored.

Ted offered to walk her home. They strolled slowly, talking about the upcoming examination. On Kirsten's front steps, Ted bent over and kissed her gently on the lips, then backed off. Kirsten was pounding, afraid to respond too strongly and ruin the moment. Ted started to turn and leave. Kirsten said, "Thanks, I'll see you tomorrow."

Ted replied, "I sure hope so," then he paused, smiled and added, "By the way, don't worry—you didn't snore." He giggled, and so did Kirsten. They were starting to know what "the other half" was thinking.

Kirsten knew she had it bad and didn't care. She loved an older man, and was falling for another—a man young enough to be her younger brother, young enough to be her husband's son.

25 Aug 2004

Señor Matos was ulcer-ridden, yet pleased that something had finally gone well. The good news was that he had found the agent that had penetrated his organization. It was a mid-level manager in the logistical section of *Mundo Nuevo*. Counter-intelligence teams, operating in the United States, had discovered a link between the agent and the British through bank accounts in Miami, Florida. Although sophisticated laundering techniques had been used, the connection was absolutely clear, particularly when the Cubans had traced debt payments for the agent's expatriate family members.

The bad news was that Matos wouldn't be able to use the knowledge to ferret out other agents in his organization. The accused agent had died a true and dedicated professional. No amount of pain inflicted had persuaded him to tell the truth, or to get him to finger other agents in the *Mundo Nuevo* project. His fatal heart attack occurred after only two days of interrogation and torture.

The poor deceased man had not been an agent at all. His wealth was created electronically by the CIA from its headquarters. Payment of his expatriate family's debts had been executed in the same manner. Forged letters in the handwriting of the *Mundo Nuevo* employee were in the hands of his family, telling them that he had become a man of means and would be helping them. Known Cuban agents in Miami had been fed rumors, and the resultant investigation provided convincing evidence. Matos had tortured an innocent man to death.

Matos was pleased that his inquisition had instilled an effective climate of fear with headquarters, a deterrent to other potential turncoats. Suddenly, his secretary broke in. She told Señor Matos that his chief of logistics, already raked over the coals during the investigation of his now expired subordinate, was nervously pacing in the outer office. The secretary said he was upset and chain-smoking. He demanded to see Señor Matos immediately.

Señor Matos waved a hand, allowing entry. The man was visibly shaken. He blurted out; "Our men in Greece just unsealed and inspected the five tanks made in Germany. They arrived late last night, moving from the ship to our front company in darkness. They are ruined, worthless! Someone has sabotaged the linings. It looks like hydroflouric acid ate the glass. We have lost millions of Euros and months of progress!"

Matos wanted to kill. He exploded, sweeping everything off his desk with a swift movement of his hand. He called his Log Chief an incompetent imbecile and ordered him out of his sight. Shaking with apoplectic rage, he vowed revenge on Britain, clearly the nation that had penetrated his operation.

Calming slightly, he knew he would have to tell Fidel. Fortunately, Fidel was on a ten-day world tour, visiting his friends in Libya, Venezuela, and North Korea. Matos would have to prepare a hell of a briefing to spin any optimism out of this debacle. The only saving grace might be that he had eliminated Britain's mole. He needed a miracle to obtain Fidel's approval for a restart of *Mundo Nuevo*. Funding, he knew, would be extremely difficult under any circumstances.

UK demolitions residue in Sierra Leone, the Russian setup in Mexico, sophisticated electronics used against the bank in Angola, penetration of *Mundo Nuevo* with British implications on the banking end, and now sabotage of critical equipment in Europe? Señor Matos smoldered. "F—— Brits!"

CHAPTER FOURTEEN

26 Aug 2004

The same rules always applied: no notes, no recorders, and no cell phones. The eldest of the group, retired General Peters, spoke first.

"Yesterday, we were entrusted with a relatively detailed briefing of the plan to eliminate the agro-terror threat. As stated, the infiltration aircraft will take off from an obscure airstrip in the States, pick up Major Trantor, fly to the Bahamas, then land and take off under another flight plan to parallel the coast of Cuba. The plane is owned by a British company, on lease through a cover."

He searched the table, his eyes flashing from one controller to the other. "The timing on the target is critical. Our scientist with the briefcase continues to depart his workplace at exactly the same time. His security always consists of two guards plus a driver. Our good Major can handle the threat that may prevent grasping the briefcase. Our British intelligence operative should be able to insert Mike in the alley at the right time, idle slowly to the pick up point, and wait. The taxi handover of the briefcase should go smoothly."

"I want to thank you all, again for your hard work. When the warehouse is closed, a sterilization crew from another agency will make sure that it and Trantor's hotel are squeaky clean. Normal attention to detail will apply. Nothing will be overlooked, every scrap of paper, every page of every phone book. Each desk drawer will be pulled... Excuse me," he paused. "You are all experts; I needn't coach."

He continued briskly. "As is customary, I would like to go around the table, and receive final comments from all of you regarding the mission."

The younger man led off. He had been Mike's biggest supporter after the incident with the car thieves in Miami. "I have no doubt Mike will get to the target. I am confident that he will obtain the briefcase. I am also confident that he will do everything humanly possible to succeed. He is stable, and fully prepared. All contingencies and branches and sequels seem satisfactory."

The other men signified their approval. One mentioned Mike's absolute composure posing as the boyfriend of Angela in the Miami hotel bedroom. Another marveled at Trantor's lack of need for more information. All of the costly preparation could not be justified for a simple snatch of a briefcase. Mike had to know that he was but a cog in a large machine, yet, he asked for not one iota of information outside of his lane. His trust and faith in his invisible manipulators was incredible.

The last to speak was Ms. Winthrop. "I want to caution this body on one thing. First of all, I agree that Major Trantor is at the top of his game. He should succeed." Her voice became harsh, virtually unfeminine. "However, I worry that if something goes awry, we will blow the whole thing with our compassion for him. Remember, the mission is to destroy *Mundo Nuevo*, not to hold a love-in for Mike Trantor." Looking over her glasses, she slowly engaged each person around the table, deliberately making direct eye contact. "We must have the courage to recommend the right decisions if the mission goes south."

Peters shivered. Her comment captured the core difference between military officers and those solely experienced in running agents. The military could never cut away a soldier. It was part of the culture, the ethic of service, and inherent love for your peers and subordinates. Ms. Winthrop placed the mission first, as anyone in the military would.

The critical difference between her and the General was that absolutely nothing else then mattered. Peters concluded, "I will report that we believe the plan is feasible and has a high probability of success."

As they exited the room, General Peters was mentally preparing his report to Ellis.

Sitting alone, he visualized an open jump door in an aircraft with soldiers exiting low-level into the black of night. One static line didn't function properly and the aircraft was literally towing a soldier, who was bouncing off of the aircraft's skin, ten feet behind the open door. The jumpmaster reached for his knife, cutting the static line. The soldier fell free without a functional main parachute; all he had was his reserve. Hopefully the soldier would have the wits and training to be able to open it before impact. The phrase *cutting a soldier away* had come, over time, to mean *abandonment or failure to offer continued support.*

The old General had no doubt that Ms. Winthrop would cut Mike away without blinking.

He called Ellis immediately with a final verbal report. Professionally satisfied, Peters considered it an honor to be able to continue his contribution to national security, even after retirement.

Ellis relayed the thumbs up to LTG Hanscom as soon as Peters rendered his summary. A positive recommendation from the graybeards had been anticipated.

* * * * *

It was time to begin the next step: physical preparation to conduct the mission. Ellis picked up his secure phone to John. "I have been instructed to place command and control in Key West. An abandoned hangar has been selected with full power, latrines, and the normal 'plug-in' needs as called for in our statement of requirements. It is in an obscure corner of an almost defunct Navy base. The cadre there has only two tenant units still operating. The base commander, Rear Admiral "Rabbit" Campbell, is read into the need for complete secrecy, nothing more. His subordinate commanders believe that there is a highly classified training exercise that is going to be conducted in the near future. The detailed cover story is written and approved. No eyebrows will be raised. You and your crew will receive a sealed packet today with status of the detailed coordination."

27 Aug 2004

The President glanced at the day's agenda, disturbed at the briefings indicating that progress with the Muslim governments in Afghanistan and Iraq were coming along a bit slower than he had anticipated. The Democrats were still giving him fits about post-invasion planning and budget implications. The widening of the war with attacks in Indonesia, Saudi Arabia, and Turkey were also nagging, in effect questioning how we would ever put the Al-Qaeda completely out of business.

In addition to a meeting on the status of the campaign in California, where Governor Schwarzenegger had surprised everyone with his leadership style and ability, the President had an agenda item with much more importance.

Late in the day was his update by the CIA on progress in destroying Fidel's *Mundo Nuevo*. The President had been supportive of their request that he speak with Prime Minister Blair. LTG Hanscom had advised the President that calls to PM Blair would be invaluable and had sent a well prepared read-ahead and a briefer to prepare the President.

The two leaders had concurred that the U.S. could continue to use the British as a front to disguise its actions from the Cubans. In addition to the initial offering of intelligence to the United States, British support would be quite substantial with their Embassy support in Havana along with one of their top operatives working directly with Trantor.

Also, a complete audit trail would be built with summaries of conversations between the leaders and all supportive actions taken by the United Kingdom. President Bush agreed to the archives to guarantee that the Prime Minister would be totally protected in case the operation against Cuba somehow turned into the equivalent of an Iran-Contra scandal due to some unforeseen complications.

Tony Blair's stand with the United States in Iraq had cost him dearly domestically, and a grateful President Bush was ensuring that he would not be damaged on this operation.

* * * * *

With the National Security Advisor in the lead presenting the Secretary of State, Secretary of Defense, LTG Hanscom and others, the meeting took less than a minute to be convened. The President's chief of staff cautioned that time was limited, and closed the door behind him.

LTG Hanscom detailed progress to date in the disruption of *Mundo Nuevo*. Hanscom observed the President's eyebrow go up when he mentioned the Sierra Leone diamond raid; the Angola non-kinetic attack; and actions in Mexico, Greece and Germany. President Bush commented, "Other than the issue in Venezuela, clearly, now, the target is Cuba."

The President had a tremendous capacity for information. He occasionally surprised his staff with his ability to remember so much as a glimmer of innuendo, a tidbit of intimation, a name of an acquaintance, or the importance of keeping a friend; although many in the press continuously presented him in a lesser light. He spoke clearly, piecing bits of information he had received in briefings over several months.

"Colin, you have done well working with Hanscom in helping to choke Fidel's desperate search for funding. Quiet diplomacy does, at times, work. As I understand it, Cuba's desire for massive investment to exploit its vast nickel reserves has completely stalled. Señor Portal, Cuba's foreign investment emissary, had been turned down by Australia, Canada, China and several European countries. The reason is investment risk, and that Fidel continues to become more dangerous. His execution of three hijackers who seized a ferry to reach the United States, and his brutal jailing of dozens of democracy activists has shaken world confidence, which we have used to our advantage."

"I have a growing preoccupation with a Venezuelan connection on Margarita Island. Khalid Shaikh Mohammed, Bin Laden's planner for the attacks on September 11, has told us from custody that Al-Qaeda has a small cell on the island. When the diamond mine was attacked in Sierra Leone, one of the calls was to Margarita.

In addition, Cuban officials, the FLMN from El Salvador, along with the Sandinistas from Nicaragua, are sending representatives periodically to the island for vacations. Even worse, Major Juan Diaz

Castillo, President Chavez' personal pilot, has now reported that Chaves has tried to funnel one million dollars U.S. into the terrorists coffers.

"In addition, the Venezuelan government tried to deny the Iraqi provisional government its OPEC seat because of a lack of U.N. recognition, indicating once again that he will do anything he can to challenge the United States. We turned that around, but I'm tired of theses two Latin American demagogues' continual challenges.

"By the way, the Iranians are still jamming the Voice of America from Cuba. Bottom line, the cell on the island may be a nexus of terrorists, drug dealers, Latin American revolutionaries, and die-hard communists. I want it addressed and put out of business. I would wager that the cell is linked to many nefarious enterprises, to include *Mundo Nuevo.*"

LTG Hanscom acknowledged that the cell would be targeted, and concluded the brief by asking for permission to begin activities in Cuba.

The President's General Council stated, when asked, that the President's previously signed finding for Cuba would cover operations in Venezuela. The President ended the discussion by simply saying, "Well done, let's get to work."

As the door closed, the President sat wearily in his leather chair. The American public and the Congress were in no mood for another alarm about a threat to national security that wasn't unimpeachably verifiable. The WMD assumption in Iraq had become a major reelection issue. He had made the right call. Cuba would be attacked in the shadows.

Key West, Florida
31 Aug 2004
LTG Hanscom answered his secure phone. It was Ellis, describing progress in Key West. "John is already down in Key West. Hybrid command and control (or C2), is installed on the Navy installation. We have 24/7 operations, capable liaison teams with full communication packages and lots of bandwidth to reach back to D.C. We will do integrated force tracking, and we reach back to you with

all we are doing. We should all be able to monitor the operation as it progresses.

"I will also have a secure portable VTC set up at the C2 node so John can video-teleconference world-wide for effective coordination and synchronization. I await written instructions from you to develop classified couriers for detailed direction, understanding that electrons are not the safest means of keeping no 'fingerprints' on this operation. John will officially activate the Hybrid in Key West, on your orders."

"Good work, especially within just two days," LTG Hanscom complemented. "I have an update for you on the CIA's work to directly target *Señor* Matos. A computer message will be sent to him in his office. It will include a complete laydown of his operation and a discussion of how OPSEC for *Mundo Nuevo* has been so compromised that the entire project has been transparent to the British from beginning to end.

"The text highlights that *Mundo Nuevo* has been briefed to the Prime Minister in London. *Señor* Matos will also be told that unless he recommends termination of the project, all the leaks and breakdowns will be made known to Fidel Castro, tainted to indicate undeniable incompetence, and possible espionage, by none other than *Señor* Matos.

"In addition, he will also be told that Britain's Prime Minister has signed an executive order that *Mundo Nuevo* is to be terminated. Matos will know that an executive order is a statement of national intent that literally removes constraints on the military and intelligence agencies of the UK to achieve a specified end. We will monitor his response by listening to his cellular and regular phones, secured or unsecured. We will reposition every available satellite to watch his movements. We will use our best men on the internet to see what he is sending, or if he is preparing any briefings. Then, we will push him over the edge by deploying Major Trantor."

* * * * *

LTG Hanscom pulled a single piece of paper out of his Top Secret personal safe. It was in pencil. He hadn't personally planned an operation since he was a battalion commander. But now he had personally written an entire execution checklist. From the time Mike took off, each minute was literally accounted for and choreographed. He would personally command the operation from his CIA office, remotely and through the cutout, Ellis.

LTG Hanscom had to brief the new CIA Director McLaughlin today, in order to gain approval to request Department of Defense UAV's (unmanned aerial vehicles) and other support required to be successful in the operation.

He would ask that the USSOUTHCOM commander in Miami be notified that a clandestine operation would be going on in his area of responsibility and that a top-secret liaison team would plug into his headquarters to keep him personally posted on events, just in case emergency conventional military support would be needed.

Additionally, he asked the Secretary of Defense for Army General Joe Cordell, full time, to help. LTG Hanscom knew the answer would be yes.

Hanscom leaned back and looked at his watch. After his afternoon meetings he was going to take a rare break and knock off early, drive home, pick up his wife and take her out to dinner.

31 Aug 2004

Kirsten grew closer and closer to Ted during the weeks Mike had been incommunicado. Their lunches at the Crossroads and their homework sessions had become more frequent.

Waking up each morning was a joy for Kirsten. She could see Ted in the weight room every other day, and he seemed to give her a much-needed jump-start. Kirsten accepted his immaturity. It was outweighed by his youthful enthusiasm and endless optimism. He cared about everything from the latest novel to the starving in the southern Sudan. They openly communicated and disagreed. Kirsten felt free to discuss anything without consequence. She was free.

Kirsten was also getting into great shape. She felt younger and younger. Her wardrobe now matched the other girls on campus, and she genuinely fit in. In fact, most students she ran into estimated her age as five to ten years less than it really was. Once, Ted and his friends had discussed how sexy they thought women's tattoos were.

The ones voted "most sexy" at the Crossroads lunch period were ones on the breast that were barely visible. The boys indicated that they were driven wild trying to imagine the tattoo and the rest of the covered terrain.

One lonely weekend, after checking with some of her female classmates on the respective stories behind their tattoos, Kirsten decided to do something daring. She drove to a pre-selected tattoo parlor and got a rose tattooed on her left breast, just high enough to peer above low cut tops.

She felt guilty, but overcame hesitancy with the rationale that since Mike was going to leave her for years on end for the rest of his career, he would have to accept that she was empowered to make her own decisions in his absence.

One day, after an initial pop quiz of the fall semester, Kirsten and Ted met to see grades posted in the hallway outside their professor's office. Their nights of studying had paid off. They had the only A's in class. They hugged with joy for each other, not with joy for their individual performances.

After the hug, Kirsten paused. She was too happy and growing too close, and knew their relationship's continuing crescendo had to stop or reach a climax, then move on to a new level.

Ted queried, "Why don't you meet me at O'Connell's tonight around eight? We'll celebrate with a few brews, and I'll teach you how to throw some mean darts."

Kirsten hesitated for only a few seconds. Her heart spoke before her brain could engage. "I'd love to! See you at eight." Then she added, since they could really discuss anything, and she didn't have to worry about hurting his feelings, "Are you old enough to drink?"

Ted ran over to her, covered her mouth with his hand, again hugging her playfully. "Shhhh, the campus cops are everywhere. I have a good fake ID. We'll be okay." Then he let her go with a hearty laugh. "Tonight at eight it is!" He made a small wave with his hand and almost appeared to float as he walked down the hall.

Kirsten watched, worrying about what she had done in committing to a date. Ted had a crush on her, she was sure. Going down the elevator, she realized that she too, was floating with joy.

She didn't care about tomorrow or yesterday. She was going to care about tonight. Tonight would be delicious.

She rushed home and cleaned house. She laid out her clothes for the evening. She selected a pair of hip-hugging tight black Capri pants, very much in style on campus, and complemented them with some platform-style high heels that were all the rage.

She then went through her selection of blouses and sweaters and found a Victoria Secrets scoop neck that was perfect, offering tons of cleavage and a hint of tattoo if an admirer looked very closely. She practiced revealing the tattoo by bending over and making selected movements in front of the bedroom mirror.

After a long shower and careful preparation of her hair, she put on her growing number of earrings, a tantalizing small necklace that would call even more attention to her cleavage. She finished with her favorite perfume.

Before leaving the house, she did a final inspection. The place was spotless, as was she. Everything was set. She closed the door, ensuring it was locked.

Ted was already inside O'Connell's. He didn't spot her among the patrons, so Kirsten made her way to the bar and ordered a pitcher of Killian's. She asked for two glasses and headed for Ted. As she approached him form behind, he turned, and started. Kirsten loved his reaction.

He was so innocent and so sincerely excited to see her. He clumsily took the two glasses and the pitcher, fumbling with them. They both laughed and huddled together up against the bar. Kirsten began. "So, explain how one plays darts." Ted jumped in excited to show his expertise. Kirsten smiled. It was to be a lovely evening.

Spirits flowed as well. Ted had to teach Kirsten how to hold and throw the darts, and finally selected one game when they could play reasonably well as a team. Each throw, each tally, each gulp of ale was a joy. Kirsten felt nineteen again, in love.

The pub was packed and vibrant with discussion of the chances for another national championship. Under Bob Stoops, the mighty Sooners of Bud Wilkinson and Barry Switzer were back. Kirsten was learning to talk the talk because Ted was so involved. She was starting to appreciate Mike's fever in regard to the team.

Around eleven at night, discussion of OU football fortunes gave way to a serious challenge from another couple. Ted accepted the challenge. Darts, to a game of twenty. When Ted threw the winning dart, Kirsten jumped into his arms and gave him a kiss on the lips, her first in public exuberance that revealed her feeling for him. He paused at first, then fully participated, lingering as long as he could.

Kirsten said, "A black and tan before we hit the road? In celebration?" She went to the bar to order. When she came back to where Ted was sitting, she leaned over from the waist and served him his beer. She moved slowly, watching his eyes focus on her tattoo. They both were a bit tipsy. It was not a relevant observation that they had drunk too much; she didn't care one way or the other.

She plopped next to Ted and snuggled up close. About halfway through her draft, she looked at him and said, "We really don't need to finish these, I have more at my place. Let's go for a walk." Ted gazed at her with laughing eyes and mischievous smile. He replied in his boyish way, "Exactamundo. I was ready to recommend a walk myself."

Halfway to Kirsten and Mike's they were holding hands. Two-thirds of the way there, they were walking arm-in-arm. Three-fourths of the way there, they had their arms around each other's backs.

On the steps, they paused. Ted embraced Kristin with the most passionate kiss she had received in years. She responded with the same. After fifteen seconds, she broke contact. She fumbled with her keys and opened the door. "Ted," Kirsten quietly said, "You're welcome to come in."

As Ted stepped across the threshold, Kirsten was thinking of it as the Rubicon. She followed; closing and locking the door behind them.

*   *   *   *   *

On the morning of the second of September, around noon, Kirsten said goodbye to Ted, walking him to the door with only her XXL T-shirt on. They had been out the night before and fell to spending the morning naked in bed. Ted was insatiable, young, and inexperienced.

He was hopelessly in love for the first time. Kirsten had made his every teenage fantasy come true.

Kirsten was taken and gratified by Ted's raw sexual passion. Mike was so much older, calm, and measured.

*   *   *   *   *

Two days later Ted called, asking to come over in the evening to work on a project in advance to get ready for the fall semester. He brought Kirsten a rose. After acting like he was studying for about an hour, Ted broke down. He moved over to Kirsten and grabbed her hand, leading her to the bedroom. They made love over and over again until one in the morning.

In the morning, Kirsten went to the bathroom, took a long shower, and dressed for the day. She was going to do some studying and also make final preparations for an upcoming trip, one which included a surprise for Ted.

Kirsten sat on the bed and leaned over Ted, kissing him gently. She was still a little sore from the night before. "Ted, I have to go. Lock up when you leave." Ted reached up and hugged her.

Kirsten added, "Go back to sleep, there is a surprise for you on the table for when you wake up." A red ribbon was tied around Mike's house key.

02 Sep 2004

The President and the Prime Minister had gotten along famously until unforeseen difficulties arose with the occupation of Iraq and in proving that weapons of mass destruction were the justifiable motivation for the invasion. President Bush tried to ameliorate the damage by conducting a visit in November of 2003, an event marred by demonstrations and wild accusations by London's socialist mayor.

Nonetheless, they remained close, and President Bush was pleased to be speaking to Prime Minister Blair over their secure NATO line. LTG Hanscom had prepared the President well and his discussion with the PM went efficiently down the main points.

The President started by profusely thanking PM Blair for the intelligence packets that had articulated the nature of the threat in Cuba. He followed with his personal assessment of the situation.

The Prime Minister was in full agreement of the need for termination of the Cuban capability and research mechanisms. Confidentially the PM expressed his opinion that the planned biological agents could easily spread worldwide and cost the lives of billions.

Precluding the development of such a weapon in the hands of an increasingly senile communist dictator clearly had UK support. However, going public or conducting overt operations was deemed to be unwise, given the Prime Minister's low popularity ratings.

President Bush articulated clearly that UK support was imperative for success of the plan as it was now formulated:

First, the UK had already accepted the pseudo-role as sponsor of the attacks on *Mundo Nuevo*. Covertly, the UK government knew that the large-scale foot and mouth outbreak the UK had experienced had been an act of biological warfare—not from Castro, but from an Al Qaida cell. As long as Fidel thought the UK was the lead nation for the effort to shut down *Mundo Nuevo*, the threat of a totally irrational response—such as launching an air armada with a few existing test bio strains that might be on hand—could be avoided.

Castro's psychological profile had been developed very carefully over fifty years by the Agency. Hatred for the *Yanquis* defined Castro's entire being. He had asked Russia to nuke the U.S. into oblivion in the '60s, and it wasn't bluff, or spin propaganda. But consensus was absolutely solid that Fidel would employ more rational thought processes when dealing with Prime Minister Blair.

Second, the UK should be prepared to intimidate Fidel for a short time period once the U.S. initiated kinetic activity against *Mundo Nuevo* inside Cuba. The President asked that the PM, at an appropriate moment, request a heads-of-state secure discussion for a serious, yet undisclosed matter. For informational buildup, it was imperative that Fidel conclude that the phone call was in reference to *Mundo Nuevo*.

President Bush added, "We will send a team of our best to brief you personally on how the operation has progressed and where we are in the scheme to prepare you for your call to President Castro. Our goal is to have Fidel off base, expecting a *Mundo Nuevo* confrontation, and then to have you steal the initiative by offering him an attractive peace offering."

President Bush added, "In other words, we request that you offer Fidel a carrot, after he has been hit with the stick, our operation." The carrot was an extension of Heathrow airport for *Cubana de Aviación* to include rent-free maintenance and storage facilities, along with subsidized utilities, paid indirectly to the UK treasury by the United States, including telephone and computer connectivity. The offer was for a free ten-year lease.

A discreet US/UK assessment team, using a U.S. front company as an investor, had already surveyed the site and drawn up an initial design and had considered environmental UK constraints. Cuba, of course, had not been mentioned. It had been a difficult engineering and environmental challenge to find a wedge in the cramped Heathrow physical plant.

The Heathrow facilities needed to be accepted by Fidel, the Prime Minister would say, because the PM was to brief a new Latin American trade initiative in a few weeks, and wanted to have the Cuban offer on the plate as an illustration of Labour's good faith and its commitment. The offer would dovetail nicely with trade initiatives that President Bush and PM Blair had discussed a few months before.

Tony Blair laughed, replying; "Your kind fellows in the Agency wouldn't want to tap in to any of the Cuban facilities, would they?"

The President laughed in return. "Only with your kind permission, sir."

The PM concluded stating that he would conduct internal briefings on the proposal and that U.S. and UK intelligence agencies would continue to link, very discreetly, on common issues. He felt assured that staff appreciation would support the effort.

The President closed, sincerely thanking the PM for his support and then buzzed his secretary. The Prime Minister had asked to delay any kinetic action in Cuba until after the mid-to-late September time frame. He needed time to build a small, discreet supportive constituency in his government.

* * * * *

LTG Hanscom looked out over the gray Potomac. He had called for Ellis. An hour later Ellis reported in to the General.

"Here are my instructions. Since the operation is delayed, we will optimize the use of additional time we have gained to refine planning for destruction of *Mundo Nuevo*. I want rehearsals and training to continue, and I want General Joe Cordell to move to Eglin Air Force Base and join a retired Air Force Colonel Reeve Baker to rehearse with some new unmanned aerial vehicle (UAV) technology that we have borrowed from Secretary Rumsfeld. We should be able to strike in surgical and discreet ways never seen before."

10 Sept 2004
Bert McNab and Amy had arrived back in D.C. in late August, shortly after the SOCEUR diamond mine raid into Sierra Leone, an action that had ended Bert's tenure with Arena Linea. Severance pay was delivered but would soon run out. On the positive side, Amy was happy to be back to her old stomping grounds near George Mason University.

One of Bert's favorite haunts was in Old Town Alexandria. Unknown to most, the bar where Bert was quietly sipping was a small, dark, alley entranceway pub that was periodically frequented by the world's best special operations forces soldiers.

Bert was sipping his favorite drink, a *Cuba Libre* (rum and coke with lime), wondering if any old friends were in town. Great news was afoot. Bert overhead a discussion disclosing that there was to be a gathering of special operators in a few days. As he recalled, usually about twice a year, someone would start informally calling around to call for a gathering at the pub.

Attendees usually numbered in excess of fifty, active and retired, legitimate and mercenary, from the young to the old. One of the huddles was to be the very next evening, Veterans Day.

* * * * *

Bert was granted another "kitchen pass" by Amy and returned the following evening to find the pub stuffed full with Special Forces, Rangers, SEALs and every other stripe of special operator known to man. Ranks ranged from four-star general to Master Sergeant. Smoke from illegally imported Cuban cigars permeated the atmosphere.

Into his third *Cuba Libre*, Bert was pleasantly surprised when one of his old running mates appeared at the other end of the walnut bar top. Bert rushed over and embraced an old buddy, whose name had slipped his mind.

"Hey Bert, did you notice the third dot on your chest that night in Sierra Leone?" his friend shouted over the noise, chuckling as he finished the last swallow of Johnnie Walker Black on the rocks.

For a moment, Bert was shocked into sobriety. The color had drained from his face, and it took him a moment to regain his composure. After a few seconds had passed, Bert started to grin, and tossed a wad of bills on the bar.

"This mother's money is no good in this place!" Bert yelled to the crowd of special operators.

"Was there anyone else aiming at me that I ought to be aware of?" Bert yelled.

No response could be heard above the clamor.

"If so, the drinks are courtesy of my severance bonus!"

Bert heard a resounding cheer, then spotted another old battle buddy—he could remember this guy's name because they had served together in the Projects in 'Nam.

By now, Bert was into his fifth drink, and he and his dear friend Art Hildebrand had exchanged business cards and caught up on the last decade or two. Art was now a DEA agent, working South America, and the money was good. Art left the 7th Special Forces Group after years of working in Latin America, but his love of the culture had led him back "down south" to his beloved portion of the world.

Before the night was over, Bert admitted that he would be coming up short in the cash department in the near future. Art told him to call in two days to see if any work was available to alleviate the hardship, courtesy of Uncle Sam.

"The DEA works with Arena Linea too, so maybe you'll have some luck if I put a few calls in," Art said.

Bert suddenly thought about Amy. He wanted to let her know about the lead from Art, so he thanked him and stumbled out to catch a taxi home.

*   *   *   *   *

Two days later, Bert gave Art a call at about ten in the morning. They met for an afternoon lunch at Clyde's, also in Alexandria, one of their hangouts from their earlier lives.

Art wasted little time with small talk. He needed someone with Bert's talents that could do some dirty work. He would have to make some bad guys and then set them up. There might be gun-play. The work concerned busting a drug cell in Venezuela.

Art had a target package put together, but Bert would have to ferret out the location of the baddies, doing a little intelligence work on his own in advance.

Bert almost choked on his steak when he heard the pay. It was incredible for two to three months of work, especially since earnings overseas for government service were tax-free. He played it cool, though, having negotiated for mercenary contracts many times in the past.

"Only if Amy goes along and is a paid participant. She is a good operator, and I have trained her with small arms and hand-to-hand combat. She's innovative and always has had ideas that make my operations better, from Bolivia to Sierra Leone. She will be a perfect cover. We'll be on vacation and madly in love. The second part will be absolutely true, and you know the best cover is always based on the truth."

Art agreed.

Bert arranged to turn over their passports for doctoring the next day. Art came to their apartment two days later with full briefing material, the passports, and the cash payment as promised. The mission seemed to be simple in concept. Finding the bad guys would be the hardest part—he was sure. Just in case the going was rougher, he mentioned to Art that he might need a certain third party who would have to ship out at the right time to assist. Art approved.

Within days, Bert and Amy had closed out D.C. and were in the air towards Miami. They were excited, Venezuela, on the beach!

* * * * *

Art called Ellis to give status as soon as Bert and Amy were wheels up. His DEA front had worked. Bert and Amy never questioned a good thing. They didn't want to.

Art now had to run down the third party. He'd lost track of Vicki Dollar years ago.

CHAPTER FIFTEEN

We see your willingness to die beautifully.
—Russian response to Castro's request to nuke the United States

22 Sep 2004

A man in blue coveralls took the Southern Design, Inc. sign off of the outside of the building and placed it in the back of his unmarked white van with Georgia plates. He went back into the warehouse for a final walk-through. It had been swept electronically and literally. Totally sterilized, it was nicely cleaned and ready for occupancy by another entrepreneur.

Sadly, Southern Design, Inc., after only a few months, had declared bankruptcy and was out of business. The front door was padlocked, and the van pulled away. The Hybrid had moved on. In Key West, it "morphed" again, this time for combat.

Mike was moved to a bachelor officer's suite at Patrick Air Force Base, Florida. His room faced the beach, and the sound of the Atlantic's waves came gently through his open window. He would sleep well. Mike's priorities were to rest and conduct mental rehearsals.

Without his knowledge, Angela had departed for England, to be turned around towards Cuba. After years of experience, fear and worry had blended together. It seemed that each birthday meant he would fear death less, while worrying more about the mission and how his peers would think of him if he failed.

Mike was dozing off, thinking of the private in his platoon years ago that was so afraid to mount the helicopters that he shot himself in the foot with his M16A1 on automatic. Three rounds shattered his instep. Several weeks later, Mike returned from the bush and visited the man in the hospital. The soldier was doing wonderfully, especially since the doctor had informed the sorry young man that the damage was so severe that he was out of the infantry. The soldier emphatically stated that the wound was accidental, having been well coached by some 'barracks lawyers,' less than stellar contemporaries, to protect himself from prosecution under the Uniform Code of Military Justice.

Mike stood up and left the man without comment, burning silently as he walked out of the field hospital. Mike couldn't understand this young man, so foreign to all Mike believed. Or was Mike the aberrant? Would he be a suicide bomber if he were a young man on the West Bank? What made him…? Mike fell asleep.

Rested, he awoke early the next morning and went about prescribed business for the day.

*   *   *   *   *

Then—the door was thrown open. The jumpmaster looked out into the blackness and gave Mike a single extended digit and yelled, "One minute." The wind bustled them both. It was brutally cold.

The jumpmaster gave the warning of "Thirty seconds!" and then shouted, "Stand by!"

The jumpmaster screamed, "GO!"

Mike was gone into the darkness.

The safety quickly ran forward in the aircraft. He dragged two bundles towards the open door as fast as he could. They were static line parachutes almost exactly like Mike's. He quickly hooked them up to an anchor line cable in the aircraft. The chutes would begin opening about twenty feet from the aircraft. He tossed them out quickly, one second apart.

The safety jumpmaster, and pilot were old pros from Air America, the agency's ex-secret Southeast Asia Air Force. They didn't even wrinkle their brows over their odd instructions. They had seen too many illogical things before. The safety closed the door, pinning it shut as he thought to himself, *Orders is orders. Where is the cold cerveza?*

He gave his partner a high five, gave the pilot a thumbs-up and sat down to smoke. *To hell with these new safety regulations*, thought the safety. They had been doing what they wanted to do with small aircraft for almost forty years.

The parachutes would fly to their designated landing points automatically. Each had a miniature ground positioning system, and a small battery imbedded in the harness to power the steering mechanism.

Each parachute would become caught in a tree or land in an open field. It didn't matter which. One would land about two kilometers east of Mike's location. The other would land about two kilometers to the west. The blocks of ice that were the weight of Mike and his equipment would be melted by dawn. The chutes would be of immediate interest to Cuban intelligence.

*   *   *   *   *

In 1993, when the last 1,600 Russian troops ostensibly left Cuba, many actually remained. "Reflagged" as civilian technicians, the Russians continued to operate their sophisticated electronic listening post at Lourdes, just outside Havana. Capabilities at Lourdes had been steadily expanded during the post-Cold War years to include eavesdropping on U.S. telephone conversations, internet traffic, and U.S. radar and air traffic control operations. Later, in 2000, Lourdes was closed with much public fanfare—while capabilities were simply moved to new locations. One of the main eavesdropping bases that replaced Lourdes was Bejucal.

One of the radar operators, a low ranking Cuban trainee, noticed three small blips entering Cuban airspace. They remained equidistant from each other, finally dropping below his radar's horizon. He immediately called for help from his supervisor. His supervisor was congratulatory. The parachutes were a good catch for a novice. The supervisor assumed that the blips were re-supply drops from Alpha 66 or another anti-Castro militia operating out of Miami. Such activity would not be unusual. The militias had been trying to operate in Cuba for decades. Persistent and brutal Cuban intelligence efforts had thwarted any real success. In fact, the biggest operations mounted by the militias in fifty years of effort had been no more than a few bombings of Cuba's growing tourist infrastructure.

In his outbox the supervisor left the report for his superior on the next shift. He gave all pertinent data and approximate location of where the blips might have landed. These Russians were no longer communists, but their leadership techniques remained unchanged. The report would be read and approved by each leader at each bureaucratic step all the way to the head of Cuban intelligence. The report would remain in the intelligence "stovepipe" for a day before anyone would take action on it.

23 Sep 2004

The drop zone was only two hundred feet below Mike's parachute. Maneuvering to the corner of the drop zone, Mike was impressed at the transcendent feeling of déjà vu. This was exactly the terrain he had seen in hundreds of virtual practices in Atlanta.

Mike stalled his chute just before impact and landed softly. He quickly scooped up his parachute and headed into the trees. His heart was racing. Mike knew it would take a little time to fully calm down. For now, he was getting his pistol laid out in case trouble arose .He quickly changed clothes and packaged his gear for the cache he was going to dig. He then froze for ten minutes. Barely breathing, he listened for any approaching footfalls. He adjusted to natural sounds in the night woods listening for predators hunting on the forest floor. Mike paid attention to the wind, in case dogs pursued him. He slowly became part of his environment, as he was absorbed into the dark Cuban forest.

Assured, finally, that he was unobserved, he marked the trees just as he had done in rehearsals, and moved into the woods to bury his cache. Mike kept his night vision goggles on throughout; giving him a significant advantage over any locals that might trip over his location.

After an hour, he closed his cache, first placing his night vision goggles in waterproof bags. He then camouflaged the hole, stepped over to the tree line and began to move towards the road. To an observer, he was Cuban. However, he was a Cuban out during the middle of the night for no apparent reason, and uncovered until link-up.

Soldiers sweat, and Mike had done plenty of it since landing in the tropical heat. He would need to clean up in the car immediately after link-up. He estimated his vulnerability to be extremely high for the next two hours, until sun-up, when the Mercedes would stop outside his final hide site. Mike found a good spot to sit and watch the road, yet remaining unseen by others. He settled in and sat ready to run, his rucksack on and his pistol by his side. He removed his hat so he could clearly listen to the heartbeat of the forest. He felt his heart rate drop to its accustomed forty-nine. Mike was now in the groove. He felt great.

*   *   *   *   *

Angela, meanwhile, was leaving the British compound in her black Mercedes. She had stayed overnight in an Embassy guestroom. The car's departure would be noted by Cuban intelligence because of the early hour. However, early morning runs to the airport to support dignitary and VIP movement were not that unusual.

Angela had memorized many different routes to Mike's link-up site. In addition, she had her own ground positioning radar on the dash, so she would always know where she was. Her maps were good. She was fresh and confident.

She was on the look out for trailing vehicles. She saw none. At a designated turnoff from the route to the airport, she took a quick left and stepped on the gas. She picked up the pace to break from the city. She then settled into a safe speed. Angela consulted her watch, then the ground positioning radar. She was exactly on time and on track.

The sun was about to rise and its rays were beginning to lighten the Cuban sky. Mike was supposed to step into the car about one kilometer ahead. Angela would make the hairpin curve, in a low spot, and stop the car for a few seconds. Worried about impact from a following vehicle, she checked her rear view mirror. The road was clear, so she need not abort the first run. As she rounded the designated curve and quickly stopped, Mike's hand was on the door and he was in the car. Angela accelerated smoothly.

Mike was overjoyed and sat in shock. He leaned over and kissed Angela on the cheek. John had sent the right person after all, knowing that it was best to keep it secret. The two of them, after all the training and preparation, felt they were invincible.

In seconds Mike was cleaning himself off with the kit from the back seat. He changed his shirt, applied deodorant, then worked on changing his pants, socks and shoes.

The sun came up and a Cuban gas station appeared on the horizon, their pre-planned stop for coffee and a key activity. Mike calmly stepped out of the car as Angela opened the trunk. He placed his mission gear and clothes in the metal box welded to the floor of the trunk. Angela locked the box. Mike breathed easier. To an observer, the couple was rearranging their luggage.

Mike was relieved. Infiltration was complete. As they sat on the porch of the dilapidated *restaurante* part of the gasoline station, with their *cafecitos*, Mike understated, "Boy am I glad to see you!" Angela roared with laughter.

Mike continued, "I'm not sure how to arrange my day. I must choose between fantastic *café Cubano*, the world's best cigars, and you."

Again Angela laughed, adding, "Mike, you choose. The day is yours." Any observer would conclude they were lovers.

In his best British accent Mike thanked the attendant for topping up the petrol. The Embassy petrol ration card worked as it should. He paid and Angela took the wheel. They headed for their hotel. As they pulled out, Angela asked Mike if she needed to touch up her lipstick. Angela was practicing their codes for talking in public. She was asking for his assessment of their being observed or tracked. Mike responded by tapping his finger twice on her arm. She laughed again. It was their touch code for *everything is okay*.

Angela drove on towards the hotel, glancing towards Mike and smiling. She was going to do her best to get Mike a good meal and lots of rest. She would be upbeat and fun. Her key task was to ensure delivery of an optimally prepped singleton to his target. She was not going to fail.

Mike smiled back at her. He typed in his initial entry report on his pager, and pushed "enter." The message was sent.

* * * * *

Mike stood aside as Angela checked in. He noted the contrast between the hotel and the poverty stricken countryside. The hotel ceiling was a dome at least forty feet high; the hallways radiating from the desk were twenty feet wide, all in beautiful pink marble. His night in Cuba was going to be five-star all the way. Mike removed the baggage for the bellboys without anyone getting a look into the trunk. He had the valet show him where to park instead of turning over the keys. Vehicle security worried him; his equipment in the trunk was their Achilles' heel.

Angela inquired about the Mercedes at the desk. She was assured the vehicle would be guarded twenty-four hours a day in the hotel's secure parking lot. Angela smiled and said, "Fine. I just hope no one bumps the car. Its alarm system is extremely loud."

As had been standard practice in the Iron Curtain countries, the hotel took the passports of the guests and kept them as long as the guests remained. This practice gave Cuban intelligence control of the tourist population. Angela and Mike, without blinking, provided their British passports.

They entered the hotel room. It was breathtaking. The view from the window was of a luxurious pool the size of a football field. A few meters beyond the end of the pool was the Caribbean Sea. The excruciating poverty they had seen along the way from the drop zone had disappeared.

The room had been set with two bottles of wine on ice and an inviting assortment of fruit, cheese, and bread. Mike put away their clothes, then playfully hollered. "Yahoo!" diving on the king-size bed. Angela had been putting things right in the bathroom, laying out her cosmetics. She heard him and joined in, running from the bathroom and diving on top of Mike. They laughed and kissed gently.

Each gave one another two taps as they frolicked innocently on the bed. Things were okay so far. Each had cased the apartment and saw no apparent bugging or video monitors.

Mike's first order of business was a quick shower to remove the evening's grime, and then he wanted to go to the gym. Angela agreed to go as well. They both needed a good two hours in the weight room to work off the kinks of traveling. Mike showered quickly and Angela changed clothes. They were off to "bulk each other up." They closed the door laughing at their imitations of Arnold Schwarzenegger's accent.

They carried their backpacks with them, to include all cash and identification. Mike had memorized the placement of every piece of clothing. Angela's job had been to memorize the exact location of everything on the tops of the dresser, cabinet and sink. Mike also, had placed the luggage so he would know if it was disturbed.

Taking turns spotting for each other, they lifted hard. Mike was impressed more each day with Angela's physical and mental prowess. He respected her technical and tactical skills as well as her dedication to being physically ready for any mission.

They ended the workout with a quick rinse off, and then stepped into the Jacuzzi. They sat close and relaxed, ordering two Perriers with lemon. Angela kissed his cheek periodically and nuzzled Mike's ear. She spoke sweet nothings.

Returning to the room, they immediately canvassed the interior without being excessively deliberate. Sure enough, drawers had been gently and professionally ransacked, and the luggage had been slightly rearranged. Angela noted that Mike's shaving kit had moved almost a quarter-inch from where she had placed it to just graze the edge of a lamp base. During conversation, at different times, they each rubbed their left arm with their right hand, a movement similar to scratching the left triceps. They both got the message easily. They were under professional observation, and without conversation Mike and Angela concluded the same thing. Cuban intelligence probably searched any suite used by foreign diplomatic personnel.

They quickly showered again and headed for the beach. Securing beach chairs and a large umbrella, they settled in, ordering Cuban sandwiches and a bottle of wine for lunch. Angela had brought novels for both of them. She wanted Mike to take a nap; he had barely slept the night before. After the hearty sandwich, two glasses of wine, and about ten pages of reading, Angela had her wish. Mike was out.

23 Sep 2004

Kirsten, at the same moment, was anything but asleep. At home, in the middle of the day, she was on top of Ted, rocking back and forth in pursuit of her second orgasm. She shuddered and held her breath as she came in a rush. Ted followed shortly. Kirsten tried to understand what was happening to her. She couldn't decide if she was trying to make up for all the years Mike had left her alone, if she was in early mid-life crisis, or if she simply wanted to be young and carefree once more.

After showers and a quick lunch, Kirsten decided to give Ted a present that he would never forget. Even though school had been in session only for two weeks, Kirsten couldn't wait to get away with Ted to have him all to herself, in an environment free from neighbors and prying students.

She was aware of Ted's age and that he still answered to his parents regarding most of his activities. His whereabouts for Thanksgiving and Christmas would probably be dictated according to Ted's recent comments.

Kirsten decided to take things into her own hands. She was going to give Ted a sexual holiday he would never, ever forget.

Since Mike had disappeared, her expenses were greatly decreased, leaving his entire paycheck as hers. She had decided to fund a trip for the two of them. All it required was for them to skip class for one week, allowing them to be gone from Saturday, October 2nd through the next weekend.

Kirsten shyly handed an envelope across the table. Ted was surprised, opening it cautiously. He couldn't believe the contents, two tickets to Key West, Florida. They were going over a thousand miles away, just to be free to be together and to be publicly in love. He could cover the week out of town with his friends and parents.

Ted was in heaven, totally infatuated. He gushed, giving Kirsten a most wonderful embrace.

CHAPTER SIXTEEN

23 Sep 2004

LTG Hanscom looked down at his execution checklist and was pleased. He looked at the scheduled time for each occurrence in the plan, and then annotated the actual time it happened in pencil next to the programmed plan. His checklist was the only one that was totally complete, including planned events in Venezuela.

The CIA and NSA checklists were missing key items that they didn't need to know about. John's version, down in Key West at the old Navy hanger, was nearly all-inclusive. It had Mike's take off, his estimated time to leave the aircraft, his initial entry report, and key measures of progress along the way. Things looked good to John, too, as he kept his higher headquarters informed.

To John, higher headquarters was only Ellis, the Chairman's cutout and front man. Ellis had his own small communications suite installed in the Pentagon. He and his few workers looked like any other of the thousands of civilian bureaucrats. Linkage to LTG Hanscom was invisible.

The Southern Command liaison team had arrived and been "read on" to the classified mission. They would be invaluable if there was some cataclysmic emergency. SOUTHCOM's control of Army, Navy, and Air Forces could come in handy. Meanwhile, General Joe and Colonel Reeve Baker had the experimental Combat Search and Rescue Force at Eglin Air Force Base, Florida, standing on its head. They were having a ball with a fleet of new UAVs and practicing every conceivable search and rescue possibility in Cuban scenarios. Their task was still fuzzy, but generally it was to help destroy *Mundo Nuevo* and maybe to save Mike if everything completely went to hell.

*   *   *   *   *

In Cuba, the first empty parachute had been found, and the local police reported by phone to the regional Cuban intelligence desk. The second was found and reported at 4:00 p.m. The two chutes generated enough concern to precipitate a message to Havana. There, it meshed with the report of the three radar blips from the night before. Havana ordered the parachutes delivered immediately for technical analysis.

*   *   *   *   *

Angela reached over and nudged Mike. "Time to wake up," she said with a gentle kiss. Mike awoke quickly as was his habit.

"How about a swim, Mike? The sea looks so inviting."

"Good idea. That sounds refreshing."

They swam, splashed, dunked each other, and held each other close. They were lovers on a beach, an unimpeachable cover. Angela felt strongly about Mike, and was trying to remain professionally distant, losing ground each day that they spent together. Mike was more detached. He could role-play and have a close relationship with Angela, yet he was pledged to Kirsten.

Angela and Mike strolled along the beach hand in hand. They paused at a beachside *bohio* and ordered Havana Gold rum and coke. Delicious. They settled into comfortable handmade wooden chairs and felt the evening breeze gently stirring. The view of the ocean was breathtaking.

Mike pulled out his pager. He typed in the code for a weather update, location Havana, next twenty-four hours. The temperature at hit operation time was to be 72 degrees Fahrenheit, the skies would be clear. Later that day the temperature would reach 95. Mike leaned towards Angela. "The weather tomorrow will be ideal."

Angela, from experience and intuition, knew that Mike was focusing more and more on the hit as it approached. She leaned over to him and put her head on his shoulder. Mike looked into her eyes; they were a beautiful deep blue as always. He stared into them, as she intently did in return. It was clear to her that there were things best left unspoken. Mike hugged her in return. They moved back to the pool, rinsed off the salt water and sand, then reentered the hotel. They cleaned up, dressing casually.

Nine o'clock was the earliest dinner reservation available. They decided to shop and explore the hotel until around eight.

Mike was getting tight. As he walked through the hotel, looking at everything from Cuban art to sandals, he kept pacing off twenty-two meters, the distance from the corner of the alley to his target. He was mentally rehearsing; playing the "tapes" burned into his memory. Angela kept things light and moving, taking charge to kill time until dinner with continuous normal tourist movement.

Shortly after eight, Mike put on the tuxedo Angela had brought for him. Everything fit perfectly, as he tied his bow tie he realized that they made a handsome couple, the opposite of what one should be when trying to operate covertly. He shook his head to himself. He was becoming anxious, getting a game face. He wanted tomorrow morning, now.

While Angela dressed, Mike turned on the television to watch one of the evening soap operas so popular in Cuba. It was nine o'clock. He didn't worry about their reservation. In the land of *siestas,* nobody was expected to be on time in the evening.

* * * * *

The parachutes had arrived in Havana. The technical inspection immediately determined that the chutes were the best British equipment available, and that the two individuals in the harnesses could have been virtually untrained in regards to infiltration skills. The parachutes had been designed to literally fly themselves.

The equivalent of an all points bulletin went to the local Cuban Army regional headquarters and the constabulary office nearest to the drop zone Mike had used. The intelligence service wanted the third parachute tracked down. Also in the all points bulletin was a requirement that all neighborhood block chiefs be given a warning that infiltrators might be in the area. All were to be on high alert for unusual activity. The analysts were tracking the infiltration closely because it was out of the norm.

The British equipment was a first, expensive and the best available. Something new was afoot. In addition, a countrywide warning was sent to all agencies mandating close scrutiny of British citizens for the immediate future. Any abnormal activity by any British citizen was to be reported immediately.

Matos and the *Mundo Nuevo* project were so highly classified that there was no crosswalk of British activity against Cuba that would appear in normal intelligence channels. In the morning, *Señor* Matos would see a full report on the infiltration. He would be the one to merge the information.

*   *   *   *   *

Angela emerged from the bedroom. Mike had moved out on the balcony. He slowly turned towards her. She was dressed in black. The dress was sinfully low-cut to just above Angela's waist. Knee length, simple, the dress focused all attention on Angela's ample breasts. It was complemented by one of the fashionable gold collars Mike had recently seen. The collar had tens of gold chains streaming down at different lengths, emphasizing the breasts even more. Mike stood up and simply said, "Wow! Are you trying to seduce me again?"

Angela laughed, replying, "Mmmm. Are you objecting?"

Mike responded, "No. You are absolutely gorgeous. In fact, I'm not sure I want to share you with the outside world. We could just have a champagne dinner sent up."

"Later, my love, later."

Angela beamed. Mike would gravitate to the truth, always. His complement meant more than he knew. Angela stated with equal candor, "Think of tonight as a reward for all the hours you've put in at work. Let's enjoy."

Mike didn't answer. He seemed to have been drawn back through the French doors onto the balcony. He was looking far out to sea, seemingly oblivious to what Angela had just said.

He appeared abnormally calm and at peace. His gaze was fixed on the horizon. Angela put her hand on his shoulder.

Softly, she whispered, "Mike?"

Mike pointed far out into the ocean. "It has been beautiful all day, and the weather reports are perfect for Havana tomorrow. Yet, in the distance, there is lightening and a storm brewing. I can feel it."

Angela hugged him tightly from behind.

*   *   *   *   *

LTG Hanscom was at home when his secure phone rang. It was the Director of NSA. They had "picked" Cuban intelligence reports from the ether. The parachutes were having an impact. Hanscom simply replied, "Great news. Implement line thirty-seven from the execution checklist."

Line 37 was an NSA action. They were to remotely turn on Mike's emergency radio in his buried cache. Although the equipment was slightly underground, it was designed to emit enough signal for Cuban radio direction-finding equipment to locate it. Someone at Bejucal would begin to see a mysterious blip.

The NSA director made a secure phone call to his operations center. Soon thereafter, a satellite over Florida sent a message to Mike's cache. The radio turned on and as planned, at Bejucal, a faint signal appeared on a bored operator's screen. This time, the cadre of signal intelligence experts was energized. The blips and two parachutes were the talk of the day.

*   *   *   *   *

Cuban military reaction was immediate. As soon as the report of the signal from the parachute landing area was reported, a combined infantry and intelligence search team was alerted and given instructions. The intelligence experts hoped the signal was from an infiltrator or infiltrators in a static position for the night.

The search team would include a company of infantry riflemen, approximately a hundred in number. Attached would be three signal-detection-finding teams who would use their equipment to locate the transmission site. By triangulating the signal from three different points on the ground, an exact fix should be easy. An intelligence officer, Colonel Baez, would lead the team.

The goal was to capture a live prisoner and his equipment. However, eliminating any security threat was also important. Rules of engagement were simple. Find the infiltrators. Shoot to wound. If the infiltrators fire back, shoot to kill.

Colonel Baez was given unlimited written authority. All government offices, agencies and employees were to provide any needed services without question. He also had the right to confiscate government or civilian property deemed necessary to accomplish his mission. Such authorizations were unheard of in American military operations. The American Constitution, values, norms, and history of protecting individual rights would never tolerate such power being granted to any one individual.

Colonel Baez began planning the operation while his forces were still being assembled. He closely examined the landing sites of the two parachutes. In between the two sites was a red dot, the site of the suspected transmission. Baez quickly selected three likely sites where he could get a fix on the signal with his portable equipment. He then had technicians check his selections to make adjustments if the terrain wasn't supportive of his decisions. Next he selected dismount positions for the three platoons that would come from the Infantry unit. He would have them come from three distinct directions to surround the suspected site.

He prepared his order, then laid out sketches and a large photo-map on the floor. He briefed the leaders and their men at all at once, so they could move out smartly. He asked the infantrymen to be mature and silent and ordered them to take exceptional care not to accidentally discharge a round giving the enemy early warning. He closed with a patriotic paragraph on the importance of their mission for state security.

Civilian vehicles were chosen for the signal intelligence (SIGINT) detachments. They would leave fifteen minutes before the Infantry. The detachments would set up to fix the cache's location, reporting immediately any findings to Baez. The three infantry platoons would pull into position as quietly as possible, then begin closing into the woods upon command. Baez would locate himself with the platoon likely to reach the site first.

Link-up from three directions was going to be tough. The men were ordered to close in almost arm in arm making certain no infiltrator ran through them. Tackling suspected infiltrators had been discussed as an option. The men were expected to be alert, disciplined, and brave. They were poorly trained, given the state of the Cuban economy, yet they understood their task and were going to do their best for *la Patria*.

Colonel Baez remembered an old American military saying, "A poor plan vigorously executed is far superior to no plan at all." He had done the best he could in a short period of time. What he *had* to do was find the site well before dawn. No competent infiltrator would stay so near his site, unless injured, for more than a few hours. He hoped he would be in time so he could make his superiors proud.

The three signal detachment cars left the compound.

*   *   *   *   *

Halfway into their hors-d'oeuvres, Angela said she had to go to the ladies' room. Mike stood up and pulled out her chair. He smiled inside at himself; she was so beautiful it seemed mandatory to give her such treatment. Every head in the restaurant had turned when they had entered to be seated.

In a few minutes, Angela returned. After Mike seated her, she reached slowly over her body with her right hand and gently rubbed her left triceps. She spoke slowly and innocently, "Mike, there is a man over in the corner that was on the beach all afternoon. He has the most beautiful dark Cuban eyes. I like the Latino look of his full moustache too. You two are the most handsome men in the place."

Mike forced a laugh. "There you go again, trying to make me jealous." He lifted his glass and made a mock toast to Angela. "You have succeeded, too." Angela laughed in reply. She had "made" a potential tail. She had given him a description. He would find a way to get a look during the evening, but would not make an immediate move to do so. Even if every word was recorded, and every action was on video, Mike and Angela were still clean.

They finished their meal and moved out onto the veranda, now in the embrace of a refreshing evening breeze. Mike ordered after dinner drinks and his favorite Cuban cigar, a Cohiba. Angela gamely acquiesced, even though she hated tobacco products.

They were served and Mike slowly lit his cigar. He had learned all the proper techniques for lighting a cigar years before the resurgence of interest in fine cigars in the mid-1990s. He removed the paper band and expertly sliced off the rounded top end of the cigar with the small penknife he carried in his pocket. He ensured that the flame never touched the cigar, only the heat. He slowly allowed the end to begin to burn, then settled in, and inhaled, fully relaxed in appearance.

"I'd really like to hit the sack early tonight. You're looking good enough to eat and I need to—"

Angela interrupted, noting that Mike was tensing up. She responded by saying, "And I thought you really wanted to dance!"

Mike laughed aloud. He signed for dinner and stood up with Angela, finally spotting the man, now sitting at a table on the veranda, that Angela had mentioned. The man paid no attention to their departure. Mike put his arm around Angela and walked her to their room.

Together they laid out their clothes for the next morning and pre-packed most of their luggage for a quick checkout. Earlier, Mike had cut a button off one of his shirts and placed it strategically in his second drawer. Anyone searching the drawer would cause the button to fall, and would not be able to determine what its initial position had been. He could now see that the button was moved, and the room had been searched a second time.

Their plan was to approach the desk with no warning, carrying their own luggage and quickly depart. Reducing reaction time for those watching them could never hurt.

It was getting harder and harder to make small talk. Mike finally said he was going to take a shower and get ready for bed.

"Clean your teeth, sweetheart—you know I can't stand the taste of tobacco on your breath."

"Well, darling, that's the price you pay for being in love with a real man!"

During mission preparation Angela and John had tried varying medications to guarantee Mike a good night's rest, but results were poor. Frequently Mike woke up sluggish, or the medications simply didn't work. They could find no adequate combination of drugs, so they gave up.

Angela knew something that might help. She stripped nude, and slowly opened the bathroom door. Mike was in the luxuriously huge marble shower. Angela slowly opened the steam-covered door behind him. Mike had his head under the shower with his back towards her. She announced, "Mike, I'm joining you."

Mike froze for no more than a nanosecond. He then returned to role-playing and answered back, "Come right in, my lady. I was just about to call you to come and scrub my back."

Mike kept his back to Angela, and she slowly began soaping his back and neck, working on his tight muscles, massaging him as they stood together. Eventually, she hugged him hard from behind, and Mike became aroused from the feeling of Angela's breasts and erect nipples pressing against his back.

Angela said, "Ummm. You feel so good, sweetheart." She slowly reached around from behind Mike, gently grasping his rock-hard organ. She was impressed. Mike closed his eyes and didn't protest. Angela moved around in front of him and bent over at the waist. The shower sprayed her hair, plastering her beautiful blonde hair around her head as she took him in her mouth. Gently, then feeling his urgent response, she directly applied her fingers and lips to his thrusts. He groaned luxuriously as all the muscles in his long, thin legs fully tightened, his hands holding her head and face tightly to him as he let go in a spurt of gloriously powerful relief.

Mike still hadn't opened his eyes nor stopped shuddering. It was as if he didn't see what had happened, he wouldn't have to acknowledge it. Angela slowly stood up tightly against him, moving in close and gently held his jaw with both hands, kissing him with all her might. Mike responded, uttering quietly, "Thanks."

As Mike slowly walked out of the shower turning it over to her, Angela tiptoed after him softly. She wanted to speak of feelings that had become stronger and stronger during their time together, strong enough to overcome her conditioning to never let personal considerations interfere with business. She held her tongue, as Mike headed straight to bed.

Mike crawled into bed and thought of Poncho Gonzalez, the famous tennis player from Mexico. He used to openly discuss the positive effects of having sex before key matches. Mike had read philosophies on the same subject by famous Spanish bullfighters. He would try to write this off as work-related. It bolstered their cover; it was operationally successful. Struggling with guilt, he would confess to a priest later. He tried not to think of how deeply Kirsten would be hurt with his betrayal. Now he had to go to sleep, the mission was at hand.

After she had dried off, Angela set two alarms, both carefully checked for functioning to make sure they would wake up on time. Mike was nearly out. She thoughtfully chose what she would say. It had to be something of value to Mike that would help him both tonight and tomorrow. Angela remembered the bug on Mike's collar in the Atlanta confessional booth. She snuggled up and simply whispered, "Good night. God bless you, Mike."

CHAPTER SEVENTEEN

This lamb can never be devoured—not with planes nor smart bombs—because this lamb is smarter than you, and in its blood there is, and will always be, a poison for you.

—Fidel Castro, January 28, 1998

24 Sep 2004

It was three o'clock in the morning. As Mike slept in Angela's arms, Colonel Baez was watching his men uncover the cache, working under the light of several soldiers' flashlights. He quickly inventoried the items and submitted an initial report by radio to his Havana headquarters. Baez ordered his infantry company to secure the site's perimeter, and to be prepared to detain, for interrogation, anyone approaching it. He reminded the commander that anyone visiting the cache might be armed and dangerous. The young officer cleared orders for further activity in a matter of hours.

Baez organized a work party to carry the cached equipment to his vehicle. He raced towards Havana, leaving the three signal intercept teams in place; also promising prompt orders if the mission evolved. Colonel Baez told his driver to speed, but not to the excess that would cause a wreck. They would arrive to meet with technical experts at five in the morning.

At six, one hour after Baez arrived in Havana, Mike and Angela's alarms went off. They packed and left the room at 6:45. The desk clerk downstairs was surprised to see them. They hadn't asked for a bellboy or a wake-up call. Both gave the hotel and staff sincere praise saying they had a lot of sight seeing to do. They were cheerful and said they would return someday. After paying in Cuban pesos, they recovered their passports, said good-bye in English and Spanish and quickly departed.

Angela started the Mercedes. They were on their way. Mike punched his report into the pager. The execution checklist line item was simply, "Departed hotel unimpeded."

At 7:30, the hotel security office received a flash request. A country wide alert was in place. All British citizens were to be closely observed for suspicious activity. Reports of such activity were to be expedited to Havana. Meanwhile, Mike, on a pre-selected sandy turnout off the highway, had changed into his native fighting gear. He was loaded and ready. He changed his contact lenses from the normal clear to brown, making his eyes blend in with those in the *barrio*.

Mike was pumped, yet calm and precisely where he mentally needed to be. He was totally confident. He looked at Angela. She was saying little, hitting the marks on route to the target within thirty seconds. She had her shades on to cut any glare and was wearing Formula 1 racing gloves. She wanted to tell Mike that she did not believe in casual sex, but controlled herself because of the seriousness of the moment. To him, she was business, all business.

*   *   *   *   *

Señor Matos went to work at 7:00 a.m. as usual. His executive support had laid out all of his morning readings and his computer was turned on, awaiting his personal codes. Being a career intelligence officer, he always read the daily intelligence updates.

On the second page, he saw the item on the parachutes. Following was the announcement of a cache of principally British equipment. Matos started to panic. He wondered if British agents could be linking up with more conspirators inside his organization. He began to sweat profusely. Trembling, he turned on his computer to log into Cuba's highest security intelligence information net. He wanted to obtain exact details about the captured cache.

He logged in and his screen turned red. There was a warning:

DO NOT TOUCH YOUR COMPUTER. GET A PEN AND PAPER. IMPORTANT INSTRUCTIONS WILL FOLLOW IN 30 SECONDS.

Señor Matos didn't know what to do except comply. He reached for his ballpoint pen and a sheet of paper. The screen flashed to a different shade of red. Instructions continued:

SEÑOR MATOS, YOUR CAREER, REPUTATION AND LIFE ITSELF ARE AT RISK. YOU HAVE FAILED TO PROTECT MUNDO NUEVO, WE HAVE PERMEATED YOUR ORGANIZATION WITH SPIES, AND YOUR ENTIRE APPARATUS IS CRUMBLING FROM A MYRIAD OF ORCHESTRATED ATTACKS.

WE KNOW ALL ABOUT YOU, YOUR IMMEDIATE FAMILY AND YOUR EXTENDED FAMILY. WE HAVE ACCESS TO EVERY PESO YOU OWN. WE CAN ERASE YOUR HISTORY, AND EXTERMINATE YOU AS WE HAVE DONE WITH THE ANGOLAN BANK ACCOUNTS.

BE ADVISED, WE ARE FULLY COMMITTED TO THE TERMINATION OF MUNDO NUEVO, TO INCLUDE SACRIFICING OUR BEST MEN TO ENSURE CLOSURE OF THE PROJECT. WE HAVE MADE NATIONAL COMMITMENT FROM WHICH THERE IS NO RETURN.

WE ARE PREPARED TO INITIATE MORE DRASTIC AND VIOLENT MEASURES UNLESS YOU REPORT WHAT HAS HAPPENED IN THE FAILURE OF SECURITY FOR MUNDO NUEVO, TAKE CREDIT FOR YOUR CLEAR AND CONCISE INTELLIGENCE APPRAISAL, AND RECOMMEND CLOSURE OF THE PROJECT TO FIDEL CASTRO.

START COPYING NOW: HERE ARE THE
UNIMPEACHABLE FACTS AND INFORMATION YOU
NEED TO MAKE YOUR CASE. . . .

Matos took notes; it was a logical analysis of the threat to *Mundo Nuevo*, and an articulate guide that one could use to support closure. The discussion of international strategic loss of face by exposure of Cuba's development of weapons to adversely affect Mexico, a fellow Latin country with a history of close relations, was one good point.

Matos wrote furiously, and suddenly, his screen returned to normal. He had captured ninety percent of the argument. Then his screen flashed red once more, this time with a skull at the top.

IF YOU FAIL TO COMPLY, WE WILL ENSURE THAT
THE NATIONAL COMPUTER NETWORK DEFENSE
CENTER IN HAVANA FINDS INTERNET TRAFFIC
BETWEEN OUR AGENTS AND YOU. THE RESULTS OF
THE DISCOVERY WILL BE MOST UNPLEASANT.

The screen went blank.

Matos removed his jacket and tie. He stood up and paced, his heart pounding. He hated being outmaneuvered. Eventually he sat down, trying to calm himself.

He looked at the notes. They were an attractive option. It would put him on the offense, taking the initiative to provide Fidel with the best advice possible under current circumstances. Yet, he hated the *gringos* and their lackeys, the British. He had spent his life fighting them and did not want to roll over. The veins on his neck were about to burst from rage.

He looked over to the wall, seeing the Cuban flag next to his beloved photo of Fidel. His dream to retire a hero was all but destroyed.

Slowly gaining control, Matos could see no good options, so he didn't need to rush. He would wait forty-eight hours. Hopefully one of the British agents would be captured and tortured to gain a true perspective of the British intent. His presentation of the bad news would have to be crafted into a positive spin. He called his secretary and asked for her to arrange a briefing for *El Lider Maximo* three days hence. Matos would stay on the fence for now.

It dawned on him that there was probably nothing the British didn't know. He was starting to realize that personal survival and retirement ought to be his primary concerns. He called his chief of security and instructed that all *Mundo Nuevo* security forces be immediately placed on maximum alert. Detailed orders would follow.

Señor Matos looked at his watch. It was 7:50 a.m.

*   *   *   *   *

Just prior to his drop-off point, Mike punched another message into his pager. The execution checklist read, "Operator on target." Angela pulled the Mercedes over and tried to say something, her eyes welling up with tears, but Mike had stepped out into the alley and was gone. She bit her lower lip, as she made no attempt to drive to the rendezvous with Mike.

Angela looked straight ahead and took off for the Havana airport as fast as she could without attracting undue attention, following the plan laid out by John and through him from the top of the mission direction pyramid. She parked in short term parking at Havana's Jose Martí Airport, leaving the door unlocked and the keys and parking slip inside. Angela headed for her flight with only a light bag.

A stranger stepped in from the shadows and slid behind the wheel. By the time Angela entered the airport, the car was out of the parking lot, on its way back into Havana. Angela checked in, and was in the air in one hour.

The vehicle was soon back at the British Embassy. All its mission-related contents were destroyed, and its license plates changed.

Angela's flight was to Canada. After liftoff, she sat forward to look out of the window trying to keep Havana in sight as long as she could. She had followed orders to the letter: (1) Deliver Mike in optimal shape to the target. (2) Abandon him and immediately leave the country.

In deepest internal turmoil, Angela was nauseated and feared falling ill. She sobbed quietly for a few minutes. The passenger next to her asked if there was anything he could do to help. Angela replied that there was nothing anyone could do. She stiffened slowly, regaining control by the time the plane had crossed into Florida's airspace.

*   *   *   *   *

Mike was rag picking in the alley. He saw the black sedan pull up at the compound's entrance at 7:55. One guard stepped out, leaning against the front fender. He looked inattentive. The other guard appeared to be resting in the front seat, talking to the driver. Mike had twenty-two meters to go.

Slowly he started positioning himself to start the run. He pulled out the pistol and held it under his shirt. Then all hell broke loose.

Matos' order to go to full security alert had filtered through the system. Alarms went off inside the compound, Mike looked up at the two guard towers that could observe the black sedan and saw a flurry of activity. Men were standing up and manning machine guns. Mike immediately focused back on the target. The guards were at full alert, and yelling at each other, questioning what was going on. Both had drawn pistols.

Mike immediately assessed that he couldn't run. The towers would spot him immediately; the advantage of speed was gone. He would begin strolling as nonchalantly as he could, hand under his shirt.

He slowly moved across the street, then began to parallel the wall of the pseudo-prison housing *Mundo Nuevo*'s bio lab. He wanted to reach the entrance at the same time the professor stepped out. He would fight closer in. The guards would die. It would be toe-to-toe.

Mike's advantages were numerous. Skill. Preparation. Audacity. Selection of time and place for engagement. Mike pulled his hat down tight and shuffled along, almost reaching the entrance when the steel gate flew open. The target stepped out, a small man, carrying a briefcase locked to his wrist. Mike was four steps away. One guard was looking directly at him, pistol not yet raised, but moving. He was looking at Mike's hand under his shirt. Mike shot him in the forehead and moved his trigger finger to engage the laser.

With his left hand, Mike grabbed the suitcase. As rehearsed over and over again, he pulled to stretch the target's arm away from his body. In less than a quarter of a second he had laser sliced off the scientist's hand just above the wrist. Vigorously Mike shook the briefcase by the handle until the unattached stump of hand and forearm dropped from the handcuff hitting the street in a splatter of blood from the severed artery.

The second guard froze in shock, fixated on the amputation. The hand had just struck the ground. Mike's pointer laser put a red dot on the bridge of the guard's nose. A bullet followed erasing the laser spot.

In one fluid motion, Mike squatted down and killed the driver as he was reaching for his hidden weapon under the dash. The right rear door had been opened for the scientist, making it an unimpeded and simple shot.

The scientist was screaming in terror, reeling backwards, which helped Mike for the first few seconds since the guards in the towers were focusing on the shocking, gore squirting, and ear piercing phenomenon directly blow them...

Mike shot the nearest tower guard with a laser beam, temporarily blinding the machine-gunner. The other tower sentinel, in the chaos, had finally spotted Mike and opened up. Mike ran a zigzag pattern towards his designated alley, feeling the chips of rock from the street hit his legs. He dove into the passageway just when a grenade went off in the opening. He realized that the tower guards must have rifle grenades, something not covered in his intelligence briefing.

Immediately on his feet, he hustled down the alley. He put his pistol under his shirt into his custom harness and began walking briskly. Two Cuban ladies quickly got out of his way. He stepped out of the alley expecting to see the '57 Chevy taxi. *Nothing.*

Mike heard sirens and whistles from all quarters. He immediately picked up the pace, yet forcing himself not to run. He threw the briefcase into a dumpster in the second alley, as planned, and covered it with waste. Then he moved rapidly to meet Angela.

He stepped out on the street. There was no black car. He was alone in Havana. The blood of the unfortunate scientist was all over his left hand. He stepped back into the alley and grabbed a piece of cloth from the trash, wiping his hand as clean as he could in a two-second pause.

Mike moved rapidly onto an adjoining small street and began to seek a puddle of water, a bucket of water, anything. He needed two things desperately, distance between him and *Mundo Nuevo*, and a clean left hand and shirtsleeve.

The Cubans must have known he was coming, as evidenced by the alarms going off just before his attack. All support was wiped out. He was on his own. Mike prayed for Angela as he walked rapidly down the back alleys and streets, angling through the poorest neighborhoods towards the British Embassy, changing direction frequently, and looking for a way to wash.

He was composed. He was unhurt. He had momentum and the initiative. Pushing his pistol deep into its hidden sewn-in holster on his vest, Mike was on the move, confident he would make it home. Mission accomplished.

*   *   *   *   *

It was 8:35 a.m. *Señor* Matos had an initial report and the recovered briefcase on his desk. He shot questions rapidly at his assembled three man security staff, standing before him. Then he picked up his phone to give a report to the head of intelligence. He started as all professional bureaucrats did in Cuba, with personal damage control.

"As I read last night's intelligence reports, I deemed it necessary to place the security forces here at the project on the highest alert. Even with appropriate measures in effect, we have had an unfortunate incident that has caused many calls to your directorate over the last few minutes."

He breathed deeply and continued. "A *Señor* Iglesias, one of our best laboratory men, was assaulted just before 8:00 a.m. as he left our compound. He was en route to a staff meeting with some of his subordinates at a minor outlying support facility. The meeting was a common weekly occurrence.

"*Señor* Iglesias was attacked by a highly skilled gunman armed with sophisticated equipment, including a hand-held laser. The attack resulted in the death of *Señor* Iglesias' driver and two bodyguards. In addition, we have one tower guard that is temporarily blind from being hit by a laser; the man is under medical care. Finally, *Señor* Iglesias' left hand was amputated to expedite theft of his briefcase. Initial reports are that the hand may be saved. Havana's best doctors are on the case.

"I sent a squad of men in hot pursuit. We lost the gunman's trail but we were able to recover the briefcase unopened. All indicators are that nothing is missing. Our supposition at this point is that our security posture surprised and disrupted the assailant and his supporters, causing rapid flight and abandonment of the briefcase. We stand by to help your directorate in anyway possible in this matter."

Señor Matos placed his security chief in charge of liaison for the investigation and handed him the briefcase wrapped in plastic as evidence.

The message from his computer, less than an hour ago, was grinding on him:

WE ARE PREPARED TO INITIATE MORE DRASTIC AND VIOLENT MEASURES IMMEDIATELY.

He sat up straight when the realities of his situation came together. *Señor* Matos realized that *Señor* Iglesias wasn't the target and that briefcase didn't matter. An enemy that would amputate an innocent man's hand to reinforce a message was formidable and committed.

Matos internally acknowledged that *he* was the target. He rubbed his wrist as he contemplated what he was up against. This was not like the *Yanquis*. It was too brutal. This sounded like the old Soviets or Bulgarians, although it was clear the British were behind the entire plot. The UK must be fully committed to see this through, with their national crosshairs placed right on him. The thought made him tremble.

In any case, the message was received and understood. He had no choices. Matos would comply and try to convince the Cuban senior leadership to terminate *Mundo Nuevo*.

CHAPTER EIGHTEEN

LTG Hanscom was receiving input from many sources. The director of NSA relayed that the computer intimidation appeared to be working. *Señor* Matos had not reported that a foreign agency was inside Cuba's intelligence internet. At the minimum he was keeping his options open. In his phone calls were also indicators that the program was still on track.

At the end of the NSA report, Hanscom paused and issued an order. "Turn Mike on; check list number 63." He knew that the Cubans would now be able to determine Mike's location. Within minutes, Mike's pager and implant would begin continuously, silently broadcasting.

Next, LTG Hanscom called Ellis. His instructions were clear. He wanted the Joint Special Operations Task Force composed of the experimental UAV unit at Eglin Air Force Base, Florida, to move immediately to Key West and join John and his people. General Joe Cordell and Colonel Reeve Baker needed to be prepared to execute two missions, a direct action destruction mission in Cuba, and possibly a combat search and rescue mission. Ellis thought, *At last, Hanscom is starting to lay all the cards face up on the table.*

General Joe Cordell and Colonel Baker promised to be in place and operating in twenty-four hours. They would answer directly to John.

Outside of Hanscom's office, in the wood paneled corridor on the outer ring of the building, a British major detached from the SAS to the British Embassy in the U.S. waited patiently. When granted entrance to the office, he saluted and carried out his instructions. He delivered a sealed personal note from the British Ambassador. LTG Hanscom thanked him, and closed his door.

The General read the note. Angela had left safely. The car was being sterilized. The Cubans had rings of security around the British Embassy and were scrutinizing every passerby. Finally, the Embassy had no indicators as to the status of the American singleton.

Hanscom quietly updated his execution checklist then shredded the note. He relayed the contents of the note to Ellis via a secure phone call, even though they had just finished speaking, in order to keep John and his Key West team up to date.

The Director of the Central Intelligence agency phoned about execution of checklist item number 77. McLaughlin asked LTG Hanscom if it was still a go, and the answer was in the affirmative. Item 77 was an agency drop of three more unmanned parachutes at two in the morning. They were programmed to land near Mike's primary EEP (emergency extraction point.)

The President's secretary placed a call to the Agency. The President asked for a progress report and was happy with the detailed, yet cursory report. The President was going to call the Prime Minister in London and give him a personal update.

An hour later, the President called General Hanscom. The UK would contact the Cuban government tomorrow on the need for their leaders to speak secure. Subject matter and agenda would be kept fuzzy.

Everything was coming together. Full cooperation from the UK was making the plan fit together like a fine puzzle.

Angela landed in Canada. Calling a pre-designated 800 number, a cutout, she received instructions. An executive Lear jet was at the executive aircraft hangar waiting for her. She would be taken straight to the small Key West airport. A driver would pick her up in a white Ford Taurus.

Now she knew where the command and control node was. John and the Hybrid had moved to Key West. Mentally exhausted, Angela tried to get some rest on the Lear, but couldn't.

24 Sep 2004

Mike moved easily but cautiously through the city. Finding a puddle to wash his hand and shirtsleeve in, he felt better. Along the way he changed hats, buying a brown baseball cap to replace the one worn on the objective. He bought it for a few pesos from a street side vendor. He spoke little, pointing to his neck. He whispered, "*Mi garganta*," and the vendor understood that his throat hurt, not pursuing any bargaining or further discussion.

Having memorized the way to the British Embassy during his seemingly endless memorization drills, Mike hit key checkpoints along the way: an old cathedral, a key intersection, a government office building, and several other places of note. His clothes were Cuban, his eyes were brown, he moved like a man with a purpose, but not too rapidly. He took evasive measures to ensure he wasn't tracked, doubling back on himself by waiting at corners right after the turn, or by switching his direction of travel for a block or two at key moments. He also crossed busy streets at the last minute to "brush off" any trailers. He was sure he was not being followed.

Mike was about five blocks out from the British Embassy when he almost froze. The antenna sticking out of the back pocket of a man leaning against a lamppost was for an MX radio or its equivalent. The antenna was black rubber and about one-half-inch in diameter. The hand-held radios were secure, had great range with just a few repeaters on the top of tall buildings, and were common equipment for Special Forces and security units worldwide.

The man was stationary, observing the street and the movement of all foot traffic. Mike turned and retreated. Moving back two blocks, he moved over three streets and again turned towards the general direction of the British Embassy. In minutes, he found another watcher, this one drinking a *café con leche* in a chair outside of a small mom-and-pop *restaurante*.

Mike then knew what he was facing. This outside ring consisted of civilian clothed spotters. Closer in toward the Embassy would be forces to arrest suspicious personnel. He waited till the spotter turned into the restaurant and stepped past him, moving closer to the Embassy. Sure enough, there were uniformed forces on both sides of the street, manning roadblocks and questioning pedestrians and drivers.

Mike did not probe further, but he knew for sure there would be a final ring just outside of the Embassy, possibly even supported by snipers. He worried about the potential of security system video coverage of his attack that morning.

Mike decided to move to his cache site, re-supply himself with ammo, batteries, and some chow, then move to his primary extraction site, a helicopter-landing zone pre-selected during his many rehearsals. Mike would be patient.

Either the British Embassy would eventually be able to dispatch a vehicle for him, or a helicopter could pull him out. He was pleased that he had his STABO harness built into his vest. From the time a helicopter hovered and dropped its ropes, Mike only needed about two seconds to hook up.

At the moment, however, he needed a safe place to hole up. Tomorrow he would work his way out of the city. He headed for the cheaper part of Havana, in the barrios on the way out of town.

From 1989 to 1993 the Cuban economy shrank 35 percent due to the elimination of Russian economic subsidies. To survive, Castro had to do what he had long tried to avoid. He "dollarized" the economy, legitimizing a black market. Farmers could increase their production of agricultural foodstuffs for private profit, and he threw the nation open for tourism and foreign investment. This lessening of controls increased Mike's survivability. He could pay in dollars for a broken down room, in some neighborhood on the outskirts of town. He would clean up and get some rest.

Mike soon found a possibility. It appeared to be a hostel. He obtained a room with public bath for three dollars, cash of course. There were no questions asked. This was a *casas particulares*, a black market flophouse outside stringent government control. He had used the throat routine once again, and figured it should be the last time, just in case Cuban intelligence discovered his method of operation. He headed straight for the latrine, a filthy place, but relieved himself and took a quick shower, drying off with the one towel in his room. He brushed his teeth and felt refreshed. He knew the water might not meet American cleanliness standards, but he cupped his hand and drank heartily, to avoid becoming dehydrated.

In his room Mike typed a report on his pager. He stated his intention to head for his primary extraction point. He punched the pager. The monitor at Bejucal picked up the surge, easy since they had been tracking the odd signal since NSA had turned it on without Mike's knowledge. Cuban intelligence computers were now keyed for the pager's wavelength and pattern. Additionally, the wavelengths were identical to the ones found in the cache by Colonel Baez.

The Cubans were on it, moving rapidly to find the signal's source.

*　*　*　*　*

Angela had arrived in Key West. She was anxiously watching the situation board and trying to maintain a degree of professional nonchalance when Mike's message hit.

She stepped to John's small office in the corner of the hangar, opened the door without knocking, and as calmly as possible relayed the wonderful news. "John, Mike is okay, he is on the run."

John gave her a quick hug and stepped out on the floor of the command and control hangar to read Mike's message himself. One of the hanging computer screens had a glowing dot to identify his location. The dot was transposed onto a computerized aerial photo of the city. The dot was on a small, ramshackle hotel.

*　*　*　*　*

General Hanscom had just received his reports. The singleton was moving. The chaos Mike created in the city was reflected on the Cuban intelligence internet. Castro would be briefed late morning.

The British agreed to increase the pressure according to plan. The Prime Minister's office had requested a secure call just prior to Castro's briefing for optimal effect. For impetus, three additional dummy parachutes would be dropped tonight, indicating a total of six infiltrators.

Hanscom reached into his personal safe and pulled out a packet. No one else knew the complete contents. It was time to turn all applicable information over to John in Key West. The rest of the fight had to be fought from there.

He asked for Ellis, simultaneously taking his aide to find a jet in the system to get down to Key West immediately. It was time for direct action. As the Cubans focused on Mike and non-existent infiltrators, the Hybrid would hit them hard. Hard enough to rock Fidel himself.

After a quick update, Hanscom called the Secretary of Defense and the President. It was proper protocol to keep them briefed on key events as they occurred.

A leased jet landed in Key West with Ellis on the plane. John walked briskly to the Lear jet and entered the plane. They had their meeting and half-an-hour later John came out of the plane with a packet in his hand. The jet took off for Washington immediately thereafter.

25 Sep 2004

Hanscom called the NSA director at his home on the secure red phone. "Sorry to bother you. I just wanted to make sure that last night we turned Mike back on in accordance with our plan."

The director answered in the affirmative. NSA operators had turned on the implant behind Mike's ear, exactly as had been done with his pager.

Hanscom hung his head. He had now put Mike at extreme risk without John, Angela, or Mike knowing. If Mike didn't make it, he would be personally responsible.

With Mike now becoming a target for the Cubans, Hanscom was confident of two outcomes: One, Mike would create chaos inside of Cuba, making the Cubans pay a heavy price as they hunted him down. And two, that the Cuban leadership would be convinced that dozens—if not more—British agents and insurgents were loose in Cuba. Hanscom sighed, "Singletons—my God—we ask so much of them. . . ."

John and Angela had the technology to "pulse" Mike and find him without the Cubans picking up his location. But with Mike now continuously broadcasting, Key West *and* the Cubans had him on their screens.

Even though Ellis had delivered close to a complete planning package to John, neither he, nor Mike, nor Angela were aware that the Cubans were operating with full knowledge of Mike's location.

For insurance, NSA had not only turned on his implant behind Mike's ear, they had also switched on an additional "tag." This one had been installed, without Mike's knowledge, in one of his teeth when he was in the dentist's chair.

CHAPTER NINETEEN

Mike snacked from his rucksack, leaving no trash in the room. It was growing dark. Mike was disturbed, the hotel was too quiet, and it was as if he were the only person in the whole building. He looked out of his window and saw a large park across the street. It was filled with the urban poor, many sipping on small bottles of rum and beer, moving out into the evening breeze after a hard day's work. There were a few stalwart trees in the center of the park, an assortment of broken down benches, and many completely bare spots where children played *beisbol*, a national passion; or *futbol.*

Mike decided to move. He picked out a tree deep in the park, yet a good place to watch the front of the hotel. He quietly went out the back door of the hotel, unobserved. He went through the trash and found a green glass bottle without a label, probably from a cheap brand of rum.

Carrying the bottle with him, Mike slowly walked around the corner and stepped lightly across the street, under the tree. He avoided contact with Cubans in the park. He sat cross-legged holding his bottle in his right hand. He pulled his hat well down over his eyes and leaned back against the tree to get some sleep. He dozed off periodically for a few moments of rest.

Three trucks full of troops dismounting in front of the hotel woke Mike. His heart rate jumped. He mimicked the reaction of the Cubans in the park, expressing interest while trying to remain distant. The troops started to move into the park.

Mike turned and moved slowly along with some of the other Cubans. He knew if he ran he was finished. He then spotted roadblocks rolling into place at all four corners of the small plaza.

Trapped, Mike quickly canvassed what was in his favor. His biggest assets were that he looked Cuban and that it was nighttime. The poorly lit streets and his years of night training would give him advantage.

He stopped for a second as the Cuban crowd moved away from the government troops. The soldiers were spreading out in a long line and would walk the length of the park in order to sweep everyone from it into the checkpoints at the end of the plaza. As he paused, Mike took his silencer out from its pocket on his vest, and screwed it into his pistol. He stood back up, putting the pistol in his belt, and moved with the crowds towards the inevitable shakedown at the end of the street.

Mike was going to fight his way out.

The best way to break out of encirclement was to place all combat power on a single weak spot and blow through the enemy. He would have to apply the doctrinal principle as an individual. Mike was confident, being free to pick the place and time for a fight. He approached the roadblock lining up with the crowd to be frisked. The modus operandi seemed to be a quick frisk, followed by several questions, then release to loiter outside of the surrounded area or return home.

The soldier doing the frisking had his rifle slung over his back. He was watched over by two troopers, rifles in hand, ready to raise and fire. They were surveying the crowd as it bunched up at the shakedown site.

Mike realized he would have to knock all three down. The two in over watch would go first; the final would be the frisker, since he had his weapon over his shoulder. Mike needed space to work, so he slowed up behind the man in front of him.

Then someone else caught Mike's eye. It was a small man, dressed in Cuban fatigues like the others, but without the standard issue olive drab fatigue cap. He had on a set of ear mikes, in his hand he had a radio direction finder, and he was excitedly looking directly at Mike. Mike had to act immediately.

He pulled out his pistol and pumped two bullets each into the head and neck of the two armed guards. As the frisker tried to bring his rifle to bear off his shoulder, Mike shot him in the chest three times. Then he fired one round at the man with the radio direction finder, causing him to duck. The crowd recoiled backwards, offering Mike a split-second to break away. Mike started to run from the plaza, quickly stuffing the pistol in his belt. He pointed back towards the dead men yelling *"Cuchillo, cuchillo, hay un hombre con un cuchillo!"*

Since he had used his silencer, the milling crowd of Cubans that had just been searched had heard nothing. All of their attention turned towards the growing chaos where the guards had been killed, since Mike had screamed that there was a man with a knife. Mike looked like a terrified *campesino* running for his own safety. The crowd looked back towards the roadblock instead of at him.

He sprinted as fast as he could, took an immediate right, and slipped into another side street. Needing distance, he began walking quickly in the poorly lit *barrio*. He would head generally towards his cache site. Mike could make it cross-country in two days from Havana, possibly in one if he could get to the edge of the city tonight.

He had to make a break from his pursuers and flagged one of Havana's famous classic taxis, a 1958 Chevrolet Bellaire four-door hardtop.

Mike asked in his best Spanish to be taken to a market place near the edge of Havana. It would save Mike hours and hours of working his way through the city.

There was another reason Mike wanted to move quickly. The man with the headset had spotted him with direction-finding equipment. Mike was somehow hot. He was going to run a test.

Mike sat low in the taxi and nervously kept a look out for tailing vehicles. He saw none. He had placed himself where the driver couldn't get a good look at him. He put his arm around the driver's neck, and held a huge tip in dollars U.S. in front of his nose. In Spanish he quietly said, "This *propina* (the tip) is for you to forget that I was ever here. One word of my movement will cost you your life. I have memorized your car tag and I can find you. Do not turn around. Do not look in your mirror. Simply drive slowly away. *Gracias*."

Mike walked through the many wooden stalls in the now empty market place. He paused, under a dim streetlight and sat on the curb. Pulling out his pager, he sent in a report:

THIS IS MY LAST TRANSMISSION UNTIL I CAN PICK UP A REPLACEMENT PAGER AT THE CACHE SITE. I AM BEING LOCATED BY HAND-HELD DIRECTION FINDERS. I WILL BE AT MY PRIMARY EXTRACTION SITE IN 72 HOURS. IF I AM NOT THERE CONTINUE FOLLOWING CONTINGENCY PLANS. ALL IS WELL. END MESSAGE.

He sent the message. Although the Cubans couldn't "break" or decode the message, they could still monitor that transmission.

Mike took out his Leatherman and unscrewed a 2"x 4" board from the plywood roof of one of the more sturdy booths. He placed his pager up in the small space above the beam, screwing the beam back into place.

Mike retreated several blocks, settled into the doorway of a locked store, and sat down in the barely lit opening. He pulled out a cigarette. He was going to relax for a while. Two cigarettes and thirty minutes later, Mike heard Cuban Army trucks pull up into the neighborhood. He peered around the corner and saw a human cordon quickly being established around the market place, and another vehicle heading towards his location.

Mike had caught forty winks back in the park. He felt fresh and strong. Slowly heading towards the edge of the *barrio* in the darkness, Mike would soon be on the edge of some farmland. Once in the woods, he would be in his element.

24 Sep 2004

It was one o'clock in the morning. Colonel Baez briefed his commander on his findings. It had taken four hours to locate the pager. The pager had not been opened or any action taken with it, since Baez and his men knew that it would automatically "zero," or terminate all of its codes and power, if touched by anyone other than signal experts. It was an even more valuable find since it was identical to the model found in the cache site. The man fleeing might be heading straight for the cache, which was still surrounded by Cuban troops.

Colonel Baez, known for his candor, explained that, in retrospect, when the agent was trapped in the plaza, he and his men had been overconfident. He concluded by saying, "It is obvious that the enemy agents are fearless and will fight to the death. We will be more cautious in the future. This is why we took so long to secure and sweep the marketplace. Every soldier in the rifle company supporting this pursuit knows that his life is in danger."

Baez's greatest concerns were the size, expertise, and equipment available to the support network of the agents, now loose in Cuba.

Mike was already eight miles into the jungle, steadily and confidently moving in the night. He was walking a 200-meter box at the moment. He turned left off of his trail and walked the box, doubling back on his trail, bringing him up to 5 meters of his original path. He put on his headnet, fastened his clothes tightly, and slipping his hands into gloves, using his rucksack as a pillow he fell asleep on the ground, his pistol in hand. Anyone tracking him would have to pass right in front of his position. In a large bush, he would be safe from observation, yet he could hear any trackers. Now he could rest.

*   *   *   *   *

Señor Matos and Colonel Baez had been practicing their briefings since six in the morning. Colonel Baez briefed General Manuel Rojas, the head of the Military Intelligence Department. The charter of the MID was to conduct electronic warfare for the Cuban state, both domestically and internationally. The Russians, of course, maintained their close relationship and shared technology, since they had no better platform for intelligence collection against the United States.

Señor Matos was working closely now with *Señor* Roberto Muñoz, the head of the Ministry of Interior. Included in the Cuban Ministry of Interior was the Directorate General of Intelligence. The DGI was founded in 1961, as Castro implemented the Soviet model for population control and intelligence gathering. The DGI's charter was to conduct all foreign intelligence operations.

General Rojas and Colonel Baez took a military staff car over to the Ministry of Interior at nine o'clock. They were escorted to the Ministry's most elaborate briefing room. *Señor* Ramos, warm and cordial, met them personally. He stated that their assignment was two-fold. They had to present their best estimate of the threat inside of Cuba, and also impart their assessment of project *Mundo Nuevo*.

Muñoz and General Rojas had coordinated their positions the night before. Their viewpoints were heavily influenced by the hard work of Matos. His analysis for the closure of *Mundo Nuevo* was particularly compelling. Of course, neither of the intelligence heads of agency knew that the structure for the argument had arrived uninvited on *Señor* Matos' computer screen.

For the Castro presentation, the lead off information would be about the immediate problem, an enemy element operating in Cuba. The element was estimated to be no more than six personnel, one or two active agents and up to four support personnel.

The intelligence appraisal indicated that the lead agent, could be a Brit, whose appearance corresponded with the initial parachute drop, and whose disappearance corresponded with the attack at *Mundo Nuevo*'s front gate.

The Brit obviously had some sort of infrastructure support to be moving so freely in the capital, as indicated by tracking of his transmissions by radio. Also, the infiltration by parachute had to be supported by a reception party. The British Embassy was under tight observation and nothing was amiss.

The visit to the hotel by the British couple was under full study and evaluation. Their passports had proven to be legitimate, but were possibly manufactured. The British Embassy plates on their car were valid, yet the car had never been previously logged or reported by intelligence spotters or Cuban guards. This meant that the Embassy had set up a spare plate.

The infiltrator had not been seen since fleeing from the *plaza*. A potential blonde accomplice had been tracked to the airport. The blond had been in country only three days when she departed. The appraisal clearly concluded that the blonde's companion was the assailant at *Mundo Nuevo*. The woman's trail came up cold in Canada.

Mike's passport photo, copied by the hotel staff, showed a man with a beard. An artist had made a composite sketch on what his appearance would be without the beard. The audiotapes from the hotel room revealed nothing, except that the two were lovers, and the resident Cuban agent embedded in hotel security had little more to offer.

Sadly, *Señor* Iglesias, while losing his hand, had been so terrified he couldn't describe his assailant. The guards and the driver had been killed, and Cubans in the streets added little to the description.

The recommendation at the end of Colonel Baez's brief was to continue pursuit of the enemy network, and to ask for Fidel's guidance in the eradication effort. It was clear that the infiltrators were using multiple infiltration techniques, commercial air and parachute.

When Colonel Baez had completed his brief, *Señor* Matos would then give his. His task was to be much tougher, but he was buoyed by the identical conclusions of General Rojas and *Señor* Muñoz. They would back his counsel to the hilt. It would be to close down *Mundo Nuevo*.

Señor Matos' final practice went well. Both intelligence chiefs were satisfied, to their chagrin, with the joint conclusion. The biological initiative was compromised. The Russian scientist framed in Mexico, the laser attack on *Señor* Iglesias costing him his hand, the breeding tanks, the diamond mine, the Angolan accounts, and penetration of *Mundo Nuevo* by British agents, all punctuated one key point. The UK was willing to sacrifice British lives, a signal of intense national commitment.

The Cuban intelligence estimate concluded that Britain might be attacking *Mundo Nuevo* due to sensitivity towards agro-terror caused by the devastation of the nation's international trade in beef during the foot and mouth disease crisis several years earlier. The cost of lost cattle, a drop in the bucket compared to the damage Cuba could cause, exceeded four billion American dollars.

Other potential players were discussed, including the Russians. There was a possibility of British/Russian partnership since the original project was brutally shut down by the Russians after a KGB analysis indicating that it could jeopardize the nation. It could be that the potential risks inherent in the development of such aggressive biological weapons had made some strange bedfellows with common interests.

Finally, strategic propaganda cost was analyzed. The UK could "go public" at any time, and, if they exploited the potential danger, they could attack tourism, the one industry keeping Cuba afloat. In addition, they could notify Mexico and other long-tolerant Latin American governments that Fidel was developing the capacity to endanger, by a simple laboratory accident, the hemisphere's ability to feed its population. This key argument, everyone in the room concluded, would carry the day.

The men went on a short break to use the bathroom and get ready for what was always an ordeal. Muñoz then stepped up to the front steps to await the arrival of the President of Cuba, Fidel Castro.

*   *   *   *   *

Muñoz was surprised. Not only did *El Presidente* Fidel Castro Ruz, arrive, but the Vice-President General Raúl Castro Ruz was also in the sedan. They would be briefing the heir apparent as well as the President.

After *abrazos*, the customary Cuban hugs, and other mandatory polite exchanges, the room was cleared of all staff. Only Fidel, Raúl, *Señor* Muñoz, General Rojas, *Señor* Matos, and Colonel Baez remained.

Baez, being junior, was more nervous than the others. Castro immediately won him over by telling him to settle down and relax, stating that he simply wanted to get to the truth. In seconds, during his first meeting of his life with *El Presidente*, Baez had already seen the charm that had won millions over to him.

Baez took a deep breath and briefed the details of the enemy situation thus far. Castro was most disturbed with the loss of the soldiers by the plaza. Upon completion of his brief about the tactical situation, Baez asked for questions and held his breath. Fidel simply said he would wait until the completion of both briefings before making comment and thanked Baez for his professional presentation.

The apparent warmth *El Presidente* displayed toward him captivated the colonel.

Señor Matos was up next. The President became increasingly agitated as the brief went along. When Matos completed his summary statement, after recommending closure of *Mundo Nuevo*, Castro exploded. He refused to believe that *Mundo Nuevo* could not be salvaged. It was up to *Señor* Muñoz and *Señor* Matos to come back to him with a plan to do so, quickly.

He viciously attacked the Russians, British and Canadians. He had worked for years to develop close relations with Canada to split them from the influence of their evil neighbors. He had signed the Ottawa Treaty against land mines that the bloodthirsty Americans had ignored. He had exploited damage to Canadian industry caused by the American Congress's embargo and had fought for Canadian rights for free international trade.

He ranted on. In 2000, he had met with President Putin of Russia to heal old wounds and foster better cooperation and trade links. On the twentieth of December, 2000, he had fostered a follow-on meeting between the Canadian PM and President Putin. As for the Brits, he cursed them, dwelling on the imperialistic attack on Argentina during the Falklands War. Frothing at the mouth, he then closed by stating that, like Margaret Thatcher during the war, the Prime Minister of Britain was in bed with the President of the United States. Fidel castigated his intelligence services for being blind to the obvious.

He closed by restating that he wanted a briefing on how to save *Mundo Nuevo* within forty-eight hours. He then had Colonel Baez and General Rojas stand up. Castro turned cold. His eyes lit up.

In a calm, chilling tone he delivered his ultimatum: "You will have unlimited resources. Men, equipment, electronic warfare gear, aviation, or anything else you need. General Rojas, you will send all requests for support that you can't fill to Raúl personally.

"I want live prisoners. I want them for exploitation. I am going to take this violation of Cuban sovereignty and shove it up the backsides of the bastard *Yanquis* and their British surrogates. I want a prisoner! You WILL succeed! We are going to exploit this in the manner as Khrushchev did the shooting down of Gary Powers and his U2!" He slammed his fist on the table.

Rising quickly, Castro turned and slapped his hat on his head. He strode down the hallway, obviously disturbed. His aide walked up to him, apologetically relaying a message to him hours after it had been received.

The British Prime Minister wanted to speak to him on a secure line in a few days over an extremely important matter. Castro was livid. He told the aide to tell the Prime Minister to go to Hell. Raúl followed quietly behind.

Matos hurried back to his office. He wrote his notes and observations from the meeting in a page on his computer. He sent his reflections to *Señor* Muñoz and General Rojas as agreed to make sure they understood all that was said. He then made a few secure phone calls on the same subject.

Tomorrow they would prepare their plan to save *Mundo Nuevo*. He hoped that the Brits, obviously accessing his computer and his organization, would realize that he had tried to close the program. The failure to do so *was not his fault*! Again, unconsciously rubbing his wrist, Muñoz thought of his mauled compatriot, *Señor* Iglesias.

*   *   *   *   *

Mike was steadily pushing towards his cache from the west. He had moved throughout the day, stopping to refill his canteen frequently in streams. He continually worried about dehydration in the Cuban heat. He had only been seen twice, once by a small boy playing in the woods, and once by a man driving cattle. He tried to be nonchalant in both encounters, and kept moving as if it was perfectly normal to be strolling through the woods.

Mike was about two miles or so from the cache site when he began to suspect trouble. He heard a lot of truck movement on the roads, although he was well off of them. When he spotted two Cuban jeeps he moved deeper into the woods.

Mike had fired almost a magazine and a half of ammunition in Havana, but had only consumed a little chow. At the cache he could replenish his supplies and obtain the back-up pager for communications.

Back in Key West, John and Angela were very concerned. The Cuban Army, as indicated by satellite photography, had moved almost an entire brigade around the cache site. It appeared that the troops were deployed in three concentric rings, one close in, and two further out. Included were reserve troops with trucks and jeeps in concentrations at two sites about one to three kilometers away. They appeared ready to pounce in response to any call for reinforcement.

Both John and Angela were extremely chagrined that Mike's tag was malfunctioning. Instead of reacting to an occasional inquiry to give his location, the tag seemed to be permanently turned on. John worked the issue discretely with Ellis and was told the technicians at NSA were working a solution.

Mike's implant gave John and Angela his exact track as he moved through rural Cuba, whereas, luckily for Mike, the Cuban tracking was much less sophisticated. At times, due to inherent inaccuracies in the Cuban equipment, dependent on strength of signal, Mike could only be located within one kilometer of his actual position.

John and Angela were holding their breath. Mike was inside their projected trace of the Cubans' outer ring. John concluded that he may have walked through an unmanned spot, or entered before the ring had closed. Worse, the sun was not yet down, allowing the enemy a chance to spot Mike easily. Angela closed her eyes for a moment. John put his hand on her shoulder. There was no way to warn him since he had discarded his pager.

Later, just before sundown, Mike paused in the low ground, near a small stream in some thick woods. He pulled his map out to do one more check before sunlight disappeared. Illumination had already dropped about 50% as the sun headed under the horizon. Mike squatted Vietnamese style with his feet flat on the ground. He heard leaves moving behind him. Warily he turned.

Two Cuban soldiers were slowly approaching, their AK-47s at the ready.

In Spanish, one soldier said, "Do not move, you are under arrest." They stopped several steps away as Mike sat frozen, with his map still unfolded across his legs. His left hand lay on top of the map. Under the map, in his right hand, was his silenced pistol.

The soldier continued, "Look at me." Both soldiers moved closer together to look at Mike again, before glancing down at a half-crumpled piece of paper containing an artist's sketch of the man at the hotel with Angela.

The other soldier smiled widely, "*Señor*, they said you were coming in from the west, and here you are."

In a flash, Mike shot him in the left eye and shot the man on his left in the heart. Dragging the bodies quickly into a thicket, Mike picked up the paper—an excellent caricature of him with a baseball hat on.

He quickly searched the men, taking some of their bread and stuffing it in his backpack. He also took six magazines of 7.62mm ball ammunition and one of their AK-47s. In addition, he relieved the deceased of their medical pouches; he might need more med supplies before this mission was over. Mike had automatically concluded that the cache was hot, and he would have to survive by scavenging.

He quickly set his old zero data on the windage and elevation on the communist-made automatic rifle. He still could recall the numbers from foreign weapons training in Fifth Special Forces Group.

Mike then tried on the men's clothes. Luckily one of them was huge, and the Cuban fatigues fit over his clothes. He pulled the Cuban olive drab patrol cap down on his forehead and began to move away to distance himself from the cache site. It had been seven minutes since he killed the soldiers. They would be missed. Luckily, it was now almost completely dark. He had to make use of the night and move out.

Mike was deeply worried as he thought of Angela. She must have been captured. The cache site obviously was compromised. The soldiers had his picture; the trucks moving into the area all day now made sense. These woods were alive with soldiers on one mission, to find him. Mike was also concerned about how they could have known he would enter the cache site from the west. A person coming cross-country from Havana would have entered from the east; it would be much easier to do so following natural lines of drift. He would sort it out later, first, he had to survive the night and get moving towards his exfiltration site.

Slowly he picked his way through the woods surveying the bush ahead as far as he could with his tiny starlight scope, then moved about fifty meters forward. Finally after about two hours of painstaking progress, Mike could no longer hear movement through the bush and trees. He felt almost certain he was free from the troops lying in wait around the cache site. He decided to pick up the pace and put some distance between himself and the threat. It was a mistake.

Not less than two kilometers further on, he walked right into a three-man position. The Cuban platoon leader had been wise. He had briefed the young men to set up comfortably in small groups along small trails, where men and animals naturally gravitated when moving in the woods. The men were keeping their weapons in their laps and quietly listening. Any man moving in the woods standing up, or any soldier doing more than relieving himself on his knees or at a crouch, was fair game for gang tackling or shots to wound.

The young man most alert commanded, "Halt, what is the password?" Mike immediately opened up on full automatic with his AK. He pumped the full magazine into the movement of the surprised soldiers directly in front of him. One return round hit his left biceps in the exchange; it burned, but didn't knock him down.

Mike took off at full speed for about five-hundred meters. He quickly slipped off his shirt, and in the dark, put the Cuban pressure dressing on his wound, tying it around his arm. He immediately slipped his Cuban fatigue shirt back on. He had to keep moving. All hell had broken loose. Men were yelling; whistles were blowing; there was movement throughout the woods. Flashlights in the hands of panicking troops were waving madly. Worst of all, it was almost moonrise. The tropical forest would lighten up considerably in about twenty minutes.

Mike ran hard, picking up the pace. He stopped every few hundred meters to listen. On his third listening halt he heard a truck stop out on the highway to his left. It was about fifty meters above him on a road cut through the edge of a hill. He was about two hundred meters laterally from the road, hidden in the low ground.

Mike grabbed quickly for his rucksack. He heard a resonant baying sound. Dogs!

Bloodhounds were being dropped from the truck. Mike held one of his mace canisters in his left hand, put his rifle across his back and gripped his pistol in his right. He started moving with a purpose.

Mike slid through the rugged terrain quickly. Suddenly he heard dogs snarling behind him. He turned and two hounds were almost on top of him. The first one leaped and Mike shot it in the chest with his pistol. The limp dog's body struck him, knocking him down. The second dog came for Mike's throat before he could bring his pistol to bear on the target. Mike sprayed it with mace, then shook himself free. As the dog bellowed and backed off, Mike put the dog out of its misery and took off. It would take the Cubans a while to figure out what had happened.

Eyes streaming from the use of mace so close to himself, Mike knew that speed would be his savior in the chaos he had created. He ran as fast as he could to gain time and space. He analyzed the terrain as he moved, and eventually did a right turn, heading straight out to the road.

He was tired of being on the defensive. Furthermore his left arm was throbbing. He needed to give the Cubans something to worry about besides him. To regain the initiative, to shape events and place himself in control was all-important now.

Mike positioned himself on the top of a rise where he could see a turn in the road. The drop off from the road was a forty-foot ditch. After pouring water in his eyes to help purge the rest of the mace, Mike settled in and picked a good prone firing position. As he lay on the ground, he placed his rifle over the top of a log and sighted the weapon into the curve. There was now enough moonlight for a good shot. Mike was adroitly making the change from ambushee to ambusher.

Mike knew to shoot a hair low when using automatic fire, because the weapon would rise. He also knew the nuances of glass shooting, having practiced the art hundreds of times. The Cubans were tracking him; somehow they knew where he was. He was going to let them get close. He placed his AK on automatic fire and waited. He calmed his breathing. Now it was his turn to be on the offensive.

Mike heard a truck coming. He steeled himself not to be blinded if its lights hit him directly.

As the military truck came into view on the winding road, Mike opened fire just below the windshield on the driver's side. He put six rounds into the darkness of the front seat, right where the driver should be; he then moved his aim to the center of the windshield as the truck started to weave. He wanted to make sure that any passenger would be dissuaded from taking the wheel. The truck became airborne as it left the road; loaded in the back with soldiers, it crumpled into the creek below. Mike heard the men's moans as he ran as fast as he could back into the woods. Mike had created a small mass casualty situation. The Cubans would have to take care of the emergency.

Colonel Baez, back in the field as leader of the pursuing forces, heard the report over the radio in his jeep. He spoke calmly to the excited Captain rendering the details. "Be sure that the wounded are taken care of. Expedite movement to hospitals as required. Render a final report to me within two hours." He ended with a curt, "Out!"

Baez threw down the mike from his jeep radio. He was furious. His driver moved away, knowing better than to be in the bursting radius of the officer's anger.

Mike moved as quickly as he could. Having broken contact with the enemy, he was heading in the general direction of his extraction point. He needed to be there by the next evening.

*   *   *   *   *

John and Angela were downloading every satellite heat seeking computerized photo they could get to keep track of Cuban activity. They merged the pictures with Mike's location on one screen. It appeared that Mike had broken free and was moving away from the defensive circles around the cache.

*   *   *   *   *

Three dummy parachutes and their blocks of ice had landed in the vicinity of Mike's extraction point. At least one would be found by morning. John and Angela were told, belatedly, about the parachutes. They were extremely displeased, but professional. They knew Mike was walking into a deliberately laid trap. It didn't take rocket scientists to conclude that the choreographer of this mission wanted Mike to stay in contact with the Cubans.

Meanwhile, General Joe, Air Force Colonel Baker and their hand-tailored JSOTF (Joint Special Operations Task Force) of high-tech gear and UAVs had arrived in full strength.

*   *   *   *   *

"Mike will probably reach his first extraction point near sundown today, according to his progress so far," Angela observed.

John agreed, adding, "His instructions are to stay by the first emergency extraction point for three days, keeping it under observation, unless the enemy occupies it. If no one comes to pull him out, he knows it's time to move to his alternate extraction location and settle in for pick up on the fourth, fifth, or sixth night.

The parachute drop should attract so many Cubans that Mike will probably bypass the site." He continued, explaining the current situation. "Until *Mundo Nuevo* is definitely shut down, pulling Mike is a mistake. I am not pleased that we were not made aware of the true intent for the use of Mike. Yet, I acknowledge that he is an invaluable asset to keep the pressure on by mucking things up in Cuba. Also, a rescue attempt by our agents in the looks impossible at the moment.

The entire area around Mike is cordoned off with manned roadblocks and roving patrols. Mike is boxed in and our agents can't get to him," John concluded. "To use American helicopters would compromise our pretense that Britain is behind everything. We need to be patient."

*   *   *   *   *

General Cordell was pumped up about his target, received in the DA (direct action) planning folder. He had not expected to be ordered to attack in the next twenty-four hours. He was going to assault *Mundo*

Nuevo directly, with some of Secretary Rumsfeld's secret toys. The special family of UAVs was familiarly known to those who shared knowledge of their existence as the "whirlies." General Joe had used a C-17 Starlifter to move mission planning equipment, communications, personnel, and UAVs. An MC-130 Hercules brought ammunition separately for safety reasons. He had enough gear and expertise on site to handle any conceivable task.

General Joe and the JSOTF staff had the entire mission planned by noon, including all communications, flight routes, loads, contingency plans, and frequencies. Mid-day, the team was authorized to stand down for a short break to enjoy the mess hall delivery of chow for the planning cell.

*   *   *   *   *

Sunrise was approaching. Mike hurried to cross the railroad track in front of him, a dangerous task. From the flanks, any hidden observer could see someone from hundreds of meters away. Suddenly everything came together as he grasped the real purpose of this singleton.

Mike paused, looking back at the railroad track through the woods and brought out his Leatherman. He washed off the blade, and opened his pack. After putting some iodine on the blade, he reached back behind his ear and awkwardly made an incision. Forcing his fingers into the opening, he pulled out the implant. Ignoring the blood all over his hands, Mike poured iodine into the wound and applied one of his bandages as best he could. He kept pressure on the wound for a few minutes until he thought coagulation had begun. Next was the excruciating part.

He grasped the Leatherman, turning it into a set of needle nosed pliers. Mike opened his mouth and one by one, twisted, turned and finally extracted the first tooth from his mouth and then the second one that the doctor had implanted in Atlanta. The pain was so great, he trembled uncontrollably. He held his breath as he shook to preclude a scream and violent oaths. His mouth filled with blood. He spat several times, washed his mouth out with water, and gathered his gear as the sun began to rise.

Mike hustled out into the open.

On the railroad tracks he placed the two teeth, the implant from behind his ear, the laser attachment from his pistol, the taser, and his small night vision device. He would toss the exhausted laser batteries into the nearest stream on his way forward. The Cubans at the cache, the dog handlers, and the actions of the Cubans in town all indicated that he was emitting a signal. He had thought it was his pager. All along it was something else.

He heard a train coming and stood back waiting until he saw the wheels crush his equipment. Quickly moving to the tracks to gather the residue, Mike was off, as the sun began to rise. Crossing a stream, Mike dumped his batteries and the remains from the train tracks. He washed the blood off his hands, arm, neck and clothes. He filled his canteens. Mike, still concerned about more dogs, moved up the creek for a few hundred meters more before proceeding. The Cubans couldn't track him now.

Mike decided to stay in Cuban soldier's fatigues, since the region was crawling with Cuban forces. If he was spotted at a distance his chances of survival were better if he were initially recognized as a soldier.

* * * * *

John went to his monitors. The area near the cache was crawling with over a thousand troops. He pulsed Mike's implant. Nothing happened. He tried again, then he looked at the console operators, "Mike's gone," was all he could murmur.

Angela was electronically proofing the situation report of the day for Ellis. John slowly walked into her cubicle with a cup of coffee in his left hand. Walking gingerly from behind Angela, he put his arm around her and spoke softly. The operators from across the room saw her shoulders visibly sag, her head lowered for a second. The operators tried to look away.

"You mean that we can't get a pulse on Mike?" she murmered to John.

"That's exactly right. As you know, we could pulse him through the implant in the pager, the one behind his ear and the emergency one in his tooth."

Angela thought for a moment and then replied, "Well, you know, John, surely he's realized by now that the Cubans also have a method of tracking him. Perhaps one of the implants is malfunctioning and is sending out a permanent signal. Maybe he's removed the implants?"

"I suppose that's a possibility. Unlikely though."

"It's what I would do in that situation," Angela remarked.

"You may be right. I'll open the package containing his contingency plan."

26 Sep 2004

It was early the same day. *Señor* Matos had come in at seven to begin building the brief on how to save *Mundo Nuevo*. He had to send a draft over to *Señor* Muñoz at Intelligence and one to General Rojas by one o'clock in the afternoon to give them time to prepare feedback. He would work, all night if necessary to build an honest, achievable plan for Fidel.

Matos turned on his computer and read the reports from the night before. Six Cuban soldiers shot to death: two by 9mm rounds and four of them by 7.62mm ammunition. Eighteen wounded soldiers from an ambush on an Army transport truck. Seven were critical and three might not survive the day. The enemy had caused a total of twelve dead and nineteen wounded, counting the plaza incident and the scientist and his bodyguards.

The damage backed the conclusion that more than one operator was working in Cuba. A support network was almost a sure thing. In addition, two more parachutes had just been found in an area distant from the cache. The news was worse in the next paragraph. Since just before dawn, no electronic tracking measures had worked. The enemy had disappeared from the electromagnetic spectrum.

Matos counseled himself. He needed to focus on his task at hand, saving *Mundo Nuevo*. Everything he was reading was in the domain of General Rojas and the military; it wasn't his direct problem. Muñoz and General Rojas would be seeing the same reports. He quickly changed his computer over to his working files. He began to type furiously, hoping the Brits got it all, seeing that Fidel was the problem, not he.

*   *   *   *   *

LTG Hanscom received his updates and was displeased that Fidel had been unwilling to grasp the obvious course of action. Mike would have to be used to continue creating chaos and increasing speculation that a determined enemy force was operating inside Cuba.

Hanscom, of course, was deeply concerned about Mike, yet the fact that he had been purposely endangered was accepted as a necessity to all focused on the strategic termination of *Mundo Nuevo*. However, off duty, Hanscom wasn't sleeping well. In the evenings, at home, strategic purpose faded and his love of soldiers took over. He had deliberately placed Mike in a nasty situation, and the General would hold himself personally culpable if Mike didn't return.

Major Trantor was by far the most resourceful and reliable operator available. Hanscom was comforted, despite the anxiety he felt, as he recalled an earlier conversation. "One can't beat the Special Forces when it comes to being singletons." Major Dick Meadows and his operations in Iran came to mind, along with Mike Trantor.

He reached for his secure phone. The Secretary of Defense, the President, the Director of the CIA, and the Secretary of State had been in conference on the secure net and now he was to join them. Discussion was short. The Hybrid was authorized to conduct a direct action mission, a kinetic strike, on *Mundo Nuevo*.

President Bush was concerned about Major Trantor. His empathy for the common soldier was evident in his many trips to visit the wounded in Walter Reed. Hanscom explained the realities, stating he had great confidence in the Major. "Mr. President, we have no status on our man. He was moving freely prior to dawn, but now, we may have lost our last tracking mechanism. I remain optimistic on his eventual recovery. He is one of our best. Our focus must remain on convincing the Cuban leadership of the futility of continuing the project. We will, as you have ordered, attack at midnight."

One hour later, the British again contacted the Cubans, saying that a secure call between the Prime Minister and President Castro would be mutually beneficial. The Cubans continued rebuffing the suggestion.

CHAPTER TWENTY

26 Sep 2004

In Key West, preparations were complete to use the whirlies for the first time in combat. Led by Colonel Reeve Baker, the crews and technicians had been playing with the equipment, conducting innovative experiments for over a year.

Six whirlies had been built so far. From a distance a whirlie appeared to be a six-foot tall R2D2 robot right out of "Star Wars." The aberration from the R2D2 appearance was a rotating head with rotor blades attached. The body contained communications, guidance system, fuel and optics so the pilot could see, day or night. Underneath the robot were several pins and metal rings for attaching all sorts of payloads. In addition there was one robotic arm that could reach about eighteen inches for limited functions.

One key concern was the range of the UAVs. Seventy percent of the size of the aircraft was to accommodate fuel. The whirlies could reach Havana and return, with about thirty minutes of flight time to spare. If they were excessively delayed, they would fall in the ocean or have to land on a sea-going platform.

One of the most controversial aspects of the program was the selection of UAV pilots. The search reached into every service, including the Army, Navy and Air Force. The critical criteria were good character and military record coupled with a severe addiction to video games. The best twelve men and women selected were between eighteen and twenty years of age. Eight were from the Air Force and four were Army. They looked like kids on the beach, cute and cool.

When they showed up at Key West, all but one was wearing the latest designer sunglasses. Two were girls. They had their sleeves rolled up and stepped out laughing and poking each other. John, coming out to meet them, had never seen such a sight among ostensibly military people. Their boots weren't shined, and they wore flight suits like pilots, but without rank or unit insignia. Every one of them, especially the girls, were pushing haircut length regulations to the limit.

John was an Agency man, used to mercenaries and irregulars in all sorts of uniforms and disarray. However, he couldn't believe that a tough old bird like General Joe would tolerate lackluster salutes and slouchy postures as the scruffy whirlie crews moved around the hangar.

John saw General Joe and Colonel Baker watching him. Reeve Baker, having read John's thoughts, strolled over. "Don't judge a book by the cover. Let us show you what we've trained these young pilots to do for the next fourteen hours. You'll be amazed."

The pilots were standing, arcade like, at their computer consoles flying virtual terrain from Key West into Cuba. Their screens were tinted simulating darkness and looked exactly like what they would see tonight with their whirlies' night vision devices. The computers had been loaded with the entire map of Cuba and a map of the ocean from Key West. The pilots were flying the whirlies into Havana at tree top level, seeking dark streets, and unpopulated areas. Intent, the pilots' biggest fear was power lines. In Cuba, due to forty years of economic stagnation, hardly any lines were underground. It took two hours to "fly in" the routes as the computers digested the findings of the young pilots.

The mission would require two whirlies. Two pilots for each would be fully prepared and ready throughout the mission. One was called, of course, the co-pilot. Control of the whirlie could be passed instantly if the pilot became fatigued or unable for some reason to continue the mission. The structure also allowed for continual exchange of advice and professional experience. General Joe and Colonel Baker took Angela and John inside a separate hangar to examine the two mission birds for that night.

One would fly all the way to Cuba carrying what looked like a six foot long "yard dart" from the game, with huge over-sized darts, popular several years ago. The dart, large in circumference, would stick in the ground when dropped from about forty feet in the air. The fatter end of the dart would then emit explosive gas. Approximately 1.5 seconds later, when the fuel and air mixture was exquisitely combustible, explosives in the dart would ignite. Anything entered or surrounded by the gas would be destroyed. Such weapons were particularly effective against urban areas, bunkers and dug-in fortifications.

The other whirlie would be flying the "mummy." A goofy idea posed by one of the young special operators about eight months earlier was to try to convince an enemy that troops were in the area. They built a few disposable sand filled cloth dummies, suspended them from the "whirlies" and pounded the ground with them several times to tamp spots in the grass the shape of a human.

John and Angela moved to an air-conditioned enclosed truck where the two pilots, the two co-pilots, and the two backups were doing pre-mission training. After watching them fly the last few blocks to *Mundo Nuevo*, and seeing them complete the rehearsal mission in less than a minute, John shook his head, silently acknowledging that Colonel Baker had been right. The kids were incredibly talented, with reactions like seasoned fighter pilots.

John stepped out of the trailer and spoke to General Joe. "Reeve is right, those kids are all business, wet behind the ears, and yet, already pros. Did you see how that one maneuvered between the virtual trees on the screen to thump the mummy up and down?"

John and Angela left them and went back to check the command and control center. General Joe reached for a cigarette. Slowly lighting up, he mused. "You know, Reeve, I think I am just out-of-date. Everything is changing so fast. Pretty soon we won't have pilots in fighter aircraft; it will be a waste of life to do so. Are we going to replace the infantryman? With what?"

Colonel Baker chuckled, "Sir, other than the fact that fewer and fewer of them smoke each year, they are just what we were. They want a tough mission. They want the best tools to do it. And finally, they want us to teach them as best we can, then get out of their way.

Who would have ever guessed we would have an Army sergeant, the young black girl on the left, fly a U.S. Air Force bird into combat? Everything is changing," he continued. "But the men and women want to fight, just as we did."

"I'll be retiring soon," Reeve concluded. "I've been a special operator for more than twenty-nine years. The chance to build this test program has been a hell of an opportunity. Molding these kids into pilots was a perfect way for me to leave the service, succeeding in one more difficult project. Now it's even better. I get one more mission under my belt before hanging it up."

The whirlies each had names given to them by the pilot and copilot. The whirlies were covered with special flat black paint to avoid radar detection, the paint and night operation orientation was reflected in their names. The UAV delivering the explosives was "Black Knight," influenced by the Army football team, its name picked by the Army female sergeant.

The UAV carrying the mummy was named simply "Spectre." The pilot, a young Air Force sergeant, had come from an AC-130 Spectre gunship unit. The unit history was full of night exploits from Vietnam, Grenada, Panama, Desert Storm, Afghanistan, and Iraq. The unit specialized in placing munitions inside windows and doorways, at night, with incredible precision, from thousands of feet in the air.

John stepped outside as General Joe was nearing the end of his cigarette, asking Colonel Baker a technical question. "Is it true Black Knight and Spectre will fly on their own to the target, using only their computer?"

Reeve replied, "They will fly themselves for over 95% of the flight route. We pre-program them to loiter short of their target. If we fail to take over the controls earlier, or at the hover location, the aircraft will call and remind us to take over manually." Reeve paused, smiling. "This means they send NO overt signals on the way in or out of Cuba, as long as we pick up control when we are supposed to. They broadcast only as we interface on the target site. We call it 'flying in black.' Once the mission is complete they fly themselves home, unless they get in trouble and call us. Watch us take off tonight. You will see us fly them until they are off the coast, then they'll go black. Another factor is fuel. The computer will direct the most efficient route, taking into account wind and humidity. Our pilots would be making continuous corrections and wasting fuel."

Reeve gave General Joe a serious look. "Sir, I'm as nervous as a second lieutenant. In just a few hours we prove ourselves. We've worked so damn hard!"

General Joe smiled at his old friend. He put his arm on Reeve's shoulder and gave him a reassuring one-armed hug. "You and your great Americans have things to do. I will see you an hour before launch. You'll do just fine."

26 Sep 2004
Just prior to his one o'clock deadline, Matos had finished his input to the MID, General Rojas, and the DGI, *Señor* Muñoz. Respective return comments had been received in his office just before five. He went home for dinner and returned at eight, refreshed by a shower. *Mundo Nuevo*'s staff had the coffee going, ready for a long night. Matos went to work.

* * * * *

At eleven thirty that night *Señor* Matos had finished his fifth and final copy of the briefing for Fidel. It would be taken to *Señor* Muñoz and General Rojas first thing in the morning. Proud of his work, he puttered around locking his safes, closing down his computers and removing their hard drives, and just relaxing from the intense mental effort of the evening. At 11:59:30 p.m. he shut the door of his car in front of project *Mundo Nuevo*, not more than two meters from where *Señor* Iglesias had lost his hand. The driver pulled out, heading towards home.

Meanwhile, the birds in the large aviary in the back of the project were all settled in for the night. Three species calmly coexisted, and were quite spoiled. They had been selected because of their instinctive desire to migrate from Cuba and nearby islands to the Great Plains of the United States. Once the full capability of Mundo Nuevo was realized, their numbers would be increased, always ready to be infected by order of Fidel. The birds were about to be abruptly awakened.

Out of the night, two whirlies arrived at opposite ends of the compound. One quickly climbed to about sixty feet, hovered, then lowered to forty. The Black Knight dropped her fuel air explosive dart and scurried away. It was 11:59:55. Matos had turned the corner, hearing nothing.

On the other side of the compound, just outside the chain link fence, Spectre was bouncing the mummy up and down in the weeds right off of the security trail around the fence. Simultaneously, the small robot arm dropped two small items in the grass. Mission accomplished, Spectre went straight up through a small hole in the trees and headed towards home. The mummy would be ejected at sea to lighten the load, reducing drag and fuel consumption.

Colonel Baker was in his trailer. Pilots and copilots took their hands off the controls. They congratulated each other with "high-fives," difficult with their eyes welded to the computer screens.

General Joe hotfooted it from the pilots' van to the command center. He wanted to watch for the report of an explosion from the satellites. On the way he was thinking about what Baker had said about kids still being warriors. If he had recorded the pilots, it would have sounded like a World War Two movie. There were more "checks, rogers, over and outs" than ever. Joe was proud of both the precision and teamwork.

The target for the night was *Señor* Matos' office building and the computer center in the building immediately adjacent. If they could both be severely damaged, it was hoped that enough hard scientific research would be lost to help force the right decision. An attack directly on the compound had to gain Castro's full attention and might force him to talk to the British.

Señor Matos was approximately one-half mile away when he heard an explosion. It lit up the Havana night sky. He ordered his driver to turn around and very cautiously approach the compound. Matos was afraid that the compound might be under attack from ground troops. His driver only had a pistol and *Señor* Matos carried nothing. As they moved cautiously back towards the building ambulances and fire trucks began to appear. Matos ordered his driver to stop the car, pulling out his badge.

As *Señor* Matos made it through a gathering crowd he became aware of the extent of the damage. His office was gone, as well as the building behind it. The largest pieces of the previous structures visible were concrete chunks, one meter by one meter. The perimeter fence was ruptured. He saw two guards being carried on stretchers. There was a small fire in another building. It was chaos.

Matos worked his way through the rubble back to his car and told the driver to go to the homes of his two deputies. He would have to brief them personally since telephone lines in this area were obviously non-functional. He pulled out a notepad and began to write, the notes would help in constructing a report in the morning. Amid the chaos and dust, he noticed, oddly, that the aviary was ruptured and jotted down a note that the carefully nurtured birds had been freed.

As his driver pulled away, the hair on Matos' neck was standing on end. If he had stayed a few minutes more he and part of his staff would have been killed. Were the Brits watching him? Were they specifically targeting him? How many men did they have loose in Cuba at this moment? In one matter there was no question. He was going to recommend that *Mundo Nuevo* be cancelled regardless of any pressure from Fidel. The Brits were coldly serious on this one, and if this continued he would simply be dead.

*   *   *   *   *

General Joe watched the growing body of data on impacts of the raid. First were the satellite impressions of the blast, followed by SIGINT with detailed comments on Cuban telephone conversations articulating the number of wounded and the extent of the damage. The icing on the cake came one hour later, confirmation that the mission had been flawlessly executed.

Cuban intelligence reported that counter-intelligence personnel had found a spot where enemy soldiers may have lain to direct the attack. Included in their findings was a cover and red lens for a small flashlight, probably inadvertently dropped by the enemy force. One guard claimed he had seen and heard a small helicopter. No one else could verify his observation.

John and Angela were ecstatic. The Cubans had to be finally convinced that there was a complex and sophisticated organization in Cuba determined to close *Mundo Nuevo.*

John looked at his watch. It was 1:35 in the morning. Black Knight and Spectre would be arriving at their loiter off the coast of Florida in minutes, asking to be flown home.

*   *   *   *   *

The whirlies were heard just west of the hangar. General Joe was amazed how quiet they were. Out of the black, the pilots were bringing them home. As soon as Black Knight and Spectre landed, maintenance crews wheeled them into their own hangar where they would be hidden. Post-operations checklists were followed to the letter. Test equipment and wrenches flew around the hangar. Each critical system was checked and rechecked.

General Joe walked over to the hangar. Not only were crews busy, but the pilots joined them. As soon as maintenance was complete, all questionable parts were replaced and the needed adjustments made, the entire team sat down together for their "hot wash."

The mission was taken apart minute by minute. Each decision was given a critique. Pilots and crew members unhesitatingly told the truth, even if errors were their own. A note-taker wrote down every lesson that was learned and every correction needed in training or maintenance. He would submit a formal report on his return to Eglin Air Force Base.

The "hot wash" was over. General Joe asked the ranking pilot, if, since none of them smoked, they had all quit drinking alcohol too. They laughed and General Joe motioned to his aide, who had the brew.

Everyone relaxed. It was 5:30 a.m. and the newly baptized combat veterans sat together around the picnic tables in the hangar, sipping beer. As they told their fresh war stories, General Joe compared memories of his first combat success as a young soldier. Colonel Reeve Baker soon joined them.

Reeve was right. Warriors are still warriors. They could have well have been centurions sitting around a fire after a battle on the German frontier. General Joe was in his element. He knew better, but he reached for his third beer. Such moments were more and more precious.

*   *   *   *   *

John and Angela couldn't pause to rejoice over the victory. The news about Cuban activity near John's choice of primary extraction site was extremely disturbing. It appeared that more troops had been infiltrated into the area, literally saturating it with soldiers. Heavy weapons were visible from the satellite observations. Mike, if alive, would, according to the plan, approach the extraction helicopter-landing zone at dark to place it under observation. He would be walking into a buzz saw, and there was no way to find him, nor any way to warn him.

Angela tried to hide a deep sense of concern. John sensed her turmoil. "The mere existence of these extraordinary efforts by the Cubans probably means that Mike is alive and kicking them in the shins. Let's watch what they do. Their actions will tell us how Mike is doing." Angela perked up a bit, staring at the enemy situation posted on the computer screen in front of them.

"Have you activated Mike's emergency evacuation plan yet?" Angela asked.

"We know where he will go. I've requested a satellite watch for the spot."

*   *   *   *   *

The President received the welcome news: initial mission accomplished. *Mundo Nuevo* was in all probability cancelled, though independent intelligence verification might take months.

The Secretary of Defense was grateful and congratulatory. He congratulated General Hanscom warmly. "The nation is in your debt and so am I. Well done."

On the secure net call, the President went on to say that he would be calling Prime Minister Blair to thank him for his support. He would also remind the PM of the tremendous importance of his coming video conference with Fidel to secure mission completion, a solid guarantee to terminate *Mundo Nuevo.*

Hanscom, a soldier's soldier, did not rejoice. He had a man still at risk. Deceived by his chain-of-command into creating chaos in the enemy's rear, Mike had been necessarily duped for a purpose no longer necessary. It was time to pull out all the stops to save him. Hanscom called Ellis, consulting his mission synchronization calendar.

Soon, Mike was supposed to approach his primary extraction site. It was the same location where Hanscom had dropped additional "enemy" parachutes, to bring Mike and the Cubans into confrontation. The confrontation was no longer necessary, but all communications were gone. He couldn't turn Mike around.

He picked up his red phone. "Mr. Ellis, Joe and Reeve need to pull out all the stops and put together an unconstrained search and rescue estimate for Cuba. We may have to fly into the middle of a Cuban brigade to save Major Trantor. The situation on the ground is ambiguous. We need a plan that is agile, creative, and flexible. I want the estimate to be what would be required to go in blind and dig Mike out. I want all the options fully detailed first thing in the morning. Thanks."

* * * * *

Señor Muñoz and General Rojas reeled under Fidel's verbal assault. They had been called to the Presidential Palace with no warning. *Señor* Matos had been saved from personal abuse because he had worked all night sorting out the damage from the Key West raid. Fidel was shaking in anger. He had ranted and raved for fifteen straight minutes, with no let up in sight. *Señor* Muñoz and General

Rojas were still at attention in front of his desk. Raúl was standing too, though more relaxed.

Not only was *Mundo Nuevo* dead in its infancy, Castro had a full-blown conspiracy operating inside of Cuba! Each night the number of wounded and killed escalated, and indicators were that the enemy might have bases and helicopters operating on Cuban soil.

Fidel eventually regained control and summarized, giving instructions that were quite clear. "*Señor* Muñoz and General Rojas, we have been friends a long time. *Mundo Nuevo* is terminated. Close it down, and sterilize it. I want no records of any kind remaining that the project ever existed." He went on, his belligerent tone softening. "We have overcome seemingly insurmountable obstacles together in the last forty years together. I will not tolerate this affront to our national sovereignty. The bastards in London still want to have a discussion, and we will." He paused to catch his breath.

He suddenly leaped up and pounded his desk looking viciously at the two terrified men in front of him. Fidel wanted blood. "The discussion will be to discuss the dead operatives I have as proof of their violation of Cuba's sacred territory. I no longer care about prisoners, although they would be an enhancement. Every single British pawn in Cuba will be eradicated! Every support mechanism destroyed. There will be no mercy! General Rojas, you have the lead. There are no limits to what you can do to achieve this end."

He continued, "Raúl, set a secure video conference, not a phone call, with the Prime Minister in ten days. General Rojas and *Señor* Muñoz, in that videoconference I am going to show the Prime Minister enemy equipment. If we are lucky, I will show him prisoners of war. If not, I will show him severed heads of his henchmen. If you fail, as you have failed in the administration and protection of *Mundo Nuevo*, you will be relieved of your positions and face other punishment as I deem appropriate."

He coldly looked at each trembling man. "Do you understand your mission?" he screamed. Leaning further forward over his desk, he bellowed, "Do you have any questions?"

Rojas and Muñoz were frozen with fear. Castro finished, "Leave my sight. You have ten days to produce or face the most horrible of consequences. Go, *NOW*!"

The men gave abbreviated salutes and almost ran from the room.

Fidel turned to Raúl and said, "Watch them like a hawk. Provide daily reports on their progress. Notify me when the Prime Minister agrees to speak. Ten days, Raúl, ten days."

As soon as *Señor* Matos broke away from the others, he moved to a secure computer to pass required instructions to *Mundo Nuevo*'s cadre. In reality, he wanted the medium to inform the British that they had succeeded. He followed with phone calls discussing the implications of the decision to terminate the project. Overkill couldn't hurt. Matos hadn't slept for over twenty-four hours. He was dead tired and needed a good rest.

He was weary and Fidel's threats were excruciatingly troubling, but at least the British would be taking the cross hairs off of him. He would throw all of his energy into tracking the UK sponsored insurgents.

Raúl contacted the British Embassy.

CHAPTER TWENTY-ONE

27 Sep 2004

It was 1:35 in the morning, and Mike was dead tired. His arm ached from his earlier wound, his head throbbed, and his jaw pained from the traumatic tooth extractions. He worried if he had done more damage than necessary behind his ear.

He had covered many kilometers of ground. Boxing his trail so he could hear any trackers, he settled in, keeping one arm through a rucksack strap, boots on, his rifle ready to fire.

Again he went through the ritual of putting on his headnet, tightening his clothes by tucking in his shirt, stuffing the Cuban fatigue pants in his shoes, putting on his gloves. His method for sleeping on jungle floor had worked for years. He was immune, at least mentally, to snakes, vampire bats, mosquitoes and anything else. In one minute he was out. He would sleep for four hours like a baby.

* * * * *

The sun was just beginning to rise as Mike eased towards his primary extraction point where either a helicopter or the British Embassy would pick him up. His instructions were to remain in this area for three days awaiting extraction, which would occur at night.

He needed, according to plan, to hide nearby and watch for enemy forces, moving on to his secondary site if this one proved untenable. If pick-up failed at the secondary, he would move again to an alternate landing zone and repeat the same procedure for the subsequent three evenings.

Mike was still two miles out, making his way carefully through the woods. He felt confident about moving in the daylight. He had his Cuban fatigues on; he carried his AK-47 like a soldier would. He knew from his map that a well-maintained dirt road, straight as an arrow, was coming up. There was heavy vegetation on both sides. It was a classic "danger area," as every Ranger knew, same as the railroad tracks had been. Moving cat-like through the dense brush, Mike saw the road appear.

He didn't see or hear anything on the other side of the road, where an entire Cuban rifle company was deployed directly facing him. The men had emplaced their weapons wisely and had interlocking fire and observation zones up and down the road. They knew what had happened to their comrades who were taken by surprise earlier in the week. The Cubans were on edge, disciplined, and absolutely silent. Each foxhole and firing position was manned by two to three of them. At least one in each position was continuously observing the company front.

Colonel Baez had changed his tactics. He had placed his men in belts, with something similar to "free-fire" zones before them. Doctrinally called "engagement areas" or "kill sacks" by the troops, the procedure was clear. Each unit was free to kill targets in the length width and depth of the area designated on their maps in front of their particular positions. Civilians in the area had quietly been quarantined into safe areas, conducting business as close to normal as possible.

Unknown to Mike, he had lost the advantage of his uniform. He was in the engagement area where anything that moved could be shot. The silent infantry company was on line, not more than ten meters to his front. Mike froze for five minutes to listen for activity on the other side of the road. The wind was blowing, which was against him, he strained but heard nothing.

Mike then crawled forward, stuck his head out of the woods and looked right down the road. He was preparing to cross casually, acting like a Cuban soldier on patrol. If he ran, he would automatically be suspect.

He then turned his head to the left and saw the muzzle of a light machine gun glint in the sun. It was moving in a camouflaged position not more than twenty meters away. The gunner was barely visible, and the muzzle was coming to bear on him.

Mike turned and ran as fast as he could. Crouched down, he sprinted at full speed. Bullets cracked overhead and the machine gun pumped out round after round.

Foliage fell all around. Luckily, as usual, ill-trained troops shot slightly high. Mike took off to his left at an angle trying to get out of the beaten zone of the machine gun. All hell broke loose a second later as the other men along the road were told to fire to their fronts. Mike ran as fast as he could in the thick vegetation, seeking shelter from more and more trees to catch much of the ordnance. Each step, as he sprinted, increased his fragile survivability.

The sounds of the Cuban weapons were fading to a degree, and there were no more clear cracks overhead. Mike was now running at full speed standing up. Then things went black. A mortar round had landed five meters to his right. The blast blew him into the air like a rag doll. He flew ten meters and landed, out cold.

Mike had been hit by what Special Forces called the "golden BB." The golden BB was an enemy round that could screw you up completely. A round that could be accidental. A round that hit just the right spot on your helicopter. A round that, by chance, could cause mission failure. A round that no matter what you did to prevent it, might still strike at just the right time and place. A pure luck round. And so it was. The mortar men were blasting unobserved harassment fire into the engagement area. No one knew Mike was hit.

Dazed, he tried to sit up. Extremely dizzy and disoriented, he lay back down on his back, worried about shock. He knew enough to keep his knees up and his head down until he was stable. Deaf from concussion, he thought he heard mortar rounds continuing in the distance, but he was unsure. His head was ringing as he tried to gather his thoughts, slowly regaining his senses. His hand reached for his right leg, on its own accord. It returned in front of his eye, colored a deep dark red. Once again, he was wounded.

Mike forced himself up and looked down at the torn leg. Bone was showing. A huge chunk of flesh was torn from the right side of his calf. He sobered quickly. The good news was that no blood seemed to spurt. Maybe he was lucky, Mike thought, "No major arteries."

As quickly as he could he applied a pressure dressing, then tied it tight to the wound. He cut away some of the fatigue trouser to work better on his leg. The pain was piercing, but not paralyzing. Mike didn't notice the blood oozing from his right ear. His eardrum had ruptured. He couldn't hear a thing.

Mike forced himself to his feet. He had to walk. Distance was now going to be his savior. Tentatively he started hobbling forward, muttering to himself, "That might not have been the golden BB, but by God, it was silver!"

Mike immediately dismissed going to his original pickup site. Angela had to have been swept up. The Cubans were ahead of him every step of the way, waiting for him in depth at both cache and exfiltration sites... As he hobbled through the woods he said a prayer for her, hoping she was still alive. He assumed that Angela would have told them about his secondary extraction location, just as she had told them about his cache and his primary exfiltration point.

Mike bet she went down hard. He wondered how many she killed before they subdued her.

Mike flashed back to Atlanta. He was sealing an envelope and handing it to John. In it was his "go to hell" plan as most Special Forces soldiers called it. If everything else in the plan broke, the soldier would execute his last gasp option. Each man wrote his own, memorized how to find the location for pickup and all terrain and population involved. He also wrote how he saw the link-up taking place—to include the signals and the final confirmation that both sides were friendly. Normally, one trusted advisor was allowed to study the plan for feasibility and supportability. Mike was so experienced, a review was waived. John had put the plan in his safe.

Mike would now execute that plan. He was pretty sure that having disabled his tracking devices John would have read his "go to hell" plan. Still deaf, limping badly, Mike struggled with his wounded leg. He would walk twenty-four hours straight if necessary to build space between himself and the Cubans.

*   *   *   *   *

John was pleased and Angela jumped for joy when the satellite overhead revealed indicators of the fight. Mike might still be out there raising hell. John passed the word to General Joe and at the same time briefed him on Mike's emergency plan. John was convinced that Mike would now be putting his own strategy into effect.

Joe was putting the final touches on the unconstrained search and rescue packet. After a forty minute brief during which time Mike's own emergency plan was incorporated, John agreed that it was good enough to forward to Ellis.

28 Sep 2004

Ellis dropped off the search and rescue estimate. Shortly thereafter, General Hanscom sat down to read.

The force package was enormous. Air Force and Navy fighters. Army Apache helicopters to kill enemy mobility. Bombers on call. Airlift enough to do the invasion of Panama over again. Almost an entire Army Division of paratroopers as back up for the Ranger Regiment and the Special Forces. Field artillery and even larger indirect weapons for more fire support. The template, outsized as it was, was about right for a completely ambiguous situation. The vast majority of the proposed forces would have to invade Cuba to create a secure bubble; enabling the rescue force could operate inside of it to find Mike, the needle in the haystack.

The operation was so huge it would have to be run by a Joint Task Force based on the Army's XVIII Airborne Corps. The Hybrid was too small to effectively command and control an incursion of such scale.

The deployment of such significant firepower would be very costly, and not only in taxpayer dollars. Political ramifications for the administration would have to be considered. The 200+ billion dollar bill for the occupation of Iraq still rankled many in Congress.

An invasion of Cuba was a guaranteed losing proposition in the Organization of American States, and the United Nations. It would also undo one of the reasons that the Hybrid's operational construct was low- viz (visibility); Latin America might explode with resentment towards the United States.

Hanscom set the document aside. He knew unconstrained the proposal had little chance of approval, but he had to at least present it as an option to Secretary Rumsfeld for an initial appraisal.

They both rapidly reached the same conclusion. The likelihood was practically nil that the State Department would approve a massive deployment to search for a single missing American, without vetted intelligence that he was alive. In addition, a military action of this size and scope just prior to the November 2004 election simply wasn't wise. The Democrats would probably declare that the Republicans were conducting combat operations simply to gain the spike in the polls that usually accompanies aggressive military activity.

Things might be different if definitive proof existed that Mike was still alive at a specific location. Although Hanscom expected negative feedback received from the Department of Defense and the head of the CIA, he couldn't rest as long as a single soldier was at risk. He reasoned that insight might be gained by having the vetting committee take a look at the plan. There was also the faint hope that Mike might make the extraction point outlined in his "go to hell" plan. That needed to be considered in the overall planning, but not yet. He called Ellis to activate Peters and his team.

* * * * *

Ms. Winthrop was furious. Peters had presented the search and rescue estimate for comment, and it was perfectly clear that the United States was about to snatch defeat from the jaws of victory. As she had predicted, the collective leadership had become enamored with Mike Trantor and had taken their eyes off of the strategic purpose of the operation.

She slowly began to speak. "I am deeply concerned. We are on a dangerous course. Without due oversight or the sensing of the Congress for an unannounced and unnecessary plan for invading the sovereign nation of Cuba . . ." She continued to unload, building the case for abandoning Mike, coldly stating the myriad of reasons why it was in the national interest to ". . . cut him away." Ms. Winthrop closed with a scenario in which the incursion was executed and Mike was not recovered, leading to disastrous consequences for the President in the upcoming election. All around the table could envision the political cartoons with George W. the cowboy shooting his six-guns.

Peters saw the logic, as did all the others. Yet, along with General Hanscom, his Army upbringing had instilled values that simply made it impossible for him to accept writing Mike off. He had never liked Ms. Winthrop. She had been an unpopular career CIA case officer and operator. Her forte was building agent networks, and then abandoning them when programs closed or national interest changed direction. She was most infamous for leaving a Vietnamese net in Saigon when she could have pulled the agents prior to the government's collapse. Even worse, she knew that the North Vietnamese would capture documents naming each one of them as American employees.

Earlier, she had failed miserably in Cuba. In fact, it was some of her agents that were captured by the Cubans and "doubled" to feed the CIA false information for almost five years.

Nonetheless, Ms. Winthrop's cold logic carried the day. The search and rescue plan was not vetted and no one saw the possibility of approval by the administration. In essence, the body fully agreed with Secretary Rumsfeld's analysis.

Peters was distraught and decided to fudge his report to Mr. Ellis. He had to give Major Trantor a chance. He reported that the committee had deemed the search and rescue plan unfeasible, but that *a covert rescue operation needed to be planned immediately for an extremely small surgical strike* that could have a degree of plausible deniability.

*   *   *   *   *

General Hanscom received Peter's recommendation and acted on it immediately. He pulled out a sheet of paper and furiously wrote out his personal intent for a surgical operation to rescue Mike. It left the "how" in the hands of the Hybrid and simply instructed John on the necessary results of the operation. Ellis left immediately for Key West to deliver and discuss General Hanscom's intent.

*   *   *   *   *

Late in the day Colin Powell, Donald Rumsfeld, and Paul Hanscom sat down in the Oval Office. The President cordially greeted them and settled in for discussion.

President Bush began, "Please accept my sincerest congratulations for a job well done. I believe we will soon have confirmation that *Mundo Nuevo* is truly out of business. Prime Minister Blair has faith that he will soon close the deal with Fidel to ensure that the defunct program is not resurrected. Now please tell me your opinions regarding what we can do for the good Major."

After twenty minutes, the President cut off their discussion on what to do for Mike Trantor. "Enough. This is simple. We have a man at risk that has carried the mail for us with incredible bravery and unquestioning loyalty. If we can locate Major Trantor, I, without reservation, approve the execution of a discreet surgical strike to recover him. Ideally, the rescue will not be directly traceable to the United States, but I will personally take responsibility and be accountable to the American public and the Congress if somehow this blows up on us. Just let me know if and when we are going to launch."

In spite of potential risk to the 2004 election, the President had decided to take the risk and approve the recovery mission.

As he pulled out of the White House's rear entrance, General Hanscom called secure to Joe Cordell with the good news.

01 Oct 2004
Moving as fast as he could, in a haze of pain, Mike had progressed to within several miles of his "go to hell" beach pick-up point. He had used the single intravenous bag in his rucksack. It should have helped for the loss of blood and his loss of water from continuous movement. He buried the bag and moved on.

Deaf in one ear, wounded twice, he had begun taking pain pills. Down to four pills remaining, Mike was spacing them out to try and obtain at least some degree of relief for the long haul. Flies assaulted his wounds, almost driving him mad. The deeper he came into the swamp that surrounded his pick-up point, the more insects he encountered.

Earlier, he had stopped to sew up his leg, using his needle and the monofilament fishing line. His Special Forces cross-training with the "docs" helped. He poured what iodine he had left in the wound, on his arm, and behind his ear.

Two days earlier, Cuban soldiers had nearly seen him as they moved through the woods on well-traveled trails. It was now apparent that he had outdistanced the military, and that he may have broken away from hot pursuit. He had fashioned a cane out of a sapling. He was having more and more trouble walking as his leg began to swell. In fact, his crude fishing line stitches looked as if they would break from the tension.

Mike was becoming sluggish. Burdened with significant swelling behind his ear, a constant fever, an infected left bicep, and a leg wound soon leaning towards gangrene, his movement was slowing. He had a little chow remaining. The Cuban soldier's bread had been a temporary lifesaver. Aware that he was losing momentum, Mike was still fully aware that it was imperative to keep his canteens full. Above all of his current problems, the greatest danger was dehydration.

Mike reckoned he was well over half way to the beach. He would soon be in the thickest part of the mangrove. The mangrove would be a lot safer, but movement would be painful and slow.

After several hours of fighting his way through the incredibly dense foliage of the mangrove swap, in between two and four feet of mucky, dark water, Mike began to slip. The heat was taking its toll, and Mike was now no longer making his normal crisp, logical decisions.

He sat down on a mangrove limb and pulled his feet out of the water. Against common sense and years of training, Mike took out a cigarette, lit it, and took a deep drag. Leaning back, his right hand was shaking as he put it to his lips. He was in such pain he was starting to not give a damn. Mike was becoming more dangerous to both the Cubans and himself.

He shredded the cigarette butt, stood slowly, with the rifle he had appropriated slung across his back. The cane was now almost useless in the mud. He carried it to keep his balance and to probe under the water for obstacles. He moved until after dark, and prepared to sleep, once again in some low branches. He was incredibly uncomfortable, yet he would wait to use his pain pills in the daylight so he could keep moving.

02 Oct 2004

John, Angela, General Joe, Colonel Baker, and four key planners were in a separate room to collaborate on a plan to meet Ellis's intent. They had been ordered to create a plan to rescue Mike with a very small force not attributable to the United States. They could take high risk, yet they were to have virtually no Department of Defense casualties. This was going to be tough.

The planners started through their normal military thought process, taking the intent and developing ends, ways and the means inherent to achieving it. General Joe watched them practice their formulas for a half-hour, growing impatient until he could stand it no longer. He told them all to sit down and listen.

He stood up in front of a blank white dry-erase board. He picked up a marker and wrote:

END STATE: MIKE GETS HOME ALIVE.
MISSION: GET MIKE HOME ALIVE.
CRITICAL TASKS: FIND MIKE. GET TO MIKE.
                        PICK UP MIKE. PROTECT MIKE.
                        BRING MIKE HOME.

"Here's how we do this," he began in staccato tones. "The riggers will fashion harnesses to carry operators from here to Cuba and back, comfortably, with straps that won't hurt their circulation, *hanging from the whirlies*! They must sew a rig to bring back Mike, even if he is severely wounded."

Next, General Joe wrote in large letters on the board COMMO. "The operators will need communications gear that plugs into headsets to talk to each other, and to the pilots back here. And," he added, growling, "on an open secure net so we all can hear what is happening.

"The rigs need to allow for AK-47s and ammunition, to include Russian hand grenades for each operator. Obtain all ex-Soviet ammunition. Remember the need for denial of U.S. involvement. We need to sterilize the whirlies, take all U.S. markings off of any parts, engines, and whatever. Check for hidden data plates. Same with any radios or devices we send along with personnel.

"We need some water and a little chow to go with each person. Add a bundle of dollars for emergencies. At least three rigs need medical kits that are identical in case Mike is in worse trouble than we suspect. Each person must carry a small emergency waterproof radio, so we can find any downed personnel at sea or on land.

"Each rig has to have multiple flotation devices built in that will float someone if required. I envision the pick up of Mike taking less than two minutes. A quick medical check, then strapping him in to his harness and take off, hopping over the trees, dodging in and out, then fleeing to open sea. We should do this at night, so the operators must all be experienced with night vision devices.

"The whirlies are going to get us in, and out. Range is critical—load up the whirlies with men and equipment as quickly as you can and see how far we can go on a tank of gas."

General Joe paused, breathing hard. Colonel Baker was smiling. General Joe, when inspired, spoke in bursts like a machinegun. He was in the zone, creating and innovating on the run. Sometimes he was best thinking out loud.

The General flipped the dry erase board over to the clean side, and drew a simple picture. It was five circles. He labeled them in seconds. Two whirlies for security, they would search, watch for the enemy, divert the enemy, and"—he paused ominously—"anything else required for success. They are Scout I and Scout II."

The circle at the center of the board was labeled "Angela."

Angela gasped. General Joe continued, "Angela is the best choice to pick up Mike because of body weight. She also knows him better than any person under our control, and she worked with him day and night 'in his shoes.' She just might have the key to overcome unforeseen obstacles. Angela has proven her worth in this operation—good with weapons and highly survivable in a Cuban environment if everything goes to hell."

Angela, inwardly screaming for approval, looked at John, pleading with her eyes while trying to remain coolly detached in front of the planners. John simply said, "I agree with your recommendation." Angela, hiding her emotions, coughed gently in her hand.

General Joe asked John if it was okay to bring the whirlie pilots in for detailed planning. He agreed. They took a short break to gather the team.

On the break, Reeve Baker and General Joe had a short conversation in the parking lot. They began with the Reeve's nominations for the last two names for the mission. They were "Robbie," the name of Sergeant Robert W. Brown, a gung-ho volunteer for Baker's whirlie program. The other was "Jimbo," Sergeant James B. Brooks, the newest soldier to pass Baker's tough selection program.

The General continued. "Of course, I'll agree with your recommendation. First of all, you know their capabilities better than anyone alive, and both Sergeant Brown and Sergeant Brooks used to be Special Forces medics. They will be really useful in an emergency. As usual, you are way ahead of me."

"Reeve, I need you to put your own fingerprints on the rig to bring Mike home with Angela. See if we can put some sort of monitor on him so we can get vital signs on the way home. Also see if there is some lightweight bio monitor we can put on the whole team, built into our communication scheme."

Inside the meeting began. General Joe asked, "Do any of you pilots feel that this is too risky? Is this feasible?" Everyone agreed that it could be done. The hardest problem would be arranging the communications and rehearsing the give and take between the suspended personnel and the pilots to get the whirlies to perform exactly what the Jimbo, Robbie, and Angela team needs of them.

General Joe concluded with two comments. "I forgot one thing. I want the lightest weight possible bulletproof vests and helmets for the team. Take an extra set with each manned vehicle for Mike. Additionally, our guidance says, literally, 'virtually no DOD casualties.' Give me an update in six hours."

He flashed a challenging, bulldog glare. "We will submit our plan two days from now *after* we have rehearsed and tested the concept. Angela, start rehearsals immediately, planners can write the plan concurrently, let's have a finished product ASAP. Let me know immediately if something comes up to preclude us from making the timeline." Once again the classic General Joe swept the area with demanding stare. "An intelligence breakthrough could come at any time and provide us with Mike's location. We have to be ready."

General Joe strolled out of the room thinking, "They are all energized, they have direction, they are focused. Now, where in the hell is Mike?" He moved out smartly to start "energizing" the intelligence analysts.

He mentally kicked himself. He had to remember that John was in charge. He was concerned that in his intensity he had stepped on John's toes.

02 Oct 04

Ted had taken Kirsten by the hand and was leading her from the Key West airport towards a taxi stand. Kirsten dropped his hand, and as she adjusted her OU baseball cap, she paused, still protected by an overhang from the gentle afternoon rain. Suddenly she was deep in thought. Ted watched her and patiently waited.

Kirsten had suddenly thought of Mike. Somehow the palm trees and rain had triggered the moment. Mike might be somewhere, once again, unable to come in from the rain or cold.

A wave of guilt hit her and she turned away from Ted, seeing her reflection in the airport's pane windows, still adjusting her hat. She stared at herself, searching her own image, realizing there were two of her; one for Ted, another for her husband.

She looked down to break the image, reaching to again grasp Ted's hand. Mike had left her alone. Alone and lonely, too often and for too long.

Kirsten and Ted didn't make big plans for their first night in the Keys. After checking in to the visiting officers' quarters, they rented some bicycles and headed for a small restaurant off the strip and stopped off for some pizza and beer.

Waiting for the pizza, Ted surprised Kirsten. "Do you see any scenario where we might have a long-term relationship? I think of you day and night. You are beyond any woman I have ever imagined, in all aspects, from intelligence, to beauty, to, well, you know, the other stuff. I have never been so happy, but I'm starting to fear that someday we won't be together. I know you are a little older, but it doesn't make a damn bit of difference to me."

Kirsten looked long at him. She reached across the table and gently held his cheek in her hand. Of course she was perfect. Of course the "other stuff" was fantastic. Ted was under the influence of teen-age hormones. He couldn't be rational.

She replied, "Ted, what will be, will be. Let's enjoy every moment we have for now. The future will come as it will, regardless of what we do or say." Ted raised his glass. He was happy. Kirsten's reply wasn't a no.

Kirsten made gentle love to Ted as soon as they entered their room.

* * * * *

Also at Key West, preparation and rehearsals continued. Angela, Jimbo, and Robbie were suspended in their rigs, separate from the whirlies, dangling in the hangar. The morning's activity was another communications rehearsal. Each man had a bone microphone on his forehead and everyone could be heard in the operations center, and at each pilot station. Their bio monitors and the one carried by Angela for Mike functioned as planned. There seemed no technical impediments to crystal-clear communication.

General Joe, John and Angela had read Mike's "go-to-hell" plan over and over again. If he was alive and had avoided capture, they had to believe that he would somehow make them aware that he was at his predetermined location.

If he couldn't, it was up to the intelligence community to produce. Time was running out. The satellite monitoring the site had not picked up any sign of him so far.

Late in the afternoon, Angela needed to take a short break from the intensive planning and preparation. She decided to walk several blocks from her hangar to the Navy Mini-Base Exchange. On the way out loudly announcing, "Does anyone need something from the exchange? I'm making a run."

Angela was allowed to use the exchange with her fake U.S. Military ID. She was dressed in a standard Army olive-drab flight suit. It fit perfectly with their cover of being guests on the Navy base in order to conduct a training exercise. "You got it," she confirmed the orders. "Two Diet Cokes, a Mountain Dew, and a pack of Camels for General Joe, coming up!" She stretched her legs and reached her arms above her head as she left the hanger, striding out and breathing deeply.

She was searching for the Mountain Dew when she looked up at the woman beside her. Angela cased her automatically. She was wearing a white Oklahoma baseball hat, a maroon low-cut halter-top revealing a tattoo, white shorts with an ankle bracelet and sandals. She was cute, and accompanied by a breathtakingly handsome younger man. Angela froze, staring. The woman slowly turned her head and looked directly at Angela.

Angela recovered quickly, breaking eye contact and searching slowly for the Mountain Dew, trying to stay in listening range. After buying some chips and dip, the couple left, holding hands. Angela watched them cross the street and enter the Visiting Officer Quarters.

Angela paid, then walked hurriedly back to the hangar. She laid the bag of goodies down on the table, singing out, "Come and get it!" She rushed to one of the intelligence computers that had been installed in their rapidly constructed operations center.

She pulled Mike's historical background and personal dossier, rapidly surfing through his personal data. The handsome young stud had called the woman in the Base Exchange "Kirsten." The woman was wearing an Oklahoma Sooner baseball cap. Angela pulled up a photo, dead center of her computer screen. The woman from the exchange, a little heavier and minus the baseball cap and earrings, stared at her.

6 Oct 04
Still wearing their "OU #1" baseball caps, Kirsten and Ted had dirty danced the night away at Sloppy Joe's. It had been great fun,

particularly dealing with the barbs, given in jest, from local Miami, University of Florida, and Florida State fans. They had consumed way too many margaritas, and were stumbling home. It was only three-quarters of a mile to the Naval Base and the Visiting Officer's Quarters, which was one of the best places to stay in Key West. And since Mike was in the *Army*, and this was a *Navy* base, she was confident nobody there would know her or Mike. Over ninety percent of the visitors were Navy or Coast Guard.

Kirsten was woozy. Staggering back on the outside of the base's perimeter fence, they paused to embrace. As they held each other Kirsten looked over at the hangars, lit up in the middle of the night. She saw soldiers in the distance working late and thought of Mike and the incredibly long workdays he seemed to love, and how little the Sloppy Joe's crowd knew about such sacrifice. Inebriated, she discarded the thought, giving Ted a passionate kiss. They only had three days left until they had to fly back to Norman.

CHAPTER TWENTY-TWO

03 Oct 04

The foul odor and growing discoloration of his leg concerned Mike greatly. He had downed two of his remaining pain pills in spite of his plan to conserve them. Luckily he still had a half bottle of antibiotics. He would need them to counter his worsening infections that would escalate in the fetid mangrove swamp.

He built himself a platform with woven saplings using bark as rope. It wasn't fancy, and it didn't look like the ideal in the old Jungle Operations Manual, but Mike's rear end was dry. He could sleep above the swamp's waterline and rest. The Viet Cong had used the same rig forty years earlier, and just like the VC, Mike's chance of being found in such an inhospitable environment was nil.

The mangrove swamp was a safe place for Mike to stand down for at least forty-eight hours. He would elevate his leg, sleep, and take his antibiotics. He had pushed himself to the limit to break contact with the Cubans and to get deep into the swamp. The cost, physically, had been high. Mike's head hurt so badly, he just wanted to lie down, but the throbbing increased in intensity when he did so. He was sure now that he had a massive infection behind his ear. When he probed the area behind his ear, the skin was soft and squishy. In addition, it was over a hundred degrees in the swamp. Mike was sure that this was why his temperature was refusing to come down, even with the antibiotics. His goal was to rest, regain some degree of strength, and then do a final push to his "go-to-hell" point.

Sitting on his platform above two to three-foot deep stagnant water, Mike elevated his leg and leaned back against one of the supporting tree trunks, again carelessly lighting a cigarette. He opened his rucksack to inventory his chow. Remaining were dried fruit, some beef jerky, and a pack of trail mix. At least he had several packs of cigarettes. They effectively suppressed his appetite, which he was losing anyway.

He promised himself he would sleep all day and all night to take the stress off his body. In bad shape, and increasingly woozy, he was sure he had finally out distanced the pursuing Cubans. The heat and his fever made him feel like he was in hell. He stretched out on his hand-made platform and used his rucksack to elevate his head to help with the throbbing.

After a few moments he fell into a deep sleep. Soon flies returned as they did at each stop, to swarm over the wounds on his arm and leg. His head was assaulted too, but his head net offered protection. He did not stir.

05 Oct 04

Fidel ripped General Rojas over the phone. *El Presidente* had given them unlimited assets and the results were next to nothing. The only proof of enemy activity was parachutes, equipment recovered from the cache, stacks of Cuban casualties, destroyed *Mundo Nuevo* facilities, and two flashlight lenses.

Furiously Fidel increased the pressure, "General Rojas, we have the video teleconference set with Prime Minister Blair for the eleventh of October. I gave you adequate time to produce. You have done nothing! Anything other than captured or killed agents is unacceptable. Also tell *Señor* Muñoz that his man, *Señor* Matos, is also going to get the sack if you fail." He slammed down the phone. "To hell with all of them," he shouted aloud, "I am surrounded by incompetents."

General Rojas put down the phone. He turned. *Señor* Muñoz was in the General's office. "Matos is gone too, if we fail," he relayed slowly. Then, more upbeat, he stated, "We are not yet defeated. Our plan for the next phase is this."

He pulled back a curtain covering a map. "The cache site and the site where additional infiltrators may have landed have gone cold. We need to expand our search and use every single resource at our disposal to look for the abnormal. I want you to pull out all of the stops. We need every Communist Party block chief in Cuba to know we are faced with a dangerous a threat. Each neighborhood must be on the alert for strangers. The police and constabulary military units must have the power to summarily detain any suspect without hesitation."

"Organize a media program to advertise on national television that at least one armed and dangerous criminal is loose in Cuba. Our sketch of this man must be in everyone's mind. We must also inform the populace that he has unknown accomplices. Make up a cover story for his crimes. Absolutely ensure that we divorce the media blitz from the truth, that the man and his supporters are enemy agents. We don't want the disaffected elements in Cuban society to believe organized resistance is possible."

The General barked on. "On our part, we are alerting a helicopter force with armed spotters in each, all with infrared night vision goggles and scopes. We will comb rural areas radiating from the location where we think we last engaged one of the agents. If the agents aren't well hidden in deep vegetation we may be fortunate enough to find them."

General Rojas was becoming animated. "We will fly every minute of darkness to try and turn up these insurgents. Hopefully we can find a two or three man cell together, hunkered down somewhere. We will then either engage the enemy with our spotters and their rifles, or we will dispatch our quick response force consisting of truck mounted and helicopter borne infantry."

As the General spoke, he pointed with his pen at a map on the wall. "We are going to focus the search on these circled remote nooks and crannies, inhospitable terrain, where enemy agents and their supporters on the run would feel safest." One of the circles surrounded Mike's swamp.

"*Señor* Muñoz, we both have a lot of work to do," Rojas concluded. "We will call each other every few hours with progress reports." Then with forced good cheer he concluded. "Good hunting!"

6 Oct 04

Mike slept for eighteen hours. He was awakened in the darkness, still groggy, by a helicopter hovering over his sapling platform suspended in the mangrove branches above the swamp. Automatically he put his arm through one sling on his rucksack and grabbed his AK-47 with the other.

The Cuban rifleman in the helicopter was looking at the hotspot in the swamp through his infrared night vision goggles. He examined what appeared to be the outline of a man. As the helicopter hovered and became stable, he put his AK on automatic, sighted and fired.

Mike had rolled off the platform just in time. Tracers and 7.62 rounds chewed up his platform, just a few feet from where he lay. The mangrove was so thick he couldn't run, falling in his attempts. He was stuck, like a fly in a spider's web. Frequently, in mangroves, a unit would only move four-hundred meters in a whole day.

Mike made an immediate instinctive analysis. He found an indentation near some large roots and put himself, rucksack and weapon under water. He pushed his mouth up to the water line and gulped a breath every thirty seconds. He hoped that the water would dissipate his body heat.

It worked. The rifleman continued to put rounds into Mike's improvised platform until it was shredded. His infrared goggles continued to see Mike's shape from his body heat, luckily causing the rifleman to focus where Mike had been in-lieu-of his current location.

As the aircraft flew away, Mike popped out of the swamp gasping. His dry platform was gone along with his crutch.

The rifleman reported on his headset that whatever had been in the swamp was dead, he couldn't verify if it was a man or not. The pilot noted the exact location with his GPS. A search party would enter the swamp and search the location the next day.

Mike had no options left. Even if he made only fifty meters by dawn, he had to get moving. Ill and throbbing, he pulled out his compass and began fighting his way through the vines, brackish swamp, mud, and mangrove. His goal was a garbage dump nearly ten kilometers away. It was his "go to hell point." He was going to have to make it without rest, with excruciating pain, and with dwindling medication and chow.

* * * * *

An infantry patrol had been slugging, cursing, through the mangrove. They had tried to stay "on-line" or abreast to sweep the area. It was impossible. Finally, the squad leader asked for a helicopter to hover over the coordinates recording Mike's location the previous night. The men walked in single file, cutting a narrow path through to right below the helicopter. After half an hour of searching, one of the men cried out. He had found remnants of the man-made jungle platform.

Raúl called Fidel immediately upon receipt of the field report. Castro was animated. "Postpone the conference with Prime Minister Blair. We assuredly are on to something in the swampy region. Woven platforms are definite indicators of human presence. Increase the pressure on General Rojas and his subordinates. Demand success, emphasize reward if they succeed, and stress punishment if they fail." Castro frothed. "Compliment them. Tell them their grateful President grants one more week, then my patience runs out!"

7 Oct 04

Mike was hunched over at the edge of the swamp. He had barely avoided the search party. There was no doubt that the helicopters would be back that night supporting ground troops. The game was up. He could barely move through the swamp with his festering leg wound. He was exhausted. Barely mobile, his ability to hunt for food was limited. He would be in serious trouble in a few days.

His damp hiding spot was ten meters from a dirt road that cut through the middle of the swamp. The road had been bulldozed and slightly built up, about three feet above the swamp, in the 1950s. At the end of the road was a large garbage dump servicing local villages. The dump was periodically torched by local authorities; and the swamp acted as a buffer, keeping rats and other vermin from spreading. At the end of the road the dump, surrounded by swamp, was situated in front of a small, white sand beach, visible except during high tide.

It was almost noon. Mike decided to get on the road and walk directly to the dump, cutting the distance and pain level to a minimum. Mike felt himself fading, muttering to himself that he was "going south." Out of options, Mike abandoned his AK-47 under water. He was going to risk everything. He took off his Cuban army uniform. He was now an ill, tired Cuban.

He stepped out onto the road and began walking on a new crutch he had quickly fashioned with his knife. Storm clouds were rising since it was time for the seasonal midday to 4:00 p.m. rainsqualls. Ill, cornered, wounded, wet and hungry, Mike was as dangerous as he had ever been. He had moved down the dirt trail for thirty minutes, a poor, down and out, crippled Cuban, when he heard a vehicle behind him. It was the army equivalent of a jeep. Mike moved as far to the right side of the road as he could. The jeep, however, didn't pass him on the narrow one-lane cut through the swamp. Instead, the jeep stopped fifteen feet short of his location. A driver stayed at the wheel as two soldiers stepped out.

They shouted out, respectfully, that they wanted to talk to Mike. Mike knew it was over. They would see his bandages and his light skin. They would notice his accent. From his condition, they could surmise he had been living in the swamp.

The soldiers held their AKs at the ready, yet they were very relaxed, slowly walking up behind the feeble man. The lame Cuban's back faced them. Mike lifted his right arm a few inches, and the crutch seemed to be falling away from his body as in slow motion. The two men fixed their eyes on the crutch as it slowly fell towards earth.

Simultaneously, Mike slowly turned, swinging his pistol around in both hands. Mike killed the men with four shots in less than two seconds. He couldn't see exactly what the driver was doing because of the shade inside of the jeep, and he couldn't run to close the distance between his location and the driver.

Mike reached down, grabbed one of the AK-47s, and put it on automatic. The driver of the jeep panicked and reached for the radio mike to call for help, instead of defending himself. Mike riddled the jeep with automatic fire. The windows shattered, the driver was slumped over the steering wheel, dead.

Mike, in great pain, dragged both dead Cubans next to the jeep. He searched the vehicle for food and found some bread, which he stuck in his shirt. He threw all of the Cuban weapons into a pile. His search of the driver resulted in more cigarettes and matches. Mike took them. Quickly, he pulled the five-gallon can of gasoline off the back bumper and poured it over the men and sloshed it all around the interior of the jeep. After opening the jeep's gas tank cap, he poured a trail of gas away from the vehicle and threw the empty can into the swamp, hoping to draw follow-on soldiers' attention in that direction.

It was starting to sprinkle. The squalls would pass through shortly. Mike threw one match, and the jeep went up in flames. The burnt out hulk would block his rear, and might give the enemy something to think about for a while. He tossed the soldier's AKs into the swamp too, ensuring they were under water. Investigators would think the perpetrators of the ambush had taken the weapons, an action which any good insurgent would take. The jeep and Cuban analysis of what had happened might steer them away from looking for a single unarmed man.

The rain was a blessing. It would erase any tracks he was making on the trail and hinder helicopters coming in. It might even cause all of the troops in the area, on foot or in vehicles, to hunker down. Hopefully, it would be hours later before the Cubans would saturate the swamp looking for the enemy that ambushed the vehicle.

Mike moved out as fast as he possibly could with one hand on his crutch. The other was stuffing trail mix into his mouth. The driving rains came in sheet after sheet.

An hour after the rain stopped, Mike arrived at the garbage dump. Making his way around the dump about fifty meters wide and twenty meters deep, Mike saw a beautiful white beach. The small isolated stretch of sand was fresh and clean. Mike almost forgot his throbbing leg and exploding headache. He dropped his crutch. God had provided numerous pieces of driftwood in the right size and configuration. Mike dragged out two of the pieces and put a "T," facing in the pre-planned direction, right in the middle of the small strip of beach.

The clouds had cleared and the sun came out brightly. The temperature rose as the humidity stayed at 99%. The sun would set in a little over an hour. Mike settled back into the swamp, twenty meters or so from the small sand dune that tapered into the beach.

He had reeds, pre-selected and cut, and found low spots where he could submerge. He would have to stay awake all night to listen for ground and aerial pursuers. If he had to, he would go under water. Hours in the water wouldn't allow for the elevation of his leg, and the pain was becoming unbearably intense. Mike feared amputation was a possibility. Yet, in his ultimate misery, he laughed at himself for his good fortune.

At least, awake and in the water, he didn't have to worry about dump rats attacking him if he fell asleep. Under light foliage to hide him from aerial observation, resting on a dry spot next to the swamp's edge, he would slither into his pre-selected underwater "hide-site" at the first sound of man or machine. He now had time for a couple of his captured Cuban cigarettes. There was no worry that trackers might smell them. The dump took care of that.

Sitting on the ground, leaning back against a tree, he smoked left handed, keeping his right hand on or near his pistol. He could no longer run, and his head had swollen to the point where his ear was just an indentation. Mike looked up through the tree limbs above him and saw bright blue sky. He didn't smile, but he was pleased. With the clouds gone, satellites were looking down.

07 Oct 04

It was 6:30 a.m., and Angela was already at work, deep into mission planning and rehearsal. She had moved her place of business to the whirlie hangar. John pulled into the lot outside the hangar and was locking the car when two of his intelligence analysts ran up to him. They were agitated and bursting with enthusiasm, hustling John over to their consoles.

They briefed him on SIGINT that indicated that the day before a firefight had occurred near Mike's "go to hell point." News of a vehicle ambush with three Cuban casualties crackled over the Cuban military channels and intelligence nets. The Cubans were deploying hundreds of troops into the swamp, and helicopters combed the area until dawn.

The entire vicinity was cordoned off in depth, including plans to move elements of the Cuban Navy in to seal off egress by small boats to the sea. The option of using the agent in the British Embassy to save Mike was now impossible unless the situation changed drastically—which was highly unlikely.

For John, the ambush indicated clearly that Mike was alive and was closing on his emergency extraction point. John called for Angela on his radio head set, telling her he had good news.

Hanging from her rehearsal harness in the UAV hanger, Angela "rogered" that she would come right over. She immediately struggled out of the rig and Kevlar protection gear.

John hovered over the two analysts' shoulders. There were three flat computer screens on the wall in front of them. On the first one was split screen satellite imagery of the burnt hulk of a jeep, now rolled over to allow vehicles to travel down the trail.

The other analyst then called John's attention to the blank second screen. An image of Cuba appeared from space. The analyst scrolled down and John took a long breath. The imagery became increasingly sharp. It revealed Mike's "T" annotated on the screen that the photo was taken at 6:00 p.m. Eastern Standard Time the night before.

John became animated, waiving wildly to Angela and Reeve Baker as they entered. The entire command center was stirring, realizing that a breakthrough was at hand. A small crowd was gathering to see what would come on the third screen.

The analyst, still calmly briefing, said, "And now for what we have this morning at sunrise. We tasked a satellite for full time coverage starting last night, and the Pentagon granted our request. Look what just arrived."

A pin drop would have resounded as the scroll down started with Cuba coming up at the viewer, then a quarter of Cuba, then the swampy region about the size of two counties. Then the beach appeared. Mike's "T" had not moved. The cursor pointed slightly into the tree line just behind the beach. Scrolling down through the leaves, the analysts stopped.

The room was silent. Everyone's eyes were on the screen. Angela was next to John. She reached over, grasping his hand, squeezing it hard. Her eyes didn't leave the image as the screen cleared. A hand, holding a 9mm pistol with silencer, was resting on top of a rucksack. It was Mike.

John barked instructions. The analysts started gathering archived satellite photography. Angela had specific requests for information, "Where would be the best places to hide? How would the enemy enter the area? What types of vehicles move in and out of the area, how often, day, night? Where are the Cuban Quick Reaction Forces? Tree height? How many and what kinds of helicopters do the Cubans use to conduct the search?"

One of the analysts, acting as scribe, copied the list. Angela stopped at forty-nine questions. The last was answered on the spot. "Do the Cubans have access to imagery as good as this?" It was about the only question the analysts hadn't already asked. A few minutes later as they worked the list, USSPACECOM returned the analysts' call. There was no Russian or commercial satellite in place at the moment that could scroll down with enough detail to match U.S. coverage.

Angela scurried to finalize the plan, while Colonel Baker and the pilots moved to have their computers updated and focused on the target area so they could begin flying virtual scenarios.

John reached for his red phone. He spoke to Mr. Ellis, promising to have images sent by point-to-point fax immediately. John moved quickly to the point-to-point secure fax with the images of the beach and Mike's hand holding his pistol. Using a heavy marker to circle the "T," he then circled the pistol and rucksack on the other image. Additionally, dates and times of the "shots" were annotated on each image to explain when Mike was seen and how the "T" had vectored the Hybrid to him.

John then wrote a quick note on the fax header.

"Eyes Only" exclusive for Mr. Ellis. The "T" is subject's marker according to plan. Subject is in place to be rescued. The weapon and rucksack are verified as the Subject's (specially designed for the mission). Also enclosed is a detailed brief and map of enemy activity in the area.

As soon as Ellis received the fax, he called General Hanscom. The President agreed to meet them at eleven in the morning.

The Secretary of Defense, also invited, led the small group into the oval office. Extraction by the agent in the British Embassy was no longer a possibility, and the massive invasion by U.S. forces, vetoed by the President earlier, was off the table. The Hybrid option was ideal. The Secretary simply summarized after a three minute brief, details obviated by the photos supplied from Key West, "Mr. President, I recommend we take measures immediately to rescue Major Mike Trantor."

President Bush only asked one question, "When will they be ready to go?"

Secretary Rumsfeld replied, "Tonight."

President Bush quietly closed discussion. "Get it on. Let me know when the Major is in our hands."

07 Oct 04

Ellis called John, instructing him to have the force ready for extraction tonight. It was nearly noon and Angela had her two Special Forces sergeants hanging in their harnesses from the ceiling. She was giving instructions as if they were on the move. They were "dry-firing" their weapons and practicing dropping their magazines to the floor, discarding them, and reloading without looking at their weapons. A young man from the operations center hanger came bursting into the room yelling, "Stop, stop. Ma'am, come quick. Hurry! John wants you."

Angela cut away from her rig harness leaving her weapons dangling by their safety cords. The rig was swinging free as she sprinted into the operations center.

She rounded the corner. John was beaming. Angela's heart raced. John saw her, "Angela, current photography is coming in, look!"

Mike was still there. He hadn't moved. The new super-resolution computer from Space Command was sending its data. She leaned over the analyst's back as the screen cleared. Through the treetops one of Mike's legs was visible from the knee down. Angela had held the custom made shoe, visible on the imagery, in her hand.

She looked over to John, and he gave her even better news, "Also, we've been ordered to go in tonight."

Angela walked over to the photo interpreter, putting her hand on his shoulder. "Watch him all day. Give me a verbal every hour on what you see. I'm going back to work. I guarantee we'll be ready."

*   *   *   *   *

On the 10th, the analysts called for John, Angela, and General Joe. The Cubans had not found Mike, and the analysts were wondering why, since Mike had not moved an inch in hours. The Cubans were saturating the swamp with troops and were keeping helicopters up. Maybe it was luck—or perhaps it was being behind the garbage dump that separated Mike from natural lines of drift—that the Cubans broke off their helicopter patrols before they could spot his body heat.

It should have been easy for the Cubans. Mike was clearly immobile. He had finally lost consciousness during the afternoon. No longer able to move, his body temperature was spiking. He was done, ready to be easy pickings. Angela glared at the image. The analysts were right. She could conclude only that Mike was severely injured.

She ran to the hangar to brief the Special Forces medics on changes to their plan. Mike was no longer able to move and was vulnerable. It was now a footrace to see who would reach him first.

CHAPTER TWENTY-THREE

Bert and Amy had done their homework. There were two main strips on *Isla Margarita*, one in the vicinity of *Playa Parguito* and one near the main beach, named *Playa el Agua*. By independently cruising the bars, eating lunch, making friends with the locals, the two had finally "made" their target.

Art Hildebrand had charged them to find the cell that was laundering money, acting as a coordination cell for international drug trafficking, and dabbling with Cuban and Venezuelan agents.

Amy's best technique was to cruise and flirt. Bert's was to drink and be a combination of David Letterman and Rodney Dangerfield in both English and Spanish. Neither Bert nor Amy asked direct questions regarding the cell, patiently working the edges and slowly developing information in an unobtrusive and virtually undetectable manner.

Prostitutes that worked the *Playa el Agua* strip hung out at a small cantina off the main drag. Amy slowly worked her way into acceptance in the pub by befriending the bartender with lively discussion and exposure of large portions of her ample bosoms via carefully selected beachware. The girls, unlike North American hookers, were true to form and quickly accepted her after they realized that she wasn't competing for customers.

Some of the women had been servicing Cubans, Colombians, and surprisingly, a few Arabs. After this discovery, Amy slowly zeroed in on the activities of the Cubans, while Bert worked the indicated neighborhoods, searching for their cell. It didn't take long for Amy to obtain a definitive description of where the Cubans had their parties. It turned out to be a large rental home, one that housed, depending on who was in town, from four to eight men.

Bert was sharply attuned to Arab involvement, which had surprised him. In his clandestine reports to Art Hildebrand, he stressed the nefarious combination of Venezuelan, Colombian, Arab, and Cuban operators. Art didn't bother to tell Bert that the Arab/Al-Qaeda connection was for the blood diamonds, recently interrupted by the U.S. raid into Sierra Leone. Al-Qaeda, Cuba's *Mundo Nuevo*, and the Colombian drug dealers from the FARC all were dirty, using the cell to garner funds for their common interest—anti-U.S. activities.

Art's reply was a surprise. Bert decoded the message three times to make sure he wasn't in error in his decryption. Oddly, he was empowered to "eliminate" the cell. Bert stroked his chin as he reread the message. He then leaned back, smiling and shaking his head. He'd been had. Art had set him up; there was no way this operation was run by the Drug Enforcement Agency.

Bert realized clearly why he and Amy had gotten the fat contract. They were dirty, tied to British mercenary outfits and the United Kingdom. If he was hit and traced, he would serve the same purpose as the phony evidence left in the raid on the diamond mine—the UK would appear culpable.

Bert typed in his acknowledgment, and asked, "Where is Vicki Dollar? Now we need her for sure." Art came back in a few minutes. "She lands at the airport at 2:50 p.m. local tomorrow. You need to meet her. She's your guest."

* * * * *

Art's request for Vicki had gone through Ellis, and then to General Hanscom. Vicki was a unique piece of work. Originally a University of Georgia physics major, she had switched to law and graduated from Stanford. She moved overseas to Paris and found subsistence employment so she could hang around ex-patriots, artists and "left bank" sorts. In weeks Vicki found that she had the ability to take foreign languages on board quickly.

It didn't take long for the American embassy staff to spot the attractive brunette, and invitations to embassy functions followed. Within two months, the CIA had made her an offer.

During the next ten years, she proved to be an incredible worldwide asset. She was brilliant, absolutely adaptable to the assigned culture. Her vast variety of languages and experiences made her covers unbreakable. Vicki, also, was not averse to having relationships with targeted men if it was necessary for completion of her assignments. This willingness led to incredible success on several high risk missions. Vicki's handlers were amazed again and again. In bed, Vicki's targets always spilled the needed information.

Vicki also had, in accordance with instruction, failed to complete selected meetings, dates, or planned rendezvous. In two instances, her men were found dead, with no clues for the local police. In a third, a man had simply disappeared, never to be seen again. A capable assassin, Vicki had made her bones as one of the best in the shadow world of espionage.

At the top of her game, she suddenly resigned. The CIA tried desperately to keep her, but Vicki was adamant that she was through. After the break with the Agency, she moved quietly to the east coast of Florida to begin her life anew; amazingly passing the Florida Bar Exam on her first try.

During her time in the agency, she had become fast friends with one special operator who had worked with her on two assignments. His name was Bert McNab. They had been through thick and thin together, and for some reason, Vicki found she could communicate anything to the rough, non-intellectual Bert, and the feedback was warming and valuable. He became her safety valve. Fast friends, they had no secrets between them. Even better, they had never had sex together, which gave Vicki's only close relationship with a man a unique character.

Once settled in Florida, Vicki, free from the CIA, called Bert. She was soon to have a baby, and she needed a new start to live up to her responsibilities. Bert never asked who the father was, and Vicki never commented on the subject. Bert was overjoyed when a beautiful baby girl, Alexis, arrived several months later. Bert was to be the Godfather, a secret to everyone except him and Vicki.

Vicki Dollar became a practicing lawyer and a doting mother. To all around her, it was clearly evident that the number one priority in her life was Alexis. Bert occasionally checked in with a phone call. He was proud of Vicki, giving up everything, foregoing the simple solution of abortion in order to have her child.

Bert also realized that Vicki's hardened core remained the same. When her law firm asked for her to defend a rich client in a child molestation case, she shocked the firm by refusing the case and openly stating that if she found out for sure that her client was guilty the man would never show up for trial. Without cognizance of Vicki's history, her peers had difficulty understanding the rabid stance. She called Bert after a hard day of climbing out of the hole she had put herself in by refusing to take the case.

Bert empathized. Vicki was a uniquely equipped and dangerous mother. Any potential threat to Alexis, no matter how far removed, would be immediately eliminated. As usual, talking things over with Bert helped. He made light of her rough day with the firm, reminding Vicki of the first rule of holes. "When you find yourself in one, stop digging."

*   *   *   *   *

Vicki stepped off the plane and walked briskly to the baggage area of the small Margarita airport. Her two bags of luggage had made it, including one with the false bottom. She knew her bags had been switched because of a small rip in the side, just enough to let her know that her handlers had succeeded in transit. In the false bottom were three pistols with silencers, nine magazines of ammo, a stack of clean $100 bills, and several bags of cocaine. The bag was full of beachwear and a belly dancing costume.

Vicki hugged Bert and Amy as soon as she broke through the doors from the baggage claim area. She introduced herself to Amy with her code name and Amy and Bert replied with theirs. They drove away in a rental car, obviously long-lost friends.

That afternoon, Vicki drove the neighborhood to see the physical layout of the target. Bert and Amy rehearsed with her drawing diagrams and schemes of maneuver as they sat around a small coffee table. That night the two girls, dressed in their sexiest outfits, went out to work the bar where the Cubans had been made by Amy. Vicki had some years on her, but she still looked damn good; while Amy was already a known quantity in the bar because of her consistently low cut tops.

The girls started drinking heavily and slowly drew the Cubans over to their location. Vicki, with her excellent Spanish, was soon speaking with the Cubans, acting tipsier than she was, laughing hilariously at their jokes and putting her arm around the most handsome one. Amy joined in, flirting outrageously. Later in the evening, the Arabs joined the Cubans. Around midnight, the girls offered to join the men for some fun in the men's apartment.

Vicki surprised the Arabs by asking them if they would like to see her belly dance, insisting that she was one of the best they would ever see. Vicki had picked up the skill as a means to get back into shape after Alexis was born.

Amy jumped into the lead vehicle with several of the men, nuzzling one of the men's ears as they pulled out of the pub's parking lot. Vicki drove her rental car, with her hand on the thigh of one of the Cubans.

Pulling up to the men's address, Vicki stumbled deliberately getting out of the car, and laughingly said that she had to get her belly dancing gear out of the trunk.

She grabbed the bag and then—arm-in-arm with the Cuban—she followed Amy and the other men into the front door of the rental. The number of pistols in the bag was now two. Bert had the other, watching discreetly from half a block away.

* * * * *

Amy quickly found the bar. She started pouring drinks for the men while Vicki went into the bathroom to change her clothes. Amy, meanwhile, was casing the joint for weapons, while continuing to hang onto the men, touching them to feel for Kevlar vests. There were four men, two Arabs and two Cubans. The Venezuelans and any Colombians, probably out on the town, were going to be very lucky.

Suddenly, Vicki literally burst out of the bathroom in a revealing belly dancing costume. Amy was amazed as Vicki moved in ways she couldn't comprehend. The two Arabs loved it, clapping loudly and excitedly speaking to each other in their native tongue. Vicki danced close to the men, sensing their excitement. After a few minutes of hooting and hollering, the men settled down, and Vicki stopped dancing. She announced, "If you think this was something, wait until the next performance." The girls, giggling, made new drinks and stepped into the small bathroom.

Vicki quickly changed clothes. As she was doing so, they gave hand signals to each other to verify that the men had no weapons on them and no vests. They took out the pistols and flushed the toilet to cover the sound of them chambering their rounds.

The bathroom door flew open and Vicki came out screaming for the men to freeze. Focusing on the left side of the room, moving quickly to the right, she saw one of the men reach for a drawer under the coffee table. She opened up, cold, dropping the men with sequential head shots. Amy was hot behind her as a back up, but was not nearly as well-trained. Luckily, Vicki had put down all of the men in the room so Amy, only trained over the years by Bert in his spare time on the range, didn't have to shoot. Nonetheless, Amy panicked, since only three men were down. One was missing!

Suddenly, she heard a crashing sound in the kitchen. Bert yelled, "It's me, I've got one down back here!"

Amy ran back to Bert, yelling "We've got them all!" Vicki had already placed the cocaine on the coffee table, and littered the $100 bills on the floor. Amy hurriedly collected the drinking glasses and bottles of booze she and Amy had touched, putting them in Vicki's bag for later disposal. Amy wiped the front door handle as well. The three casually walked out of the back door, and the girls took off, slowly meandering towards the dark and now isolated beach. Bert wiped the rear door handle. Prints were probably all they had to worry about. Hairs and DNA evidence would not be collected in this part of the world; if they were, their aliases meant that no match could ever be made anyway. Vicki and Amy would toss the weapons in the surf. The pistols could be found later without ramification since they were untraceable. Besides, by tomorrow noon all three of them would be in the air headed to Miami.

Bert, carrying Vicki's bag, recovered the rental car from its location a safe distance from the targeted house, driving slowly away. The silencers on the pistols had worked. There was no sign of *La Policia*, and no evident concern from the neighbors. The girls would get home later.

* * * * *

Upon landing in Miami, the three claimed their bags and hugged each other goodbye. Bert gave Vicki a kiss on the cheek. He thanked her for coming back to work with him. He had sincerely missed her. After accepting a gift that Bert had purchased on the Island for Alexis, Vicki smiled, saying, "Just think of it. Two days' work and I have completed Alexis' college fund. Four years at Stanford!"

Bert laughed, put his arm around Amy, and walked away to continue on through customs and catch the next flight to Dulles. He punched his cell phone, leaving a simple message that Art would pick up. "Everything completed as planned."

CHAPTER TWENTY-FOUR

The sun had set. All was ready. John had Angela. Jimbo, and Robbie, the two Green-Beret trained medics, staged for one final intelligence "dump." General Joe and Colonel Baker looked on. The weather was perfect. Winds were not to exceed fifteen kilometers per hour anytime during the mission. No rain was forecast and the temperature was not to fall below 65 degrees Fahrenheit.

Of significant concern was evidence of enemy activity in the immediate area of the garbage dump. Continuous satellite observation revealed the closest search to the garbage dump had been approximately three hundred meters away. The only activity observed near the dump itself was one truck, apparently with two workers in the back, shoveling out a heap of refuse. The truck had departed.

Other than the enemy, the major concern was Mike's condition. A rapid medical assessment might be the key to his survival, and it would have to be conducted after sunset with night vision devices on.

Angela led the team outside. The pilots were all at their consoles. The crews were with the whirlies, and the whirlies sat still in the dark, as the three-person rescue force strapped themselves into their harnesses. Angela's UAV had an extra harness strapped below hers, to a separate cable from the base of the whirlie for Mike. The other two also carried spares, just in case the unthinkable happened to Angela.

Final communications checks were made. Call signs were simple: "Angela, Robbie, Jimbo, Scout I, and Scout II." Pilots of the whirlies were simply "Angela P, Robbie P, etc." All calls for command and control were simply "John." John added that he might

turn C2 over to Joe if shooting started and things got crazy. He told
the operators not to worry about voice recognition. Whoever used the
word "John" was definitive boss in this crisis.

The two unmanned whirlies cranked simultaneously. They lifted
up and headed out over the ocean, taking the lead. The other three,
Angela and her two Special Forces teammates, gently rose, and in
formation moved to join their two scouts.

The five aircraft would fly to Cuba in as low-level formation as
possible. Angela and her wing mates had Kevlar helmets, night
vision goggles, Nomex aviator gloves, black flight suits, black knee
and elbow pads, but had tossed off their dog tags during sterilization
inspection. Nothing was traceable except for equipment from the UK
or other international manufacturers.

Scout I and Scout II were up front, Angela centered, and Jimbo
and Robbie to the rear, confident, and ready. They would arrive
comfortably, ready to fight if necessary. Once out over the open
ocean, the whirlies spread out, just barely visible to each other. As
briefed, the pilots would now put the birds on "black." The UAVs
would fly themselves without electronic emission to a rendezvous
point off the coast of Cuba, out from Mike's beach. Angela and her
fellow operators would sustain radio silence unless there was an
emergency.

John called Mr. Ellis with a verbal update. He then joined
General Joe over by the analysts with the current infrared picture on
their screens. They would look all night for any enemy activity.
Collectively they worried about three things. First: Mike's condition.
Second: the Cuban helicopters. Third: Cuban interception of the
necessary signals between the three rescuers in search area.

Mike was delirious; his fever was over 104 degrees Fahrenheit.
Flies covered his wounds. He faded in and out. He needed water, but
couldn't gather his thoughts long enough to take a drink. He had
stopped worrying about the rats from the dump. It was over, and
Mike fell unconscious, his head resting at the base of the tree.

One hour after nightfall, about forty minutes before the whirlies
would rendezvous, the imagery analysts raised their hands, spotting
trouble. There were hot spots, probably helicopters. Currently four
were flying; the analysts could find no others on the ground or in the

air. The choppers were searching an area two miles inland from Mike's location. It appeared they were still centering on the "ambush site" from two days earlier.

It would be critical to brief Angela and the rest of the team on the helicopter threat as soon as radio silence lifted. Angela, Robbie, and Jimbo knew that the Cuban helicopters could mass on Mike's site in minutes. John told the analysts to pick apart the helicopter operational concept. He wanted to know how the Cubans were selecting their routes and what patterns they were establishing. This had been done for days, yet John closed with, "Observe behavior again *tonight*, draw conclusions, and prepare concise directions for Angela within the next forty minutes." He called Ellis.

John was concentrating. As soon as the pilots took control of the whirlies, Cuban SIGINT would see five blips. Assuming the search was surely now Fidel's national priority, it would probably take only minutes for the blips to be noticed, analyzed and forwarded to Havana. A simple radio transmission to the helicopters could turn their attention towards the garbage dump. John thought that only about two minutes on the beach would be a safe window—then they would have to run to the sea and disperse.

Something else was worrisome. The helicopters could chase the whirlies down out over the ocean, since they fly much faster. Angela would lose in a game of hot pursuit. Worse, if any Cuban naval craft were at sea, it could be an enemy sandwich. Luckily, so far, no Cuban Navy vessels were indicated to be in the area of the beach.

John called General Joe over to the white board. They stared doodling their courses of action for contact with one, two, three, or four helicopters. They made the assumption that each helicopter would have a door gunner, a machine gun or two, and night vision capability.

General Joe and John had their headsets on. The whirlies were to be at their rendezvous point in one minute. Sixty seconds later, the pilots, over their headsets, all checked in that the five UAVs were in place, hovering. John quickly gave the intelligence rundown, and said at the end of his long count, the pilots would take over and the team would be heading inland. He counted in order that all on the headsets could hear.

"10, 9, 8, 7, 6, 5…"

Angela, Robbie and Jimbo removed the straps from their AK-47s, loading thirty round magazines of 7.62mm armor-piercing ammunition mixed with tracers. The tracers burned in flight, leaving a streak that looked like a laser. Tracer fire was designed to allow a shooter to 'walk' his weapon onto a target by just watching where the rounds were going. The downside of tracer is that the enemy can see where the firing is coming from. The upside was that these particular ones were of Soviet manufacture, burning green, so they would seem that a Cuban was firing his weapon. Confusion always added to the element of surprise in battle.

They each adjusted themselves in their harnesses one last time for comfort. They each checked the location of their hand grenades and other critical equipment.

"…4, 3, 2, 1, Go!"

Scout I and Scout II, the unmanned vehicles, led the way. Scout I flew to the front or road-side of the garbage dump about six feet off the ground, slowly moving up the trail towards the village. Scout II moved over the dump, looked at the beach, saw nothing dangerous, and moved above the trees, using its night vision camera to try and find Mike.

Scout II spotted something behind where Mike had been laying. The pilot for Scout II, back in Key West, relayed this to Angela, Robbie and Jimbo.

Moments before, Mike had awakened, delirious. Two rats had been chewing on the bloody bandage on his arm. Mike screamed, leaped up, ran blindly into the edge of the swamp approximately thirty meters, hit a tree, and fell backwards into black water about two inches deep. He was knocked out cold. Luckily his mouth was above the waterline.

Angela quickly took the report from Scout II's pilot. She directed Scout II to move deeper into the swamp, but stay above the tree line serving as an observation post. She ordered Jimbo to hover slightly off the beach to cover her and Robbie's rear. She told Robbie to switch his night vision goggles from passive to infrared, picking up heat, as she was doing.

Angela, speaking to the "Angela-P," her pilot in Key West, began sweeping the swamp. She moved above the tree line very slowly. In one minute, she saw a hot spot below, the shape of a man, but she couldn't land due to the trees.

Angela immediately ordered her "P" to hover her craft, thereby remaining stationary. She then ordered Robbie to hover just above the beach, drop out of his harness and move through the swamp to right under her whirlie. She had her AK ready and was scanning the area for more heat emissions. She was a sitting duck and knew it. In Vietnam over 50% of Army pilot deaths were during hover operations.

Back in Key West the analysis desk exploded. "Thank God! We've got him!" one of the men yelled out.

Many kilometers away, two of the Cuban helicopters had just landed to refuel and change pilots. Immediately after they landed, the two others had taken off. Refueling stops, over the last few nights, had taken up to thirty minutes. None were working the Mike's immediate area at the moment, and two was the maximum number of helos that Angela's team had to worry about, unless they were seriously delayed.

In addition to fresh crews, the two Cuban helos lifted off with Colonel Baez in the lead aircraft. Plugged into the helicopter's radios with his headset, he could command and control the helicopters and receive instructions from Havana. He was frustrated; he wanted to engage the enemy desperately, and the search seemed fruitless and endless. The other helicopters, refueling, faded into the background as he gained altitude.

General Joe was thinking that the helicopter threat was diminished simply due to coincidence, or as Karl von Clausewitz deemed it, the "fog and friction of war," events that no one could positively control. The helos had needed fuel at just the right moment to increase the survivability of Angela, Robbie, Jimbo, and Mike.

As Angela, Robbie and Jimbo were being notified to be on watch for the two helicopters, Robbie landed, hopped out of his rig, and left the whirlie hovering just above the beach. He hurried into the woods. Using the sound of Angela's whirlie to guide him, Robbie quickly picked up the heat of Mike's body. He grabbed Mike by the drag strap, sewn on the back of his vest. It was precisely where the strap was supposed to be, between his shoulder blades on his tailored gear. It was Mike, all right.

Robbie exploded on the radio. "Mike is in hand, I verify, Mike is in hand."

There was momentary rejoicing in the operations center. John pumped his arm and cried out, "Yes!" Then, annoyed at his burst of exuberance, he cautioned everyone that there was lots of work and danger still ahead.

As Robbie struggled through the swamp to pull Mike's limp body out to the beach, Angela ordered her "P" to hover her near Robbie's whirlie.

Robbie broke out of the foliage, dragging Mike through the sand and did a quick triage with Mike laying in the prone. Robbie took extreme risk as he turned on a flashlight without filter. He had to go "white light," after removing his night vision devices, to adequately assess Mike's condition in the dark. As many Special Forces Medics do, he put the small flashlight in his mouth. It was a proven technique, and the only way to accomplish all the tasks at hand.

Mike's leg wound was gangrenous but with the enemy minutes away nothing more could be done. He quickly took vital signs with his medical equipment, talking continuously to describe Mike's condition over the radio. The doctors with their headsets on in the operations center relayed advice. Robbie quickly administered two shots in accordance with pre-arranged instruction. He finished, putting an IV in Mike's arm to provide vitally needed liquids.

Robbie called for Angela's whirlie to hover over to his location. Angela's feet were only a few inches off the ground. He immobilized the injured arm against Mike's side and muscled him up into position. Angela helped him snap Mike into the rig using the STABO harness. They struggled for a few moments, finally succeeding in positioning Mike right under Angela and facing her.

Accidentally knocking the Kevlar helmet off her head while rigging Mike's IV on her harness for gravity feed down to him, Angela announced, "To hell with the helmet! Done! Mike is strapped in! Great job, Robbie! Lift me off, NOW!"

Mike was now linked to the bio monitoring system, feeding data into Angela's radio. Robbie watched Angela slowly lift off. Mike was propped up, head in her lap, ready to go. Mike's feet cleared the beach and they were off.

Meanwhile, the Cuban SIGINT center was reporting possible insurgent or agent transmissions at coordinates near the garbage dump. Colonel Baez and two Cuban helicopters, with machine guns and two soldier spotter/snipers each, were screaming their way towards the beach.

The Cuban pilots were excited. The veteran pilot, with Baez aboard, was talking to the younger one on the radio. He mentioned that he hadn't been given a "free fire" zone since he was in Angola as part of the Cuban contingent fighting guerrillas for the Angolan Communist-leaning government.

The senior pilot took the lead and the second helicopter followed him about three hundred meters behind. They flew just over the treetops toward the garbage dump. They would search for an estimated half dozen enemy agents judging by the havoc created in the last few weeks, and the number of SIGINT "blips." Baez smelled blood; he had trapped them at last, their backs to the sea.

Back in Key West John was starting to sweat. He told the current operations computer expert to merge the enemy and friendly actions onto a common operating picture. The results were extremely troubling. John immediately began shouting into his microphone. "Bogies, Bogies! There are two helicopters approaching your position from the inland side. They could be at your location in less than three minutes."

Angela, cool as a cucumber, gave instructions. "Scout I and Scout II, fly on line, about a hundred meters apart. P's head them straight towards the helicopters so we can get as early of a warning as possible. I want to know immediately what they are seeing."

"Jimbo, fly up the trail. Quickly find a hole in the trees to hide and hover. When you hear an enemy aircraft pass by you, pop up and put as many rounds as possible into the following bird. Thereafter, take immediate action to hop and hide until you can get safely out to sea."

Angela's shrill voice dominated the radio transmissions. "Robbie is almost ready to lift, listen for his command."

Robbie had struggled to get Mike's bulletproof jacket on him. In addition, he had to give up on Mike's helmet because of the swelling of his head. Luckily, Angela's fallen helmet fit in Robbie's nylon bag as well. Fortunately for Angela, her bone mike was on a separate nylon web around her skull, not part of her helmet, so communications would still be up. Robbie was picking up all of his medical equipment to "sterilize" the beach and leave no trace of what had occurred. Mike's weapon and rucksack or anything else he had carried was clean as a whistle and of no concern.

Robbie had just completed snapping his harness, and extinguishing the "white light" when he heard the sound of helicopters. Scout I and II came scurrying down the trail with the two Cuban helicopters in hot pursuit. Suddenly all hell broke loose.

Jimbo had heard the helos and waited till the first passed. The worst thing he could do would be to shoot at the lead bird so the second could engage him. He ordered his "P" to pop him up and he held his AK steady, not moving it. He aimed the barrel to a point in space in front of the second helicopter. By holding the AK steady, the helo would fly right through his rounds. As the aircraft came into the right of his peripheral vision he lined up the barrel and squeezed.

For the pilot who saw a stream of green tracers in front of his windshield there was nothing he could do.

Seconds later, Jimbo was screaming into his radio, "Helo is down, trail helo is down!" Jimbo shouted. "Put damn near a full mag in her. They were flying so low, either the pilot flinched or I got him as he flew through my burst. The helo has crashed and rolled. I'll evade the other helo and head to sea. Awaiting orders."

Robbie had not yet lifted when the lead chopper came over the garbage dump. Scout I and II were trying to lure the remaining helicopter out to sea, but one of the spotter/snipers saw a whirlie with a man on the beach. Baez told the helicopter turn back and ordered the spotter/snipers to be prepared to fire.

Robbie shouted for his "P" to lift off immediately. The whirlie rose just as the helicopter was beginning to bank towards his position. Robbie screamed in his radio, "I'm in their sights, MOVE, MOVE, MOVE!"

Suddenly, the helicopter was dotted with green tracer fire from out at sea. Angela had unloaded, trying to cover Robbie. She had pumped a full thirty round magazine at Colonel Baez's helo, trying to draw him away from Robbie on the beach. Robbie quickly realized that she was risking the mission to save him.

Two of Angela's 7.62mm rounds went through the helicopter's windshield. The pilot automatically broke away and headed inland to regroup. One of the spotter/snipers was hit in the thigh by a third round. The sniper cursed violently on the radio as the crew chief moved over to rip open his fatigues and stop the bleeding.

Baez was furious. "We had one in our sights!" He screamed at the pilot. "You coward, if we had remained steady for one more moment we would have had a kill! Turn immediately," he shouted. "NOW!" The pilot obeyed, flying a U-turn over the still burning and smoky hulk of his sister chopper.

Colonel Baez gave a spot report to Havana, "We are engaging the enemy and are in hot pursuit!"

General Rojas himself came on the radio, "Pursue them to their deaths!" he screamed. "Finally we have them! Do not let go. Stay in contact with the enemy. The other two helicopters are on the way!"

General Rojas was sweating. Solid proof for Fidel's video teleconference with PM Blair was almost in their hands.

General Joe grabbed John, heatedly, but not in anger, discussing something literally nose to nose. Workers in the operations centers turned their heads, but the conversation was over in seconds. John was on the radio. "Get to sea, get to sea immediately, put as much distance as you can between you and the remaining choppers!"

Angela countered, "No, I won't go farther out until I see Robbie clearly off the beach."

Robbie answered, "I've lifted and I'm clear! Head for home! Head for home!" Just then the helicopter came over the edge of the swamp.

Robbie had just made it. The whirlies all headed for the sea. Angela screamed, "P's, disperse Robbie, Jimbo, and me. Spread out, spread out! The helo can't chase all of us. Mike is the precious cargo.

They might pursue Robbie or Jimbo or the Scouts. Scout I and II lag behind, get in the way of the helo. Stop it!"

But, Colonel Baez, following Robbie as he broke for the open sea, had seen the flying machine carrying two personnel. He couldn't believe the long blonde hair flowing from the top figure's head. It stood out with great intensity through the night vision goggles, reflecting the moonlight. He ordered the veteran pilot to focus entirely on the aircraft carrying the two insurgents and to ignore the others.

The pilot dodged Scout I and II and left them behind with the helicopter's superior speed, shouting into his mike once again that he hadn't had such a rush since Africa. The helicopter rapidly closed on Angela; as Scout I and II, in trail, fell further and further behind.

The helicopter caught up to Angela, and then paused, hovering to give the sniper a stable platform. The choice to use the unwounded sniper instead of the helicopter's machine gun was a fatal mistake.

Angela was silhouetted against the reflection of the moon on the sea. The sniper assumed that the top position on the odd contraption would be the pilot. A woman pilot? He wondered, staring at the flying hair.

Suddenly a stream of green tracer bullets erupted from the blonde witch's AK-47 causing the chopper pilot to momentarily lose his hover for the sniper's precision, and guaranteed, kill. Angela was still wildly firing across her body as the whirlie crabbed to try to get away.

Angela's pilot, without command, turned her whirlie to run full speed. Angela concurred, screaming, "Faster! Faster! Get me some distance!"

Angela, as she tried to flee from the once again stable and hovering helicopter, couldn't see the red dot of death centered between her shoulder blades. The sniper controlled his breath and slowly squeezed the trigger.

Colonel Baez saw the top suspended body with the yellow hair snap violently forward and bounce on impact from the sniper's bullet. The whirlie reacted to the blow, dancing in the air for a moment.

A split second later, in his headset, Colonel Baez heard the wounded spotter/sniper on the other side of the helicopter shriek into his intercom. "Jesus help us!"

They felt the helicopter shudder, then the aircraft, fire breaking out in the engine, plunged towards the ocean. Scout I's "P," in Key West, without instruction, had chased and caught the helicopter as it hovered. Scout I had flown directly into the main rotor blades. The helicopter was now an earthbound multimillion-dollar piece of twisted wreckage.

The pilot for Scout I came up on the radio, "Scout I is down. Helo has been struck. Need assessment from others if you can see anything. I am blind. Out."

The Cuban helicopter dropped like a rock, coming apart on impact with the water, yet the threat wasn't over. The two Cuban reinforcement helicopters were closing, just minutes out.

John called out over the airwaves asking Robbie if he could spot Scout I. Robbie replied in the affirmative. "It's floating on the sea below me."

John called out orders. Robbie, in reply, pumped Scout I full of holes, and dropped a couple of hand grenades, cooked to go off at the water level, for good measure. John wanted Scout I to sink. Robbie also raked the downed helicopter with a tracer-filled coup-de-grace fire as he pulled away.

Angela had gone dead on the radio. The pilots were still flying, moving the formation out to sea. Angela wasn't answering. John didn't know what was wrong with Angela, and it couldn't matter at the moment. The fresh Cuban helicopters were bearing down on the beach.

John only had one choice, given the fuel available and the threat. He told the whirlie pilots to go black in five seconds, and to program the most direct route back to Key West. Then John pleaded, "Whoever can see Angela and Mike, give me status, quickly! Monitors," he yelled in the control center, "give me the bio metrics on Angela."

Jimbo answered, "I can see clearly, both are hanging limp in the harness." Then the control room went stone quiet. Everyone was in black. The only blips on the screens were the Cuban helicopters.

A red phone rang. It was from the pilot's desk in the hangar. It was Angela's copilot. "Just before going black, I pulsed the bio meters. Both Mike and Angela are alive, but appear unconscious. The doctors are doing a detailed analysis now."

John answered, "ROGER." Hanging up the phone, he said a quick prayer.

The Cuban helicopters arrived moments after the whirlies had dispersed in the night. Inland, the Cuban intelligence screens were blank; no vectors were available to guide the pilots to the whirlies. They had simply disappeared.

The combat action had taken place so quickly that the remaining two helicopters never received an accurate description of what to look for. They combed the beach and the sea, fruitlessly, looking for helicopters, not small UAVs. As the remaining two Cuban helicopters searched the area, they radioed for rescue assets for the still blazing downed aircraft, and the other one, now sunk, with floating debris, barely visible, went unnoticed.

Fortunately for Mike, small naval craft to cordon the area weren't arriving until the next day. The Cubans would use the assets to contribute to an extensive land, sea, and air search. Of course, no agents, insurgents, helicopters, or enemy of any kind would be found.

John and General Joe, inviting Colonel Baker to come with them, went to get a cup of coffee, still listening on their headsets. John said, "I must call higher with an update."

General Joe replied, "Yes, but first listen. Give them only things we positively know. One, we have recovered Mike. Two, Mike is alive but severely injured. Three, we have lost one test UAV at sea. Four, the remaining four UAVs are en route back to Key West. Five, one of our operators may have been wounded. Six, we will not have solid medical status until return. Seven, enemy losses appear to have been two helicopters and crews. Reinforce that this is an initial report."

In his quarters at the top of Fort Meyer, General Hanscom had not yet gone to bed. Ellis was calling on his secure phone. The General looked at his wife. She had watched him during the evening and it was apparent that he had been carrying an extra burden. As he put down the phone he seemed relieved and at peace.

General Joe left the operations center. He was in his element. He had seen far too many operations screwed up at the end simply because units thought the hard part was over. He would get everyone refocused on the tasks at hand. Joe firmly believed that Yogi Berra was right. In combat for sure, it ain't over 'til it's over.

He verbally fired up the medical unit. Trauma specialists and surgeons received special attention. He made them tell him every single thing they would do from the time Angela's bird landed until casualties were loaded in the waiting MEDEVAC aircraft for transport to Walter Reed Medical Center in Washington, D.C.

If emergency surgery was necessary, they had the finest state of the art Army gear all set up right on site, to include x-ray machines, scanners, everything.

General Joe then went to the crews and asked how they would handle all the birds coming in—disposal of ammunition, maintenance, damage from enemy fire if any. Finally, he went to find the pilot of Scout I. The pilot was a bit saddened. Although Scout I had been the savior of the day, the pilot and the whirlie had been a team for almost a year. It was a personal loss.

The General understood, thanking the pilot for a great job. "Mission success lies on your shoulders. You saved lives tonight, and the best thing is, you didn't wait for orders. You made the call to knock down the helicopter to save your buddies. Fantastic."

The airman beamed.

General Joe walked back into the operations center. Thirty minutes had passed. There was an odor of pessimism in the place. Joe couldn't stand it. He waved at John and shouted, "Huddle, huddle!" The key operations center players gathered around. Joe started off: "I want an immediate assessment of what will happen if we turn Angela on, just her. What will the Cubans see now, since she is far off their coast? What will the cost to the mission be if they track her to the U.S.? I want an estimate in five minutes." He walked out and spoke to Angela's pilot. The pilot was ready.

The answer came back. The leaders all huddled one more time. They decided to take a small degree of risk. A single emitter probably wouldn't cue much for the Cubans. A single blip could simply be a small Piper Cub or the equivalent.

The pilot immediately took Angela's craft off black. John spoke clearly and loudly, "Angela, this is John. Angela, this is John."

For a full ten seconds there was nothing. John looked at General Joe. Then the radio cracked, "John, Angela here." Her voice was faint.

John asked, "Angela, what is your status?" She replied, "I just came to. It feels like a sledgehammer hit me in the back. I think they shot me dead center of my 'chicken plate.' I can't find any blood but I am having some trouble breathing. Maybe I've some broken ribs. Mike is still breathing, and I can feel his pulse in his neck."

John replied, "The doctors are going to take over now, they will be reading your bios, work with them to get the best advice for you and for Mike, we'll see you soon."

John and General Joe spoke about how armored vests save Special Forces' bacon every time they go out. Clumsy, hot, and uncomfortable, they are the cats' meow in every fight, especially when the heavy "chicken plates" are installed.

More good news came in. Cuban radio traffic analysis indicated that no one had reported accurate information on the whirlies. The Cubans continued to call them helicopters, but had no real description. The traffic also indicated that the Cubans were pulling out all the stops to intensify their search.

Things were looking up until the crew chief for Angela's whirlie came running in. The airman demanded, "Quick, have Angela jettison her weapons, ammunition, pistol, all emergency gear, etc. We are low on fuel. The fight took longer than we had anticipated, and the wind has turned unfavorable. The wind and the combined body weight of Angela and Mike are sucking the tanks dry."

Angela was called and immediately started dumping everything loose in her kit minus medical equipment for Mike. She also kept her radio.

John asked the pilot if Angela would make it. He replied, "They may not." John demanded, "Is it really that bad?" The airman nodded. John asked, "Would fifteen miles make a difference?"

"A critical difference," the airman replied.

John told the pilot to fly the whirlie to a public beach fifteen miles south in the Keys. The marker would be the Army ambulance with the light on the roof turned on and spinning. The trauma team and the best doctors were dispatched immediately. As General Joe frequently said when the troops really got motivated, "Assholes and elbows start flying."

And they were. In minutes a convoy sped off the base towards the beach. John called in an additional transportation crew. He told them to get one of their trucks and a bunch of canvas down to the beach to hide the whirlie.

A forklift on the back of another truck would follow to lift it into the truck. He wanted as few people to see the UAV as possible. So much for operational security!

The pilot was shouting into his microphone, "May Day, May Day! I'm virtually out of fuel. On the beach I will hover in place for a second. The reception crew must immediately cut the straps to Angela and Mike, then I will fly away, heading in the direction of the truck. Crew, drop the sides of the truck and I will try to put the whirlie directly in the back. Everyone must stay clear. If I run out of fuel and crash the spinning rotors could be fatal. I repeat, stay away from the truck. Also, tell me when Mike and Angela are cut free. Just yell, 'FREE, FREE, FREE,' so I know I can break for the truck."

"The computer says I have almost no fuel left. I am ONE MINUTE from your location! Here I come!"

The reception team had surgical knives from the doctors. The whirlie came in from the sea and quickly hovered. The straps were immediately severed. The crews cushioned Mike and Angela's fall while screaming a chorus of "FREE, FREE, FREE!" which echoed on the radio net.

The whirlie headed toward the back of the truck, hovered momentarily above it and fell like a rock. The truck bounced crazily from the shock to its suspension system. The pilot saw the computer screen flash red in the bottom right quadrant. FUEL EXPENDED was flashing over and over again. Success, in this case, measured in seconds.

Soldiers, as they always do, had innovated on the spot, somehow managing to land the UAV in the back of the flatbed, allowing it be covered by canvas immediately and transported back to the base. John called the unneeded forklift to turn it around. During the beach operation, the other three remaining whirlies had landed at the base as planned. All were low on fuel.

John and General Joe were glad to MEDEVAC both Angela and Mike to Andrews Air Force Base, near D.C. If Mike came around it would be therapeutic to have her with him.

The MEDEVAC aircraft took off and John submitted additional reports to Mr. Ellis. Immediately, the operation started closing down and sterilizing. Quickly, piece parts of the team started folding up and leaving. The cover with the Navy had worked. Everyone on base thought it was just another exercise.

Mike, still unconscious, was on a stretcher in the MEDEVAC bird. Angela was lying on the cot next to him. She had taken some painkillers and had fallen asleep holding his hand.

Later in the night, General Joe and Reeve Baker had a few beers, once again, with Robbie and Jimbo, the pilots and crews. There were new war stories stirring their blood.

The next morning General Joe, Colonel Baker, and John said their good-byes. Cuban intelligence reports still indicated that the whirlies had not been compromised. The soldiers and airmen would be returned to Reeve's unit in one more day. The members of the disbanding Hybrid all promised to keep in touch, the way soldiers always do.

Late that night, the President received a call. Mrs. Bush watched him hang up the phone. He paused, closing his eyes. She looked at him quizzically. His only comment was, "Honey, some days I'm simply proud to be an American."

CHAPTER TWENTY-FIVE

13 Oct 2004

President Bush had been a pleasant surprise once again. He had ordered the entire operation to be classified as TOP SECRET and non-releasable for twenty-five years. Election or no election, he wanted no credit, no spin, nothing. The Hybrid was too valuable an investment to be exposed. The war on terror would probably necessitate reactivation over and over again.

One of his closest advisors had reminded him of Chancellor Schmidt's "outing" of German Special Forces, called the KSK, immediately before his failed attempt at reelection in the late '90s. The German unit had just completed the German Army's first combat operation since World War II, with complete OPSEC. Years of hard work were sacrificed on the front pages of German newspapers for political purpose.

Overall, the interagency, distributed unit concept was working well. Press leaks did not happen. Players were beginning to trust the "non-organization." The final determination of complete success would be on Friday, the fifteenth of October, when Castro and the Prime Minister spoke. The videoconference had been moved up three days. President Bush had faith that PM Blair could close the deal.

The strategic decision of most benefit, General Hanscom believed, was the use of Britain as the U.S. front. President Castro would negotiate with Britain, whereas he simply couldn't work with the United States because of the decades of animosity.

Ellis summarized for Hanscom: "I am most proud of how we can pick the best personnel, regardless of agency or department. Major Trantor had the right skills to begin. We brushed him up to increase survivability. We did not know if events would force him to survive in the field, his natural element, or whether he might have to try the high road as a tourist in an urban setting. His instincts were superb. The chaos he created was the ideal complement for our non-kinetic activities. Other bright lights were Angela from British intelligence and the UAVs."

He concluded, "Our biggest operational lesson is that we need to develop long distance weapons as a major defense effort. The UAV is a part of the program. Think what incredible things we could do with unmanned platforms if we made them a number one priority. If we can wean the Air Force from its fighter pilot mentality, the possibilities are endless."

Hanscom nodded. "Good job. I want you to take a week off with the family, then we'll begin another project." He paused, asking, "How are Angela and Major Trantor?"

Ellis replied, "When the MEDEVAC landed the Agency had their ambulance on station and took Angela away. She has two broken ribs, severe bruising, and is doing well. She could be released today. British intelligence says they'll never keep her in a hospital for long. She is known as a tough cookie.

"As you know," Ellis continued, "Mike is still in Walter Reed. His leg is so infected that his wound is being reopened, cleansed, and then will be maintained open for several days. His arm is in pretty good shape. The infection behind his ear is serious, but can be controlled. Doctors will measure the amount of damage as Mike begins to respond. He is still not fully conscious. The doctors say he may come around sometime tomorrow."

Ellis started to leave, then halted. "Two other things, sir. After Mike recovers, we will conduct a final after action review to capture all the lessons from this operation. Secondly, as you know, for security, we have legal exemption and authorization to wiretap U.S. citizens, even though we can never use it for criminal charges, and we cannot store the information. We inadvertently captured proof of Mrs. Trantor having a torrid affair with a student. Meanwhile, Mike is delirious in the hospital asking for her. I have grown to respect Mike greatly. Is there some way we can influence the situation?"

"There may be something that can be done," General Hanscom responded. "Thanks for caring about one of my soldiers. Good day." Mr. Ellis left and Hanscom buzzed for his executive officer.

When the executive came in, General Hanscom gave instructions. "Please call the Army staff to stop official notification to Mrs. Trantor that her husband has been hospitalized. Then get me the Army Chief of Staff on the phone. We need some help."

*　*　*　*　*

General Cordell landed his Army executive jet at Oklahoma City's Will Rogers World Airport. His rental car was ready, and he headed south towards Norman on I35. Within two hours he found Kirsten's house, looked over the campus, and had walked into the university weight room.

In-lieu-of immediately finding Kirsten, General Joe decided to wait until the next morning. Although Mike had severe wounds and was extremely ill, his life was not in question, Joe could take a little more time than the usual casualty notification. By Army regulation, a casualty notification to a relative was done in a dress uniform, frequently with a Chaplain in attendance. General Joe was going to forego normal protocol. He intended to use his visit to start bringing Kirsten back into the fold.

The tapes from Mike's phone revealed that Kirsten and Ted would almost always lift weights early in the morning. Joe wanted to contact Kirsten in front of Ted to start building a wedge between the two, not because of Army business, simply because he loved Mike and wanted to ensure that Mike would have at least a fighting chance at saving his marriage. Joe checked into his motel and went to bed early. The next morning he ran before the sun came up, and ended his run at the OU Student Athletic Center.

Kirsten and Ted, not feeling a bit guilty about skipping a week of school, were pumping hard. Kirsten was lifting as Joe walked into the center. She was in better shape than General Joe had ever seen her. The handsome, clean cut young man with her had to be Ted. Kirsten was doing sets, concentrating, dripping with sweat.

General Joe walked straight towards her. She was still lifting so he was a blur as she focused on the bar. She finished her last "rep" with Ted spotting. She sat up and Joe was three feet away looking dead into her eyes.

As Kirsten focused, her jaw dropped open. General Joe seized the initiative. "Kirsten, it has been a long time. I'm glad I found you. Is there somewhere we can have a talk? It is about Mike."

A wave of nausea hit Kirsten. She quickly stood up, shaking as she tried to towel off, looking for her gym bag, stammering and confused. She was in shock. Mike was either wounded or had been killed, otherwise the General would have never been sent.

The General said to Ted, "Young man, could you hand me her bag?" Ted responded without saying anything. He wanted to help Kirsten, but didn't know what to do. Joe looked Ted dead in the eye, cold, as Kirsten was still distracted. "Young man, this workout is over. This is a private matter, government business, and about Kirsten's husband. Leave us alone."

Joe immediately grasped Kirsten by the arm and started moving her towards the door of the fitness center. Ted was standing still. Dumfounded, he hadn't moved.

Crying, Kirsten demanded, "Is he all right. Is Mike all right?"

As soon as they got out the door, General Joe answered. "Yes, he will live. He has been through a lot. I will explain."

Joe started the rental. He asked if he could drive her home or if she needed a cup of coffee or anything to help. Kirsten wiped tears from her eyes with the towel. She asked that he pull into a small diner she had come to enjoy. They could sit and talk over coffee.

They sat down, and Joe began. "There has been a terrible training accident. . . ."

Kirsten, trying not to make a scene, leaned over the table, clenched her teeth and grabbed Joe by the shoulder pulling him towards her. "Don't hand me any of that Special Forces bullshit! I know goddamn well that Mike was on another one of his goddamn secret operations. You bastards are going to keep him away from me my whole life, and my reward is that you are eventually going to bring him home in a box! Tell me the truth or I am going to walk out of here and never look back."

General Joe was amazed at the strength of her grip. He was glad to see her anger, and glad to hear her complaint up front. He hoped he could start healing the wounds now. "Okay, Mike has been shot in the arm; he has been hit in the leg by what we assume from the jagged wound was shrapnel, maybe from a mortar or artillery round. He has a severe cut on his head which is acutely infected and which has him delirious at the moment. His hearing may be diminished. He is receiving a regimen of antibiotics and other care that should have him coming around late today or tomorrow. How this happened to Mike is not what is important."

Kirsten was calming; she was concentrating on the wounds, trying to comprehend them. Her adrenaline level was coming down from her eruption a moment earlier. Kirsten softly said, "Go on."

Gently General Joe set the stage set for maximum impact, "What is important is that the doctors want you to come be with Mike. Drugged and ill, in and out of the edge of consciousness, he is asking for you."

Kirsten started crying again, softly. The General continued. "I want to leave not later than four o'clock from Will Rogers' executive lounge. We can be in D.C. by eight, and with luck at Mike's side by nine. I will have a car waiting in D.C. I have already made a hotel reservation for you. I'll pick you up at three this afternoon, if that is agreeable."

Kirsten nodded, dabbing her eyes. She would need to pack, contact all of her professors, and talk to Ted. "How many days?" she asked.

General Joe replied, "Pack for four." He was moving to pay for the coffee they had ordered. He came back, escorted Kirsten gently out, and dropped her off at home. Her eyes were rimmed in red, and she was shaken.

Kirsten packed quickly, called three professors and had to leave messages for two. Her neighbors would pick up her newspaper and gather her mail. She would not call Mike's family until she had seen him.

She was now in a quandary. She loved two men and one of them needed her this minute. There were no good options. She felt awful, a headache was coming, and she had no appetite. She had put off calling Ted till everything else was arranged. Slowly she dialed the phone. He picked up. "Hello?"

Kirsten thought that a direct burst was best. "Ted, I am doing okay. I have to leave. Mike has been hurt in a training accident and is in the hospital. I need to be with him."

Ted asked, "How long will you be gone?"

Kirsten replied about four or five days and added, "I will call you from Washington."

Ted said, "I'm sorry, and I sincerely hope Mike is okay. I'll miss you." He hesitated, and then continued, "Call when you have a return flight. I will come and pick you up. Kirsten, I really love you."

Kirsten replied, "I love you too." She hung up. Ted had rehearsed his comments. He had let her know that he was supportive and that he loved her. She walked over to the mantle, picking up the poems Ted had sent her and set them gently back down. She put her arm on the mantle and leaned her head against it staring into the fireplace.

*   *   *   *   *

Kirsten sat down and strapped into her seat on the executive jet, mentally exhausted. She was next to the window and Joe had the aisle seat on her right. They took off, making small talk. After the plane leveled off, she asked for a pillow, telling the General, "I am strung out. I'm going to rest so I can be fresh when I see Mike tonight. Sorry."

Joe pulled out safety instructions from the seat pocket in front of him. He nonchalantly acted as if he was reading it. He swallowed, and without turning his head, he began to speak. Kirsten, while fluffing her pillow, paused to listen. Joe began, "I've had a lot of fine soldiers get wounded through the years. Each family has to handle it their own way. The really sad cases were those at the end of Desert Storm and Vietnam, where the wounded would come home to find their wives either gone or on the way out."

Kirsten looked at Joe, but he still stared straight ahead. "Many of the wives didn't realize that their men needed them desperately, and would forgive anything that might have come between them. God didn't make men or women to be angels. Frequently the men, after the trauma, were better husbands, more supportive and understanding. The lucky couples were those that could communicate, and work things out as a team. I think the bottom line to reconciliation after time apart, particulary in the military, is simple forgiveness."

He paused, looked into Kirsten's eyes and said, "I do it every day."

Kisten, tired, bags under her misting eyes, replied, "Can I borrow a strong Army man's shoulder?"

General Joe gallantly answered, "Sure, anything for a pretty young lady."

Kirsten put her pillow next to Joe's shoulder and placed her head softly against him. She reached over, squeezed his arm before dozing off, and said, "Thanks."

15 Oct 2004

As Kirsten dozed, her head on General Joe's shoulder, Fidel Castro was walking into his secure video teleconferencing studio. Raúl and a single, trusted stenographer were present and would watch off camera. Being a few minutes early, Fidel took his seat, and asked if the screen and audio were activated. The answer was that the studios were linked. On the screen was a briefing room in London.

There was no audio; everything would be muted until the Prime Minister showed up. Fidel began, "His audacity confounds me. The United Kingdom has invaded Cuba, killed over two dozen of our citizens, may have founded an insurgency, and now demands that this video teleconference be moved up in time. Lastly, the Prime Minister sets the schedule, and makes me sit. We have one minute till this starts. What the devil is the PM up to? Does he want war?"

He asked Raúl, "You do have the evidence?" Raúl nodded.

Laid out, in an adjoining small room were the pager, parachutes, all the cache equipment, and an assortment of large blown-up pictures of the chaos: the crashed helicopter and several photos of the destroyed buildings of the *Mundo Nuevo* compound.

The PM entered the picture ten seconds early. He sat down smartly and pushed a button on a small console in front of him. Raúl, out of sight, did the same. The two rooms now had audio.

PM Blair began, "Mr. President, it is so good of you to change your schedule to accommodate us. I am greatly appreciative."

Fidel replied, "Good day, Mr. Prime Minister. I hope the family and the baby are well." Raúl smiled off camera. Fidel, the charming diplomat, was at work.

The PM smiled, "We are all are quite well, thank you. I also hope things are fine with you and yours." Fidel nodded.

The PM went directly to business, "The purpose of this VTC is to make a proposal. Frankly, I need your help. Give me a few minutes to explain, if you please."

A chart with a blow up of Heathrow Airport was handed to the PM. Looking directly at Fidel, he began. "In a little over two weeks, I brief Parliament on my plans to build bridges to Latin America to increase trade and to enhance relationships. We, frankly, have not kept pace with recent US, Japanese, and Chinese initiatives. I would like to use Cuba as an illustration of our commitment."

The PM then turned to the chart. "The area in red is where I envision a *Cubana de Aviación* operational hub. Space and access to Heathrow are at a premium, as you know, yet, we are prepared to provide a twenty-year lease at no cost, to include *gratis* installation of requisite computers and telephone links. We are willing to redesign the associated hangar, within some budgetary constraints, to your desires. I sincerely hope our offer will bolster Cuban tourism, thereby setting the stage for improved relations between our nations. Nothing could be better to signal our intent throughout the hemisphere. With your concurrence, our embassy in Havana will set up a visit of representatives to Britain to begin negotiations on realizing this initiative."

Raúl watched Fidel's body language. He was stroking his beard deep in thought. His eyes were on fire. It was obvious that Castro was disturbed. He had come to the VTC to try and find a way to reach through the electrons and choke the PM. He now had to quickly sort through options. A master at strategic issues, Castro immediately shifted to horse trading. He began, "Your proposal fits perfectly into our schemes to enhance European access to our beautiful beaches and climate. On the surface, your offer seems quite attractive, yet," he paused for at least ten seconds for emphasis, "there are some issues outside of this one that impede my outright acceptance."

The Prime Minister seized the opening, "Absolutely true. In the past we have had some differences over weapons of mass destruction. Our policy is that we simply can't tolerate proliferation."

Castro stiffened, Raúl's eyes opened wider. Surely the PM would not openly acknowledge *Mundo Nuevo* and UK involvement.

The PM continued quickly. "I am speaking of the '60s missile crisis, of course; but now, I think we are ready to move beyond past concerns. In fact, I see a new day coming. One where the entire world respects the sovereignty of the Cuban nation. One where we work communally to solve problems. We and Cuba, as we know, will always work in pursuit of our respective best interests, and friendly inter-state competition will always be a part of our lives. Nonetheless, our two great nations can, undoubtedly and mutually find ways to move forward."

Fidel weighed the proposal. The offer on the table was clear. If Fidel guaranteed termination of *Mundo Nuevo*, the Brits would terminate their military activity in Cuba, return to normal "competition," and would fund a foothold into a key tourism market. The proposal made absolute sense for the cash-strapped Cuban nation. The hub in London could prove to be a bonanza. Politically, Cuba could use the UK effort to embarrass the United States.

Raúl watched and took mental notes. Fidel was about to vote. Raúl, as the heir apparent, would eventually be making weighty decisions, as this one, himself. Fidel spoke, "Mr. Prime Minister, I agree in principle. There is a lot of work to be done. We will have a team in London within thirty days. Everything collapses, of course, if we do not immediately, this moment, return to your stated 'friendly inter-state competition.'"

The PM grasped the opportunity to close the deal. "I am quite pleased to hear your comments. I agree wholeheartedly. We look forward to hosting your representatives in London. Thank you."

"One other thing," Fidel added. "We need to synchronize the announcement of our common enterprise. I would like to ensure that we both simutaneously let our constituents know that we are taking this step."

The PM simply said, "Agreed."

"So be it. Good day," Fidel concluded.

The screen went blank, Fidel spoke to Raúl. "Great, now I can be first to announce our new relationship with Britain and stick it up the *Yanqui* backsides." Fidel ordered the stenographer out of the room, telling Raúl to come and sit by him and take notes. He told him exactly what he wanted to do to monitor the entire country to see if the British were truly going to take apart whatever organization they had created. The full intelligence capability of the nation would focus on one single item for the next fourteen days: Indicators of hostile activity inside Cuba by the UK or UK-sponsored actors would be briefed daily on results.

He closed by saying, "I want General Rojas, *Señor* Muñoz, and *Señor* Matos standing in front of my desk in one hour."

* * * * *

The three were at the position of attention in front of the President's desk. General Rojas seemed controlled and resigned to his fate. *Señor* Muñoz was worrying that Fidel might see his legs shaking in his slacks. He was terrified, trying to be brave. *Señor* Matos, a man who had tortured for Castro for thirty years, was cold and detached. He knew that death might be imminent. If so, he wanted it quickly.

Castro left them at attention to keep them uncomfortable. He began quietly.

"I am upset that we have lost so many good men because of your incompetence. The funeral of Colonel Baez will be tomorrow. He was an innocent, fine young man, serving his nation proudly. He tried to fix what you had broken, yet he failed.

"Collectively you have his blood, and that of the others, on your hands. If you had been able to keep a secret, if you had been able to execute your charter and keep the nation safe from external threats, none of this would have happened."

"Therefore, it is your duty, now, to help the families that have sacrificed so much. We must let them know we love their sons and husbands. Tomorrow, Colonel Baez will be interred after a small military funeral at his brigade headquarters. I will attend since he is the highest ranking man to die. You three will also attend, to carry the casket since you helped fill it. His family will consider it an honor; I have spoken to his wife. The casket will be carried all the way to the burial site, on foot. It is seven kilometers. I want each of you to think of Colonel Baez' blood oozing needlessly from his body as you sweat in your service to him."

"The day after tomorrow you will all resign from government service. General Rojas, you will retire in the grade of Lieutenant Colonel, move immediately from your home, and lose all general officer privileges. I think one step below Colonel Baez' rank of full Colonel is an appropriate retirement grade to remind you of your failure. *Señor* Matos and *Señor* Muñoz, you will retire with the same civilian equivalent of grade. You too will be stripped of all executive privileges. Of course, your retirement payments will be reduced accordingly."

Castro concluded, "We have come many miles together. I know you feel this punishment is just and merciful. Today I have done the best I can to repair the damage in negotiation with Prime Minister Tony Blair. I believe I have the sincere commitment of the UK immediately to cease any military activity in Cuba. In addition, you will soon hear of UK economic reparations to pay Cuba for damage done. You are dismissed." General Rojas smartly saluted, while the others stayed at attention. They turned and rapidly exited the office.

Fidel looked down at an open folder on his desk. On the left was a 8"x10" glossy of Colonel Baez along with his biographical sketch. On the right was an award citation for one of Cuba's highest defense medals. Fidel was using the information to mentally prepare his remarks. He would award the medal to Colonel Baez's wife. Pausing, he found himself wandering in thought through the last fifty years, thinking of the heroic sacrifices of his loyal followers. Castro looked up and called for his secretary. As she entered the room, he requested that Raúl be sent in.

A few minutes later, Raúl entered. Castro was sitting rigidly, looking out of his window. He turned slowly and had Raúl take a seat. "Raúl, my health is not what it once was. I will not hide from you, as I will from all others, my absolute certainty that the United States was behind our recent debacle. Their British lackeys, I am positive, are simply covering for their ally. I fear that I will not be here to witness America humbled and humiliated. You, as my heir apparent will now hear the unspeakable, and learn what should not be known, outside of a few trusted men of parallel purpose."

Castro slowly stood and walked wearily over to Raúl. He leaned over and grabbed both of Raúl's hands in his, highly agitated and shaking. Taken aback, Raúl had never seen Fidel in such a state.

"On my recent trips to Palestine, North Korea, China, and Venezuela, I reaffirmed our commitment to help those pledged to destroy *Yanqui* imperialism and its corrupting influence on the poor and oppressed nations of the world. You must promise that if anyone of these nations, or their surrogate organizations, even Al-Qaeda, come to you, you will provide comfort, aid, and assistance."

"Their triumph over *Mundo Nuevo* was only a temporary setback in the struggle. Even though our bio program is dead, attacks on the U.S. occupation forces in Afghanistan and Iraq are a continuation of our fight and we must be cautiously in support. There is a new breed of warrior unafraid to die, rising from the desert, that will strike America for us. Swear now that you will unquestioningly support their requirements with all of our nation's resources. I hope with all my heart that I can live to see America's blood running in its streets."

Castro was out of breath, still shaking with intensity. Raúl answered, "I so swear."

* * * * *

In London, the PM had already relayed the agreement to the President of the United States, George W. Bush. The information was quickly passed to the Secretary of State, Secretary of Defense and the CIA. In a word: *success*.

Simultaneously, Fidel was told that his cell on Margarita Island had been attacked and his agents had been found murdered. Fidel clutched his chest and ordered his secretary to leave the room. He could barely catch his breath. In severe pain, he swore Raúl to another oath: an oath to someday, somehow, kill President Bush and destroy the United States of America.

CHAPTER TWENTY-SIX

CIA Headquarters
Langley, Virginia

LTG Hanscom called the NSA director to thank him for all of his hard work and support. He followed with calls to other personnel whose assistance had been critical.

The latest reports reavealed that Castro was almost bedridden, propped up on drugs for the funeral of Colonel Baez. LTG Hanscom had privately hoped that the Margarita information would be the final blow that would give Castro a heart attack and put him away. However, for fifty-four years Castro had faced setback after setback at the hands of the United States with little or no apparent effect.

LTG Hanscom looked down at two open folders on his desk. The file on the left contained a photo of Major Trantor, his biographical sketch, and a draft citation for an award for valor. On the right was a file with the same information regarding Angela. The general looked deep into the photos, silently declaring that someday he would thank the two heroes personally.

The new director of the Central Intelligence Agency was next in line for a phone call. "Angela, from British Intelligence, was singularly responsible for the success of the mission to recover Major Trantor. I will send you a written summary of her actions from our perspective. Your endorsement of the CIA's highest award for heroism would be great news."

The director replied, "I'm all over it. My staff already has a draft of their own on the Intelligence Star. Consider it done."

The Chief of Staff of the Army was next. Hanscom concluded, "My executive is sending a draft award citation for Major Trantor. A

Distinguished Service Cross, the nation's second highest medal for bravery, might be appropriate. A Medal of Honor would gather too much attention in Congress. The draft citation offsets his actions to Iraq, and will serve to hide the real mission. A Purple Heart, for his wounds, is also offset in time and place. These actions will allow Major Trantor to be appropriately recognized for his contribution to national security. I personally thank you for allowing us to deploy one of your best and brightest. We are in your debt."

The Chief of the Staff of the Army agreed to accept the packet and thanked LTG Hanscom for taking the time to ensure that an Army officer was being appropriately recognized for distinguished service to the nation.

Hanscom hung up. Ellis reported that General Joe was working with the U.S. Air Force and U.S. Army to obtain recognition for the pilots and their crews, especially the two young Sergeants that were Angela's wing men.

Hanscom leaned back in his chair. Daydreaming black and white, he pictured the foyer inside the grand entrance of the CIA. The design was simple. The large hallway was all marble, to include the walls. On the left was a statue of Major General Donovan, the founder of the Office of Strategic Services, or OSS, which eventually became the CIA. On the right was a simple desk, with a book. In the book were inscribed the names of agents who had given their lives for their country. He envisioned a small gathering of Angela's friends and family. Angela was bowing slightly, a ribbon, attached to the CIA Star, was being placed over her head.

He then saw Major Trantor, in the Chief of Staff of the Army's office, having a small private ceremony. Mike was moved receiving his medals from the leader of the U.S. Army, thinking he didn't need all the attention.

Hanscom sighed, looked at his daily agenda, brushing it aside. He was proud of the interagency teamwork in the Hybrid. He was having one other pleasant daydream before plunging into work.

He envisioned a barbecue going on at Eglin Air Force Base behind an old hangar. Several picnic tables were set up on a concrete pad, and several iced-down kegs of beer had been tapped. In a crowd of servicemen and women were General Joe, Ellis, John, Major

Trantor, Colonel Baker, and a good many pilots and crewmen. Almost everyone appeared ten years older. The old warriors were intermingled with young special operators in fatigues and flight suits. Angela was there too. Some had a snoot full and all were enjoying themselves in the warm Florida sunshine. It was a reunion of veterans that had formed the Hybrid. A small gathering was forming at the edge of the runway behing the hangar.

Several warriors were arm-in-arm, beers raised to give a toast over at the edge of the concrete. A few feet from in hangar, protected by a small scrub oak, was a tiny tombstone. It was the only concrete evidence that the Hybrid existed. The stone was symbolic and the engraving simple, SCOUT I.

Washington, DC
Walter Reed Army Hospital
Angela was released from the CIA-contracted hospital at six o'clock in the evening. She had raised hell all day with its residents and specialists to go home. Finally she was given a clean bill of health, minus broken ribs. Her chest was wrapped tightly and she had medication to help her sleep.

The British Embassy had called her on her secure cell phone. Angela was to report in the next day for onward movement to Otrano, Italy, her favorite spot on the Adriatic. There she would have some precious solitude, intermixed with British Intelligence psychiatrists and other selected debriefers. British Intelligence had determined long ago that a decompression period after each mission was extremely valuable to avoid any ill effects. She would sunbathe, dance with handsome young men if she chose, read several novels, and work out to the degree possible, given her ribs.

She took the instructions, and acknowledged compliance. Then she surprised the intelligence officer at the Embassy. Angela spoke into her cellular, "Would you find out where Mike Trantor is? Immediately! I am very concerned about him. He was my responsibility only hours ago. To me, he still is." The intelligence officer said he would call right back.

A few minutes later Angela's cellular phone rang. Major Trantor was in Walter Reed, bedded down in the secure ward and cared for by cleared personnel in case he divulged classified information under the influence of drugs. The intelligence officer cautioned that public linkage of an Army Major to Angela could endanger her on future missions. Angela responded that she would be careful.

She stepped out into the street and flagged a taxi. Paying the fare, she walked into the entrance of Walter Reed. At the information desk she asked where she could find a Major Michael Trantor in the secure ward.

The elderly lady politely responded, "I'm sorry, no one by that name has been admitted."

Angela felt foolish, the secure ward existed for a purpose. She tried again. "Can you tell me where the secure ward is?"

The elderly lady politely responded, "West wing, fourth floor. Take the elevator straight ahead on your right." Angela thanked the lady for her help.

Riding up in the elevator, she was trying to develop a story that would allow her to enter the secure floor. Not being able to fashion an immediate plan in almost any crisis was unusual. Her emotions were interfering with a normally smooth decision-making process.

The door of the elevator opened. Angela's heart rate was going up. She approached double doors and tried to pull one open. They were locked. A young soldier, standing behind a window cut into the wall, spoke through a speaker.

"Ma'am, please identify yourself for admission. This is a secure hospital wing. You must have permission to enter."

Angela didn't know what to say. Her hands were slightly shaking as she opened her purse, trying to buy time by seeing if her identification might somehow gain permission.

She asked, "What is needed to obtain entrance?" Angela was hoping she would get an answer she could exploit.

The answer was, "Ma'am, you need a code number provided by the patient's sponsor."

Angela knew Mike was steps away through the door; she desperately had to make sure he was all right. She replied, "I think I left it in the car."

Quickly turning, she walked around the corner, out of sight of the guard and pulled out her phone.

* * * * *

General Joe woke Kirsten up as the plane made its final approach into Reagan International Airport in Washington, DC. As they waited for their luggage, an Army sergeant found the general and told him that the staff car was waiting outside to move him and the lady directly to Walter Reed. The General's cellular rang. He stepped a few feet away from Kirsten.

"General Cordell speaking."

"Joe, this is Angela. I have a favor to ask of you. I'm here at Walter Reed, and—"

"Just a minute," the General interjected. "Are you all right? I didn't think you would be in Walter Reed."

Angela was speaking rapidly, "No, no. I'm okay. I would like to see Mike before I leave."

General Joe replied, "I'm going secure." He pushed the secure/encryption button and after thirty seconds saw that both phones were TOP SECRET.

"Angela, that would be impossible. I give codes and social security numbers to the Army Surgeon General's office and they set in security. The office isn't open at night. I might be able to do something once I get to Walter Reed. I should be there in forty minutes or so. I'm escorting Mike's wife in from Oklahoma. She'll be with me."

Angela kept her voice under control. "Joe, please listen. I can be in Mike's room in seconds. I've been on this mission from the very beginning—a long time—I even took out two Cuban spies in Panama so that our embassy could receive documents vital to this mission. I have worked closely with Mike and have built a close rapport with him. He was my buddy in this mission and you know what that means. I need to see him before I leave. Please, reconsider."

The General stepped a bit further away from Kirsten. He reached inside his coat and pulled out a small notebook.

He continued, "Do you have a pen?"

Angela replied, "Yes." She pulled out a pen and small piece of paper.

General Joe continued, "Your code number is XC1703. Here is your social security number." After giving the number and ensuring she had copied it correctly, Joe said, "Your name is Kirsten Trantor." Angela gasped.

General Joe quickly took charge, "You have forty minutes or less. Make sure you are gone when I get there. Good luck."

Angela burst out, "Joe, thank you."

She punched the cellular dead and ran for the entrance to the building. Breathing hard, she went up to the third floor and found the women's restroom. She canvassed to make sure she was alone. She hopped up on the sink and lifted a ceiling tile. She put her purse on top of the tile and put it back in place. She had to make sure that she couldn't be asked for a driver's license or any other secondary identification. She headed out of the bathroom towards the Army guard. She was studying a piece of paper in her hand. Her eyes were red and she was disheveled.

She told the soldier, "My code is XC1703, my name is Kirsten Trantor, and I am here to see my husband."

The guard asked her social security number, and Angela gave Kirsten's from memory.

Angela grabbed the initiative. "Please don't ask for anything else. I'm so desperate, I can't think straight. I've left my purse down in the car getting my code. I need to see my husband now."

The soldier said, "Okay, ma'am. I hope everything is all right." He buzzed the door.

Angela rushed to the desk.

"Please," she asked, "where is Major Michael Trantor?"

*   *   *   *   *

Kirsten sat in the back of the staff car with General Joe. She was quiet, looking out the window at the D.C. skyline as they pulled away from the airport. Finally she spoke. "Joe, you need to help convince Mike to let me go home in a few days. I need to get the house ready for his homecoming, I have exams to take, and a whole mess of other housekeeping that has to be taken care of."

She was going to burn the letters, wash the sheets, and ensure that Mike would find no trace of what she had done. She looked pleadingly into the General's eyes—he understood.

"Of course I'll help."

Kirsten was thinking. She wouldn't call Ted except to tell him it was over. She would take a taxi home from the airport. Kirsten simply said, "General, I'm going to start over."

He replied, "I'll be with you all the way." He reached over and squeezed her hand.

"I know you will," she answered. She then looked out the window in silence. She closed her eyes, wishing with all her might that she would be strong enough to keep her word.

* * * * *

The nurse looked up at Angela. "My goodness you're early," she said, getting up from her duty station.

Angela quickly answered, "Yes, the General is parking the car now. May I see Mike?"

"Of course, I'll take you to his room," the nurse replied. "Mike is slowly regaining full conciousness. We're not too concerned, but it has surprised us that it is taking this long. His vital signs are positive, and we have reopened the leg wound to cleanse it. We're confident he will fully recover, with the possible exception of some hearing loss, which we can't fully evaluate until he's awake. The doctors say his overall health and physical conditioning have really pulled him through."

The nurse walked on slowly continuing to explain. Angela wanted to run to Mike. Each second was valuable.

Finally they reached the room. Angela asked if she could be alone with him and the nurse nodded her head, showing Angela the button to push if she needed anything.

The nurse slowly closed the door, saying, "The note on the table arrived a few minutes ago. You should be very proud of your husband."

The nurse looked in through the window as Angela looked at Mike, tears running down her face. His leg was bandaged from the knee to the ankle, and was elevated. His arm was wrapped from the elbow to the shoulder, and his head was wrapped in gauze, except for his face.

He had on a blue, Army hospital robe. His face was pale and sweaty, and swollen, and covered in bruises. IVs were running into the backs of both hands. His head was slightly elevated with several pillows. Angela gently kissed his forehead.

She kept her hand on his arm, as if keeping contact with him would bring them closer. She reached over and picked up the envelope. It had the White House logo in the corner. On the front, it merely said,

Major Trantor, U.S. Army

She opened it.

Dear Mike, the nation and the Bush family thank you for your patriotism, tenacity, sacrifice, and dedication to duty. Your selfless service to others is a model for us all.

Respectfully,
George W. Bush

Angela kissed Mike's forehead again. He didn't respond. She then placed the note carefully back in the envelope. Suddenly, the events of the last few days and lack of sleep all weighed down. Fatigued, and near collapse, Angela moved a chair up close and sat down. She placed her head on Mike's chest. Her right hand gently held his right shoulder.

Mike's breathing was light and reassuring—he wasn't struggling. Angela held still, closing her eyes, feeling Mike's warmth in bed for the third time in her life. It seemed that if she didn't move a muscle, the moment could be sustained. Angela fell asleep, eventually dreaming that Mike had just stepped out of the Mercedes. She was leaving him again....

Angela startled, and awoke.

Looking at her watch, she jumped up, realizing Kirsten was probably already in the hospital. She leaned over and kissed Mike softly on the lips, saying, "I love you Mike Trantor, I truly do."

She turned, and prepared to leave, still looking down at Mike. He suddenly moved his head slightly in her direction, and opened his eyes for a fleeting moment. As he slipped back into sleep, she reached for his hand.

Somehow, Mike squeezed her hand twice.

Angela looked at the clock on the wall, grabbed her left hand with her right, and clutched its message to her heart as she left the room. She stepped out of the secure wing's double doors and headed, at a trot, for the elevator.

Tears were evident on her face, and the soldier on guard noted that she was grasping one hand with the other. Angela stopped at the closed elevator doors, turning and looking back towards Mike one last time. The doors opened.

General Joe and Kirsten looked up. Angela froze, not wanting to make eye contact with General Joe. Kirsten's eyes met Angela's.

Florida. Key West.

Kirsten stepped out of the elevator as a distraught Angela stepped in. The elevator doors closed with the two gazing intently at each other.

General Joe would order the guard to strike any record of the earlier visit from his log. For now, Joe tried to gently guide Kirsten towards the soldier, having already signaled him to keep quiet by pinching his own lips when Kirsten wasn't looking.

Kirsten stared back at the elevator, then glanced at the entrance to the secure wing of the hospital. She turned once more, fixated by the closed elevator doors and the distracting recollection that she might have seen Angela in Key West.

Two veterans suddenly rounded the corner in their blue robes. One was in a wheelchair with a clearly evident stump from a recent amputation. The other was on crutches. As they brushed by Kirsten, she withdrew in horror, sensing the future and the dawning full reality of the inherent danger of Mike's career.

The culminated stress of the last twenty-four hours and her internal struggle were coming to a crisis. Kirsten was trapped between Ted and Mike; between love and responsibility; between being with a kind and loving man or being alone and supportive of an absent husband; between staying young and growing old; and between the freedom of the college campus and the truth awaiting her on the hospital floor. She wanted to run. It was simply too much. Kirsten, overloaded, simply didn't know what to do. Frozen, she couldn't move.

CIA Headquarters
Langley, Virginia
John, Mike, General Joe, and many others were gathered in a secured classroom. They assembled to conduct the Hybrid's final After Action Review (AAR) for the Cuban operation. Critical comments were to be gathered in the following areas: command and control, intelligence, signal interface, mobility, operational security, weapons and individual equipment, planning sufficiency, interagency synchronization, logistics, and personnel. The observations would be archived for recall if, and when, the Hybrid came back to life.

General Joe had begun by saying how proud he was to finally be part of an information age outfit that understood that *influence operations* were the primary effort and that fighting was secondary.

Still resolving some issues from his wounds, Mike was glad to be back in the Special Forces business full time. He had asked permission to terminate graduate school, promising himself and the Army personnel center that someday he would return and complete his course of study. The Army agreed because of the ongoing requirements of the war on terrorism.

Mike asked if Angela was going to be able to attend the AAR. John responded, shaking his head, "Sorry. She's being re-tasked; she isn't Angela anymore."

Mike was inwardly crushed. Leaving Kirsten to stay at the University of Oklahoma with a separation agreement had been heart wrenching. Mike, while he hoped that before the divorce became final something would change Kirsten's intent to leave him, had looked forward to being with Angela again. He had planned to confess how fond he had become of her and how much she had been missed. Now it was not to be. Visibly downcast, his chances of finding her would be zero without agency help. *Hell*, he thought, *I don't even know her name.*

Mike looked up and Joe was intently looking at him. Joe gestured for Mike to come over, and put his arm around him. Joe left the room with Mike in tow.

CHAPTER TWENTY-SEVEN

Three days earlier, Abu and his fellow terrorists had been surfing the Internet, pausing to do their daily check-in with a camouflaged al-Qaeda website. On the second page, an icon had appeared in the lower left-hand corner of the web page. It was a small scimitar, pointed downwards. Abu yelled for the others. The scimitar was the symbol to activate their plan. They were being called into action, ready to give their lives to force Great Satan's infidels to withdraw from their Holy Lands.

The four men immediately went back onto the Internet to purchase plane tickets from Bangkok to Honolulu, then on to Los Angeles. In the airport at LAX, inside a rental locker, would be instructions, cash and cell phones. A copy of a key to the locker had been mailed to them months in advance. One of the men had the key on a chain around his neck. He grabbed it with one hand, nervously making sure it still hung there, while his other hand nervously fingered a set of worry beads.

A Thai Counter-Terror (CT) Agency sedan waited outside of the men's apartment. The intelligence fusion center had picked up the ticket data overnight. Four Thai police, armed with M16s and black flak vests, piled out of the van. Other uniformed policemen surrounded the apartment building.

The take-down was professionally executed—only one casualty: an al-Qaeda member, a swarthy, dark man now in surgery with a bullet wound in his left arm. He had exchanged fire with the CT team before leaping through an open window in his apartment.

Thai agents waited outside of the operating room until surgery was complete and then moved into the recovery room with the young man, who appeared to be not more than twenty-five years old. His reaction was cold and stony.

The agents remained in the room, silently sitting there for over an hour. The wounded man became more and more irritated at their calm demeanor, and then the door opened. It was Bert McNab, now on contract to the Agency.

The young AQ operator lost control upon seeing an American. He kicked out, trying to land his foot in Bert's chest, an incredible insult in the Middle East. Bert instinctively blocked the kick and followed up with a straight right hand palm-heel strike that broke the terrorist's nose with a crunch. The two Thai guards intervened and cuffed the man accordingly.

In a van, they drove directly to a holding cell for interrogation. The other three men had already been initially screened and were already in solitary confinement in a Thai prison. A bloody nose and a bullet wound didn't dent the young man under scrutiny at the moment, however. He was clearly the leader and a totally dedicated asset: one of Osama's better products.

The combined Thai/US interrogation process was great. Information gleaned from the prisoners was blasted back to the U.S. immediately—allowing designated forces to chase down hot leads. The leader, in this case, however, was completely tight-lipped.

After the Thai police were through, Bert had a chance to interrogate the young man through an Arabic translator. He also failed to make any progress. Suddenly, with no notice, he grabbed the AQ and threw him on the floor, hog-tying him and placing a bag over his head. The AQ felt himself being lifted up, carried out and placed in the trunk of a car.

The AQ's head was debagged and his feet freed so he could walk from the car, where he had been held for endless hours, towards a military C-130 Hercules transport.

Bert, the translator, and two policemen accompanied the hardcore AQ as he moved slowly towards the plane.

Men in military uniform stepped off the trail ramp of the C-130. Tough, unsmiling, business-like, they were imposing and intimidating. Still in cuffs, the young terrorist's eyes widened as he realized he was being handed over. He then recognized the uniforms. They were Russian.

"Sign here," instructed Bert, as a massive Russian stepped forward. "In accordance with Thai/US/Russian cooperative agreements, we hereby officially turn this fine fellow over to you for exploitation. Please promptly relay to us what this man knows."

The two Thai agents literally tossed the young man forward, still barefoot in his hospital pajamas. The Russians roughly caught him.

One Russian said to the other, in Arabic no less, "Wonderful. We have another Chechen, another killer of school children!" Sweat beads were appearing on the prisoner's brow. He looked over his shoulder to Bert and the Thai police. They were smiling and waiving goodbye.

As the AQ was forcibly strapped into his nylon seat, he looked across at the Russians. They were cold and quiet. The engines cranked and the tail ramp came up and locked into place. The terrorist yelled over the noise, trying to cover his growing fear, insulting the Russians.

The ranking Russian pulled out a human finger, showing it to the bound AQ, and then the other Russians. They broke out in fits of uncontrolled laughter.

The young Arab inwardly quaked. He remembered the stories of what the Russians did to the terrorists who shot a Russian Embassy employee in Lebanon two decades ago. The men's bodies were delivered to their families with their testicles in their mouths.

As the plane took off, Bert turned to return to work. He would do his best to help in the war on terrorism, including using Russians, if need be, to gain information about compartmentalized AQ operations. The AQ would never know that the finger came from an approved medical cadaver, the body of a soldier, who in his will, legally donated his body for the cause. Bert felt great; he could still operate and contribute to his nation's security. Amy loved Thailand and its kind and gentle people. Even Vicki and Alexis were coming for a visit.

Bert was thinking that if America and her allies could win this damn war, everything would be perfect.

Kyrgyzstan
19 Jan 2005

The Hybrid, back in action, included Mike. In flight, he was reading a copy of the latest *Washington Post* handed to him by one of the crewmen inside the C17 transport. The Presidential Inauguration, set for the next day, was headline news. Mike folded the paper and handed it back to the airman.

Joe might have been right; maybe Cuba *had* been his last singleton. Fully recovered from his wounds just in time to launch, he still had a war to fight—but on this mission he wouldn't be alone. Mike looked out of the porthole window, gauging the craggy mountains below. They were one hour out from landing. They would meet their contacts and begin a long hard trek to the brutally cold snow line.

Still intently looking out of the porthole, Mike unconsciously reached for his partner, feeling her long blond hair as he gently squeezed her shoulder, twice.

EPILOGUE

CIA Headquarters
21 Oct 04

LTG Hanscom was reading the morning's intelligence estimate. Included was an analysis of Fidel Castro's collapse during a public appearance lauding Cuban artists. He fell—in full public view—breaking his leg and arm. He was also captured on Cuban TV sweating profusely.

Hanscom rubbed his chin and leaned back in his chair. He was thinking of all he had learned over his long career: As a young officer, he had been pure kinetic energy and bullets. And now—he let this sink in—he was a master of the non-kinetic approach, with potentially valuable second- and third-order effects. The possibilities were endless. He wondered if Raúl was ready to take charge.

BIBLIOGRAPHY

Cuba and the Biological Warfare Threat. Ken Alibek with Stephen Handelman, Biohazard, Random House, New York, 1999.

The Economist, "Biotech in Cuba, Truly Revolutionary," November 29 – December 5, 2003, Vol. 369, Number 8352.

Garcia, Luis. "More Facts Uncovered in Chavez-Al Qaeda Collaboration," *<http://www.MilitaresDemocraticos.com>*

Jamming of U.S. Satellites:
J. Michael Waller, "Homeland Insecurity – Iran, Cuba zap U.S. Satellites," News World Communications, Inc., August 7, 2003.

Lack of Investment in Cuba:
The Economist, "Nickel, but no dimes," September 20-26, 2003, Vol. 368, Number 8342.

Margarita Island Connection:
"Nexus of Cuban, Venezuelan, FARC, AL-Qaeda Interests?" Special Warfare Magazine, April 2003.

Werlau, Maria C. "Does Cuba have biochemical weapons?" The Cuban American Foundation, *<http://www.canf.org>*